THE NAME BENEATH THE STONE

—— SECRET OF THE ——
UNKNOWN WARRIOR

THE NAME BENEATH THE STONE

—— SECRET OF THE ——
UNKNOWN WARRIOR

ROBERT NEWCOME

Universe Press

First published by Universe
an imprint of Unicorn Publishing Group LLP, 2019
5 Newburgh Street
London W1F 7RG
www.unicornpublishing.org

10 9 8 7 6 5 4 3 2 1

ISBN 978-1-912690-55-8

A CIP catalogue record for this book is available from the British Library

Typeset by Matthew Wilson

Printed and bound by Jellyfish

Front cover artwork by Battlefield Design,
front cover illustration by Claudia Newcome

Interior photographs from Mirrorpix

PROLOGUE

May 1916

The sound was of thunder, pealing across open country, unbroken by landscape, enveloping the Western Front in a familiar vibrating rumble.

The Reverend David Railton paused briefly, noted the flashes on the horizon, then looked back into the opening at his feet. Eight feet by four feet, edges neatly squared but deforming rapidly, water already gathering at its base.

'Ashes to ashes, dust to dust,' he said, not reading from the prayer book he sheltered as best he could from the persistent rain. He looked across at the General standing opposite him and at the four soldiers surrounding the grave, their heads bent, their hair matted, their eyes to the ground.

'How strange,' thought Railton, 'how strange to be here, now, with this small group of men, briefly united in the solemnest of tasks, strangers one moment, comrades the next, likely never to meet again.'

'Railton?'

It was the first word the General had spoken since they had met fifteen minutes earlier. Raindrops formed dark marks on his coat, merging even as they multiplied.

'And so, dear Lord, we commend this soul to thy mercy...' continued Railton, his eyes closed, mouthing words he could recite in his sleep, words he had spoken in the past year more often than he dared count. When he had finished the General reached down to pick up a handful of earth and threw it into the hole. The two officers and four soldiers then stood in silence for a few seconds before the General stepped back.

'Thank you Railton,' he said.

'Sir.'

The soldiers were already shovelling mud onto the exposed body as the officers turned away and began walking towards their staff car. Railton looked across at the General but he appeared to have retreated once more into a dark contemplation.

'You knew him, sir?'

'Yes.'

'I'm sorry.'

'Thank you.'

They walked on in silence, passing through a large makeshift cemetery. Railton looked about him at the rows of wooden crosses. 'Another one gone,' he said.

'Indeed.'

The General was a tall man but he walked slowly, limping slightly, his shoulders stooped, his right arm hanging loosely by his side.

'I'll write the letter,' said Railton.

The General stopped and looked into the distance. 'Loved by his comrades, ... a good soldier, ... died painlessly?'

'That sort of thing, sir, yes.'

Railton thought he detected the smallest shake of the head. Then they carried on, heads bent against the wind and rain, not speaking. The sound of a loud explosion carried in the light wind.

'And so we continue,' said the General.

'Yes, sir.'

They passed the perimeter of the graveyard and a soldier opened the door of the car.

'Well, keep up the good work, Railton.'

'Sir.' He saluted and the General raised his cane with his left arm before climbing into the back seat. As the vehicle moved off Railton looked in through the misted window at the senior officer's profile, at the pronounced eyebrows, at the firm jaw, at the lines of exhaustion etched across the man's features as he stared ahead of him, not turning, not smiling, facing with a grim composure the certainty of the decisions he must continue to make; decisions that would result, inevitably, in thousands more advancing to their deaths in the coming months.

Later that day David Railton stepped out of his billet for some fresh air. The clouds had passed and as he stood alone in the small garden he noticed how still was the evening, how peaceful was this small patch of rural France. Even the guns seemed to be resting. Behind him light seeped out from one of the downstairs windows and he could just hear the voices of his fellow officers, laughing at some joke, enjoying a cigarette and playing cards after their evening meal.

He looked up at the clear sky, at the sun that was now sinking behind the horizon, at the stars that were just beginning to appear, and began walking in no particular direction. It was a small garden, walled, surrounding the house on all sides, and having completed a circuit he decided on a second. It was then that something caught his eye. A wooden stake, driven into the ground, over in a corner, half hidden by weeds. He walked towards it and crouched down. It was not just a stake, it was a cross and someone had carved an inscription at its top. Railton rubbed away some dirt and, moving close in the fading light, read the words:

'An unknown soldier (of the Black Watch).'

He stayed squatting until his legs began to ache and then slowly he stood up. He shook his head and his thoughts turned back to the funeral service he had led earlier, then to all the other burials he had conducted in his time as a padre at the front line.

He wondered how many more there were, like this one, whose names were not known, whose deaths would never be recorded and whose families would never know the circumstances of their loved ones' final moments.

As he returned inside he imagined what it must be like to wait, day after day, perhaps week after week, to hear news of a husband or son – only to finally be informed he was 'Missing in Action.'

Railton went to his room, picked up his diary and paused for a moment. Then he began writing:

Wednesday, 16 May 1916: 'I found a grave in the garden of my billet today. On the wooden cross a fellow soldier had written 'An unknown soldier (of the black watch).'

He paused again, holding his pen in mid air before beginning a new paragraph.

'How that grave caused me to think... But who was he? And who were his parents?' What can I do to ease the pain of the father, mother, brother, sister, sweetheart, wife and friend?'

He stood up, paced up and down his room, then sat down again. All these people needed something to grieve. They needed a coffin, a service, a funeral. They needed to watch a box being lowered into the ground and to dare to believe it was their son or lover being buried.

He picked up his pen. 'Let a body,' he wrote, 'a symbol of him – be carried reverently over the sea to his native land'.

He looked at the words he had written. 'And,' he noted, 'having had this idea I was happy for about five minutes.'

CHAPTER 1

September 2011

Sarah Harding looked down at her father and spooned some soup into his open mouth. He spluttered but managed to swallow a little before nodding his head for more. When the bowl in Sarah's hands was empty she put it to one side and stood up.

'Well done, Dad,' she said, 'you can have a nice sleep now.'

He tried to raise himself from his armchair to speak but only managed to lift his head a few inches. Sarah bent down and put her ear to his mouth.

'Thank you,' he whispered, his eyes closed.

She helped him onto his bed and tucked a blanket around his frail body before leaving the room quietly. His nurse would be back soon and they would need to talk about arrangements now that Stanley's mind and body were fading so fast. His long resistance to being packed off to an institution seemed to have paid off – his last days would be spent in his own home after all.

Downstairs she helped herself to a sandwich before returning to the lengthy task of organising her father's affairs. On the dining table were piles of documents she had earlier extracted from his old wooden filing cabinet and then grouped under various headings: Army. Investments. Certificates. Letters. Photos. House.

She flicked through the Investments folder and felt her heart sink at the complexity. Share certificates, ISA records and various savings in different bank accounts were all jumbled together and would take some unravelling. She sat back and had a rare moment of wishing her methodical ex-husband with his love of order and process was still around to help out: lists, spreadsheets and meticulous filing had never been her strengths and she wondered at her ability to sort out this mess on her own.

Her eyes moved to the letters pile. There were four folders, each a different colour, each with a name written on their cover.

One had the name 'Peter Harding' typed on its white label. Peter had been Stanley's father, her grandfather. The folder was faded red and looked as if it hadn't been opened in years. Carefully, she unwound the string from the circular piece of cardboard in its centre and then opened the flaps outwards. Inside, letters were neatly divided by pieces of foolscap paper into three headings; Friends. Family. Joyce.

Joyce. Sarah pictured her grandmother, Peter's wife, who had died in 1982: standing at the Aga issuing instructions as she cooked large meals for the family, down on her knees playing games with her grandchildren, laughing and reminiscing in that infectious way of hers while Peter sat quietly in the background.

She put the friends and family letters to one side and began reading the first letter under Joyce's section. It was dated 1971 and was a description of her visit to friends in Switzerland where she had stayed for a week to benefit from the fresh mountain air. The following letters were in chronological order going back in time, one or two a year, mostly from abroad.

Sarah skimmed each letter, working her way back to 1926, enjoying Joyce's descriptions of the places she had stayed and the people she had met. Sandwiched between her letters were Peter's replies; more formal, less poetic, written with a military brevity. It seemed Joyce had travelled extensively without her husband throughout the later decades of their marriage which would make sense – while she was always adventurous and interested in meeting people Peter had, as far as Sarah could remember, been a solitary sort of man, a keen gardener, more devoted to his flowers and his fishing than to people.

Then, at the very bottom of the pile, Sarah came to three letters in stark contrast to the others. Each was written on sheets of crumpled paper torn from a pad, the writing was in pencil, there were no addresses at the top. The first was dated 6 June 1917. 'My darling Joyce,' the letter began and it was signed at the bottom 'your love for ever, Daniel.' The next two were dated 16 July 1917 and 18 August 1917.

Sarah sat up. She read the letters slowly then re-read them a second time. Daniel. No one in the family had ever mentioned his name. He was clearly a soldier, the first letter reflecting on his visit home from France the previous month when he and Joyce had spent two days in a small hotel overlooking Brighton pier.

'That was grand,' he wrote, 'sitting on that bench and looking out to sea while you joked around. I even managed to forget about this place for a while. But it was odd too. Walking the streets, not ducking or diving for cover. All the lads say how tough it is dealing with all that.'

The second described his return to the trenches and the pattern of life rotating between the reserve, support and front line before being part of a major advance. 'It all went well,' he wrote, 'better than any of us could have hoped.

Some lads didn't make it and the new young officer was upset but he'll get used to it soon enough.'

In the third he was looking forward to another visit home.

Sarah noticed her hands were trembling as she read. In places the writing was faded and hard to decipher but there was no mistaking the dates.

She sat thinking for a few moments before putting the letters down and reaching for the 'Certificates' folder on the other side of the table. The very first document was her father Stanley's birth certificate: he had been born on 3 February 1918.

She stared at first the birth certificate and then the June letter. 'May 1917' she whispered to herself. 'My God,' she said out loud and her hands instinctively went to her mouth. 'Oh my God.'

She stood up, walked to the kitchen and poured herself a glass of wine. Then she paced the length of the dining room, stopping every now and then to re-examine the letters. Was this man Daniel her real grandfather? She'd known since childhood that Stanley was born two years before Peter and Joyce's marriage but whenever she'd asked him about this he'd always been evasive, only saying that his mother had had 'a romance' with a soldier. 'Peter has been a good father to me,' he once said, 'that's all that matters. The rest is best forgotten.'

But it hadn't been forgotten. These letters had been carefully filed away and now here they were, filling in a gap in Sarah's background that had been nagging at her for as long as she could remember.

She'd often wondered about the soldier who'd 'had a romance' with her grandmother. Over the years she'd found herself drawn to books and documentaries about the Great War in what she realised was a deep need to discover more about her ancestry. She would look at photos of men in the trenches and see in their faces an echo of her past. And now, with these letters, she had something tangible to focus on. She imagined Daniel in uniform, standing on the pebbled Brighton beach, or sitting on a bench and looking towards France, his strong hands holding those of his girlfriend Joyce. Her grandfather Daniel.

A cough from upstairs interrupted her thoughts. She stood for a few seconds, holding the letters, caught in a moment of indecision as to what she should ask her father. He coughed again, as if summoning her to speak to him. Slowly she climbed the stairs, gripping the handrail to steady herself, sensing a moment of great significance unfolding. In his bed Stanley had his eyes open and was staring at the ceiling. Sarah walked across the room and sat down beside him.

'How are you feeling?' she asked.

He nodded and gave her a weak smile.

She gazed at him, her heart racing. 'Dad,' she said, 'who was Daniel?'

Stanley remained completely still.

'I found these,' said Sarah, holding the letters close to Stanley's face, 'in a file of Granny's.' She swallowed and took a breath. 'They're from a man called Daniel. To Joyce. To your mum. Love letters from the trenches.'

Stanley's eyes blinked but he said nothing.

'Was he the one, Dad? Was he the soldier?'

Stanley's head stayed facing upwards but his eyes moved to look at her. He held her gaze for a long while before nodding.

'So he was your father?'

Another nod. Sarah closed her eyes. The room seemed suddenly cooler. 'So he was my real grandfather.'

Stanley raised his right hand slightly and motioned for her to come closer.

'Unknown,' he said weakly.

'What was that?'

'Unknown,' he said again, slightly louder this time.

'Yes, Dad, unknown. I've never heard of him.'

Stanley was attempting to shake his head.

'Not unknown?' said Sarah.

He motioned again and she placed her ear to his mouth.

'Unknown ... Soldier.'

Sarah didn't move. 'Unknown Soldier?'

He nodded and suddenly he was gripping her hand with a strength that caught her by surprise. 'Unknown Soldier,' he repeated and stared back at her, not smiling, holding her attention with a fierce sense of purpose. She leant back and looked at the shrivelled old man lying in front of her, his body decimated from eating almost nothing this past week, his face folding in on itself, his eyes glazed and exhausted.

'What does that mean, Dad?' she asked, but he turned his head, closed his eyes and went back to sleep.

CHAPTER 2

March 1917

Private Daniel Dawkins, known as DD to his friends, was lying on his bed in a corrugated iron hut in a base camp to the west of Ypres when the new recruits arrived. He put down his magazine and stepped outside to watch the men as they marched in, their new uniforms showing no signs of wear, their boots well dubbined, their faces clean.

He had seen it all many times before.

One of the earliest volunteers in 1914 he was one of the longest serving war time soldiers in the British Army and was considered a lucky charm by the few men who had survived alongside him.

He watched as the men formed three rows in what had been designated the drill square before being assigned beds and heading off in small groups to their billets. Four of them began walking in his direction.

Murphy, the terrier who had joined them six months earlier, nuzzled against his leg.

'New troops,' said Daniel, 'poor bastards.'

One of the many dogs trained at the dog training school in Scotland to take messages between the lines, Murphy had arrived one day looking for food and had been adopted as a pet by Daniel and his mates in 5 Platoon.

Daniel bent down and patted Murphy on the back. He watched as a fresh young officer spoke to a sergeant who then saluted before the two of them moved off in different directions. The four new recruits arrived at the door of his hut.

Daniel watched them without speaking as they looked inside. 'Not too fucking bad,' said one of them.

Daniel waited in the doorway, observing with a cool indifference as the new recruits laughed and joked with each other as they chose somewhere to sleep. He felt no inclination to talk to these excitable youths, separated from them as he was by the gulf of his own experience. Except for one of them. This man was standing apart form the others, not joking, unsmiling. He was short, with thin, whispy hair and pale skin that suggested a life of undernourishment. He seemed unable to stop his left leg from moving in a strange circular fashion. Daniel indicated for him to step outside and offered him a cigarette.

'Been to the line before then, son?' said Daniel.

The soldier turned to him slowly and nodded.

'I'm Dan.'

'I'm Pete,' said the man quietly and his hand was soft and trembling when Daniel shook it. 'Pete Jackson.'

'Who were you with?'

'A Company.'

'Thought I recognised you.'

'You're Dawkins.'

'That's right.'

'I took one.'

'I can see that.'

'They've sent me back.'

'There's a surprise.'

The soldier looked down at the ground. 'It ain't fair,' he said.

Daniel shrugged. 'Nothing's fair out here, Pete,' he said, 'surprised you hadn't worked that one out by now.'

'I've got this terrible ringing in my ears, stops me from sleeping.'

Dawkins watched Peter's leg as it formed repetitive arcs, lifting his foot an inch off the floor with each swing.

'Seen that before,' he said, 'too many times.'

'Can't think straight,' said Peter.

'No one can out here, son.'

'Not so bad as this.'

Dawkins stepped closer too him. 'Well there's no profit feeling sorry for yourself here, Jackson,' he said, 'you're stuck in this nightmare and that's that. Make the most of it – that's all you can do.'

Peter shook his head and Dawkins grabbed his shoulders. 'Listen,' he said, 'I'll see you allright but not if you snivel around. If you try to make a fist of it I'll keep an eye out for you but if you go soft on me you're on your own.' He lifted Jackson's chin. 'Got that?'

Jackson looked back at him through eyes brimming with tears. 'Got that Dan.'

'Good. And don't, for fuck's sake, let the others see you blubber.'

* * * *

That evening Daniel Dawkins went with his mates Timmings and Fletcher to an estaninate in Dickebusch. It took them half an hour to walk to the town and another fifteen minutes to find the bar.

The large room was packed with soldiers.

'Beer,' said Fletcher when asked by Dawkins what he wished to drink. 'Vin rouge,' said Timmings.

Dawkins bought the drinks with the few francs he had remaining from the last pay day and sat down with his friends at a small table. They had found this place the previous week on a suggestion from a corporal in the Signals who Daniel had befriended on a spell back at staff. They had liked it as the landlord was welcoming and it seemed to be a magnet for French girls from the local towns.

'Just enough for two or three,' said Dawkins, 'then we'll head back.'

The three men had been together now for over eight months and their friendship had been sealed in frequent visits to the front. They had seen more than half their company lost in that time and the recent batch of recruits were just the latest in a long line. They drank slowly, watching the girls squeeze through small gaps between crowded tables.

'Can't stop thinking about that order not to stop for any bugger what's wounded,' said Timmings. He was only nineteen years old and easily angered by the inconsistencies of those in authority.

'Ignore it,' said Dawkins, 'it's bollocks.'

'I tell you, if I see a mate go down no bloody brass hat's going to stop me helping him.'

'Written by some bloody fool whose boots ain't never seen a bit of mud.'

'Bastards,' said Timmings, 'they think they can fight this war with pencils and paper.'

'You can't take a trench without casualties but there's one thing saying they're unavoidable, there's another saying they don't matter,' said Dawkins.

'It's not right.'

'As I said, ignore it. You do what you think is right, Timbo. We need to look after ourselves. Don't listen to those idiots.'

Fletcher, a married man and the oldest of the three who often sat back and listened to such debates now joined in the conversation. 'Give them a chance,' he said.

'Give them a chance?' said Timmings incredulously, 'they need to give me a fucking chance.'

Dawkins leant forwards. 'What are you saying Fletch?' he asked.

Fletcher looked at his two friends. Better educated than the average private soldier he often took an impartial view in discussions. 'You're right,' he said slowly, 'that it's our job to look after each other.' He pushed his glasses back onto the bridge of his nose. 'We're the ones fighting, we're the ones who need to make the decisions at the time. But the brass hats have a different job. They can't think about individual men. We're just material to them, one bit in the whole battle. They have to plan as best they can with what information they have and they can't get too wrapped up in what happens at the sharp end.'

'Fuck me,' said Timmings, 'can't get too wrapped up? So just send us all to our deaths then.'

'Hear the man out,' said Dawkins, 'he's not all piss and wind.'

'I don't get it,' said Timmings, 'all I know is we're the bastards what get killed, not them.'

'Plenty of them get it,' said Fletcher, 'if the brass think too hard about us poor bloody infantry they'd never send us over the top at all.'

'Yes, but to say we can't stop to help a wounded mate...'

'That's a mistake,' said Fletcher, 'and good officers like Major Witheridge will let them know that soon enough.'

Dawkins had often heard Fletcher talk like this. 'You're so bloody reasonable, Fletch,' he said, 'you confuse me at times.'

Fletcher nodded. 'Everyone's confused, Dan,' he said.

Dawkins gave a wry smile. 'That's true. I doubt if even Field fucking Marshal Haig has a bleeding clue what's going on these days.'

A woman on a small stage started singing and they sat back and listened. Soon a waitress arrived at their table.

'Encore?' she said.

'Oui, bon,' said Fletcher. She smiled at Dawkins and headed back to the bar.

'She's got you lined up,' said Timmings to Dawkins.

'Has she?'

'I saw that smile.'

'She can smile at others.'

'What's your secret, Dan?' said Timmings, 'They make straight for you, you bastard.'

'Not interested,' said Dawkins, 'I've got my girl.'

'So what? She's back in blighty.'

'So everything, Timbo. You'll find that out one day.'

Timmings, never short of words with his older friends, told a story about his last visit home and a night with a woman twice his age.

'So, heard from the lass?' Fletcher asked Dawkins when Timmings had finished.

'Expecting to, Fletch.'

'Having the fucking postman as we speak, I 'll bet,' said Timmings.

'Steady, Timbo,' said Fletcher who seldom joined in the crude banter of the soldiers around him.

Dawkins leant forwards and took hold of Timmings' shirt. 'You don't know Joyce,' he said, 'and maybe you don't know me so well.' His eyes were fixed on Timmings. 'So you can shut your fucking mouth now Timbo.'

Timmings held up his hands. 'No offence, Dan, just a joke.'

'Not a very good one, lad' said Fletcher.

'No offence taken,' said Dawkins, leaning back, 'and I'll tell you one more thing. I ain't taking no itching back as a little present from the front.'

The waitress reappeared with their drinks. She sat on Dawkins' lap and ruffled his hair. 'Vous aimez moi?' she said.

'I do, love,' he said, 'you're a picture.' She was; a rarity amongst the women attracted to the drinking holes of the British Army. 'But I have a girl back home.'

The waitress shrugged, 'that is not a problem for me,' she said and giggled.

'My friend Timbo, however, might be interested,' said Dawkins.

The girl looked at Timmings. 'Maybe later, my darling,' she said and left them with a smile.

They watched her approach another table to be greeted by a roar of approval and they sat back and listened to the singer at the far end of the room who was singing a medley of upbeat French songs.

'I'll miss Mr Allard,' said Fletcher after a while. The others nodded. 'Decent enough bloke,' he continued, 'did his best.'

'He was that,' said Dawkins.

The three men sat in silent contemplation, reflecting on the events of the previous week when Lieutenant Allard, who had only been their platoon commander for six weeks, had been shot in the chest whilst out on patrol. It had been Fletcher who had sat with him as he died, apparently in no pain as his mind slowly closed down on him.

'Not like Mr Horrocks,' said Fletcher, happy to change the subject.

'No. Fucking cunt, that one,' said Timmings.

'That he is.'

'He had it in for you, Dan,' said Timmings.

'He had it in for all of us.'

'But why did he hate you so much?'

'No idea, Timbo.'

'It's because Dan wouldn't be intimidated by him,' said Fletcher, 'you were the only one who really stood up to him.'

'Remember that time you told him we needed more men on that patrol,' said Timmings, 'I thought he'd fucking hit you.'

'Nearly did,' said Dan, ' he put me on a charge anyways for insubordination.'

'Didn't know that Dan.'

'Just before he was transferred to A Company. Major Witheridge took it on and cleared me. He said there was no breach of discipline.'

'That's because he knew you were right,' said Fletcher.

'Yes, well, thank fuck for an officer who knows what he's doing.'

Dawkins had grown to know Major Witheridge well over time. The previous November they and ten others had been cut off from the rest of the company, caught in a trench that had been taken to the north and south of them and had held out until a reserve force had come to their rescue some six hours after their first detatchment. Dawkins had subsequently been promoted, a position he held until a month later when he had been caught acquiring extra rations from the back of a supply wagon.

'I saw the new officer earlier,' said Dawkins.

'What's he like?'

'Young.'

'They all are these days.'

'Young as you Timbo.'

'Bloody hell,' said Fletcher, 'if he isn't older than Timbo let's hope he has more brains.'

The men laughed and sipped at their drinks.

'What's with that lad in our billet?' asked Fletcher.

'The one with the shakes?'

'That's him.'

'Somme.'

'Thought as much.'

'Sent back because there's nothing wrong with him.'

'Nothing wrong with him? My arse.'

'I talked to him,' said Dawkins, 'nerves are shot. Ringing in his ears. Whole of his section lost in one advance and he took one on the side of his head. Should never 'ave come back.'

'Poor bastard.'

'We're all poor bastards, mate.'

It was past midnight when they rolled back into their hut where they found the four new recruits in their bunks. All were fast asleep except Peter Jackson.

'Can't sleep, mate?' said Dawkins.

'No,' said Peter, 'like I told you.'

'Well, shake us in the morning,' said Dawkins, 'I won't say sweet dreams.'

CHAPTER 3

September 2011

Sarah Harding sat at her desk and switched on the anglepoise lamp clipped to its side. 10.20pm. She typed in the words 'Unknown Soldier' on her laptop. Immediately a mass of information appeared on her screen and within minutes she was completely absorbed in an event that had gripped the nation nearly a century earlier in 1920.

By 11.30pm she had pieced together a story that began in 1916 when a padre called David Railton came up with the idea of disinterring a body of an unidentified soldier from one of the battlefields of the Western Front, taking it back to England and burying it in Westminster Abbey to represent all those who went 'Missing in Action' in the Great War. She discovered that he had kept his idea to himself until the end of the war when he wrote to Lord Douglas Haig with his suggestion. Dismayed to receive no reply he would have quietly forgotten the whole outlandish scheme but his wife urged him to persevere so in 1920 he wrote to Bishop Ryle, the Dean of Westminster.

Ryle then wrote to King George V, the Prime Minister and the War Office.

King George was highly sceptical. He said the idea of a symbolic funeral two years after the end of the war should 'now be regarded as belated'. But Lloyd George was enthusiastic and made a strong case for having a burial on Armistice Day: 11 November 1920. The King slowly came round. A Committee was set up chaired by Lord Curzon. The idea gathered momentum and when it was finally approved in October 1920 the extraordinary challenge of organising a major event in the heart of London at short notice was under way.

Meanwhile the concept of burying an unknown soldier captured the public imagination way beyond anyone's wildest expectations. It seemed Railton's idea had struck a nerve, not just with all those who'd never been able to bury their loved ones, but with the whole nation. Soon the entire country was gripped in expectation and by the time the body was carried through London on 11th the streets were packed with massed crowds. It was then buried in the Abbey. *The Times* reported the next day that the service was *'The most beautiful, the most touching and the most impressive this island has ever seen.* Thousands formed long queues for days afterwards to see the coffin.

Sarah stared at the articles she had printed off and were now spread out across her desk. She remembered the funeral of Diana, Princess of Wales in 1997 and how the whole country had come to a halt. She had been amazed at the public outpouring of grief at the time and had imagined this was something new for the British people but it seemed that that event paled into insignificance when compared with the burial in 1920. She took a sheet of blank paper out of a drawer and wrote at the top the words 'Unknown Soldier'. Beside it she drew a large question mark. Was this event what her father had been referring to? If so, why, and why had he spoken about it when she asked about Daniel?

Below this she wrote the names 'Daniel', 'Peter Harding' and 'Joyce' and started filling in details:

Daniel. Soldier fighting on Western Front. Home on leave in May 1917. Writes letters to Joyce. Nothing more known of him.

Peter Harding. Born 1896. Marries Joyce 1921. Remains married to Joyce until his death in 1976.

Joyce. Born 1899. Sent letters by Daniel 1917. Gives birth to Stanley February 1918. Marries Peter Harding 1921. Dies 1982.

Sarah's pen hovered over the page. Stanley's reluctance to talk about what must have been a shameful birth out of wedlock for his mother was understandable but now, all these years on, it seemed that he hadn't wanted to entirely eradicate the memory of Daniel – otherwise why had he held on to those letters? Perhaps Joyce had kept them hidden away from Peter and passed them on to Stanley before she died. Perhaps he simply didn't have the heart to destroy them.

Sarah wished she had asked her grandmother about it and not been steered off so easily. She looked at the clock. She had a busy day ahead so reluctantly switched off her computer, tidied up the papers and was in bed by midnight. But it was a while before she fell to sleep. Stanley's words kept coming back to her. What could he possibly have meant? She found herself thinking about Daniel and wondered what sort of man he was. His letters had been matter of fact, talking mostly of his mates and the mundanities of life in the trenches. Yet there was tenderness also in the way he referred to his visits home and his feelings for Joyce. Sarah lay on her back, closed her eyes and considered the various possibilities those letters had thrown up. Daniel. Unknown. She would dearly love to know what that was all about.

The next morning, in a coffee break from comparing samples of material for a room she was designing, she re-read one of the articles she'd printed off the previous day. Describing life in the trenches from the point of view of a corporal in the Seaforth Highlanders and based upon his letters home it had struck a chord with her. The gut-wrenching fear of the man who had *'held his wife's present to him, a simple bar of chocolate, a link to home, a temporary remembrance of a distant life'* had come across to her in vivid detail. She picked up her phone and dialled the number of the historian who had written the article.

'James Marchant.'

'Oh, James, I didn't expect to get through that easily.'

There was a pause at the other end. 'Who is this?' His voice implied generations of well-bred reserve.

'I'm sorry, I'm Sarah Harding, and I read your article about men in the trenches last night.'

'I see.' Another pause. 'And?'

'Oh, I am sorry, I'm not making much sense, am I?' Sarah, unusually for her, was suddenly feeling a little flustered by Marchant's brief responses. 'It's just that I was rather impressed by the way you described the men's lives, you know, the camaraderie as well as the horror.'

'I see. Well, thank you for taking the time to tell me that.'

'No. I mean, yes, that's fine, but it's not what I was calling you about.'

'Go on.'

'Well, I came across some letters from a soldier yesterday, writing to my grandmother from the front. They've been hidden away in a file for years. I thought you might be interested to see them.'

'Possibly.'

'He talks about some of the battles he was in – ones that you seem to know about.'

Another pause.

'Yes, that might well be of some interest to me.'

'Oh good. You see I think he might have been my grandfather.'

'Your grandfather?'

'Yes, you see my father was born nine months after this soldier, called Daniel by the way, was back home on leave.'

'Intriguing.'

'It is, isn't it? I'm going to try and track him down, find out a bit about him.'

'That should be possible.' Sarah could sense Marchant weighing things up. 'Well look,' he said, 'would you like to post me the letters so I can have a look at them?'

It was Sarah's turn to pause. 'Well, there is something else. Something related to the letters.'

'Yes?'

'Um. I think I'd like to talk to you about it in person.'

'In person?'

'Yes. Are you based in London?'

'I am.'

'Then perhaps I could drop the letters by one day.'

'I see.' Marchant sounded cautious, as if meeting a stranger after just one phone call was somewhat irregular.

'I'll buy you a coffee.'

Yet another pause.

'Then that will be hard to resist. Let me get my diary.'

Two days later she came in on the train to Waterloo and filled in time in a café just up the road until twelve o'clock, when her appointment with Marchant was due. She looked up at the flat in Redcliffe Square and checked she had the correct number then pressed the buzzer.

'Hello, it's Sarah Harding.'

Almost immediately a voice answered. 'Sarah. Hang on there and I'll come down.'

Sarah waited. The door opened and Marchant appeared. He was wearing an old pair of corduroy trousers, a tweed jacket, a check shirt and a striped tie.

'The flat's a little untidy at the moment,' he said, 'I hope you don't mind. I thought we'd go to the café just up the road. They do very good pastries.'

'That would be fine.'

Marchant started walking swiftly in a slightly strange manner, his heels raising unnaturally high off the ground with each step as if he was subconsciously attempting to skip.

'I did enjoy your article about the front line,' said Sarah.

'Thank you.'

She glanced sideways at him, trying to reconcile the old fashioned academic beside her with someone who could write such a moving article about men at war. He was hard to age but she guessed he must be in his late thirties or early forties.

'Nice square,' she said.

He stopped and looked up. 'Yes. I love it. Built in 1860 and designed by a man called Godwin. The name Redcliffe comes from his association with Bristol. Lovely period of architecture don't you think?'

'Beautiful.'

They carried on walking. 'Of course, I couldn't possibly afford to buy here nowadays on my salary but I was fortunate enough to be given a legacy as a young man and I've been here ever since. It's terribly convenient for town.' He spoke swiftly as if keen to disseminate as much information as possible in the shortest amount of time.

'And what do you do?' asked Sarah.

'I write, I lecture, I do research. I'm called upon by organisations now and then who need an expert.'

'Well, thank you for seeing me.'

'My pleasure.'

Sarah smiled. Had Marchant been wearing a trilby she had no doubt he would have raised it at that moment.

In the café the Croatian waitress Sarah had chatted to earlier immediately perceived the slight awkwardness surrounding her return and smiled conspiratorially.

'I think I'll have one of your delicious croissants,' said Marchant.

'You need not tell me,' laughed the Croatian. She turned to Sarah. 'He always have the same thing.'

Marchant looked surprised. 'Lord, am I that predictable?' He adopted an expression of mild embarrassment. 'A creature of habit, I fear.'

They sat down and Sarah opened the folder she had bought with her.

'So,' she said, 'Here they are. The letters.' She placed the sheets of paper on the table between them.

Marchant took out a pair of horn rimmed spectacles and started examining them.

'On a first inspection they seem entirely authentic,' he said after a minute, 'this is just the sort of paper the soldiers wrote on.'

'That's good.'

'Not that I expected them not to be. Where did you say they've been all this time?'

'In a folder in my father's house – he's dying so I'm going through his things.'

'I'm sorry.' Marchant was reading the first letter. 'Do you mind leaving me to look through these for a few moments?'

'Of course.' Sarah stood up, went outside and lit up a cigarette. She looked in through the window at Marchant who was reading intently. There was something about him that hinted at a life lived in his own private world, or even, Sarah imagined, a solitary life, perhaps a lonely one.

She left him for ten minutes, before going back into the café.

'If he did die soon after writing that last letter it's really very moving,' said Marchant.

'Yes.'

'And, from a historian's perspective, fascinating. His description in the first letter of the attack on Messines Ridge is actually of some significance.'

'In what way?'

'Well.' Marchant leant forwards. 'How much do you know about the Great War?'

'A certain amount. I did it in History at school and have read a few things since then. I've got a rather unusual taste for those films. '

'All Quiet on the Western Front?'

'The original version, yes.'

'Paths of Glory?'

'Yup.'

'Oh! What a Lovely War?'

'Years ago. I remember seeing it with my parents.'

'Blackadder?'

'Of course.'

'War Horse?'

'No. Not yet.'

'Well, what's the picture painted in the public imagination by the world of entertainment of the generals and officers who commanded in the war?'

'Well, in Blackadder, Rowan Atkinson's character turned out to be a brave man.'

'Yes. That was clever. How about Hugh Laurie's?'

'Dopey upper class toff?'

'How about General Melchett?'

'Idiot. Out of touch.'

'Exactly. Now, of course, these were caricatures and they were playing for laughs – brilliantly I might add – but they did help perpetuate this image of remote generals sending thousands of men to be slaughtered unnecessarily. Have you heard the expression 'Lions led by Donkeys?'

'Yes, I think so.'

'It sums up that viewpoint. But a number of historians these days are questioning these long-held views. They are pointing out that, yes, mistakes were made, sometimes on a colossal scale, but that the generals and their staff were learning all the time, trying out new tactics as the war progressed. We are fed images of callous generals sitting in Chateaux while soldiers spent months in sodden trenches, but in fact high numbers of formation commanders were killed in action. Fundamentally, they were fighting an almost impossible war.'

'I see.'

'And Messines Ridge is a very interesting case in point. It was a good example of new tactics working and this letter very much supports that.'

'I see. That's rather exciting.'

'Yes. Thank you for showing them to me.'

Sarah sat back and took a deep breath. 'So, what next?'

'Well, I'd like to examine these in a bit more depth. But you said you think Daniel may have been your grandfather?'

'Yes.' Sarah explained the chronology to Marchant.

'And you'd like to track him down.'

'Yes, of course.'

'Do you have anything more about him?'

'Only these letters and the name Daniel.'

'He's never been talked about in the family?'

'No.'

'So no second name anywhere?'

'No, I'm afraid not.'

'I see.' Marchant studied Sarah's notes. 'Well that certainly gives you plenty of scope for narrowing things down.'

Sarah watched his face, unsure if he was being purely factual or if he was making a wry comment.

'But,' he said, 'there's enough detail in these letters to make a start.'

'Good. I was hoping so.'

Marchant finished his coffee.

'Another one?' asked Sarah.

'Oh, I think it's my turn.'

'No, you look at these again, I'll get the coffees.'

When she returned he was writing in a small notebook.

'What happened to Joyce?' he asked.

'Granny? She went on to marry a chap called Peter Harding.'

'What was she like?'

'Oh.' Sarah stopped to think. 'I only knew her as a child but my memory is of someone who was outgoing. Always interested in people. A bit like me I suppose. I think she and Peter must have rather drifted apart because she often seemed to be going off to places on her own. In fact Dad once said he thought she might have had a lover in Italy – which wouldn't be too surprising as Peter was a dry old stick.'

'And what else do you know about Peter?'

'Well, he's the man I've always called Grandpa – even though I've known for a while he wasn't my actual grandfather. He died when I was five so I never really knew him.' she paused for a second, 'but I thought you might ask about him so I've bought in a few bits and pieces.'

'Thought I might ask about him?'

Sarah bit her lip but looked him in the eye. 'I was rather hoping you might be intrigued enough to want to help me find out more about Daniel.'

Marchant looked back at her and a smile slowly formed across his face. 'That was a fairly shrewd assumption I'd say.'

Sarah felt a tremor of excitement, sensing that this moment might be the start of an intriguing adventure. 'That's marvellous.'

Marchant reached forwards. 'Hand them over then,' he said, 'and let's get started.'

Sarah handed over various documents to Marchant related to Peter Harding. He looked through them quickly.

'So, he only joined the Army towards the end of the war,' he said, 'as an officer in the artillery – so there's unlikely to be any connection there.'

'No,'

'And you say he was a dry old stick.'

'Yes, by all accounts. Joyce seems to have been the one everyone remembers with affection.'

'And you say she was a bit like you.'

Sarah thought she detected the mildest of smiles. 'People have said so.'

'Well, it might be worth my looking into his time in the Army. At least we have more than just his first name to go on.'

Sarah watched Marchant but, again, his expression gave nothing away as to whether he was speaking factually or ironically.

'It would be so good to find out more about my true grandfather,' she said, 'it's a gap in my past that's become rather important to me for some reason.'

'I understand.'

'There is one other thing, though.'

Marchant waited for her to speak.

'Dad did say something funny the other day when I asked him about Daniel.'

'After you'd found the letters.'

'Yes.'

Marchant detected her hesitation. 'And this is the thing you thought might be of interest to me.'

Sarah smiled. 'Well deduced.'

'I've been waiting for it to emerge.'

Sarah paused, suddenly doubting the wisdom of revealing the route her thoughts had taken her these past days.

'Go on,' said Marchant, 'I hear all sorts of strange things in my job.'

Sarah gathered herself. 'Well, when I asked Dad about Daniel he said 'Unknown Soldier,' to me.

Marchant gave her a long look. 'And?'

'I didn't know what to make of it but I googled 'Unknown Soldier' and came up with all sorts of information.

'You mean about the burial of the Unknown Soldier in 1920.'

'Yes.'

'And you think there might be some link?'

'I have no idea, it's just that it seemed odd.'

Marchant's eyes remained on hers. 'Did he say anything else?'

'No, he's very frail and barely able to talk. I haven't had another word out of him since.'

'I see. But what are you suggesting?'

'Nothing.' Sarah felt herself beginning to blush. 'I don't know what I'm suggesting. It's just it was an odd thing to say.'

Marchant looked down at Daniel's letters on the table. 'Your father was probably implying that Daniel was one of the thousands of men who were killed but there was no record of their death. The body buried in Westminster Abbey belonged to a soldier bought back to England from the Western Front in 1920. They went to extravagant lengths to ensure it was completely unidentifiable.'

'I know, I've read it up.'

Marchant finished his expresso. 'So if there is any link it would be purely circumstantial.'

'Yes, of course.'

'Of course it's quite a thing isn't it?'

'What is?'

'The Unknown Soldier. Or 'Warrior' to give him his proper name. A body belonging to no one knows who is buried amongst royalty in one of the most hallowed places in the country and is revered over decades. The dead man could have been a private soldier, an officer, a good man, a wicked man, a brave man, a coward – no one will ever know yet that body has come to hold almost mythical status.'

'No one will ever know? No one will ever find out who it is?'

'Of course not.'

They sat in silence for a few seconds.

'Well, as you say, quite a thing,' said Sarah.

'Anyway, Let's focus on finding out more about this chap Daniel. I'll see if I can identify which regiment he was in and at the same time I'll look up details of Peter Harding. I feel quietly confident that something will crop up.'

'Great. Is there anything I can do?'

'Not for the moment but there probably will be.'

'Thanks.' Sarah closed her folder. 'I guess that's it, then.'

'For the moment, yes.'

'And what shall I pay you for this?'

'Oh, I hadn't thought of that.' Marchant looked momentarily non plussed. 'I don't often work on behalf of individuals.'

'Perhaps you can email me when you've given it some thought.'

'Well, in a sense I've already received some form of payment in being able to see those letters.'

'I'm sure we can do better than that.' Sarah smiled. 'How about as a start I buy you some lunch?'

'What, now?'

'Yes.' She looked at her watch. 'It's 12.45, we both need to eat something.'

Marchant looked surprised at the suggestion. 'Well, I suppose so. I normally just have a sandwich.'

'Well why not go wild for once?'

Marchant smiled wryly at her. 'Are you implying,' he said, 'that I might be a bit of an old fogey?'

CHAPTER 4

April 1917

The Regiment was on the move again. Kit was packed, the men fell in, and they set off in an easterly direction.

'Back to the line,' said Dawkins.

'Be nice if they told us what the fuck was going on,' said Timmings.

'Can't do that,' said Dawkins, 'we might wander over to Fritz and tell him we were about to attack.'

They marched along narrow roads and as they progressed a light drizzle dampened their webbing. They passed through small villages where the locals stood and waved and asked where they were headed.

'Don't ask us,' replied Fletcher humorously, 'we're only the poor bloody infantry.'

'Ypres, that's where we're headed,' said Dawkins, 'I've been down this road before.'

The new Platoon Sergeant, Sergeant Barnes appeared beside them. 'What's your name son?' he asked Timmings.

'Timmings, sarn't.'

'You're a big lad, we've got a Lewis with us, you can carry it after the next halt.'

'Yes, Sarn't.'

'And who are you?' he asked Daniel.

'Dawkins, Sergeant.'

'Ah, so you're Dawkins.'

Daniel raised an eyebrow. 'I'm famous then Sergeant?' he said.

'Infamous more like,' said Sergeant Barnes.

Daniel looked across at him. 'Did they mention my promotion then Sergeant?'

'Demotion, Dawkins, or demotions more like. That's what was mentioned.'

'The Regiment's loss, Sergeant.'

Barnes didn't smile. 'Time will tell,' he said, 'it always does.' He moved on to talk to the other soldiers in 5 Platoon.

'No messing with him, then,' said Timmings.

'Fought at Mons,' said Dawkins, who always seemed to have inside information about everyone, 'one of the old regulars.'

'Lucky to still be alive then,' said Fletcher.

'Been in a training depot since the first Christmas,' said Dawkins, 'back for a second crack at Fritz.' He shifted his webbing on his waist. 'Bit of a bastard by all accounts.'

After two hours the battalion came to a halt and the men sat down on the grass verges. Hot tea was issued into mess tins and they lit up cigarettes. The rain had stopped and the sun appeared infrequently between gaps in the clouds. Dawkins, Fletcher and Timmings sat apart from the rest of the soldiers, comfortable in their own company and wary of being drawn into conversations about the front with the new recruits. In the distance a sound of shells being fired carried to them on the light wind and the men stopped talking and looked in the direction of the guns. Lieutenant Jeremy Latham, the officer who had arrived the day before and their new Platoon Commander, came walking down the line of soldiers and stopped to talk to them. They stood to attention and saluted.

'Good morning,' he said.

'Morning, sir.'

'I gather from Sergeant Barnes that you're the old guard here.'

'You could put it that way, sir,' said Fletcher.

'And you are?'

'Fletcher, sir. And this is Private Timmings and this is Private Dawkins.'

Latham looked at Timmings. 'How old are you, Timmings?' he asked.

'Nineteen sir.'

'And how long have you been out here?'

'Over eight months sir.'

'Well, you're ahead of me on one score at least.' He turned to Dawkins. 'So you're Dawkins.'

'That's right, sir.'

'I hear you've been with the Battalion since it was formed.'

'Yes, sir.'

'Not too many like you still around.'

'Like me, sir? Not sure what you mean by that.'

Latham smiled. 'Your reputation preceeds you.'

'Should that worry me?'

'I don't know, should it?' Latham stood facing Dawkins, aware that while he was judging the men in his command they were, in turn, judging him.

'It worries some.'

'Well, I'll form my own opinions.' Latham smiled again. 'Anyway,' he said, 'I look forward to serving with you.'

'Very good, sir, likewise,' said Dawkins and Latham moved on to speak to the next group of men.

When he was out of earshot Timmings looked at his friends.

'Fuck me, he's got you marked, Dan.'

'Major Witheridge'll have told him about me, that's all. Anyway, he seemed all right. Spoke to us without looking down his nose like that bastard Horrocks. That's a start.'

'Liked the look of him,' said Fletcher, 'but fresh. Just out of private school I'll bet.'

'He'll learn fast enough.'

'As long as he doesn't fuck us about he'll fit in.'

'As long as he doesn't send us to our fucking deaths, you mean.'

Dawkins looked at both his friends with a quizzical expression. 'Isn't that what he's here to do?' he said.

Only two days earlier Lieutenant Jeremy Latham had been savouring his last evening meal with his family before heading out to France, enjoying the taste of the meat and the vegetables and wondering what the food would be like in the trenches.

'Jane's doing well at St Bart's,' his father had said, sitting to his left, at the opposite end of the mahogany dining table to his mother.

'Good for her,' said Jeremy, 'she'll make a fine nurse.'

'Now,' said his mother, 'do you have enough warm clothes? It's still cold out there at night.'

Jeremy laughed. 'I'll be absolutely fine, mother, ' he said, 'I've been issued with plenty of kit.'

'I hope so, I don't like the thought of you sitting in one of those trenches freezing to death.' She stopped and put her hand to her mouth as if trying belatedly to stop the word from slipping out. 'You know what I mean,' she said.

'I do. I'll be fine,' said Jeremy, 'anyway spring is upon us and it can be beautiful over there at this time of year.'

'It can,' said his father, 'it will be a great adventure.'

A maid appeared and took away their plates. Jeremy Latham, aged nineteen and diverted from his plans to go to university, chose not to respond to his father's statement. Each day both men would read the papers, but it had seemed for some time that while Jeremy could see past the deception of the journalists who wrote of great advances on the Western Front, his father had decided to accept without question the unbridled patriotism that coloured the reports from across the Channel. The previous year Jeremy had been struck, in particular, by his father's reaction to the documentary *The Battle of the Somme*, that they had seen together.

'A fine record of our brave men,' his father had said as they left the cinema.

'Father, have you read the details? Twenty thousand killed on the first day? No ground gained?'

'Don't be defeatist,' his father had replied, 'that sort of talk will get us nowhere.'

When the time had come for Jeremy to enlist he had done so with a sinking heart that he had kept from his parents. It was out of a sense of duty that he volunteered his services, a feeling that he must play his part in spite of the horror of a war based on the tactics of attrition. He had read Bloch's thesis, written nearly twenty years earlier, that the modernisation of weaponry combined with the state's ability to mobilise industrial resources would result in stalemate. He was, he suspected, about to enter a conflict that anyone with imagination could see was insane but from which there seemed no escape.

In his training he had kept quiet about his thoughts. He had performed his tasks, had practiced the drills, had appraised himself of the tactics and the weaponry of the war with Germany and had diligently learnt the duties of a junior officer on the Western Front. When assigned to the 6th Berkshire Light Infantry as a Second Lieutenant he had quietly studied their recent history, noted their formation in 1915 and read the casualty figures. Fewer than a quarter of the original volunteers had survived those first few years.

'When's the train?' asked his Father.

'Ten. The boat leaves mid afternoon. We'll be in Flanders by early evening.'

'We'll drive you to the station,' said his mother.

'Are you sure? I can always catch a bus.'

'No,' said his father, 'I think we can see you off on this occasion.'

* * * *

But in the morning Jeremy's mother remained in their front hall to see him off.

'I have one of my boring headaches,' she told him, straining to hold herself together.

'I'm sorry,' he said, 'you go and rest, I'll be fine.'

She held him tightly to her as he kissed her on the cheek then she turned abruptly and went into his father's study without speaking.

'Let's be off then,' said his Father.

In the driveway the Lanchester had its roof down and it's 5.5 litre engine started with an impressive roar. As his father turned the wheel to head them out towards the Bath Road Jeremy looked back and saw his mother standing in the study window, staring out, not waving.

It was a crisp, sunny day. The wind whistled past as the powerful engine propelled the light blue car along the empty road and Jeremy settled back in his seat, looking at the passing landscape, concentrating on all the familiar landmarks to ensure they were recorded in his memory.

They spoke little until the car was approaching Reading.

'It's a fine thing you're doing,' said his father and, when Jeremy didn't reply, he added, 'I wish I were coming with you.'

'Sadly you're too old.'

His father looked over at him, unsure how to take this. 'They're saying one more offensive might do it. Maybe you'll be home before long.'

Jeremy smiled. 'One way or another,' he replied.

His father breathed heavily but said nothing and concentrated on his driving. Soon they were nearing the station.

'You can drop me off here,' said Jeremy.

'It's not a problem, I can take you to the door.'

'No, I'd prefer to be dropped off here, thanks.'

'If you so wish.'

They stopped in a side street and Jeremy took out his bags.

'Well, I guess this is it then,' he said.

His father reached out his hand and Jeremy noticed his lower lip had a slight tremble to it. 'I'm proud of you Jeremy,' he said, 'It's a fine thing you're doing for a fine cause. Be strong and come back safely.'

Jeremy shook the hand. 'I'll do that,' he said, 'Goodbye father.'

* * * *

By evening 5 Platoon was established in a reserve trench and for the following three days very little happened apart from night time patrols, shoring up of the trenches and the occasional burst of fire from both sides to keep the enemy on edge.

On the morning of 17 April Dawkins was resting against the side of the trench having a cigarette when Lieutenant Latham appeared by his side.

'How's it going, Dawkins?' asked Latham.

'High on mud and shrapnel, sir, short on women.'

'Aren't you due some leave soon?'

'Yes sir, as soon as we're relieved here.'

'That won't be too long.'

'Just have to avoid the triple fucking whammy in the meantime then sir.'

'Which one's that?'

'Over the top, in the rain, being shelled by our own side.'

'I think that's unlikely for some time yet.' Latham peered through a periscope. 'Perhaps we're saving that one up for your return.'

'Very good, sir. But it's my job to provide the black humour. It's yours to send us to our instant deaths.'

Latham laughed drily. 'I don't recall that phrase being featured in the pamphlets at officer training.'

'Fritz has gone very quiet for the moment,' said Dawkins.

'Conserving his energy like us,' said Latham.

'Any news of an assault?'

'None. Then again I'd only find out just before you. But staff must be planning something.'

Dawkins looked through the periscope. Ahead of them the ground sloped upwards gradually until, in the middle distance, it rose to a height of about eighty metres. 'That ridge will be our objective before too long I'd guess,' he said.

'Not much to shout about, ' Latham replied. The ground in this part of Flanders was low lying and criss crossed with small streams.

'It least it's not raining,' said Dawkins. He sat down on a ledge in the trench.

'You've seen a fair bit of action,' said Latham.

'I have that, sir.'

'I gather you were cut off in a trench with Major Witheridge last year.'

'That's right.' Dawkins leant back against the earth and Latham waited for him to continue.

'We got isolated in a forward trench. Fritz was advancing and broke our lines to the left and right of us, wiping out the rest of the Platoon. The Major was on a visit at the time and we ended up fighting them off. Fuck knows how, we were down to bayonets by the end.' Dawkins shook his head. 'There were twelve of us at the start and by the time the reserves arrived and drove Fritz back it was just me and the Major. Close fucking call it was.'

As Dawkins spoke dispassionately about an episode that had become something of a legend amongst the whole battalion, Latham watched him with interest. 'And you were promoted after that,' he said.

'Yes sir.'

'What for?'

'My Corporal took one early on and I took over.'

'And demoted since.'

'Yes. Then promoted again. Then demoted. Three times in all.'

'How come?'

Dawkins studied the young man who was the latest in a long line of officers fresh from Sandhurst who had been his Platoon Commander. 'People say I have a problem with authority.'

'And do you?'

Dawkins stubbed out his cigarette and looked intently at Latham. 'Only when it doesn't know it's arse from it's elbow.'

'I see.' Latham smiled. 'Then I'd better be sure of my anatomy in the weeks ahead.'

Dawkins laughed. 'Your arse looks in the right place to me, sir.'

Before Latham could answer Timmings appeared with Murphy the dog on a makeshift lead and Murphy leapt up to lick Dawkins on the face.

'It's somewhat irregular to have a dog in the section, isn't it?' said Latham.

'Hundreds of 'em in the lines, sir,' said Timmings, 'trained for comms.'

'I thought there were signallers for that.'

'Lines break all the time, sir. Murph takes messages between us and reserve.'

'I see.'

'And sometimes takes food and water out to men trapped in No Man's Land.'

'So, a useful fellow.'

Timmings offered Latham a cigarette.

'I don't smoke thanks,' he said.

'What were you back home then sir?' asked Timmings.

Latham patted Murphy on the head. 'I would be at university now, reading law.'

'Sounds a fucking boring thing to read if you'll excuse me, sir.'

'I'm sorry. I meant studying law. I plan to be a lawyer one day.'

'You'll learn enough about law out here, law of the fucking jungle.'

'Ah.'

'Only law we get out here is when we're on a charge or a court martial,' said Timmings.

Latham observed him. 'I assume you've experienced the former but not the later,' he said.

'Don't know about fucking formers or laters if you'll excuse the expression sir but I've been on enough charges.'

'Have you now.'

'Mind you, I was at Billy Spencer's court martial last year,' said Timmings, 'witness number one, I were.'

'What was that for?' asked Latham.

'Cowardice. He wouldn't advance. Said we could all rot in hell and called Mr Horrocks all manner of names.'

'What happened to him?'

'Hard labour. Not the firing squad, thank fuck.'

'Can't have men refusing to advance,' said Dawkins.

Fletcher, who had appeared while they were talking, joined in the conversation. 'You're right Dan,' he said, 'but Billy was spent. Reduced to a wreck of a man. It was inhuman to send him over.'

'Then he should have been sent back down the line. Shouldn't have been there at all. That's where the mistake was made.'

'But he was.'

'Then he had to advance. No discussion.'

'That simple is it Dan?'

'Need to keep things simple Fletch or we're all fucked.'

Latham watched the two friends discuss the rights and wrongs of military discipline and guessed this conversation had been played out in many variations over the past year.

'Anyway,' said Fletcher, 'Timbo and I are on our way to report for duty. We can't stay here chatting all day. '

'See you later then boys,' said Dawkins, 'behave yourselves.'

'Well, I must be getting on too,' said Latham but he didn't move straight away.

'Got a bird lined up have you, sir?'

'That would certainly be an achievement out here.' Latham stood up straight, the top of his head just below the top of the trench. 'Do you have a girlfriend back home?' he asked.

'Bloody right, sir.'

Dawkins reached into his pocket and pulled out a small metal container which he opened. Inside the container was a photograph of a woman with long, curly hair. On her head was a straw boater at an unusual angle. He handed it to Latham. 'Joyce, sir, known her since school.'

'She's very beautiful.'

'I'll be seeing her when I get back. Second thing I'll do is put down my kit bag.'

Latham laughed. 'Well, send her my regards,' he said.

'Thank you sir, I will.'

Jeremy Latham made his way towards the dugout that served as platoon headquarters. Life at the front had proved, so far, to be surprisingly comfortable. With little rain for a while the trench where 5 Platoon were based was dry and bearably warm. As Dawkins had observed, the Germans had gone very quiet. The Platoon Commander's dugout had space for Latham to sleep out flat and his orderly saw to most of his basic needs. Living in close proximity to his soldiers he had quickly become familiar with the various routines they had adopted to make life in a hostile environment bearable.

He sat down on a chair fashioned out of duck boards and considered writing a letter home. It would be a while before he had some leave but, having spent two thirds of the last ten years at boarding school, he was used to being separated from his family and the communal life of the regiment quite suited him. He looked about him at the confined space that had become his habitat and it felt little different from his study at Harrow. If it were to rain, as Dawkins had suggested, then the situation might be very different. The low lying land would quickly become saturated and life would become unpleasant. Any assault, he realised, would be highly dependent on the weather.

Sergeant Barnes appeared at the entrance and saluted. 'I've told the platoon I'm having an extra kit inspection at 1600hrs,' he said.

'Oh, why's that?'

'I'm not happy with standards. The men are getting sloppy.'

'I thought they seemed OK.'

'Got to keep on top of it, sir. It's discipline that'll win this war.'

'Very well, Sergeant, but don't ride them too hard.'

Sergeant Barnes, squat and red faced, stood facing his young Platoon Commander. 'The moment you stop riding them hard is the moment they start fucking it up,' he said.

'I see. Well, carry on.'

Sergeant Barnes left and shortly after this Major Witheridge, the Company Commander, strode into the dugout.

'Hello Latham,' he said.

'Hello, sir.'

'How are things?'

'Quiet.'

'Keeping the men busy?'

'As busy as can be.'

'Good.'

Witheridge sat down opposite Latham and they talked about the mundanities of life in the front line.

'Any concerns?' asked Witheridge.

Latham thought for a few seconds. 'Just the one, really, a man called Jackson. He seems quite disturbed.'

'I know him. He had a rough time of it at the Somme.'

'He was sent back out on the same ship as me. He's clearly out of sorts.'

'Unhinged?'

'I'd say so. He has this constant twitching, he hardly speaks, he looks withdrawn all the time. He's rather spooking the other men.'

'Nothing to do about it I fear.' Witheridge reached into his pocket, removed a flask and took a swig. 'If the doctors have decided he's fit to fight, he's fit to fight. I've had a few battles on this one and never got anywhere.' He offered the flask to Latham who took a small sip of whisky. 'He was a good man,' continued Witheridge, 'a brave bugger, in fact, but we all have our limits. I guess he's reached his.'

They sat quietly, both considering the possibilities this statement raised in their minds.

'I'm getting to know Dawkins,' said Latham.

'Dawkins.' Major Witheridge smiled. 'He'd be a Sergeant Major by now if he wasn't so bloody insubordinate. He's a good man to have beside you in a scrap though.'

'Yes, I heard about that.'

'He seems quite fearless.'

'Is that rare?'

'Yes, it is. We're facing death all the time. If you're not afraid you're not alive.'

'What is it then? Lack of imagination?'

'He's a hard man to read. Lack of imagination?' Major Witheridge stopped speaking to think this through. 'That's sometimes the case but not, I suspect, with Dawkins.' He shook his head, suggesting an uncertainty in his judgement. 'No, it's more that he seems unconcerned about being killed.'

'Unconcerned?'

'Yes, he shows no apprehension when faced with danger.' Major Witheridge looked at Latham. 'In fact it's almost as if he welcomes it.'

Latham nodded slowly as he related the Major's words to the soldier he was just getting to know. 'So, a bit of an enigma,' he said, 'but I find I rather like him.'

'He's likeable enough but he's not the type you'd want to fall out with. Good friend, bad enemy, that sort of type.'

'I'll remember that.'

'And how are you finding Sergeant Barnes?'

Latham chose his words carefully. 'Highly professional. As you said, uncompromising. Not exactly a bundle of laughs.'

'That sounds about right.'

'I'd say I've developed a working relationship with him – but not exactly a warm one.'

'It doesn't need to be warm.'

'I know that. It's just that I'm not sure he has much time for officers.'

'Well, there's history there. There was something about him having an altercation with his Platoon Commander on the retreat from Mons.'

'Altercation?'

'I read it in his file. He felt the officer was abandoning their position too readily.'

'Lord.'

'It was all dealt with at the time but rumour has it that the brass rather felt Barnes was in the right. Anyway, the officer in question was killed soon after and it was all glossed over.'

'How interesting.' Latham recalled some of the conversations he'd had with Sergeant Barnes. 'I wonder if that might have something to do with his being held back in England for so long.'

'Could be. He certainly has a short fuse by all accounts.'

'Yes, I've noticed that.'

They ran through other men in Latham's command and then moved on to the wider picture.

'Now, nothing is confirmed as yet,' said Witheridge, 'but it seems ever more likely that we'll be going over in early June.'

Latham did some quick calculations. 'So, about eight weeks.'

'Something like that. There's been a lot of activity going on recently putting in water pipelines and building light railways to bring ammunition and supplies to the front. It looks like they're really planning this one in detail.'

'That sounds encouraging.'

'It is. And the good news is we've got Plumer in command.'

'General Plumer. Isn't he the one they call 'Daddy'?'

Witheridge laughed. 'True. He looks a bit of a blimp but he's very shrewd. He's one of the few generals I'd feel truly confident in and he has a chap called Harington on his staff who is a first rate planner.'

'And what's the plan?'

'I don't know the details but it seems Messines Ridge will be the first objective.'

'I thought that might be the case.'

'And if it's 2nd Army who are given the job then we'll be the ones at the sharp end.'

'So, another big push.'

'It looks like it.'

'Eight weeks.'

'Yes. Eight weeks. There will be practices between now and then, some men have leave, and, of course, there will be a bloody great bombardment in the build up.'

'Good.' Latham said the word without irony but he knew well enough the statistics of all previous big pushes. 'Well,' he said, 'it gives us something to think about.'

Witheridge looked at him. 'No,' he said, 'Don't do that. Don't think ahead, Latham. Live day to day, hour to hour, minute to minute. ...' He looked up as a plane flew overhead. 'These are the most extraordinary circumstances in which we find ourselves,' he continued once the plane was past. 'Death ..... and mutilation... you'll see plenty of that. Over time men can get used to it. Perhaps I have. But I've seen men under my command driven to the point of insanity – some beyond – by what they've experienced. Those new to the lines... such a contrast….the horror…' His words tailed off for a moment before he re-focused. 'So, detach yourself. Learn to go somewhere else in your mind. Don't think too much. Don't ask questions.'

Latham waited in silence for Witheridge to continue and the Major turned to stare at him, the intensity of his expression that of a man who had gone beyond the bounds of normal human experience.

'Hate,' continued Witheridge, 'that's something the men do. They demonise the Hun and it helps them when it comes to killing.' He faced Latham once more and his eyes seemed temporarily softer. 'But for the thinking man that's not so easy.' He turned away again. 'So just accept. Accept one's lot, accept the fact that it's kill or be killed. That's the only way.'

He stood up to leave.

Judging that his Company Commander had finished speaking Latham stood to attention and saluted.

'Thanks for the advice, sir,' he said.

Witheridge laughed uncomfortably. 'Advice?' He shook his head. 'I'm not sure advice is of any use here, Latham. You must find your own way.'

'Very well, sir.'

Witheridge turned to go. 'One more thing, I want you to carry out a stunt this evening.'

'A stunt?'

'A raid.'

'Ah.'

'You know what that involves, don't you?'

'Sort of. We covered raids at the depot but it was rather rudimentary.'

Witheridge eyed the green young officer in front of him. 'Well, you'll learn soon enough, they're not that complicated.' He smiled, as if amused by the thought of a mere boy with minimal training leading battle hardened veterans out into No Man's Land. 'There have been reports of the Bosche setting up a forward post in some poplars seven hundred yards from our front line, about a hundred from theirs. We need to check it out and destroy it.'

'Right. Of course.' Latham held Witheridge's eye. 'This evening – what, before it gets dark?'

Witheridge laughed and put his hand on Latham's shoulder. 'Only if you have a death wish, Latham.'

'Well, I don't have that.'

'Good. No. After dark. No one goes out on patrol in daylight unless they're a complete fool. And I hope you're not that.'

'So do I sir.'

An hour later Dawkins listened as his new Platoon Commander issued instructions for the raid. Twelve men were to head out after dark and work their way to the small wood where, once they had located the German post, they were to bomb it and kill all inhabitants.

'What kit shall we take, sir?' asked one of the selected soldiers.

'Well....' Latham hesitated.

'Rifles, bandoliers and grenades,' said Dawkins, 'that's all we'll need.'

'Very well, rifles, bandoliers and grenades.'

More questions were asked and Latham answered them as best he could. One soldier in particular seemed unconvinced by the wisdom of the raid and kept questioning the finer details.

'Listen, Henderson,' said Latham eventually, 'I know no more than I've told you. We just have to get on and do what we've been ordered to.'

Henderson, a soldier who always managed to find fault with any instructions he received, opened his mouth to speak again but Dawkins turned to him. 'Shut you're fucking mouth, Henderson,' he said, 'you've heard the officer, you know the drill. Just fucking get on with it.'

Henderson made to reply but this time one of the two corporals on the raid told him to quieten down or he'd be up in front of the OC. Soon after that the briefing came to an end.

Thirty minutes later, with the light gone, they assembled in the trench, their faces darkened, two scouts to go ahead and the bombers staying close to Latham.

They worked their way as quietly as possible along the trench and then out through a gap and into the open. Dawkins and Timmings stuck close together.

'Does he have a fucking clue?' whispered Timmings.

'Doubt it,' whispered Dawkins back. 'But Corporal Stephens knows the ropes well enough.'

It took them about half an hour of walking, crouching and waiting for long periods before they came to the wood. Dawkins crawled up to the side of Latham who was lying on his front, peering into the darkness.

'They're reported to be at the far right,' whispered Latham, 'in a dip in the ground.'

'Can't see it myself.'

'We'll need to get closer.'

'Send the scouts on.'

'OK.'

Latham motioned for the scouts to join him and he talked to them briefly before they set off again towards the wood. The remainder of the raiding party lay flat, waiting in silence, staring ahead towards the enemy lines.

'Fucking lice,' whispered Timmings to Dawkins, 'I can feel the little buggers all over me legs eating me up.'

'They'll be eating dead flesh unless you fucking pipe down, Timbo,' whispered Dawkins.

The scouts returned twenty minutes later and Dawkins listened in as they spoke to Latham.

'Heard em, sir,' one of them said, 'they was talking quietly. Three or four of them in some sort of dugout.'

'How easy is it to get close?' Latham asked.

'There's a bit of a dip leads up to them.'

'Is there someone on guard?'

'I think they're all inside.'

'Very well.' There was a silence as Latham considered his next move. 'Very well,' he said again, 'I'll go forwards with the bombers, the rest can observe from here.'

Dawkins touched his arm. 'Take a couple more, sir,' he said quietly, speaking only to Latham, 'minimum six, and get Corporal Batchelor to flank round with two men and cover from the left, Corporal Stephens to cover from the right.'

Latham was breathing heavily. 'Right, Dawkins, sound plan,' he said.

He signalled for his corporals to join him and issued his instructions. Then the two bombers, Dawkins, Timmings, Latham and one of the scouts waited for the covering parties to get in position.

'Ok, let's go,' he whispered after five minutes.

The ground was soft as they crept along, the night air cool, the jagged silhouette of the trees against the clear sky grew larger as they approached.

'Down here,' whispered the scout.

They followed him down into a dip and then he stopped and pointed to a shape up ahead. 'That's it,' he whispered. The six men advanced as quietly as possible until the shape became more distinct and they could make out a hide carved out of the earth with fallen branches and some kind of sheeting providing a door and a roof.

They turned their heads to hear better and, almost immediately, became aware of the sound of two men speaking in low tones.

The plan, discussed at the briefing, was for the raiding party to get as close as possible and for the bombers to throw their bombs directly into the listening post but the opening between the walls was so narrow there was little room for error.

Dawkins tapped Latham on the shoulder and, through hand gestures, suggested he would go forward and, on a given signal, pull apart the sheet covering the entrance so that the bombers could throw their bombs right into the heart of the post.

Latham nodded and Dawkins crept forwards. He stepped lightly but just as he was a few feet from the hide he stepped on a branch that cracked loudly. Shouts came from inside. Dawkins ran the last few paces, no longer caring about noise, ripped apart the sheeting and threw himself to one side as, all at the same time, the bombers threw their bombs and shots came whistling out fom the post. The men dived for cover as the bombs exploded inside and suddenly all went quiet. Dawkins ran to the entrance which, seconds earlier he had revealed and peered inside.

'Got em,' he shouted, 'All dead. Let's go.'

But then more shots were ringing out, coming from above them and to the left.

'Fuck, sentry,' shouted Timmings as he aimed into the darkness.

At that moment the flanking teams opened up and for a few seconds the sound of intense rifle fire sent senses reeling as Latham's team hugged the ground. Then, as if from some unspoken order, all firing stopped at exactly the same moment. A complete hush, in stark contrast to the cacophony of the previous moments, descended on the wood.

Dawkins ran up to Mr Latham. 'We're not far from their lines, sir,' he said, panting, 'all hell's going to break loose in a minute, we need to get out of here.'

Latham was already on his feet. 'Of course,' he said, 'Everyone here?'

'I'm here,' said the scout, 'Josephs, sir.'

'Timmings?'

'Yes.'

'King?'

'Sir.'

'Henderson?'

No answer.

'Henderson?'

Still no answer. 'Anyone see what happened to Henderson?'

'I saw him throw his bomb,' said King, 'then we both went to ground.'

'Show me.' Latham and Dawkins followed King to where the two bombers had stood and immediately they found Henderson, lying face down a few yards from the hide.

King shook him but there was no response. Latham bent down and listened for breathing, then tried to find a pulse. Dawkins felt the other wrist. 'He's dead, sir, let's go.'

'Dead?'

'As a doornail. Nothing we can do for him.'

'We'll take him back with us.'

'Can't, sir, they'll be onto us shortly.'

'But we can't leave him.'

'We'll come back tomorrow. We'll just risk more lives taking him.'

Latham froze in indecision.

'Sir, I've been here many times,' said Dawkins urgently, 'it's the living that count now. We must go.'

Latham still hesitated.

Dawkins leant towards him and spoke quietly into his ear. 'Sir. Trust me. I know this. Leave him and go.'

Latham had his eyes closed as he considered what to do. Dawkins leant forwards and grabbed his arm.

'OK,' said Latham, 'OK.' He stood up slowly. 'Very well,' he said, his voice sounding hollow, 'Follow me.'

The men gathered together and started running out of the dip into the open and Latham shouted to Corporals Batchelor and Stephens to follow. Suddenly a machine gun opened up from the German lines and then rifle fire sounded out along a wide front.

'Keep running,' shouted Dawkins, 'they can't see us, keep going until they throw up light.'

The flanking groups caught up with them and all eleven men were going at top speed when they heard the dull sound of a mortar being fired.

'Down,' shouted Corporal Stephens and the men dived to the ground before a thin white light lit up No Man's Land.

'Jones is hit,' shouted Corporal Batchelor.

'How bad?' asked Latham.

'We'll get him back.'

The light faded and the land slipped into darkness again.

'Keep low, move slowly,' said Dawkins, 'they didn't spot us or they'd be giving us hell.'

The men moved on, this time taking it steady, hugging the terrain, Jones being supported by two men, his left leg dragging along the ground. The machine gun opened up again but its aim was way off and then, as if having lost interest in their elusive prey, the enemy lines fell silent. The raiding party continued on their way, skirting shell holes, negotiating wire defences, stepping carefully to avoid the detritus of broken machinery and severed limbs that were the fabric of No Man's Land.

'Keep your eyes peeled,' said Corporal Batchelor, 'most dangerous time on a patrol' and the men looked about them for signs of movement but they were lone figures in the landscape as they cautiously crossed the open land towards the safety of their trenches.

Sergeant Barnes was waiting for them when they returned.

'All back, sir?' he asked Lieutenant Latham.

'Henderson's dead, Jones was hit in the leg but he's made it back.'

'What happened to Henderson?'

'Shot as we took out the post.'

'What did you do with him?'

'We left him.'

'Left him?' The tone in Sergeant Barnes's voice expressed incredulity.

'Yes, Sergeant Barnes, we left him. There was no option. We'll need to go out and recover his body later.'

'And risk more lives?'

'We'd have risked more if we'd tried to bring him back.'

Sergeant Barnes shook his head. 'Well, sir, I'm glad it's you not me who writes to his family,' he said. 'Where's Jones?'

'Over there.'

'Right. I'll get him on his way back to a field station.' He made a point of speaking loudly so that all the men could hear him. 'At least we can make sure one of our soldiers gets the attention he deserves.'

Latham was left alone with Dawkins.

'Fuck,' said Latham.

'Don't listen to him, you did the right thing, sir,' said Dawkins.

'I'm going to go back for Henderson.'

'Don't do that. They'll be alert now. Do it tomorrow night.'

Latham sat down, exhausted. 'Shit!' he said.

'It was a successful raid,' said Dawkins. 'We did as well as could be expected.

'And we lost a man.'

'Seldom don't on a raid. And he was a useless bastard anyway. Better off without him.'

Latham didn't reply. 'Speak to Major Witheridge in the morning', said Dawkins, 'tell him what happened, he'll say you did the right thing.'

Latham nodded slowly then held out his hand. 'Thanks Dawkins, you helped out there,' he said.

'Only looking after myself,' said Dawkins, 'that's all I was doing. And killing Fritz. That makes it a good night's work.' He shook his Platoon Commander's hand. 'And now, if you'll excuse me, I'll get some kip then I'm off on some well deserved fucking leave.'

CHAPTER 5

May 1917

George Latham, father of Lieutenant Jeremy Latham, was celebrating his sixtieth birthday at a quiet dinner with old friends but it was proving to be a sombre occasion. Apart from George and his wife Elizabeth, of the four couples present one had a son who had been killed in action the previous year and one had a son who was back home badly wounded. They had all agreed early on in the evening to avoid talking about the war but this was proving difficult to achieve and, by the time cheese was being served, George was engaged in an argument with his oldest friend about why the conflict had started in the first place. He believed firmly that the expansionist Germans were the sole cause, that they must be defeated at whatever cost and that the British were fighting for a just and noble cause. His friend was taking a more dispassionate view and talking of rival empires jockeying for position in a new world order.

'What rot,' George said, temporarily losing his customary politeness, 'are you telling me we should have simply accepted the Hun's aggression?'

'No, George,' his friend, a writer with connections in the War Office, replied, 'I am simply saying it was more complicated than just good versus evil, right versus wrong.'

'Well you don't have sons,' said George, 'you can stand back and take an intellectual view if you want but for most of us it is a matter of life and death and that is indeed a simple matter.'

Elizabeth, recognising a discussion that had taken place on a number of previous occasions and that always ended in disagreement and bad feeling, placed her hands on both men's forearms. 'George, Ralph,' she said, 'we've been here many times before. Let's move on.'

'Of course,' said Ralph, 'I apologise.'

George, a man of firm opinions and less able than his friend to distance himself from an argument sat staring at his cutlery and it was only a conversation about his favourite topic, motor cars, that finally calmed him down.

Later, in the billiards room, with only the men present, he was unable to resist bringing up the subject again.

'What are all our young lads out there dying for if not our freedom?' he asked. 'I am proud of their sacrifice. I am proud of the noble thing they do for us.'

'So am I,' said Ralph, 'So am I, George. Every one of them.'

'But?'

'But nothing.'

'I don't believe you.'

'But nothing, George. They are brave men all of them.'

'And?'

'George.' Ralph clipped the end off his cigar. 'I am not that distant from you in my views. I am not, and you, of all people, should know this, one for standing back in the face of an aggressor.' He leant on the green baize of the table, picked up a red ball and rolled it straight into the top corner pocket. 'I am not an apologist. I understand that the Kaiser is the initiator of all this. I know he must be stopped. I am simply observing that we seem, and by we I mean the European powers, to somehow have landed ourselves in the most godforsaken mess which looks set to wipe out a generation of our youth across the continent. I find it hard to see anything noble in all of that.'

'So what's your answer.'

'George.' Ralph patted his host on the back. 'No one has an answer. That is the tragedy of all this.'

George sighed heavily. He picked up a cue and began potting at balls. 'One needs to be certain, Ralph,' he said. 'Prevarications are an insidious thing in times like these.'

Ralph, aware that his friend's bluster hid a deep concern for his son and that any admission of doubt might bring the whole pack of cards tumbling down, nodded in agreement. 'You're right, George,' he said, 'let's leave it at that.'

Two days later an article in *The Times* caused George to reflect on that conversation. The article highlighted the enormous financial and human cost the lack of progress in the past three years had wreaked on the nation and it painted a vivid picture of destruction, loss and economic hardship. George sat back in his armchair, put the paper to one side, and found himself doing just what he had advised against two nights earlier; questioning the very core of his own certainties.

Elizabeth entered the room and he looked up at her.

'Any news?' he asked.

She held out a letter. 'He seems fine,' she said, 'there's not much happening by the sound of it.'

George read the letter in which Jeremy talked of his time in the front line and his relationship with his soldiers. 'He's doing well by the sound of it,' he said.

'Yes, he is,' said Elizabeth.

George took out his pipe and tapped it on the table. 'I've been thinking through the conversation with Ralph,' he said.

'I know you have.'

'I am right, Liz, aren't I?'

'Yes dear.'

'No. Be honest with me. We've never really talked this through. Do you really think I'm right? Do you agree with me it's a great thing Jeremy is doing?'

Elizabeth could see in his eyes the conflict that had recently been troubling her husband and she put her hand on his shoulder. 'We can't know, can we darling,' she said. 'If he comes back fit and well and we win this war then we'll know we were right.' She sat down beside him. 'But if .....' she struggled to find the right words, 'if ...... that doesn't happen then perhaps we will think differently.'

George closed his eyes and rocked back and forth in his chair.

'Then let us just pray for the former,' he said.

Mrs Margaret Jackson sat in her small living room in her house in Reading and held onto the photograph of her son, Peter, as if her life depended on it. She often sat like this after returning from work in the clothing factory, thinking of him, imagining what he might be up to, reading and re-reading his letters.

She reflected on the day a few weeks earlier when he had been sent back to the front. Straight from seeing the medical officer he had sat with her in the corner café at the end of their terraced street in Reading.

'They can't do that,' she had said, holding his hands fiercely across the wooden table, 'they can't.'

'They have, mum.'

'But you're not well.' She had begun weeping and Peter had handed her his handkerchief.

'You're not well,' she repeated, 'they can't send you back.'

'Mum, please.' Peter had looked towards the couple at a nearby table who were casting glances in their direction. 'There's nothing to be done, Mum, nothing. I have to go, I have no choice.'

'But it's not right.' Margaret's sobs were growing in intensity. 'It's not right. You can't go, you can't go back, you're all I have.'

On the way home she had noticed his leg twitching involuntarily as he walked and had let out a loud cry of despair. 'Look at you,' she said, 'look at you. You're no good. You're no good to no one.' The sky was overcast, the terrace of narrow red brick houses faced straight on to the pavement, the street was covered in a greyish dust.

'You'll just have to cope, Mum,' he had said, 'I'll be all right. I'll be back before long, I promise.'

The doctors said they had found no physical reason for the shaking and one had even accused him of malingering and said that he was trying to delay his return to the front.

In the house as he had started making a sandwich for them, Margaret noticed that his left hand, like his leg, was also shaking. She watched him as he stared at the hairs on his wrist, at his knuckles, at the tips of his fingers that were moving up and down in small but rapid jerks. He closed his eyes and stood still for a few seconds.

'God save you,' she had whispered and then watched as, with an effort of will, he continued spreading the butter.

She now put down the photograph, cooked herself a simple meal, ate it alone in silence and then walked into town in the forlorn hope of meeting someone to talk to. An old acquaintance of hers had taken to having tea parties for mothers with sons at the front but after a few visits Margaret had been politely asked not to come again. She had remonstrated, saying the get togethers were all she had to look forward to each week, but her friend had said her continual weeping was unsettling the other mothers.

In his latest letter Peter had mentioned two people. Firstly, a fellow private called Dan who Peter said was one of the few men prepared to talk to him without laughing at his twitches, and secondly an officer, his Platoon Commander, called Mr Latham, who he described as 'educated but decent'. Margaret knew the name Latham. Some years earlier she had been employed as a cleaner at a large house in Sonning and that had been the name of her employers. The man of the house had been a rich businessman and quite distant and the lady had been formal to the point of awkwardness, but nevertheless Margaret had been treated well and had left with good references. And there was a son who would be about nineteen or twenty now and, if he was serving, would almost certainly be an officer. Perhaps, Margaret thought as she walked home, Mrs Latham might be able to help her.

The next day, after work, she went into town to check bus times out towards Sonning. A man in his fifties helped her with the timetables. As expected, with many buses commandeered for transportation in France and half the drivers now enlisted, bus schedules were greatly reduced but she found what she was looking for; a bus left for Slough via Sonning each weekday morning at 10am and returned in the evening at 4pm.

She had a day off the following Friday and as she walked along the canal towards her house she resolved to go to visit Mrs Latham. She would check she had the right Lathams and, if she did, she would tell Mrs Latham, mother to mother, about her son Peter. She would say he was a sick man who had done more than enough for his country, who was now damaged, who would never hurt a fly and and who must be sent home straight away.

On the Friday the bus, driven by a lady, was precisely on time. Margaret sat near the front and watched the streets pass by. The weather had deteriorated in the past twenty-four hours and the houses along the Bath Road seemed drab and unappealing in the grey light. At Sonning she stepped down onto the pavement and looked about her; the buildings were bigger here, set back from the road with their own driveways and she recalled the feelings of envy she used to have when arriving here from her little terrace in the new town estate.

As she approached the Latham's property she had misgivings about her decision to visit but steeled herself for what lay ahead. The worst that could happen, she reasoned, was that she would be turned away and all that would be lost would be a bus fare.

The gates were open and she walked up a path to the front door and rang the bell. A maid appeared who immediately recognised her.

'Margaret,' said the maid, 'it's been a while. What brings you here?'

Margaret was ushered into the pantry where she explained her purpose for coming and the maid confirmed that the son was indeed serving in France.

'It must be him, then,' said Margaret.

Mr Latham was up in town for the day and Mrs Latham was out visiting but would be back shortly. Margaret sat and waited, accepting a cup of tea from the maid and as she examined the rows of dishes laid out neatly on a dresser that was almost the size of her kitchen she started feeling nervous again. Half an hour later the front door opened and soon after that the maid, who had been carrying out her duties in another part of the house, appeared.

'Mrs Latham will see you now, Margaret,' she said.

Mrs Latham was standing in the drawing room, dressed in a navy blue dress with a brooch on her left lapel and a set of pearls around her neck. Her silver hair was swept up and back giving her a regal air.

'Margaret,' she said, 'what a pleasant surprise.'

Margaret executed a slight curtsey. 'Hello madam,' she said.

'And what can I do for you? Are you looking for a job?'

'No, madam, not at all. I work in Paterson's now.'

'Ah. So you are a shop worker.'

'No, madam, Paterson's the factory. I make uniforms.'

'Oh. Very good, that's most worthwhile.'

After this brief exchange Mrs Latham appeared to have reached the limits of her small talk and she stood smiling benignly at Margaret who smiled nervously back.

'Did Sarah offer you some coffee?'

'Yes, thank you, Madam.'

'Well, as I said, it's very nice to see you again.'

They stood facing each other.

'Sarah tells me your son Jeremy is with the 6th Berkshire Light Infantry in Flanders, Madam,' said Margaret.

'He is, yes.'

'So is my son Peter.'

'Oh, is he?'

'Yes, Madam, I've had a letter. I believe Jeremy may be Peter's Platoon Commander.'

Mrs Latham looked surprised. 'Well, that is a coincidence.'

'Not really, Madam, it's a local regiment, all from round here. It's not that surprising.'

'I suppose not.'

'Would you like to see the letter? Peter says nice things about your son.'

Mrs Latham nodded slowly, as if winding herself up gradually to engage fully with the woman opposite her whose desire to share personal information was proving unsettling. 'Yes,' she said, 'I would like to see it.'

Margaret handed over the letter and Mrs Latham sat down on the sofa to read it. Margaret leant over her shoulder and pointed out the relevant bits.

'Educated but decent,' read out Mrs Latham with a laugh, 'as if those two were contradictory.'

'Peter's a simple lad, Madam.'

'Oh no. I didn't mean it that way. It's rather a sweet view of life really.'

'The thing is,' said Margaret, 'Peter's not well.'

'Oh. I'm sorry to hear that.'

'He was wounded in the Somme. He came home for a while until he was fit again and they sent him back but he wasn't well. Not in the head, anyways. He shouldn't be out there, Madam, it's not right.'

Mrs Latham looked up from the letter and noticed for the first time the redness around Margaret's eyes. She patted the sofa beside her. 'Why don't you sit down and tell me about it,' she said, relaxing for the first time since Margaret had entered the room.

CHAPTER 6

October 2011

Sarah Harding's second meeting with James Marchant took place in his flat in Redcliffe Square. It was a typical batchelor's apartment with overfilled book cases, antique furniture and walls crammed with oil paintings. The yellowing woodwork of the door frames and skirting boards suggested there had been no redecoration in many years.

'Very nice,' said Sarah, admiring the ornate mouldings, sash windows and high ceilings. There was a smell of furniture polish throughout the rooms.

'Sorry, bit of a pong,' said Marchant, 'the cleaner was in this morning and she's rather heavy-handed with the fluids.' He ushered Sarah into a tall armchair and offered her a drink. As he busied himself in the kitchen, from which the sounds of a gurgling coffee machine soon emanated throughout the flat, Sarah examined his books. Most were historical but there were two shelves of fiction, mainly classics she noticed, although the blue cover of the John Updike rabbit trilogy stood out beside the equally thick but shorter Wolf Hall. On a side table was a photograph of what appeared to be a young Marchant with a woman Sarah took to be his mother. There were no other photographs to be seen.

He reappeared with two mugs of coffee on a tray with some digestive biscuits on a plate.

'I laid in some provisions,' he said, smiling.

'Your mother?' said Sarah, pointing at the photo.

'Yes.'

'Any brothers and sisters?'

'Sadly not.'

'Sadly?'

'I think siblings are a good thing, don't you? Good for company.'

'And father?'

'Good heavens.' Marchant looked slightly taken aback, 'you're full of questions.'

'I'm sorry. I'm prying.'

'No, no, not at all.' Marchant smiled. 'Interested in people I think you said. Or was that your grandmother?'

'My grandmother. But well remembered.'

'It's my job to remember things.' He picked up the photograph and studied it. 'My father died when I was in my twenties. He was a historian like me ...' he paused as he reflected, 'but better known. He wrote a number of books that were well received.'

'What was his name?'

'John Marchant. You might have come across his work if you did history at school.'

'Sorry, no.' Sarah wanted to ask more but sensed his reserve was being tested already. 'Anyway,' she said, 'how have you been getting on?'

Marchant went to his desk, picked up a folder and placed it on the low table in front of her.

'Well,' he said, 'I've found out a bit more about Peter Harding.' He opened the folder and showed her a few documents. 'He saw some action in the battle of Amiens at the end of the First World War and remained on as a soldier and fought quite extensively in the Second World War by which time he was a Lieutenant Colonel, commanding his regiment.' He pointed to a photograph. 'That's him. He seems to have had a fairly conventional if unspectacular career in the Army, rising to be full Colonel by the time he retired in the 1950's. As you know, his son, your father, Stanley, followed him into the Gunners but only for a short while.'

Marchant ran through various cuttings and reports, fleshing out the details for Sarah of her grandfather's time in the army.

'Nothing very exciting, I'm afraid,' he concluded, 'but there is one thing that might be of interest.'

'Oh yes?'

'Yes. It relates to what we talked about before. The Unknown Soldier.'

Sarah sat up. 'Go on.'

'Well, it's probably nothing at all, but, interestingly, Peter was present at the Abbey.'

'At the burial?'

'Yes. It seems he was officiating in some way.'

'Officiating?'

'Yes. They'd have had plenty of soldiers showing people to their seats, acting as a Guard of Honour, marshalling the crowds, that sort of thing. There was a reference to it in his file so he was definitely present. Which is slightly odd.'

'Why's that?'

'Well, his regiment was still serving in France at the time. He should have been out with them throughout 1920. I can't see why he would have been back in England other than on leave but in which case why was he on duty at the Abbey?'

'Maybe they needed extra men.'

'Yes, but there would have been plenty in England, let alone London. It's all a bit odd.'

'Gosh!'

'Well, don't get too excited. Him being there means nothing in itself – but it does provide some kind of link to what your father said.'

'Which is rather intriguing.'

Marchant nodded slowly. 'Yes, it's a link, albeit a tenuous one.'

'Mmm.' Sarah was watching him to try and gauge his thinking. 'But, as a historian, you must admit your interest is piqued.'

'I wouldn't be much of a historian if it wasn't. But .... '

'But what?'

'Well, you set me thinking the other day when you asked if anyone might ever identify the Unknown Soldier.'

'Which you said would never happen.'

'And I meant it, but should, say, just should, by the remotest chance, someone came to claim they knew who was inside that coffin they would never let even the faintest hint of that escape.'

'Who is they?'

'The Establishment.'

'Why not?'

'Because there's too much invested in the whole concept. It's part of the fabric of the nation and though the average person in the street today probably knows little about the Unknown Warrior that's certainly not true of those in authority.'

'You mean the Government.'

'The Government, the Military, the Church. Royalty, senior civil servants. There's a tremendous emotional attachment to what has become an iconic symbol not just for this nation but for many others as well. It's really unthinkable – it would go against the grain of history.' He stopped himself, perhaps aware that he was speaking too quickly.

'I see. And are you part of that establishment?'

Marchant smiled as if at some private joke. 'You may imagine that to be the case' he said, 'but appearances can sometimes be deceptive.' He stood up. 'More coffee?'

'I think I need something stronger.'

'Good idea.' He looked at the clock on his mantelpiece. 'Eleven thirty. I think that's a perfect time to break open the gin.'

He poured them both a strong gin and tonic and sat down again. 'But that's all a bit of a distraction. What we're really here for is to discover more about your real grandfather Daniel.'

'Yes. I'd love to know what sort of man he was.'

'Well, I haven't made much progress there, I'm afraid. I've pinned him down to a few potential regiments but I can't get much further until I have a surname. I did briefly follow up your grandmother, Joyce, to see if there was anything that might link her to him but came up with a blank.'

'What sort of thing.'

'Well,' Marchant looked at the pages on his desk. 'I found out that she lived in a village called Taplow and so I checked to see if there had been any announcement of an engagement to Daniel in the local papers. But, as I say, I didn't spend much time on this.'

'An engagement?' Sarah considered the likelihood. 'That seems unlikely. Joyce didn't come from a grand family at all – not the sort to put announcements in the papers.'

'Ah. I didn't realise that. Her engagement to Peter was in *The Times*.'

'Yes, but he came from an altogether different background.'

'I see.' Marchant thought it through. 'How about schools then?' he said, 'Joyce would probably have gone to a local school in Taplow, or, if not there, a town nearby. Perhaps that's how she knew Daniel.'

'Good thinking.'

Marchant handed Sarah a few notes on Joyce. 'Would you like to look that one up while I continue researching Daniel and Peter?' he said.

'Yes, I can do that.' Sarah smiled. 'This is all rather exciting.'

'Let's see.' Marchant held his hands out to indicate caution. 'There's often a lot of digging around before one uncovers anything of substance.' He studied the file then looked up at Sarah. 'But we've made a good start.'

'We have.' Sarah looked at the antique carriage clock on Marchant's mantelpiece. 'So how about some lunch?'

'Well,' Marchant shifted in his seat,' well, that's a kind offer. Are you sure you have the time?'

'I am. It's part of the deal, isn't it?'

He took her to a pub nearby where they were able to sit in a small courtyard and enjoy one of the rare days of sunshine that summer. While waiting for their food to arrive they chatted about the First World War and the other pieces of work filling Marchant's week.

'So, what else should I know about you?' said Sarah.

'Oh.' Marchant took a sip of his pint. 'What sort of thing are you thinking of?'

'Well, your family, for instance. You said there are no brothers and sisters, how about cousins?'

'Hmm.' Marchant paused as if trying to recall if he had any close relations. 'Quite a few actually. My mother has two brothers and three sisters and they all have children so there are, let me see,' he counted on his fingers, 'nine cousins in all.'

'And do you see much of them?'

'Some of them live abroad now but I do see my cousin Hattie who is a step cousin, quite frequently. She lives in Clapham.'

'Step cousin?'

'The daughter of my aunt Barbara's second husband.'

'Married?'

'Yes. To a solicitor. They have two children so I'm their uncle. Or step uncle to be precise. In fact I have a total of twelve nephews and nieces.' He smiled at Sarah. 'I remember that number as I have to buy them all birthday presents.'

'But no children of your own.'

Marchant gave a small, dismissive laugh. ' You saw where I live, does it look like it?'

'No. Silly question, sorry.'

'Don't be sorry. I like living alone. I like having children who visit and then go home at the end of the day.'

Their baguettes arrived.

'But what about you?' he asked.

Sarah finished her glass of wine. 'Single girl,' she said, 'one brother who I seldom see, mother died a few years ago, father, as you know, going the same way. No children, one ex-husband.'

'Oh.' Marchant seemed at a loss to follow up with another question so Sarah answered what she guessed he might like to have asked.

'It was a short marriage. He was charming, successful and, as it turned out, completely self-centred. He didn't really have room to love anyone else in his life other than himself.'

'What did he do?'

'Something in the City. It was his only topic of conversation.' Sarah laughed as she reflected. 'My God, the terrible tedium of some of our dinner parties with his friends who only wanted to talk about trading commodities or to show off their latest gadgets. I was a sort of trophy wife – someone to look glamorous, serve food and listen.'

'Sounds like American Psycho.'

'You read that?'

'My reading is a little broader than you might imagine.'

'Actually, you're right. I think he did have psychopathic tendencies. When we divorced he had absolutely no concept of doing the right thing – he hired the best lawyers to stitch me up and I got virtually nothing.'

'I know the type.'

'Anyway, it's all in the past, thank heavens. I haven't spoken to him in years but apparently he's remarried to some other poor woman.'

'Maybe to someone who can just enjoy his wealth.'

'Do you think that's possible? To enjoy living with someone purely for the money?'

'People do, surely.'

'Yes, but I can't imagine they're happy.'

Marchant finished his beer. 'Another?'

'Why not? I'm only working from home today.'

'I never asked. What do you do?'

'I'm an interior designer.'

'Oh dear. I can't imagine what you made of my flat.'

'That sort of look is coming back in. I was only disappointed you didn't have flock wall paper.'

When he returned with the drinks they talked about her job and then, speaking rapidly again, he told her about his passion for fishing which seemed incomprehensible to Sarah. She told him about her recently acquired taste for ceroc which seemed equally incomprehensible to him.

'I don't think I've danced in over ten years,' he said.

'Then you must come along one evening.'

He held up his hands in a gesture Sarah was beginning to recognise. 'Let me think about that one,' he said.

'Do you have many friends?' she asked.

Marchant raised his eyebrows. 'Yes,' he said, slightly affronted by the question, 'why, do I come across as a hermit?'

'Oh God. There I go again. I'm sorry, that's not what I meant at all. I just wondered where your friends come from. Are they mostly academics like you?'

'Not at all. I have two friends who run nightclubs, a couple in a rock band, one who writes pornographic films, that sort of thing.'

Sarah stared back at him blankly.

Marchant laughed. 'Not really. It's as you might imagine, mostly crusty batchelors like me who regard a good night out as a lecture at the V&A.'

'And women?'

'Well, there's Hattie. I do see a lot of her.'

'I meant women who aren't your cousin.'

'Ah. You want to know if I'm gay.'

Sarah laughed. 'Well you are surprisingly camp. I mean look at those polished brogues and moleskin trousers – they're wearing nothing else in parts of Soho these days.'

Marchant looked down at his clothes. 'How nice to be a trend setter,' he said, 'Hattie has always said that if I dress this way long enough fashion will come round to it again one day.' He reflected a moment. 'But, as a matter of fact, I'm not gay. It's just that I don't get to meet too many women in my line of work.'

'Then I feel privileged to be a rarity.'

'That,' he said, 'is certainly true.'

They moved on to other less intimate topics and Sarah bought a third round of drinks. They discussed films they had both seen and realised they shared a taste for slightly off beat directors such as the Coen brothers and Wes Anderson and they talked about where they liked to go on holiday and realised they both struggled with lying on a beach.

'Good Lord,' said Marchant finally, 'three o'clock. I've got to write an article before the end of the day.'

'And I've got to look for a whole load of samples.'

'I'm not used to three pints at lunch time.'

'You'll probably write fluidly and lucidly.'

'I'll probably fall asleep at my desk, more like. Anyway,' he stood up, 'it's been very pleasant.'

'Good. And interesting.'

At the street they were heading in different directions. Marchant held out his hand. 'It's been a pleasure speaking to you,' he said.

Sarah smiled at his old fashioned courtesy and reached forward to kiss him on the cheek. 'So,' she said, 'film or ceroc?'

'That,' he replied, 'is the easiest question you've posed all afternoon.'

CHAPTER 7

May 1917

Daniel Dawkins, home on leave, did not, as he had predicted to his Platoon Commander Jeremy Latham, make love to Joyce Sheppard before putting his kit bag down, but it was a near run thing. They met at Taplow station and walked to her parents' house where she was still living and after she had served him a meal of bacon, eggs and chips and he had luxuriated in a hot bath she led him to her bedroom where she removed her clothes and they climbed into bed together. It was all over swiftly.

She waved away his apologies saying she understood his needs and when, later that day, after a walk along the River Thames and a drink by Maidenhead Bridge, they lay together again he was more tender and considerate in his love-making.

'Welcome home,' she whispered in his ear.

'Not for long,' he said.

'Forget that. Just enjoy being here for the time being.'

Joyce went downstairs, brewed them a pot of tea and returned to the bed.

'Remember when we first met,' she said, 'at the school. You were larking around playing football.'

'I remember it alright.'

Joyce had come out with her family from London around the same time as Daniel, who had run away from an impoverished life in London and been taken in by a farmer at Taplow. They'd both been enrolled in a school in Maidenhead but they didn't meet until one day in the playground when Daniel had kicked a ball in her direction and it had landed at her feet. Her friends looked on as he shouted over to her.

'Kick us our ball back then, darling.'

Joyce picked up the ball. 'Why don't you come and get it?'

He walked across the yard. 'Can't kick a ball then?'

'Course I can.'

'Then you can join my team.'

Joyce looked across at his friends. 'I'd rather be with the others.'

61

'No you wouldn't. Now, let's have the ball.'

'Only if you tell me your name.'

Daniel had smiled. 'Dan,' he said, 'and you're Joyce.'

'You know who I am?'

'I've asked around.'

Joyce blushed. 'So you've seen me about then.'

'I have that.' Daniel reached forwards and took hold of the football. 'Noticed you a while back. Now, give us the ball and I'll see you later on the bus.' He grinned. 'I'll save a seat for you.'

Joyce laughed. 'I might want to sit with my friends.'

'Don't mind, they can join us if they want.'

Joyce handed over the ball and Daniel walked back across the yard without turning back.

The girls with her were giggling. 'That's Daniel Dawkins,' one of them said, 'there's a queue for him.'

Joyce watched as Daniel made a long pass to one of his friends before looking over to her and waving. 'Looks like it's my turn then,' she'd said.

She lay on the bed now, her legs linked in amongst his. 'I've often wondered if you kicked that ball at me on purpose,' she said.

'Of course I did. I'd been eyeing you up for some time.'

'You were a cheeky bastard – though I did fancy you.'

'Not half as much as I fancied you.'

Joyce ruffled his hair. 'You made that clear enough.'

'No point in being shy.' Daniel stroked her back. 'But you never made it easy for me did you.'

'I left that to the other girls.'

Joyce recalled the days when Daniel would wait for her outside the school gates, surrounded by his friends who would whistle when she appeared. 'Remember the time we bunked off to Slough,' she said, 'and you took me to the pictures.'

'Got into trouble for that one.'

'You were always in trouble.'

They had begun going out soon after meeting and by the time war had been declared they were inseparable and talking jokingly of getting married one day.

While he was working at the farm, she was working in a shop and studying in her spare time to become a secretary.

Joyce looked at Daniel, their faces close together. 'You said you'd be back before long', she said, 'and that was over two years ago. What's happened?'

'We've got bogged down in a stalemate,' he replied, 'that's what's happened.'

'So many dead,' said Joyce, 'most of your old friends from school are gone.'

'I know, love, I know.' Of Daniel's gang of five who had joined the Berkshire Light Infantry together only he was still alive. 'But it can't go on for ever. Something has to give sooner or later.'

With her parents away until the end of the month they spent the next morning idling around the house but Joyce sensed a restlessness in Daniel who seemed unable to stay doing one thing for long. She borrowed a bicycle from a neighbour and the two of them set off for Windsor along the tow path. It was an unusually bright and sunny day and the water of the Thames was clear and slow-moving. At Bray lock they stopped and watched a barge negotiate the lock gates. At Eton they sat in a grassy field eating sandwiches and looking across to Windsor. Daniel lay back on the rug Joyce had bought and closed his eyes. She lay down beside him and for a while neither of them spoke.

A dog appeared and started licking Daniel's face, waking him from his daydreams. The owner rushed up apologetically but Daniel held the dog and stroked its head.

'What's his name?' he asked.

'Monty.'

'Monty? He laughed. 'My dog's called Murphy.'

Joyce sat up and looked at him. 'You have a dog?'

'Yes. He lives with us.'

'In the trenches?'

'Yes. And in reserve.'

The woman owner, sensing she was intruding, put Monty on the lead but Daniel placed his arms around the dog. 'Can he sit with us a minute?' he asked.

'If you want.'

The woman, in her twenties, dressed plainly but with a warm smile, sat down on the edge of the rug and Joyce offered her some squash.

'I love dogs,' said Daniel, 'always know what they're thinking. Loyal – you can trust them.'

'So you're on leave then?' said the woman.

'That's right. Ten days, then back again.'

'Where are you serving?'

'Flanders.'

'Oh.' The woman began stroking Monty at the same time as Daniel. 'That's where my man is.'

'Who's he with?' asked Daniel.

'Coldstreams.'

'What's his name?'

The woman looked away. 'Dave'.

Joyce looked at her face and noticed the strain in her eyes, the tension round her mouth. 'What's your name, love?' she asked.

'Barbara.' She said it quietly and looked down at the ground. 'But I've not heard anything from him for two weeks. He normally writes every other day.' She looked up at Daniel. 'Why might that be?'

Daniel knew that the post was often disrupted but it was unusual for a two week delay. He also knew that the Coldstreams had been having a tough time of it lately.

'Post does go missing from time to time,' he said.

Barbara nodded but turned away. Joyce caught Daniel's eye.

'I'm sure you'll hear from him soon,' said Joyce but Barbara's eyes were misting over so she moved closer to her and put her arms round her shoulder. 'There,' she said and Barbara leant into her.

'I'm so worried,' said Barbara, 'I don't know what to do with myself.'

Daniel stood up and walked off down to the river where he found a stone and threw it into the water. He found another and threw it further, aiming for a branch moving slowly down stream. The towers of Windsor castle gleamed above the rooftops and the town seemed quiet and peaceful in the afternoon sun. He knew Dave would be dead and he knew, if Barbara hadn't received a letter, that no one had seen him die and sooner or later he would be reported as 'Missing in Action'. She would likely never know what happened to him. He looked back at the two women who were holding on to each other, their heads bowed, with Monty watching on uncertainly, and he knew in that moment the pain of those left behind. He skimmed a third stone across the Thames and, as it finally sank beneath the surface, he sensed that in Barbara's anguish he was witnessing the future for Joyce. It seemed strange, he thought, to be foreseeing the mourning of one's own death. He imagined her at his funeral, staring through tear-stained eyes at his coffin, placing a flower, being held by her father as her legs failed to support the weight of her grief. He watched as the ripples on the calm water slowly faded to nothing, leaving no trace of their existence, there one moment, gone the next, and it seemed to him that that's how life was, had always been and always would be. Then he wandered off in the direction of the bridge, feeling the need to be alone, not wanting to talk, but as he crossed over into the streets of Windsor people spotted his tanned face and short hair and they wanted to shake his hand and tell him how proud they were of their boys. They wanted to ask him how it was going but he felt a distance from them that could not be crossed and the civilians looked bemused as he backed away, not responding, walking amongst them but apart from them, in his own world, detached, remote. He turned and walked hurriedly back over the bridge to return to the field, away from those who had not seen what he had seen and could not know what he knew. How could they understand the withdrawal into themselves of men who had lived through the annihilation of all around them? How could they possibly imagine standing beside men as their brains were blown apart, watching their severed bodies fly through the air, being covered by their innards? How could they imagine the stench that lingered for days? How might they comprehend the guilt of the survivors, the deep hollow fatalism that haunted their every waking moment? So Dave was dead. But the living dead continued for another day, another advance, a further descent into the depths of desolation. As pavement turned to field his breathing slowed and he realised, in a moment of clarity, that he felt no anger towards these civilians, no resentment, only a deep and unbridgeable separation.

He found Joyce and Barbara chatting like old friends, Barbara having recovered her composure, and he sat down beside them again.

'Barbara lives in Dorney,' said Joyce, 'not far from me, so we can meet up.'

'Good.' The image of them supporting each other at the loss of their men came to him once more but, as he had learnt to do over the past years, he was able to banish such thoughts as soon as they arrived and he moved on to consider their journey back. 'Perhaps we might go past there on the way home, then,' he said.

They finished their picnic and pushed their bikes along the road to Dorney where Barbara brewed them some tea before swopping addresses with Joyce and saying goodbye.

'What do you think?' asked Joyce once they were back on their bicycles and heading towards Taplow.

'About what?'

'About Dave. Her husband.'

'He'll be dead,' said Daniel.

Joyce stopped pedalling and let her bicycle freewheel to a halt. 'Just like that?'

'What do you want me to say?' he said over his shoulder.

'I don't know. Something more.'

Daniel turned back and came to a stop beside her.

'I'm sorry, love,' he said, 'but that's it. Fact. There's no words will make it better.'

Joyce sat on her bicycle, not moving. 'That's brutal,' she said.

He sat on his saddle, his feet on the ground, his body still, his face without expression. 'That it is.' Then he turned towards Taplow and started pedalling again. Joyce followed but he was driving his bike forwards fiercely and she struggled to keep up with him.

'Dan, slow down,' she shouted, but he was pushing hard and she could find little strength to speed up as she watched him disappear into the distance. Finally, she rounded a corner and he was sitting on a wall, his bike on its side.

'Let's not talk like that again,' he said.

She nodded. 'I'm sorry, Dan.' She sat down next to him and put an arm over his shoulder. He leant into her and she stroked his hair.

'Good old Dan, everyone's tower of strength,' she said, ' except his own.'

He had both his arms around her, his cheek against her chest.

'It's only you who knows me,' he said, 'only you who sees that.'

Joyce could feel his hard, muscular body against hers and she imagined him going into battle, leading the way, his courage encouraging the other soldiers. 'I know, Dan.' She kissed the top of his head. 'And that's why I love you so.'

Two days later they made a trip to Brighton, staying in a small hotel on the front where they could lie in bed and watch the sea break over the pebbled beach. That evening they had a meal in a pub and went to the theatre at the end of the Palace Pier where they watched a variety show. They found somewhere to have a few more drinks after the show so that by the time they were making their way back to the hotel, arm in arm, they were weaving an erratic course and having to stop and laugh each time Daniel impersonated one of the performers.

They found a bench to sit on overlooking the beach. 'Oh, my God,' said Joyce, 'I'd almost forgotten how much you can make me laugh.'

Daniel chuckled. 'And you, me. You know, you're the only one I can be like this with.'

'Go on,' I bet you're like this with all the lads.'

'Not in the same way. You're the only one I've ever been really happy with.'

Joyce held his face and turned it towards her. 'Is that true, Dan?'

'It is.' He pulled her towards him. 'I've been thinking about it these last few days. Since we had that chat. I've come to realise it's only when I'm with you that I can really unwind.'

She squeezed his waist. 'My coiled spring Daniel,' she said.

He laughed. 'That's about it.'

They sat, holding each other and watching the moonlight ripple on the waves as they enjoyed the warmth of each other's body.

'I couldn't imagine life without you,' said Joyce, 'you're my rock. There's no one else like you in the whole world.'

Daniel stood up and walked to the balustrade. He leant forwards and clasped his hands together, looking out to sea. Joyce came and joined him. 'There's other men out there,' he said, 'better men than me.'

'No Dan. Not for me.'

He looked away. 'You'll see,' he said quietly but Joyce couldn't catch his words.

'What's that, Dan?'

He turned back to her and kissed her on the lips. 'Let's get back to our room,' he said, 'It's been a grand evening but I reckon the best bit's still to come.'

The following morning they returned to Taplow and for the next few days they kept themselves busy going for bike rides, walks and visiting pubs. But though the sun shone for much of the time, and though they joked and reminisced about their days together before the war, behind every pleasant experience lurked the knowledge of Dan's impending return to the front, a knowledge that insinuated itself into their thoughts and ambushed their moments of peace. They made love frequently but for Joyce there was now no moment of reckless abandon. Unlike their early days together she was unable to submit totally to the present and so she pretended for Daniel even though she suspected he was aware she was never truly with him.

Daniel visited the farmer who had taken him in at the age of thirteen when he had escaped from London and he told him about the soldier's life in France and the farmer listened, shaking his head at the stories of terrible suffering the young man had been forced to witness.

They also visited Barbara a couple of times.

'Still no news?' asked Joyce.

'No.' Barbara seemed more in control than before, more reconciled to events. 'It's the not knowing that hurts,' she said.

Daniel became even more restless over the final couple of days, as if mentally distancing himself from home. He spoke less and went for walks alone. Joyce observed but said nothing, not wanting to intervene in his thoughts.

Then, on the last evening, after a period of quiet, he suddenly said 'Will you marry me?'

Joyce was too surprised to reply.

'It would be good,' he said, 'I'll feel better about it. It will be good having a fiancée.'

They were in the kitchen, she was sitting at the table, he was standing by the stove.

'Come here,' she said. He sat down beside her and she took his hand. 'Of course I'll marry you. But it might have to wait a little.'

'Fine by me,' he said, 'I'll be busy for a while. But when I get back. Later in the year perhaps.'

'Of course.'

'Sorry I don't have a ring.'

'I can wait for that too.' She leant forwards and pulled his head to her shoulder and he put his arms around her and they sat like that for a while, not talking. He sensed her wiping her eyes behind his hair and he wanted to turn around and comfort her; to tell her how much he loved her, to reassure her that he would come back from the front and they would live a fine life together. But he knew it would be a lie. He knew that he was too far gone, too removed from her world, too ravaged by war to fully return. So he looked out of the window and watched the sun set over the trees and as the darkness enveloped the land he kept to himself the cold, inescapable certainty of death that had been his constant companion these past years. A certainty that had stalked him on his very first advance as men fell around him, had gradually taken control of his senses, had tightened its grip with each attack and now shrouded him in its all consuming embrace.

CHAPTER 8

7 November 1920

Captain Peter Harding walked into his Commanding Officer's office and saluted.

'Ah, Harding,' said the CO, 'Thank you for coming so promptly, something's cropped up that needs urgent action.'

Peter Harding, aged twenty-two, had been a serving officer for three years. He had been commissioned into the Royal Artillery in early 1918 and had served as a gunnery officer for the final parts of the war, seeing action with the 2nd Division Artillery in support of the 4th Canadian Division at the battle of Amiens. Although this never necessitated him being within five miles of the front line the experience of being part of the final push to defeat the Germans was one that would remain with him for the remainder of his life.

Harding was a man who understood military procedures well and enjoyed the discipline of the armed forces. He was the first to admit that he was not a man of great imagination, indeed, he took some pride in his methodical, pragmatic approach to life, and while he saw the more colourful characters of his Regiment as an occasional amusing source of entertainment he noticed, on the whole, that they were often unreliable and, at times, a liability.

He was, therefore, a suitable candidate for the task his Commanding Officer was now about to hand him.

'Sit down, Harding,' said the CO, 'I have a job for you that comes all the way from Whitehall.'

Harding sat down as asked, his face registering no surprise at this sudden eventuality.

'What I will do now is to read out your brief,' said the CO, 'and then you can ask me any questions. Although I have to tell you now that I'm unlikely to have any answers.'

'Very well, sir.' Harding always spoke in slow, measured tones that many found reassuring, some found laboured.

'So. Here we go'. The CO looked down at a paper in front of him.

'You are to travel to the battleground of Ypres straight after I have read you this order. You will travel in a Field ambulance and take with you two other ranks. You will be equipped with shovels and sacks. You will visit a cemetery there where you are to find a grave marked 'an unknown British soldier' and exhume a body.'

'Exhume, sir?'

'Yes, Harding, exhume.' The CO looked up. 'Dig up the bones of a dead soldier.'

Harding's expression remained fixed. 'I see, sir.'

'The body must be completely unidentifiable,' continued the CO, reading again, 'apart from the fact that it must be clad, or at least partly clad, in British khaki material.' He looked at the brief as if it contained a terrible blasphemy. 'The decomposition of the body must be sufficiently advanced so as to obviate the need for cremation.' He looked up. 'Ideally the soldier will have fallen in the early years of the war.'

Harding took a deep breath. 'My God,' he said.

'Yes. My God.'

Both men sat contemplating the macabre nature of the task facing the young officer.

'You are to confirm by means of any scraps of uniform, boots, buttons or other distinguishing features that the body does indeed belong to a British soldier. However, if you find any means of identification that indicates who the soldier was you are to reinterr it at once and find another body.'

Harding sat in an incredulous silence.

'Once you have a body that meets the above description you are to place it in a sack, fill in the grave, and take it in the ambulance to General Wyatt's HQ at St Pol-sur-Ternoise, to arrive there at exactly 1900hrs, no sooner and no later, where you will unload the body at the chapel of St Pol. The Reverend Kendall will receive the body. You will confer with nobody and once the body has been received you will return immediately to your unit.'

The CO turned the paper over and looked at Harding. 'The two soldiers, who are currently waiting outside, know nothing of this and you will read this brief out to them on the journey to Ypres. You must swear them to silence as you will, in turn, remain silent. Here's a map of the area with the cemeteries marked. Any questions?'

Harding's remarkable phlegm was being tested. 'What's this all about, sir?'

'They haven't considered it appropriate to tell us that.'

'Good heavens.'

The CO handed Harding the brief. 'However, I've heard there is a plan to bury a soldier in Westminster Abbey on the second anniversary of Armistice Day,' he said, 'so it must be something to do with that.'

'I'd heard something along those lines.'

'And as I understand it there are at least three other teams heading out to other battle areas with the same instructions. I can only assume a choice will be made at some point as to the body they will ship back to London.'

'The Unknown Soldier.'

'Exactly.' The CO stood up. 'Now, you'll need to move fast, Harding. That deadline is critical, I'm told. The ambulance is waiting outside with the soldiers.'

Harding stood up and saluted. 'Thank you, sir,' he said, 'should I assume this is a great honour?'

'Honour? It may turn out to be a great burden, Harding. You may become part of a secret that you will need to take with you to the end of your life.'

The journey to Ypres was a long and uncomfortable one. Before setting off Peter Harding read the instructions to the two soldiers who appeared remarkably undaunted at this most unusual of duties, but once they were on their way he heard them talking quietly to each other in conspiratorial tones. The ambulance made good speed but just past 09.30 it struck a sharp boulder and veered sharply across the road.

'Fuck,' shouted the driver, struggling to keep the vehicle under control but finally bringing it to a halt. He jumped down to inspect the damage.

The ambulance was tipped at an alarming angle, its narrow wheels on the left hand side perched on soft ground.

'I nearly fucking lost her, there,' said the driver.

'We need to get it back onto the road,' said Harding, 'or it will start sinking into that mud.'

Moving quickly, Harding and the two soldiers pushed at the rear while the driver revved the engine and engaged first gear but the vehicle moved forwards only a matter of inches before the wheels started digging themselves in.

'Stop,' shouted one of the soldiers. The driver jumped down and inspected the wheels, now buried at least four inches into the ground. 'She'll just dig herself deeper,' said the soldier, 'seen it hundreds of times.'

'What's the answer then?' asked the driver.

'Walk.'

Harding groaned. 'That's not an option,' he said.

The three men looked at him. 'Well she ain't coming out of there wi' just our efforts, sir,' said the second soldier.

Harding looked at his watch. They still had a good distance to travel yet had to find their body and return to St Pol by 1900hrs. 'We have to get it out,' he said.

The driver looked at him. 'Any ideas then, sir?'

Harding turned and looked up and down the road. 'We'll need to be pulled out,' he said.

The driver looked towards the empty horizon. 'We may have a long wait then.'

'We have no option. In the meantime let's get some blankets under those wheels.'

'Blankets, sir? In that mud.'

'Yes, Corporal. In that mud. And fast.'

With the driver mumbling under his breath about ruining his precious blankets they created a form of matting under the wheels as best they could and one of the soldiers had the good idea of cutting branches from a nearby tree and placing them on top of the blankets and jamming them under the wheels.

Harding kept looking at his watch.

'What now, sir?'

'Baxter, start walking the way we are headed and see if you come to a village. Do you have any French?'

'A little, sir.'

'Then if you find someone try to get some help. What we need is a lorry with a tow rope.'

'Not sure my French goes that far sir.'

'Then use hand signals, man. Now go.'

With Baxter gone the other three waited.

'Bloody strange job, this one, sir,' said the other soldier.

'I know. And if we don't execute it .... I hate to think.'

'Couldn't be helped, sir.'

'That won't stand up as a plea of mitigation.'

The soldier smiled wryly. 'Best off as a bleeding gunner, sir.'

Harding shook his head. 'That's what I will be if we don't get help soon.'

'Wait,' said the driver. 'Sshhh.'

They stopped talking and listened.

'What is it?'

'Vehicle.'

'I can't hear nowt,' said the soldier.

'There.' They all heard it this time.

'You're right,' said Harding. He leant his head to one side. It was clearly the sound of an engine.

'Coming along from behind,' said the driver, 'truck, I'd say.'

Thirty seconds later a lorry appeared driving slowly along the road and they watched its steady progress.

'Come on, come on,' said Harding under his breath.

Finally it arrived and they waved it to a halt.

'Monsieur, aidez moi s'il vous plait.'

The lorry driver examined the ambulance, shrugged in gallic fashion, shook his head a few times at the severity of the situation but then pulled out a long rope from his cab. They attached the ends to each bumper, the ambulance driver revved his engine, the lorry eased forwards and, with a shudder that at one point threatened to tip the ambulance on its side, the unstable vehicle lurched onto the road.

'Merci Monsieur, merci beaucoup,' said Harding and offered the man some francs but he waved away the gesture and set off again up the road with a cigarette dangling from the corner of his mouth.

'We need to move fast now,' said Harding but the ambulance driver was carefully examining his damaged wheel.

'It's bent all out of shape, sir,' he said, 'we'll need to change it.'

Harding sighed. 'Then we'd better get on with it.'

'Never done one of these before,' he said.

'What?'

'Only been doing the job a while.'

In an unusual momentary loss of control Harding struck the bonnet of the ambulance with the flat of his hand. 'For God's sake man, you must know how to change a bloody wheel.'

'Steady on, sir.'

'Bombadier,' said Harding, reddening in the face, 'It's not good enough. We have a critical mission to achieve in a very tight timescale. It is imperative you change this tyre as swiftly as you can.'

The Corporal's face suggested his very existence had been questioned. 'I'm a Corporal, sir,' he said, 'I'm not in the Artillery. And I'm doing my best, I can't do more than that.'

'Right,' said Harding, so what do we need to do?'

'Well, we'll need the tools in the back I suppose.'

Fortunately for the driver the tools were in the correct place but it still took them thirty minutes to change the wheel and they were only on their way at 1045 hrs, stopping after ten minutes to pick up Baxter who was walking back towards them.

'How long from here?' asked Harding.

'Hour at least,' said the Corporal who had slipped into monosyllables since his rebuke.

'Well, go as fast as you can.'

The Corporal kept his eyes on the road and drove at a speed just fast enough to prevent further cajoling from Harding but just slow enough to indicate he wouldn't respond to undue pressure. They finally arrived at the first cemetery at 1155 hrs.

'Shit. Take a look at that!' said Baxter.

Stretched out in front of them were wooden crosses in long rows, snaking over the folds of the land. They appeared to have been hastily assembled, made of rough wood, jammed close together.

'There's thousands of 'em' said the second soldier.

The four men stood in silence, humbled by the awful magnitude of this memorial to the dead.

A man with a limp approached them. 'Digging party?' he asked.

'Yes,' said Harding.

'I'm one of the caretakers. Expected you some time back.'

'We had a problem with the vehicle.'

The man, an ex-soldier Harding assumed, eyed them cautiously. 'You'll needs be getting to it then.'

He told them he had received a message informing him that a team would arrive, would need to exhume a body and that he was to assist them in any way they required.

'Damn queer thing,' he said.

'We won't bother you too much,' said Harding.

The man led them to a part of the graveyard where the crosses had noticeably less writing on them. 'These'll be what you're looking for,' he said, 'I'll be over in that shed over there.'

Harding bent down to look at the first cross. The simple inscription read 'A British Unknown Soldier.'

'We might as well start with this one,' he said.

The two soldiers, now confronted by the reality of their task, hesitated.

'I know,' said Harding, 'not easy. But it has to be done. We'll take turns.'

Military protocol would have had the soldiers dig while the officer stood to one side but with time now against them they worked two at a time while the third rested. Fortunately, the ground was soft and they made good progress to the point where, by soon after 1245hrs, they had the remains of a badly decomposed body laid out on the ground beside the grave. The soldiers stood back, leaving Harding to inspect the corpse. He worked quickly but methodically, fighting the desire to look away, ignoring as best he could the stench of putrefied flesh, at times pausing to hold back the impulse to vomit. The soldier had been buried in his service kit and Harding went through each pocket to check for any means of identification. At first he found nothing to connect the dead man to any unit, no link to any person or institution, no suggestion as to who he might have been and Harding began to hope that the very first grave they had struck upon would reveal what he had been tasked to find but then, on feeling inside the man's top left pocket, he found a letter, tucked in deeply and in poor condition, with the soldier's name clearly visible on the envelope. He opened up the pages. '*My darling boy*,' he read, '*how are you doing my lovely son? We all miss you so much.....*' Harding read on, unable to tear himself away from the writings of a mother to her son, her musings about Auntie Doris, her description of a prayer group in Felstead village hall, her plans for the party they were organising to celebrate her son's return on leave the following month.

'This one won't do,' he said.

The two soldiers looked at him inquiringly.

'We know who he is. We'll need to put him back and dig up another.'

'So why mark it 'Unknown Soldier'?' asked Baxter.

Harding considered the question. 'I can only guess he must have been one of so many dead at the time that they only made cursory checks.'

'Fuck me. So no one knows what happened to him.'

Harding held up the letter. 'Not even his mother.'

A breeze caught the pages and they flapped in Harding's hand. He looked down at the letter and imagined a woman sitting in her home in Felstead, agonising day after day as to what might have happened to her son, wondering beyond all hope if he might have somehow become detatched from his unit, if he was in a hospital somewhere, if he would reappear some time with a smile on his face and an apology for the worry he'd caused.

'We's ought to let her know,' said the second soldier.

Harding nodded. He looked at his watch again. 'Yes,' he said, 'we must.' He looked over to where the caretaker was watching them from a distance. 'I'll make a note of these details for the authorities and you start putting him back in the ground and filling in. Then we'll start on another.'

In the next grave a cap badge informed them of the dead man's unit.

In the one after that a sergeant's stripes on the shredded left arm of the soldier's uniform was deemed by Harding to be too significant.

'We have time to dig up one more,' he said.

Baxter leant on his shovel. 'What if that's no good?' he asked.

'We'll deal with that eventuality when it happens.'

'Seven o'clock at St Pol,' said Baxter, 'it'll be tight.'

'Then we'd better start digging.'

The earth seemed harder this time and the men were nearing the end of their strength when they finally had the bones of a human being laid out in front of them.

'Not much left of 'im,' said the second soldier, already becoming inured to the gruesome nature of their task.

'This does look more positive,' said Harding.

In the festering swamps of Flanders most bodies would have decomposed rapidly and there was no knowing how long this one might have been in the ground.

'Looks like an old'un,' said the second soldier, echoing Harding's thoughts.

'What would you say, three, four, five years?'

'Easy.'

'Weren't we meant to find one from the first year?' said Baxter.

'No real way of telling. There's no date on the cross.'

'I reckon this might be it.'

The clothes of the dead man were tattered and had rotted badly but were unmistakeably British khaki. It seemed the body might have been gnawed at by rats. The bones below the left elbow were missing.

'Poor sod,' said Baxter.

Harding began his inspection but there was little to check.

'This is it,' he said, 'this is the one.'

'Thank fuck,' said Baxter.

'I'll put the remains in a bag, you fill in the grave and we'll be on our way.'

Carefully, trying hard to disturb the bones as little as possible, Harding picked up the body and eased it into the bag. What clothing there was held the limbs together in a fashion but as he slid the final leg into the sacking he noticed a piece of material he had missed on first inspection. He looked closer and it was the remains of a pocket. He fiddled with a button, opened it and his fingers met a small metal container. For a few seconds he held the container, not moving. Slowly he eased it out of the pocket, then tried to prise it open. The clasp was jammed so he had to work at it but then, with a press of his fingers, the lid sprang up. Inside he could see a piece of card and realised he was looking at the back of a photograph. It was about an inch square, with no writing, peeling at the corners but otherwise in remarkably good condition. Slowly he turned it over. Facing him was a photograph of a woman. She was young, with long hair, wearing a boater and he thought how beautiful she was. He stared at her, not moving, feeling strangely overcome by his find. A laugh from the trench broke his concentration and he looked over to see the two soldiers shovelling earth into the grave, joking at something, happier now that their job was almost finished. He gazed at the photo again, his mind racing, considering his options. There was nothing to say who she was, no name on the back, she could be anyone. He looked at his watch; they would be pressed to make it to St Pol in time. In truth there was no option. Watching the soldiers, he carefully placed the photograph back into its metal container and slipped it into his pocket before tying up the bag with the remains inside.

'I'll take this to the ambulance,' he said, 'five minutes and we must be off.'

CHAPTER 9

30 May 1917

'You look well rested, Dawkins,' said Lieutenant Latham.

They were standing on the edge of a field, waiting for their instructions as staff officers riding back and forth on their horses marshalled soldiers into battle formations. Officials with coloured flags had been moving forward ahead of B Company for the past two hours, simulating the rear impact of a barrage behind which the troops would need to follow at a safe minimum distance. Forward Observation officers had been trying out methods of communicating with their guns. Platoon commanders had been practicing the coordination of assault and machine gun sections.

In the distance the sound of heavy guns firing at the German lines gave the impression of a continuous and remorseless peal of thunder.

'I am that sir. They're pounding Fritz I see.'

'For over a week now.'

A Major with a red band around his hat approached and shouted at Latham. 'Subaltern, move your men to the left flank.' As Latham's platoon started moving he shouted again, 'get on with it, man, move those men faster.'

The practices had been proceeding since early morning and the officers on horseback were beginning to appear hot and flustered as the complexities of controlling large numbers of men became apparent to them. The Major, full of a sense of self-importance, was particularly aggravating the men with his high-handed attitude and his endless repeating of orders that, by the tone of his voice, implied that all those beneath his rank were either hard of hearing or incompetent. The result was that the formations under his command moved slightly slower than elsewhere, their responses marginally delayed, their handling of weapons a touch less crisp. This was infuriating him to a point whereby his face was reddening to an alarming degree and sweat was trickling in rivers down his sideburns and congealing on his moustache.

Latham executed the required manoeuvre with his men and, in a subsequent halt in proceedings, Major Witheridge approached. 'Humour him Latham,' he said quietly, 'or we'll be here all night.'

Latham looked towards the Major who was dismounting and beckoning for a stable lad. 'I was concerned back there we might be further delayed by having a heart attack on our hands.'

Dawkins was close by and couldn't resist chipping in.

'If you don't mind me asking, sirs,' he said, 'why is it that we need to keep practicing walking in a straight line?'

Latham suppressed a smile but Major Witheridge looked unamused. 'Are you questioning a senior officer's instructions, Dawkins?'

'Certainly not sir. I was just seeking clarification on the benefits of shagging ourselves out repeatedly for no apparent purpose.'

Witheridge gave him a long look. 'Just get on with it for once, Dawkins,' he said with an air of resignation, 'timing will be the key to the assault and we need to know how quickly ground can be covered as we progress under a rolling barrage.'

Dawkins resisted a reply and Major Witheridge pointed in the direction of a huddle of senior officers. 'See that General there?' he asked.

'Yes, sir.'

'That's General Plumer and he has proved himself to be an exemplary tactician. And the man with him is Sir Charles Harington and he's the man who has been planning everything in detail for the past few months.'

Dawkins nodded. 'I know about them, sir.'

'Good. Because we both know what happens when things aren't executed properly.'

Dawkins nodded slowly in recollection of the events of 1916. 'True, sir. Thank you. I will advance with increased enthusiasm from now on.' He saluted and departed swiftly before Witheridge had time to rebuke him.

'Cheeky bastard,' said Witheridge to Latham, 'he's the only man in the company who could get away with that sort of behaviour.'

'He does have a point.'

'I know. But never let a soldier criticise an officer to you. Never. It can only lead to trouble.'

'I understand that.'

'Good.' Witheridge looked across to where Sergeant Barnes was patrolling up and down 5 Platoon checking the men's kit. 'I know what the men think,' he said, 'that all this practice is just so the staff can say they did all they could in preparation.'

'To cover their backs?'

'In a phrase, yes. However I do believe it will be different this time.'

'In what way?'

'I think we might actually get it right for once.'

The Major with the red hat band was walking in their direction and Latham wondered if Major Witheridge was indulging in wishful thinking.

'Let's hope so,' he said.

'Witheridge,' said the Major as he approached, 'prepare your men. We will practice that all again in twenty minutes and I want no sloppy performances this time.'

Practices continued for two more days until Dawkins, Timmings and Fletcher were thoroughly bored and cynical. They were sleeping in a large barn with fifty other men which soon became airless and odorous and in the evening Dawkins walked the couple of kilometres to the nearest village to see what alternatives there might be. He passed a number of houses that appeared to have been requisitioned but down a side street he came across a woman hanging out washing outside her small cottage.

'Bonsoir, Madame,' he said.

'Bonsoir, Monsieur.'

He smiled at her and watched her peg sheets and clothing on the line.

'Vous cherchez quelque chose?' said the woman.

Dawkins had picked up some limited French over the past couple of years but not enough to converse in any detail.

'Parlez-vous Anglais, Madame?' he said.

'Un peu.'

He explained in a mixture of English and French that he and his two friends were looking to spend the night somewhere other than the unpleasant accommodation they had been allocated for the past few days. The woman seemed to understand but told him hers was only a small building and that she had already turned away many requests from the British Army.

'Ça va,' said Daniel, 'mais c'est un jolie maison.'

The woman, in her late twenties and with hair tied behind her head put down her basket.

'Voulez-vous quelque chose à boire?' she asked.

'Ah, oui, Madame, s'il vous plaît.'

Inside her cottage she indicated for Daniel to sit on a wooden chair in the small kitchen and poured him a glass of water. He asked her where her husband was and she stood facing out of the window as she said 'il est mort.'

'I'm sorry,' he said. 'Soldier?'

'Oui. Verdun.'

'C'est terrible.'

'Oui.'

Daniel sipped at his water and the woman began peeling potatoes. He chatted to her about her life alone in the village and when she asked him how long he had been in France he told her about how he had enlisted. In a break in conversation he looked at her meagre supply of food. 'Perhaps je acheter de fromage et legumes,' he said, illustrating his offer with hand gestures.

'Pour moi?'

'Oui. Peut être mes amis et moi arrivons à huit heures avec … avec some food.'

'Monsieur c'est bien.'

'Good.' He stood up to leave and touched her arm. 'Qu'est que votre nom?' he asked.

'Eloise.'

'Alors, à huit heures then, Eloise,' he said.

'Bon, à plus tard.'

Back in the barn he woke Timmings and Fletcher who were dozing on bales of straw.

'Right lads,' he said, 'I've booked us an evening out.' He explained the situation and Timmings' expression indicated his interest was piqued in more ways than one.

'No, Timbo,' said Daniel, 'none of that. She's a decent-looking woman.'

'Who's been on her own for months. She'll be desperate for it.'

'Calm down, lad,' said Fletcher, 'we'll treat the French woman with respect.'

'Well,' Timmings said wistfully, 'you never know. If she shows an interest whose going to miss the fucking opportunity?'

Dawkins and Fletcher both shook their heads. 'Let's face it,' said Timmings, 'it might be our last ever chance to have a woman.'

Ignoring this point, pertinent as it was, Dawkins instructed Timmings and Fletcher to find the nearest estanimet and buy some wine. When they had left he went over to the cookhouse and spoke to Corporal Green.

'Greeny, chance to repay me that favour,' said Dawkins.

Corporal Green looked up from his pots. 'Oh yes? Which favour was that then, DD?'

'That extra duty, for one.'

'I don't remember that.'

'Yes you do. Now, this is what I need.'

Ten minutes later Dawkins left with a bag full of meat, vegetables, bread and cheese. He checked for officers and NCOs and made his way discreetly back to the barn where he hid it under some straw just before Sergeant Barnes appeared.

'What are you playing at Dawkins?' asked Sergeant Barnes.

'Nothing Sergeant. Just been sorting my kit out.'

Barnes looked him up and down and stepped in close so that their faces were only a few inches apart. 'I don't believe you Dawkins, you're always up to something.'

'Not this time, Sergeant. Not a lot to get up to round here.'

Barnes didn't move. 'I don't like you Dawkins,' he said. 'I don't like the way you talk to me, I don't like the way you toady up to the officers and I don't like the way you wind up the men. I've seen your type before and I don't fucking trust you.'

Dawkins stood his ground. 'And what type would that be Sergeant?'

Barnes came even closer. 'The worst fucking kind. Soldiers who think they know better than their superiors.'

All kinds of responses came into Dawkins's head but he'd been around long enough to know that answering back to his Sergeant would only land him in trouble.

'Well, I'm sorry you see it that way, Sergeant,' he replied.

Barnes stared at him before finally backing away. 'I'm watching you,' he said, then turned and walked off to find someone else to abuse. Dawkins watched him leave. 'And I'm fucking watching you, my friend,' he said under his breath.

At 7.45pm the three men slid out of a side door of the barn and made their way towards the village.

'We're doing nothing wrong,' said Timmings, 'there's nowt to say as we can't go into fucking town.'

'Not with a bunch of food from the cookhouse,' said Fletcher.

'We're going for a frigging picnic, that's all we're doing.'

At the cottage Eloise welcomed them with a warm smile and Daniel handed over the supplies.

'Et du vin,' she said, 'merci.'

He helped her prepare the food while the other two stood in her small back garden smoking and drinking. When the meat was cooking she sat down and Daniel sat opposite her. 'You must get lonely,' he said.

'Oui.'

'But no children.'

'Non. We are married only one year. Philippe wanted children but now is better with none.'

'I think so.'

'And you, monsieur?'

'I have a fiancée.' Daniel opened his metal container and showed her his photo of Joyce.

'She is very beautiful.'

'She is.'

'You will be very happy.'

'I hope so.'

Eloise reached forwards and took Daniel's hands in hers. 'You can sleep here tonight,' she said, 'in my bed. I will sleep downstairs.'

'No. That's not right.'

'Please. I would like it.'

He looked into her eyes and could sense her deep need for company. 'Very well,' he said, 'Merci. But I will need to leave early.'

Fletcher and Timmings came inside. They had bought four bottles of wine and proceeded to drink most of it between them. Eloise had only one glass which she sipped slowly, Daniel, unusually for him, also drank in moderation.

As they ate the cheese and bread at the end of the meal, Fletcher stood up, his shadow flickering in the candlelight, his glasses glinting.

'Merci, Madame,' he said, 'this has been a special evening. Tomorrow, if I'm not mistaken, we march to the front.' There was a slight catch in his voice. 'The memory of tonight will be a grand thing to take with us.'

Their glasses were empty by this time but the three soldiers and the French woman chinked them anyway and then they sat without speaking, enjoying the quiet, considering Fletcher's words, each responding to thoughts of what lay ahead in their own individual way. When it was time to leave Daniel spoke to the others outside.

'I'm staying the night, lads,' he said.

'You bastard,' said Timmings.

'It's not like that. I'll not bed her, she just needs the company.'

'My arse.'

'Be sensible, lad,' said Fletcher, 'you've just got engaged.'

'I know. I will be.'

Fletcher gave Daniel a long look. 'All right, DD,' he said.

Timmings was shaking his head but he could see there was little point in pursuing the matter and reluctantly he followed Fletcher down the road. Daniel went back inside and Eloise was standing at the sink. He came up behind her and put his arms around her waist. She let her head fall forwards and he kissed her neck and then she turned round and her lips were touching his.

'Daniel,' she whispered, her eyes closed and her body pressed against him. She leant her head against his shoulder. Then he led her upstairs and they lay on her bed fully clothed and he held her tightly for a long time until eventually she fell asleep. Daniel lay with his arm around Eloise's shoulder, feeling her warm body against his, looking up at the ceiling, studying the cracks, listening to the bombardment that continued in its ceaseless assault on the senses. He thought back to that last evening with Joyce when they had sat in the fading light with her warm tears touching the back of his neck. He wondered why he had asked her to marry him. Was it for his own benefit? A doomed final attempt to provide him with a reason to live? Or was it for her? Something for her to hold onto when he was gone? Perhaps it had been cruel of him. He wasn't sure. The certainties of life that had seen him through this far weren't quite so clear now.

He closed his eyes. Over the past year he had come to terms with his own death. He knew it must come and so he had stopped fearing it. He had escaped it too long, had seen so many fall around him that it was only a matter of time before a bullet or a shell would find him. He had been lucky, that's all it was – and his luck had to run out one day.

An exceptionally loud bang rattled the windows and Eloise stirred. Daniel stroked her shoulder and she settled back to sleep. It was looking like Fletch had guessed right about moving in the morning and Daniel's thoughts turned to the trenches, the anticipation, the whistle to advance, the feet on the ladders, running across open land. He shivered and though it was a warm night, pulled a blanket over him. Then he turned on his side and curled up, his knees to his chest the way he used to lie as a boy in his uncle's house, and for a while he fought the images that so plagued him at night before eventually drifting off into a shallow, uneasy sleep.

* * * *

He woke early and, after a tearful Eloise had kissed him goodbye, he hurried back to the barn only to find the whole company already assembling. Fletcher and Timmings had packed his kit and they handed it to him, helping him adjust his webbing.

'Barnesy's on the warpath,' said Fletcher, 'he asked where you were and I told him you'd gone for a walk to get some fresh air.'

Seconds later, just as Dawkins straightened up his last item of clothing and as Timmings handed him his weapon, Sergeant Barnes appeared in front of him. 'Where have you been, Dawkins?'

'For a walk, Sergeant.'

'At six in the fucking morning?'

'I couldn't sleep, Sergeant.'

'I'll speak to you later.'

After the parade Barnes took Dawkins to one side.

'Now where were you?' he asked.

'As I said, I went for a walk.'

'Don't you fucking lie to me you bastard.'

Dawkins held himself loosely, not matching the Sergeant's aggressive posture, his casual demeanour letting it be known he would not be intimidated. 'I'm not lying Sergeant. I've just been for a walk into the village and there's no rule says I can't.'

'Kit inspection. Now,' said Barnes.

He went through every item of Dawkins' clothing and equipment but it was all in order.

'Want to charge me for something then Sergeant?' said Dawkins.

'You insubordinate bastard. You shut your bloody mouth. Just shut your mouth.' In his rage Sergeant Barnes was projecting spittle from the corners of his mouth. 'You're a disgrace, a fucking disgrace, a fine bloody example to the new men and I'll have you, I'll fucking have you before this war is over.' He stood fuming, tormented by the mildest smirk that had crept across Dawkins' face.

Major Witheridge appeared. 'Hurry the men up, Sergeant,' he said, 'I'll address them in fifteen minutes.'

'Yes sir.'

Witheridge walked off and Sergeant Barnes, as before, moved up close to Dawkins.

'You're a live cunt, Dawkins,' he said, 'but you'll be a dead one soon.'

Dawkins was standing tall now and he looked down at the Sergeant who was half a head shorter than him. 'Tell me something I don't know, Sergeant,' he said, 'and you might have me worried.'

Major Witheridge did not shout or adopt theatrical gestures when he spoke to the men. He spoke in a friendly, unconventional way and his quiet authority was reassuring to the soldiers, leaving no room in their minds for doubt or confusion. He didn't speak of patriotism and nobility but he talked of the practicalities of warfare and the importance of support. He told them they would be marching to the front and that they would be part of a major offensive preceeded by a heavy bombardment. He told them that, in his opinion, lessons had been learnt, tactics improved. He explained there would be more guns per hundred yards than ever before, that they were more accurate and that there were better communications with the artillery. He reminded them of the important elements of the practices of the past few days and how these would result in better drills for assaulting trenches. He encouraged them to check their kit carefully before the advance.

There would be a period before the assault, he said, a time of waiting as the barrage destroyed all before them, and they would only move from the reserve to front line trenches in the final hours.

'I wish you well, men,' said Major Witheridge as he came to the end of his orders. His eyes travelled round the barn as he paused so that every man in the company knew he was speaking to them alone. His voice lowered, 'May God be with you.'

Lieutenant Latham, standing with the other subalterns off to one side, remained perfectly still as a deep hush descended on the assembled body of soldiers. For most of them, new to the battlefield like himself, this moment had been long-anticipated. It was a dividing line between familiarity and the unknown, a step into an existence for which they had no experience to draw upon, no reference to steady their imaginations. He prayed silently for strength.

The Sergeant Major was now issuing orders and the officers stepped aside for a final few words from Major Witheridge.

'So, this is it,' he said. He reminded them of the key elements of firepower, communications, momentum and resupply. 'Be resolute,' he concluded, 'show courage, be an example to your men.'

'Thank you sir,' said one of the subalterns.

Witheridge looked taken aback. 'Thank you for what?'

'I think what you said will be good for morale.'

Witheridge looked at the others. 'I think it will take more than a few words from me to raise the men's morale. They know the truth – more will die than will survive.'

The subaltern flushed at having appeared naïve.

'And there I was feeling positive for a few minutes,' said Latham.

Witheridge smiled. 'That's a dangerous state of mind where we're going,' he replied.

At 0830hrs exactly the men assembled and began the march towards the front. As they left behind the unloved barn Dawkins walked behind Peter Jackson who, as always, appeared to be conversing only with himself. Two of the newer soldiers were beside Jackson and started taunting him.

'What's up with your fucking leg, Jackson?' asked one, 'can't you walk in a straight line like any normal bloke?'

'Don't fancy being alongside you when we advance,' said the other, 'Fritz'll be picking off the weak straight off.'

'It's all for show,' said the first, 'nothing wrong with him really.'

'Just wants to fuck off home, get himself a blighty.'

'Leave us to do the dirty work, is that it, Jackson? Got a yellow streak have you?'

Jackson mumbled something.

'What's that? Can't hear you. You got nothing to say for yourself you miserable bastard?'

'He's fucking simple, that's what it is. Can't even talk proper.'

'He fucking spooks me the useless sod.' The first man shoved Jackson so that he stumbled a few paces, nearly falling to the ground. Both men laughed and the first man was about to shove him again when suddenly he was struck from behind. He turned just in time to see Dawkins' fist coming straight at his face. Hit on the side of the chin he staggered back and fell to the ground. Immediately Dawkins was on top of him and aiming vicious blows into his body and face. The second man tried to intervene and Dawkins turned to him and punched him violently in the side so that he too crumpled. Then Fletcher and Timmings were pulling Dawkins away and it took the two of them to hold him back. The men gradually rose to their feet, looking shocked at the force of nature that had just overwhelmed them.

'Steady, Dan,' Fletcher was saying, 'Steady, lad. They're just kids. They don't understand.'

Dawkins' eyes were blazing but the fury that had consumed him was already dying down as fast as it had erupted. He stood facing the two men who were cowering in anticipation of a further beating. 'Let's see if you're so brave after you've faced the Hun,' he said, spitting out the words in a menacing whisper, 'when you've seen bodies fall all round you, your best friends blown to bits. Let's see if you're so fucking brave then.'

Lieutenant Latham appeared and quickly took in the scene: Jackson standing to one side looking bewildered, the two soldiers rubbing their limbs and Fletcher and Timmings still with their arms around Dawkins. 'What's going on here?' he asked.

Fletcher stepped towards him. 'All sorted, sir. A bit of a disagreement. All sorted now.'

Latham looked at Dawkins. 'Dawkins?'

'No problem sir, as Fletcher says, all sorted.'

Latham looked back to Fletcher who made an expression that implied it would be best not to intervene.

'All over here sir,' he said, 'nothing to be concerned about.'

Latham nodded. 'Very well,' he said, 'but there's no time for stopping, we need to keep a good pace up.' He gave Dawkins a long look and then headed off to catch up with the line of men already some distance further up the road.

'Let's get going before fucking Barnesey comes back to stir it up,' said Timmings. 'he won't see sense like Mr Latham.'

'Alright. You can let me go now,' said Dawkins to Fletcher and Timmings, 'I've calmed down.' Then he turned to the two men who were watching him cautiously and reached out to shake their hands. 'That's that, then,' he said, 'we'll not talk of this again.'

'Thanks for that,' said Jackson when they were on the move again.

'It was nothing,' said Dawkins, 'you'll be by my side when the day comes.' It was as if he had already forgotten the whole incident had taken place.

They talked about home. Daniel described Taplow and Jackson talked about his mum who lived in East Reading and he described how she had once worked for the Lathams.

'She went to see Mrs Latham not long back,' he said, 'asked her to get something done about me.'

'Fuck's sake.'

'The old man sent her packing in the end.'

'It don't work that way, does it.'

'Suppose not.'

Daniel considered the absurdity of it but he knew what those at home were going through. 'You'll do fine,' he said.

Jackson walked alongside Dawkins, every now and then his leg veering off at an angle that maked him appear disfigured. 'Tell me, Dan,' he said, ''why do you do it?'

'Do what?'

'Help me out.'

Daniel shrugged. 'Right thing to do,' he said after a while.

'It's more than that. There's a reason you stick up for me,' said Jackson, 'I know that.'

Dawkins looked across and studied Jackson's unassuming features. 'Perhaps there is, Pete,' he said, 'and perhaps you ain't as simple as you make out.'

A few minutes later they came to the village where Daniel had spent the previous night and the villagers, aware that the soldiers who had been billeted in their vicinity for the past week were now marching to the front, were out in the street to see them off. Old men and women, mothers, children, they stood outside their houses watching and waving. Their faces were smiling but their deep concern for the departing troops was evident in their demeanour. After three years of seeing off the troops they were all too aware of what lay in wait.

Daniel spotted Eloise standing alone and he waved at her.

She waved back, blew a kiss and turned away. Then he was past and he kept his eyes on the road and as the long line of soldiers left behind the village they fell, to a man, into a silent contemplation, troubled by the pity in the villagers eyes, more unsettled by this unspoken compassion than by any set of orders or talk of close counter battle.

CHAPTER 10

October 2011

James Marchant arrived at Stanley Harding's house and greeted Sarah with enthusiasm. To her surprise, he was wearing jeans and an open necked shirt.

'You're looking very casual,' she said.

'It's Hattie. She keeps trying to modernise me.'

Sarah considered the possibility that Hattie had known about this visit and insisted Marchant divest himself of his fusty image. She led him into Stanley's study.

'How is he?' asked Marchant.

'Still the same, very weak. He's dozing most of the time. We'll need to keep our voices down.'

'It would be extremely helpful if we could speak to him.'

'I know – but we'll have to get him on a good day.'

'Anyway, you said you had something for me.'

'Yes.' Sarah showed Marchant a photocopy. 'I've looked up Taplow school records and not found anything but I widened my search and discovered that there were two boys called Daniel in a secondary school in Maidenhead between 1912 and 1916 – Daniel Rodgers and Daniel Dawkins. Joyce was also there at the time.'

'That's significant,' said Marchant, 'well done. That gives me something to go on.'

'Rodgers would have been younger than Joyce,' said Sarah, 'Dawkins a bit older.'

'I'll start with Dawkins then. That's really helpful.'

'And what about Peter Harding? How have you been getting on?'

'I've been wading through documents but I can't say I've made much progress in finding anything linking him to Daniel. That's why I asked if we could meet here so I can check if there's something you might have missed.'

Sarah pointed to a pile of files. 'This is everything I can find. A lot of it is official military stuff and I can't say I've gone through it all.'

'I don't blame you.'

'So, I'll leave you to it,' she said.

Marchant looked at the pile. 'Ok. I should only be about ten hours.'

Sarah smiled. 'I'll make some tea then.'

'Thanks. Two sugars please.'

'I know that.'

Sarah left him and went into the kitchen. As she filled the kettle she thought about the correspondence that had been going back and forth between them over the past weeks. His emails had started to contain little jokes, one or two even containing the lightest hint of what might be construed as flirting. Mostly the two of them discussed their research but Sarah had started to add in small bits of information about herself; she mentioned her busy schedule, he suggested she needed to go out more. She said she had been out shopping for clothes, he said he looked forward to seeing them on her. She described a film she had just seen, he said he wanted to see that himself and perhaps next time she should call him first.

Face to face he was a model of propriety but, as Sarah had discovered once or twice before, a certain type of English male found expressing his feelings, no matter how obliquely, that much easier on paper.

And he was, in his way, quite good-looking. She imagined him on one of the makeover shows and smiled at the thought of him in tight trousers and a designer shirt.

She could do with a man in her life. Since her divorce two years earlier her confidence had been knocked and she had relied on a few close female friends for company. One of them had suggested dating sites but she dreaded the thought of awkward dates with men who could only talk about themselves. So, she had relied on meeting members of the opposite sex at work or on social occasions but the only men she met in the design world were either married or gay and the ones she was paired up with socially all tended to have good reasons for still being single in middle age.

Marchant was hardly the sort she fancied but his old world charm intrigued her. She wondered if he had ever actually had a girlfriend and suspected not. She guessed their meeting might extend into dinner and imagined how he might loosen up after a few glasses of wine.

She put his tea on a table but he scarcely looked up so she left him and carried on with some work of her own in the next room. Fifteen minutes later she was interrupted by a shout of 'yes!'

She hurried into the study. 'What is it?'

'Look at this.' Marchant handed her an official letter dated December 1920. It was from a Reverend Kendall thanking Peter for his assistance at the service in Westminster Abbey where he had assisted at the burial of the Unknown Warrior.

'I'd missed that,' said Sarah.

'Easily done, and we already know he was at the service so that's not news but look at the bottom of the page.'

At the very bottom were the letters 'PTO'. Sarah turned the letter over and in neat handwriting were the words; 'you will be pleased to hear we were able to contact Charlie Matthews mother. It's never nice confirming finally to a woman that her son is dead but it does at least close this sad chapter for her and her family. Thank you for your part in this. GK.'

'What's that about?' said Sarah.

'In one sentence,' said Marchant, 'I think it means Peter Harding was more involved with the unknown soldier than just officiating at the Abbey.'

'What?' Sarah struggled to make sense of what he was saying. 'In what way?'

'Well. We can assume from this that Charlie Matthews was a soldier who had died on the battlefield some time in the war but was reported as 'Missing in Action'. And somehow Peter, in 1920, helped identify that he was dead. Hence the bit about final confirmation. So how might that have happened?'

'Might he have come across some documents relating to Charlie somehow?'

'Yes, but that's unlikely. What's the most probable way he could have discovered that Charlie was dead.'

'By finding his body.'

'Exactly. With some kind of identification on it.'

'I see.'

'And why might an Artillery officer in 1920 be coming across the body of a soldier who had died some years earlier in the war?'

'Might he have just come across it? I read that bodies keep turning up even to this day.'

'Yes, but by farmers digging up fields. By excavations.' Marchant was standing now and pacing the room.

'So are you saying he must have dug up Charlie's body?'

'That's exactly what I'm saying.'

'But why?'

'You read that there were four teams, sent out to different battlefields to disinter bodies.'

'Yes.'

'George Kendall was the officer who presided over the bodies being delivered to a village called St Pol.'

'My God!'

'So, think. What if Peter was in charge of one of those teams?'

'In which case Charlie Matthews was one of the bodies he dug up.'

'Yes. But not the body. Not the one they took back to England. There's no way Kendall would be writing anything down if that were the case. As I've said before, the bodies were explicitly to have no means of identification.'

Sarah was shaking her head. 'So, in other words,' she said, 'the most likely explanation is that this was one of the ones he had to leave as it had clear identification on it.'

'Correct. We can't be sure of it but it seems a real possibility. What I need to do now is start ferreting around to see if I can find any formal evidence of who was on those digging parties.'

'Although it doesn't tell us any more about Daniel.'

'But it is another link to the Unknown Soldier.' Marchant stopped his pacing and faced Sarah. 'And it would explain why Peter was at the funeral – the four officers involved would be bound to be invited.'

'This is incredible.' Sarah was looking at the letter again. 'So are you suggesting Daniel was in that grave?'

'Wait,' said Marchant, 'No. Absolutely not. Let's not leap to conclusions.' He began walking round the room again, his excitement causing him to gesticulate as he spoke. 'All we can speculate is that Peter was involved in the process of finding a body.' He paused to think. 'In which case he may have told this to his son Stanley at some stage.'

'So why would Stanley say 'Unknown Soldier' to me when I asked him about Daniel? Why would he link the two together?'

'Why indeed?' It certainly raises a whole load of questions. And problems.'

'Go on.'

'Well, firstly, if Peter had found some means of identifying Daniel then he would have been going against explicit instructions. From what I've seen and heard he was hardly a reckless sort so that seems most unlikely. Secondly, even if he did know the identity of the body he handed in there were three others delivered to St Pol, possibly more, so he simply couldn't have known which one was chosen. That's what the whole process was set up to achieve – complete anonymity.'

'Yes, I see. But it is intriguing.'

'Oh, it is that.'

Sarah watched Marchant as his mind ran through all the possibilities. 'I haven't seen this side of you before,' she said.

'What side?'

'On the hunt. Like a dog that's sniffed a scent – all alert and energised.'

As if this might be a mild reprimand he sat down and remained still for a few seconds. 'I'm sorry – us historians get a bit like this when we feel we're onto something.'

'Don't be sorry. I find it rather exciting.'

Marchant laughed. 'Well, I'll take that as a compliment,' he said.

'So, what now?'

'More research. I'll look at Berkshire Regiments during the war and see if I can find any reference to this chap Dawkins.' He tapped the table with his pen. 'After all, that's what we're looking for here – I mustn't get too distracted by this unknown warrior business.'

'I think you'll find that hard.'

'I will.'

Sarah sat down and leant towards him. 'I mean, let's just hypothesise. If, just say *if* you somehow found out that was Daniel in that coffin, what would that mean?'

'I don't think we should even go there.'

'Yes, but play along with me for a second, what would it mean?'

'It would certainly be a massive story.'

'It would make you famous.'

'Yes, but for all the wrong reasons.' Marchant shook his head. 'Like commiting sacrilege for a start. Remember what I said about the Establishment.'

'I do.'

'So perhaps we should forget the whole thing and just concentrate on Daniel.'

'Maybe.'

Marchant gave a wry laugh. 'Bugger! I've got my blood up. I'm excited. I'm possibly onto something that every historian would dream of yet it's something I need to keep under wraps.'

'Then you've got a dilemma.'

'And I know what I need right now.'
'A drink.'
'You said it.'

 They went to a pub and moved on to talking about other projects Marchant was working on and he asked about Sarah's current design assignments. In a break in conversation he went to the bar and bought a second round of drinks. She asked him about Hattie and he told her about his cousin's marriage to the solicitor and how it appeared to have gone stale. 'I think they stick together for the benefit of the children,' he said.

'That's a shame, but you two look very close.'

'What, me and Hattie?'

'Yes. In the photo, you look very comfortable together.'

'How interesting.'

'You must be a comfort to her.'

'A comfort?' He seemed surprised at the concept. 'Yes, I suppose I might be.'

'Someone to talk to.'

'Possibly.'

'I looked up your father by the way.'

Marchant held his pint in mid air. 'My father? What on earth for?'

'Oh, just out of interest. As you say, he was pretty well known.'

'He was indeed. I suppose these days we'd call him a minor celebrity.'

'And how do you feel about that?'

'Feel about it? Lord!' Marchant looked bemused. 'Well, he was certainly a lot to live up to.'

Sarah studied his face. 'You're not really used to conversations like this are you?' she said.

'Conversations like what?'

'Conversations about people, feelings.'

'Oh.' He shifted in his seat. 'Possibly not. I'm sorry.'

Sarah smiled. 'No, it's me who should be sorry,' she said, 'I'm being nosey.'

He turned to her. 'You see I live rather a solitary existence,' he said, 'and the only other women I find myself talking to tend to be Directors of Museums or researchers who aren't at all like you and then conversations are strictly about military history.'

'If they're not like me what are they like, these women?'

'Well, rather serious and business-like.'

'Whereas I'm all fluffy and frivolous.'

He laughed. 'No, I didn't mean that. Perhaps I should have said not attractive in the way you are.'

'Oh.' Someone was squeezing past their table and Sarah moved her chair to give them space. Marchant looked away and fiddled with the menu. 'Then it's my turn to take the compliment,' she said.

'Well you are.' In the dim light of the pub it was hard to tell but Sarah thought she detected a slight reddening in his face. He held up the menu as if to signal the end of this passage of conversation. 'Anyway, I think it's my turn to buy food.'

It was past eight thirty when they left the pub.

'I'll walk you to the tube,' said Marchant.

'Thanks James.'

As they walked she slipped her hand through the crook of his arm. 'That was a lovely evening,' she said, 'and you were right, I do need to get out more.'

'I enjoyed it too.' He was looking straight ahead. 'I hope you didn't feel I was a bit forward earlier,' he said.

'Telling me I was attractive?'

'Yes.'

She squeezed his arm. 'I think you just about got away with it.'

He looked at her to check her expression. 'So you weren't offended?'

Sarah laughed. 'James,' she said, 'what woman would be offended by being told they're attractive?'

He smiled. 'I have a bit to learn don't I?'

It was Sarah's turn to look ahead. 'You're doing just fine,' she said, 'here's my tube.'

They faced each other and this time he leant forward and kissed her on the cheek.

'I'll look forward to our next meeting then,' said Sarah, 'and I'll try harder to remain all serious and business like.'

'Don't do that,' he replied, 'I'm beginning to rather enjoy the frivolous bits.'

CHAPTER 11

6 June 1917

'Home sweet home' said Daniel Dawkins as he climbed down into the trench. 'Regent Street' said Fletcher, reading a sign that had been nailed to a supporting beam, 'we've been in this one before.'

'All look the fucking same after a while,' said Timmings, implying a familiarity with the front line that belied his age.

They had marched for two days under skies heavy with the bombardment that had accompanied them ominously for the past two weeks.

'Those fucking guns must be worn out by now,' said Timmings.

'They say there's more than two thousand of them,' said Fletcher.

'Longest I've heard in three years,' said Daniel, 'they mean business this time.'

'Pity poor fucking Fritz.'

'He'll be dug deep.'

Their arrival here was the last in a long series of activities building up to the final assault. Throughout the day the men of the 6th Berkshire Light Infantry had grown quieter as they had withdrawn into themselves, thinking of the past to avoid thinking of the future, speaking in brief, disjointed sentences lest their unease be revealed to those around them by the tone of their voices. They busied themselves with small tasks, checking their kit repeatedly, cleaning their rifles, examining their ammunition. Any serious conversation was greeted with ironic and often caustic humour. Some spoke rapidly and loudly, bolstering their own confidence with their upbeat demeanour, others chose to preserve their energy by remaining quiet.

The weakest became targets for an anxiety that needed dissipating. Dawkins noticed that Sergeant Barnes lost no opportunity to belittle the more vulnerable members of the platoon and if there was a dirty job to be done it was often Jackson whom he favoured for the duty.

'What will we do with Jacksy?' asked Timmings.

'He'll be by my side,' said Daniel.

'Do you think he'll make it?'

'No.'

'Nor me.'

'Shot in the head in the first wave, I'll wager.'

'Poor fucker.'

Once they had settled in Lieutenant Latham came to join them.

'When do we go over, sir?' asked Daniel.

'In the morning, I imagine.'

'In the morning.'

'That's not confirmed so don't go spreading it around but I've been led to believe that's the best bet.'

The three men looked at each other and then at their officer. Daniel noticed that Mr Latham was holding himself more rigidly than normal. 'It'll be a cushy one this I imagine,' he said, 'Fritz will have been softened up something rotten. He'll have bugger all guns left, that's for sure.'

'Let's hope you're right, Dawkins.'

'I'm up for it,' said Timmings, 'I'm right fed up with all this fucking waiting and practicing and fucking preparation.'

Fletcher shook his head slowly. 'A great adventure then, son,' he said, 'that's the spirit.'

He caught Daniel's eye and there was a glance of understanding between the two men, veterans of previous attritional advances. Mr Latham asked some questions about their preparation and conversation drifted on to what variation of stew they might expect that evening.

'Dawkins,' said Latham, 'I was hoping you might keep an eye on Jackson when we advance.'

'I was planning on that sir.'

'Thank you. We don't want him to do anything silly.'

'I'll shoot him straight off if he does sir.'

A look of shock flicked across Latham's face. 'You .....' he said, 'You ......'

'It would be best for everyone, sir.'

Latham looked at Fletcher who was watching his friend closely, then back at Dawkins. 'You're not being serious, surely.'

Dawkins shrugged.

'Of course he's not,' said Fletcher, 'he'll look after Jackson all right.'

Dawkins took some time to speak. 'I'll do what's right at the time,' he said.

Latham looked at each man in turn, trying to make sense of this turn in the conversation. 'You scare me at times, Dawkins,' he said.

'Scare myself at times, sir.'

Timmings put his arm round Dawkins' shoulder. 'Dan's only joking with you sir,' he said.

'Let's hope so.'

'Sure I am,' said Dawkins, 'I'll leave the killing to Fritz.'

Timmings laughed nervously. 'After you Fritz,' he said, 'no, after you DD.' 'No, I fucking insist, after you.'

The others started laughing also. 'I'm not sure the Germans will know enough English to converse in quite that depth,' said Latham drily.

Timmings gave Latham a friendly slap. 'You're a fucking card, you are man … sir,' he said, 'excusing my language.'

Fletcher, who had a gift for mimicry, then began imitating a German soldier emerging from his bunker after three weeks of shelling and, in a disorientated state, inviting the British over for a cup of tea. Before long the four men were rocking with laughter and they stood in a circle, their respective ranks temporarily forgotten as the tension in their bodies released itself in loud guffaws.

Alerted by the noise Sergeant Barnes appeared angrily. 'What the fuck is going on here?' he shouted, before noticing Mr Latham was at the centre of the group. Dawkins, Timmings and Fletcher, men who showed little regard for their sergeant's posturing, who knew how to do just enough not to land themselves in trouble and who, he suspected, talked badly of him when his back was turned, were Barnes's least favourite soldiers in the platoon.

'Mr Latham' he said, 'I didn't notice you were here, sir.'

'That's all right, Sergeant Barnes. Just sharing a joke with the men.'

Barnes was at a loss as to what to say next and he stared furiously at Latham who looked back at him coolly. 'We'll do an inspection at 1830hrs, Sergeant.'

Barnes's eyes moved from one man to the other, his distaste for what he was witnessing only tempered by the presence of an officer. 'Very well, sir,' he said pointedly and as he walked off the three soldiers looked at the ground as Mr Latham gazed impassively into the distance.

'Right,' said Latham, 'until 1830,' and headed back to his platoon headquarters, only allowing himself a wry smile once his back was turned from his men.

Sitting at the small table that served as his desk Latham looked at his watch. The inspection would be in ninety minutes. He reached into his field box, took out his pen and some paper, wrote down the words '*My Dear Mother and Father*' then sat for some time considering what to say. Early the next day he would be leading his Platoon in the first wave to attack the German lines. Dawkins's words about this being a cushy one had been a subtle and kindly attempt to calm nerves but he knew the odds of survival were low. Major Witheridge talked of improved tactics, of a rolling barrage and targeted fire, but the image of walking, exposed, across uneven ground towards an enemy with fixed machine guns, their sights aimed directly at him and those around him, was vivid and inescapable.

It was not so much death that he feared, it was losing his courage. How would he be when the time came to order the men over? How would he respond when men around him started falling? How clear would his mind be when he needed to make decisions that would determine whether men lived or died? Hearing that Private Jackson, a broken man, had once been a good and brave soldier had preyed on his mind recently; 'we all have our limits' Major Witheridge had said and it was a phrase that kept coming back to him.

He must not break.

His pen hovered over the paper and he closed his eyes. 'Lord,' he whispered, 'help me be bold.'

He began writing. Small, inconsequential details of the routines of the past week. descriptions of what he had eaten. Passages from the book he was reading.

'We are due to advance shortly,' he concluded. 'All the practices over, the preparations complete. When I write again it will be as a seasoned soldier. I hope you will find reasons to be proud of me, your loving son, Jeremy.'

He looked down at the paper and as he folded it up slowly he brushed his eyes with the back of his hand.

'Latham!'

He looked up to see Major Witheridge. 'It's confirmed. 0310hrs tomorrow.'

Latham swallowed involuntarily. 'Ten past three. Good. At last.'

Witheridge settled himself opposite where Latham was sitting and noticed his pen and paper. 'Final letter?'

'Final?'

'I'll rephrase that. Last letter before we go over.'

Latham nodded. 'Yes. To my parents.'

'I've just written to my wife.'

'Your wife? You've never talked about her.'

'She exists all right. And two small children.'

A particularly loud explosion sent tremors through the earth.

'Relentless,' said Witheridge, 'there won't be much left standing after all this.'

The sound of a shell coming towards them in retaliation had them both duck instinctively but it fell off to the south. 'Never hear the one that gets you,' said Witheridge.

'But they still have some guns left.'

'Can't be many. In the past they've sent as many back as we've been able to lob over. This time they are few and far between.' Witheridge smiled at Latham reassuringly. 'I do believe it might have worked this time.'

They sat listening to the bombardment which, after nearly three weeks, seemed to be reaching a peak of intensity.

'Rising to a crescendo,' said Witheridge, having to speak loudly to be heard, 'all the instruments coming together in the last moments.'

The ground shuddered again and a scattering of earth fell onto the table between them.

'Boys or girls?' said Latham.

'What?'

'Your children, boys or girls?' he repeated, almost shouting.

'Ah. One of each.' Witheridge waited for a break in the noise. 'Not much to say really. A typical family. Boy and a girl. Cat and a dog. Standard stuff really.'

Latham tried to imagine Major Witheridge as a family man but found it hard to equate the battle hardened officer opposite him with someone sitting at home, playing with his children, taking the dog for a walk and settling down with his wife to read a book.

'Sounds nice,' he said.

Witheridge nodded his head slowly. 'I miss them rather a lot actually.'

As if on cue Murphy scampered into the shelter and nuzzled up to Witheridge who stroked him under the chin. 'My God,' he said, 'is this fellow still with us?'

'Somehow. Dawkins and his mates feed him.'

'I'd have thought Sergeant Barnes would have put paid to that.'

'I think even he realises that would cause more trouble than it's worth.'

For a few minutes they discussed the tactics of the advance. Witheridge reminded Latham that the front trenches of the German lines would likely be only lightly manned and that the danger would come from the second line of defence and counter attacks, but other than that there was little to be said that hadn't been covered many times over the past week. Bored by a lack of attention Murphy wandered off along Regent Street.

'When's your inspection?' asked Witheridge.

'Shortly,' said Latham.

'Let's just run through a few last details.'

Witheridge quizzed Latham on how he would organise his sections, how he would break into the enemy trenches and how he would communicate with the other platoons.

'Good,' he said once he was satisfied with Latham's preparations, 'well then, all there is to do now is to wish you good luck.'

The two men stood opposite each other, Major Witheridge tanned, experienced, his face hardened from warfare, Latham, still almost a boy, his skin fresh, his hair slightly longer, his body slim and lanky. They shook hands formally.

'I will see you in the morning,' said Witheridge. 'Sleep well.'

After the inspection Latham briefed his Platoon. He told them that the bombardment would cease at 0250hrs and that they would ascend the ladders shortly after that. He reminded his men of the key lessons from rehearsals but kept it brief. He finished by wishing them luck. Sergeant Barnes then walked along the trench giving final instructions, checking ladders and speaking reassuringly to the younger soldiers.

Latham followed him and found himself next to Dawkins.

'Good one, sir,' said Dawkins.

'Thank you.'

'None of that 'for God and country' shite.'

Latham smiled and they stood together, their backs to the enemy, facing west and letting the evening sun warm their faces. A sudden thunderstorm came from nowhere and passed almost as quickly as it had arisen.

'We don't need rain,' said Dawkins, 'that would truly fuck us up.'

'It's just a shower,' said Latham, 'we should be OK.' He looked up at the sky, clear again.

'So what was going on on the road back there?' asked Latham.

'With Jackson?'

'Yes.'

'Being bullied.'

'And you stepped in.'

'That's right.'

Latham said nothing.

'Saw it too much when I was a kid,' said Dawkins, 'first my Dad then my Uncle.'

'Where did you grow up?'

'East end of London. My Dad used to beat my Mum something rotten. Usually when he was pissed.'

'And you came between them?'

'I tried to but he was a big bugger. Anyway, one day he just didn't come back from work. I lived with my Mum from then on. We lived in a row of houses with twelve families sharing one tap and two outside toilets. I remember Mum emptying slops into the street. There was sod all food around and what few scraps we had were often scattered over the slimy brick floor.'

'My God, that sounds grim.'

'When I was twelve my Mum died of tuberculosis. Took a long time, that did. I was taken in by my aunt and uncle and shared a mattress with their boy. The uncle was worse than my Dad. I think he couldn't stand the fact he was such a fucking loser and he took it out on his son. He was well angry when I arrived and he took to caning me as well.'

'Lord.'

'I was another mouth to feed, see. He used to have rules that he changed all the time and we got beaten if we didn't get it right.'

'How did you cope?'

'Oh, I was OK. I could take the beatings but my cousin cried himself to sleep at night.'

'How long did that go on for?'

'Three years I was with them.'

'That must have been tough.'

'It was that.' Dawkins smiled. 'But good training for the trenches.'

'More so than my upbringing.'

'We don't choose where we're bought up,' said Dawkins. 'I won't hold it against you.'

Latham smiled and they stood in silence.

'But it got sorted in the end,' said Dawkins after a while.

'Sorted?'

Dawkins looked across at Latham who recognised the still intensity that sometimes came over him. 'That's right. One night we went to the alehouse with him and sat outside while he got pissed. When he finally came out he tried to hit us but I blocked him. The way home was alongside a canal and about half way home he fell in.' Dawkins stopped talking.

'And .... ?'

Dawkins was looking at the ground.

'And the fucker drowned before we could pull him out.'

'My God.'

'Can't say I was too upset.' Dawkins laughed awkwardly. 'Anyway, I buggered off soon after that and found my way to a place called Taplow where a farmer took me in. That's where I met Joyce and that's where I was when war broke out.'

'And you were one of the first to enlist.'

'It beat working in the fields all day.'

Latham nodded but though he wanted to learn more he sensed Dawkins had said enough so they stood listening to the strange cacophony of sounds as shell after shell flew overhead with a high pitched scream before exploding in the distance with a dull thud.

'So who are you fighting for then?' asked Latham, 'if not God and country.'

'Who am I fighting for?' Dawkins seemed amused by the question. 'Me, I guess. Fletch. Timbo. All the boys. We fight for each other.'

'Surely your fiancée.'

'Joyce?' Dawkins considered the suggestion as if it were a novel idea. 'I suppose so .....' He looked upwards for inspiration. 'Would like it to be, but .... that's a long way off. Too far away.'

'Too far away?'

'You blot it out. Forget it. That's why I don't write much. Best not think of it.'

'I see.'

'In fact, can't think of it.' He turned to face Latham. 'Can't even see her face at times. I look at that photo and nothing comes.'

Latham gazed back at him, at a loss for words. 'That sounds a bit sad to me,' he said after a while.

Dawkins looked his Platoon Commander in the eyes. 'Maybe, sir,' he said, 'but perhaps it's for the best out here.'

'Keeps the emotions at bay, you mean?'

Dawkins leant back against the wall and closed his eyes. 'Put it like that sir, yes.' His head turned to the side as if he were looking away from his past. 'Don't need them getting in the way. Learnt that a long way back.'

Latham observed Dawkins' face and suddenly saw him in a new light. He could only assume from a distance what life as a young teenager with no support might be like and Dawkins' powerful self-reliance now made sense. 'My father thinks it's a noble thing we're doing,' he said.

Dawkins opened his eyes. 'Well, if you'll pardon me sir, he hasn't been out here.'

'No. But his heart's in the right place.'

'How about you, sir?'

'Me?'

'Who are you fighting for?'

'My family. My mother, my father, my sister. Funnily enough, God.'

'God?'

'Yes.'

'Blimey.'

'Why blimey?'

'Fucking odd God who lets all this shit happen. I'd not fight for him.'

'Well there's a bit more to it than that.'

Dawkins eyed Latham. 'So he gives you strength then?'

'Strength?' Latham pondered this concept. 'Yes, I believe he does.'

'Need to find strength from somewhere or you won't survive out here.'

'Yes, I can see that. How about you? Where does your strength come from?'

Dawkins grinned as he sometimes did when being asked such questions. 'I guess I just don't give a fuck any longer,' he replied.

Murphy bounded up to them and Latham bent down to stroke the terrier.

'Will he be coming with us?'

'Oh yes. He's well used to bullets and shells. It's a nice walk for him.'

'Well,' said Latham, 'let's hope it's a nice walk for all of us.'

Timmings and Fletcher were next in line and Latham chatted to them before moving on to pass some time with every one of the soldiers in 5 Platoon. Mostly they talked of small matters, joking uneasily, ribbing each other and their young officer, not mentioning home or what lay ahead. Then he held a final briefing with his Corporals before returning with Sergeant Barnes to his dugout.

'We're as ready as we'll ever be,' said Barnes.

'Good. I suggest you get some rest.'

'There won't be much sleep in the lines tonight.'

'No. I imagine you're right.'

'Well, sir. Good luck to you.'

'Thank you and good luck to you Sergeant Barnes.'

Barnes saluted and left. Latham lay down on his bunk, closed his eyes and considered the strangeness of the past thirty minutes; the conversation with first Major Witheridge and then Dawkins, the inconsequential chatting, the pretence of normality, the unreal calm that seemed to have taken hold of the trenches. He listened to the guns for a while then closed his eyes and prayed. 'Lord give me strength,' he began as he always did, 'Lord be by my side and those of my men …'

When he had finished he lay looking up at the cold earth above him and before he slipped off into a shallow sleep he imagined his homecoming, being greeted by his parents and sister, driving home in the Lanchester, eating at the dining table and finally lying between crisp sheets with a pillow below his head and a glass of water by his side.

CHAPTER 12

7 June 1917

At 0250hrs on 7 June 1917 the artillery bombardment over the Messines Ridge stopped and the eerie silence that descended on the trenches infiltrated minds already taut with tension, filling soldiers with a sense of dread as they hunched against the earthen walls.

Nobody spoke.

For twenty minutes nothing happened. Flares lit up the sky as the Germans watched eagerly for any movement of British troops.

'Fuck it,' said Daniel Dawkins to Fletcher, 'the same fucking mistake. Fritz will be climbing out of his dugouts and manning his guns as we wait here like fucking sheep to the slaughter.'

Further along the trench Lieutenant Latham awaited his order to move, wondering for an irrational moment if he had somehow missed something and that his platoon alone from the 2nd Army was caught in motionless anticipation.

Then, at 0310hrs a series of enormous explosions ripped through the air. Their magnitude sent shockwaves through the land, causing the ground to rock, buttreses to fall, bodies to move as if caught in waves on a beach. After a moment of intense silence, a colossal noise filled the skies, deafening ears unprepared for such a titanic blast. Pillars of fire reached up into the darkness of the night sky illuminating the countryside with a bright red light.

'Christ,' shouted Dawkins, 'Mines. They've mined Fritz's trenches.'

A ripple of excitement travelled along the line and men readied themselves, fiddling with belts and buckles, gripping their rifles.

Within seconds the order to move came through and Latham raised himself. He blew on his whistle, then shouted 'Advance' but the word came out hoarse and cracked. He placed his left foot on the ladder but Dawkins was ahead of him, climbing at speed, the soles of his boots scraping each rung, his body jerking left and right as he ascended towards the sky. Latham followed, concentrating only on the legs moving ahead of him, forcing from himself an immense effort to overcome the weakness in his knees until he was at the top and he looked around him and bodies were emerging on either side, shadowy and seemingly distant as they formed into a line across the decimated landscape.

Even as they formed up the barrage recommenced and exploding shells created a wall of fire and smoke ahead of them. Latham started walking and the men on either side of him followed his lead, finding their way through gaps in the wire that had been cut earlier that night. The ground was broken and they had to veer repeatedly to avoid bomb craters filled with stagnant water, but the barbed wire defences they came to had mostly been destroyed by the bombing and the long line of soldiers advanced at speed.

To his right Latham could see Dawkins with Jackson by his side, occasionally holding the man's webbing and propelling him forwards. Beyond him were Fletcher and Timmings with Murphy trotting along incongruously beside them. The soldiers all walked with a slight hunch as if to diminish themselves as targets but no shots rang out from beyond the advancing barrage and within minutes they were approaching the German front line.

With the gun teams providing cover the grenadiers ran forwards and threw their grenades. They were followed immediately by the rest of the platoon, bayonets fixed, who scrambled over and into the trench. The reason for the absence of shots became instantly apparent; the infantrymen awaiting their arrival lay strewn across the ground, their bodies ripped apart by the mines. Arms, legs and torsos were scattered along the bottom of the trenches, helmets and rifles strewn across the vast craters that had formed only minutes earlier. Three German soldiers, dazed and wounded, not knowing where they were, half-crazed with fright and shaking uncontrollably, raised their arms in surrender and a corporal signalled for them to stay where they were. The men of 5 Platoon then clambered down into what little remained of the trenches, stepped anxiously over the bodies of the dead Germans and peered forwards at the ground ahead of them that rose gradually towards the Messines Ridge.

Sergeant Barnes appeared by Latham's side. 'We're ahead of six and seven platoons,' he shouted. Latham climbed up to the rim of the trench and looked back to see the rest of the company who were still some fifty yards behind. 'We'll wait here until they catch up,' he replied.

Sergeant Barnes went off to check on the men and soon the order came to hold their ground to give time for the divisions of the second army to regroup.

Barnes returned to inform Latham that they hadn't sustained a single casualty. 'Fritz must be totally buggered,' he said.

Ahead of them, the vicious barrage continued and Latham searched the ground up to the ridge for any sign of life.

'Pillbox on the lower ridge,' said Dawkins who had crept up beside him, 'over there on the western flank.'

Latham peered through the smoke filled landscape and spotted the low grey building, nestling in a small fold in the ground.

'No sign of life,' he said.

'But still intact. We'll need to watch it.'

Beyond Dawkins Timmings was grinning at them with Murphy the terrier sitting beside him, alert, his ears up, looking excitedly at the flurry of activity all about him.

A runner appeared and told Latham that they would be holding this position for at least an hour before moving on to the next objective.

'Fuck that,' said Dawkins, 'we need to keep moving.'

'We don't know what's happening elsewhere,' said Latham, 'there's a whole bloody army to coordinate. Let's see what unfolds.'

And so they waited. There was little conversation and the men looked ahead to avoid the sight of the dead and mutilated German bodies lying all around them. This first taste of battle, so anticipated, had passed quickly, no more than fifteen minutes, and each man reflected on the ease with which they had advanced and they dared to believe that perhaps this was how it would be, that maybe the Germans were finally on the run and the worst was over.

Latham looked over to where Private Jackson was curled up, apparently asleep.

'Leave him be,' whispered Dawkins, 'he's untroubled for the moment.'

Minutes passed slowly, the sounds of fighting all around them came and went and it was as if 5 Platoon was held in an oasis of peace, a bubble of calm while all about was noise and confusion and gunfire.

At 0500hrs they were ordered to move again. The pause had played with nerves and the sense of unease was palpable as the men advanced into the open. The barrage, reaching a peak of intensity, preceeded them again and Latham took some comfort in the fact that timings were proving robust and accurate. He kept glancing in the direction of the pillbox but could see no movement. Each step felt like a small victory, an advance towards their destination unopposed, a testament to their overwhelming power.

'Down.'

It was Dawkins shouting and Latham hit the ground as the sound of bullets whistled overhead. He looked to his left and saw two soldiers, not alerted by Dawkins' alarm, fall to the ground.

'Pillbox,' screamed Dawkins, 'machine gun.'

'Return fire,' shouted Latham and men opened up on either side of him but they were out in the open and fatally exposed. 'Lewis gun' he shouted but even before the words were out of his mouth a gun rattled into action off to his right and then smoke grenades were landing between him and the pillbox and smoke drifted across the ground, obscuring the gunners view.

'Crater to our left,' shouted Dawkins and six of them ran to the safety of the giant hole. Latham found himself beside Fletcher who peered above the lip of the crater.

'One machine gun,' he said, 'in the pillbox, a hundred feet away.'

Latham was breathing heavily from his dash to safety.

'Three men hit that I can see,' continued Fletcher, his voice calm and measured, '6 Platoon are ahead of us, on the flank, taking casualties.'

'Can we get close to the bunker?' asked Latham.

'With smoke we can get close enough for a rifle grenade.'

'Have we got one here?'

'I have, sir,' said Timmings.

Seconds passed while Latham tried to work out a plan.

'If we can lay down smoke Timbo can go off to the right and get into a good position to fire,' said Fletcher.

'How much smoke have we got?'

The men spoke up in turn and between them they had eight smoke bombs.

'That will have to do,' said Dawkins.

'It's a risk,' said Fletcher, 'Our smoke won't get close to the pillbox. Timbo will be a long way off.'

'I can fucking try,' said Timmings.

'Wait.' Latham could see the plan had only a limited chance of success. More seconds ticked by.

'Well, sir?' said Dawkins.

'Wait,' said Latham again. He knew that others would see they were pinned down and artillery spotters might at that very moment be calling down fire. 'Give it a minute.'

Dawkins looked impatient but said nothing, Timmings held his rifle across his chest, ready to move, Fletcher leant against the side of the crater, the other two soldiers remained crouching, waiting.

'We can't stay here much longer,' said Dawkins but a second later a series of shells landed ahead of them and then the ground all the way up to the pillbox was covered in smoke.

'Now,' shouted Latham and without hesitation Timmings was out of the crater and running straight ahead.

'Weave,' shouted Dawkins and Timmings moved left to right before becoming lost in the cloud.

The men in the crater all peered over the top, staring into the smoke, trying to catch sight of Timmings.

'He should be near them now,' said Fletcher.

Then suddenly the smoke cleared temporarily and they could see Timmings, on one knee, his weapon pointed at the pillbox, no more than twenty feet away from the concrete bunker. They watched as the German machine gunners looked up and they could see the barrel of their gun traverse to point straight at Timmings before the familiar rattle of an MG 08 sounded across the battlefield at the very moment Timmings fired and his rocket appeared to miraculously fly straight through the slit in the pillbox. There was a flash from inside followed by silence. The smoke returned. The men of 5 Platoon strained their eyes to see what was going on.

'Think I saw Timbo go down,' said Fletcher.

The smoke ebbed and flowed, the bunker came and went, there was no movement ahead. On either side of 5 Platoon the sounds of battle continued. In the distance heavy guns were firing and explosions were ripping the land apart all around.

'We need to ....' Latham began to say but Dawkins was already out of the crater and running towards the bunker.

'Not enough smoke ...' shouted Fletcher and even as he spoke visibility cleared so that they could see Dawkins zig-zagging at top speed towards where Timmings had last been seen.

'Shit,' said Latham and the men waited for the sickening sound of machine gun fire but none came. Soon Dawkins was at the spot where Timmings had last been seen and they saw him drop to one knee. Seconds later he was waving for them to join him.

'Come on,' shouted Latham and clambered out of the crater, closely followed by the others. No shots were fired and it wasn't long before they arrived at where Dawkins was now standing beside a bewildered Timmings who was sitting up and looking round him, his helmet off and rubbing his head.

'Bashed his head and knocked himself out,' said Dawkins, 'stupid bastard. He'll be fine,' and with that he ran off towards the bunker. Fletcher followed on immediately and the two of them kicked in the door of the pillbox and disappeared from view. Seconds later they emerged and Dawkins shouted 'all dead!'

One of the soldiers helped Timmings to his feet and the six men then advanced towards the next German line which they found deserted. They had covered perhaps two hundred yards at speed and they fell, exhausted, into the safety of the trench. Soon others who had also taken cover at that first salvo appeared alongside them. Latham looked around him at the men under his command, panting from their exertions, bent double as they regained their breath, marvelling at still being alive.

Sergeant Barnes appeared, wheezing heavily, and began making his way from one end of the trench to another, finally reporting to Latham that four men from 5 Platoon had been killed, three wounded.

'Four men? Which ones?'

'Jenkins, Marlowe, Black and Campbell.'

Latham pictured each man in turn. Jenkins, the oldest in the platoon, Marlowe, a quiet, reserved sort of fellow, Black, a powerful beast of a man and Campbell, a wisecracker who, like Dawkins, had little time for rules. 'God,' he said, 'oh my God.'

'Got off lightly,' said Sergeant Barnes, 'could have lost many more.'

Latham stared at him. 'Got off lightly?' he said, 'four men dead?'

Barnes seemed not to be listening. He stood up and looked about him. 'It was the pillbox that fucked us,' he said. He sniffed the air, as if seeking out the smell of death lingering over the enemy trench. 'Light, I'd say. Light casualties. Brass will be pleased. Expected much higher I'll bet.'

Latham watched his Sergeant with a deep and growing hatred. It seemed Barnes was enjoying the moment, relishing the victory, unconcerned about the men who minutes earlier had been under his command and who now lay dead.

'Four of our men are dead, Sergeant,' he said. 'Four lives. Four sacred lives.'

'Sacred?' Barnes laughed. 'Nothing fucking sacred out here.'

Latham shook his head. 'You're wrong Sergeant Barnes,' he said, 'you're wrong. Every life is sacred.'

Barnes leant towards him, his face red from his exertions, sweat dripping from his chin, his lips pursed. 'They're soldiers, Mr Latham,' he said, 'soldiers. Here to fight and die. That's war. Think otherwise and you'll go mad.'

Two hours later fresh troops arrived, spoke to them briefly and then moved on towards Messines. Major Witheridge appeared and told Latham that the company would now stay in reserve and wouldn't move again until the following day.

'The whole operation has gone as planned,' he said, 'it's been a great success.'

'A success. Good.'

'Light casualties, but nothing like in the past. How many have you lost?'

'Four killed, three wounded.'

'Who was it that took out the pillbox?'

'Timmings.'

'I'll see he's rewarded for that.'

Witheridge took a small flask out of his side pocket and handed it to Latham who took a long swig of whisky then spluttered as the back of his throat felt the heat of the liquid.

'Well done,' said Witheridge, '5 Platoon did well.'

'I lost four men.'

'I know. I'm sorry. But it could have been much worse.' He studied his young subaltern. 'Death is what defines us out here, Latham,' he said, 'you'll get used to it soon enough.'

Latham made to say something but decided against it.

'So,' said Witheridge, 'we'll consolidate once the ridge and surrounding area are secure. That will take a day or so, I imagine. Then it will be on to the Gheluvelt plateau. That's the main objective.'

'Jolly good,' said Latham and the sarcasm in his voice was evident.

Witheridge put a hand on his shoulder. 'I felt the same way the first time,' he said, 'everyone does, but that changes.'

'That's what worries me.'

The two men stood together, the adrenalin that had filled their veins these past hours now dissipating and leaving them feeling utterly drained.

'Those mines did the job,' said Latham.

'They did indeed. Let's hope Plumer has some more tricks up his sleeve for the next phase.'

A few light drops of rain fell between them and both men looked skywards.

'One thing we don't need now is rain,' said Witheridge, 'this whole place would turn into a quagmire in hours.'

'Does that mean we'll advance while the weather's fine?'

'Don't bank on it. We'll need to pause to regroup and that'll take a few days.'

'Shouldn't we press on while we have the advantage?'

Witheridge shook his head. 'That would make sense but if the past years have taught us anything it's not to outrun our guns and supplies. My guess is we'll pause a while.'

The shower passed and Dawkins appeared.

'That looks good, sir,' he said, noting the flask still in Major Witheridge's hand.

'Whisky is strictly forbidden in the trenches, Dawkins, you know that as well as anyone.'

'Understood, sir.'

Witheridge passed over the flask. 'Just a small sip, this has to last a while.'

Dawkins put the metal rim to his mouth and briefly upturned the small leather container. 'Fuck me,' he said, 'If that's what's issued to officers I'll apply for a commission.'

'Now there's a thought to play with.'

They began discussing the assault but were interrupted by the sound of a shell landing off to the south of their position.

'Fritz still has a few guns left then,' said Dawkins.

Witheridge was turning his head from left to right. 'I'm not sure that wasn't one of ours.'

'Our own side?' said Latham, 'shelling us?'

'It happens when advances are taking place. The whole line becomes disjointed and it's ruddy difficult for the gunners.' Witheridge stood up. 'I must get a message to the OPs immediately.' He was already walking. 'I'll speak to you later, good work again,' he said over his shoulder as he headed off along the line.

Dawkins went off to his position leaving Latham on his own. He reflected on the assault, coming under fire from the pillbox, Timmings's advance into the smoke and then Dawkins's dash forwards with no cover, apparently oblivious to the dangers he faced. It had been an act of almost suicidal bravery and Latham marvelled, not for the first time, at Dawkins's apparent lack of concern for his own safety. He considered his conversations with Sergeant Barnes and Major Witheridge and wondered if he would one day be as they were, seeing death as merely a statistic, seemingly immune to the personal tragedies being acted out all around them, losing sight of the fact that a life was God's gift and not to be taken lightly.

Sergeant Barnes appeared from the direction Dawkins had recently left by and began running through details of ammunition and rations.

'What about the casualties?' asked Latham.

'The wounded have been sent back to the field hospital, the dead will wait for transportation back down the line.'

'I suppose they have little option.'

Sergeant Barnes smiled. 'That's it sir. A bit of humour. That's what's needed now. '

'Humour. Ah, I see. I'm being humorous. Excellent.'

Latham looked at Barnes who was no longer smiling.

'Now, ammo, sir,' said Barnes but he was interrupted by the sound of another shell.

'That's close,' said Latham and they both ducked. With an intense high pitched scream the shell approached their position and it seemed bound to hit them but just as they braced themselves for the impact it fell short of where they were pressed against the walls of the trench and exploded some fifty feet away. They looked up to see earth flying through the air and clods landed all around their position. Reverberations shook the ramparts and a low wind whistled through the line.

'Too fucking close,' said Barnes, 'that nearly had us.'

Latham looked towards where a cloud of smoke was rising up above the point of impact. 'That's where Major Witheridge was headed,' he said.

Without another word being spoken both men stood, their legs unsteady, their heads still spinning, and started running.

Ahead of them they could see Dawkins already racing through what remained of the network of German trenches and soon they came to a large hole, still smoking, twenty feet across, forming a perfect parabola as it straddled the defences. Two bodies, badly disfigured, lay perfectly still on the edge of the crater. Further towards the middle another body, its torso separated from its legs, blood streaming from its head, formed a broken shape where it had come to land. Dawkins was lying on the earth beside this body and talking quietly.

Latham approached and could see Major Witheridge's face, eyes open, staring up into the sky, not moving. Then he caught sight of the severed and pulped tops of Witheridge's legs and, overcome by dizziness, he turned away and vomited. He crouched on all fours, his mind unfocused, his vision blurred and when he turned back Dawkins was still talking to his Company Commander.

'......and then we stayed there for over an hour, waiting for the reinforcements...' he was saying, '...and you told me about your family and what you'd do when you got home...' With that Dawkins voice tailed away and he sat in silence for a few moments before reaching down and closing the eyes of the Major's shattered face with the tips of his fingers. Then he stood up, looked neither to the left nor the right, turned and walked away. Latham remained where he was with no strength to move, staring at the mutilated corpse of his Company Commander, facing the true reality of war for the first time.

'*Death is what defines us out here, Latham*', Witheridge had said only minutes earlier and his words sounded in Latham's head. He looked about him at the stretcher bearers who were already gathering up the dead bodies and he squatted on his haunches, sucking in air, taking his time to clear his mind and compose himself.

He felt a hand on his shoulder and turned to see Sergeant Barnes standing over him.

'Come on, lad,' said the Sergeant, 'there's nothing we can do for him now.'

CHAPTER 13

7 November 1920

It was 1855hrs when Captain Peter Harding, still urging his driver to speed up, arrived at St Pol-sur-Ternoise with five minutes to spare. For three of those minutes they drove through the small town while Peter studied his map, finally finding the narrow road to the St Pol chapel, an undistinguished corrugated iron hut.

As the ambulance drew to a halt, the Reverend George Kendall emerged from the small building and signalled for the driver to back up to the door.

Peter stepped down and saluted. 'Captain Harding, sir,' he said.

'Well done Harding,' replied the Reverend Kendall, 'spot on time. You have your body?'

'Yes sir.'

'Exactly as required?'

'Yes sir.'

'Definitely British?'

'Yes sir.'

'But no means of identification whatsoever?'

The Reverend's eyes were fixed on Peter's.

'None sir.'

'Good. Have your men bring him inside.'

Peter stood to one side as Baxter and the other soldier opened the rear door of the ambulance and he watched as they picked up the sack containing the soldier's remains. He walked beside them as they carried their load, little more than a collection of bones, into the chapel. There were already three other sacks in the building, identical to theirs, laid out in a row on stretchers in front of the altar.

'Place it there, please,' said Kendall, pointing to the remaining space, the furthest to the right.

They placed their body on the stretcher then stepped back. Kendall led them outside where the driver was standing waiting for them then he addressed the small group.

'Now,' he said, 'I am going to say to you something of the utmost importance.'

The men stood in a line, facing the chapel, observing the Reverend.

'The task you have just undertaken is one of the gravest significance. One of these four bodies will be chosen to be taken back to London for burial in Westminster Abbey. This will be the body of the Unknown Warrior. It is absolutely imperative that there is no way of knowing who that dead soldier is.' He looked at each man in turn. 'So, I will ask you now, can you confirm you have absolutely no knowledge of who it is whose remains are in that sack?'

Baxter, the most loquacious of the group, spoke up immediately. 'None sir,' he said, 'We 'ad to dig up four of the buggers, beggin your pardon, sir, before we got 'un with now't on it. The Captain was most particular.'

The Reverend smiled and looked at the others, each of whom nodded in ascent.

'Good,' he said, 'now I will ask you to speak to nobody of what you have done today. You are not to talk of where you found the body, nor where or when you delivered it. I have said exactly the same thing to the other parties. Is that clear?

'Yes, sir,' said each man in turn.

'Good. Thank you and God bless you. You have been involved in a noble thing today and you will have cause to feel pride in what you have done. You will now return directly to your unit and, if asked, will say only that you have been involved in an administrative task for staff.'

Back in the ambulance Peter sat in the front beside the driver who, now that he was heading home, was finally driving at speed. He let his fingers glide over the narrow metal container in his pocket. He repeated the words of the Reverend Kendall in his mind: 'can you confirm you have absolutely no knowledge of who it is whose remains are in that sack?' He could remember the sentence word for word in its entirety.

He gazed ahead at the narrow French road and questioned his own judgement. When asked to confirm to the Reverend that there were no means of identification he had, quite simply, lied. At the most critical moment he had come up short and this went against the very core of his being.

Thoughts revolved inside his head in ever-decreasing circles and the countryside passed unnoticed as he berated himself for his weakness.

But then the driver came to a junction. 'Which way, sir,' he asked, 'Left or right?' Pulled out of his reverie Peter needed to consult the map and the interruption cleared his brain. 'Right,' he said.

The driver engaged first gear with a loud grating sound and as the ambulance picked up speed again Peter felt a renewed sense of purpose; what had happened had happened. There was no turning back. Decide what to do now and move forwards. The solution was simple: on his return he would burn the photograph and all evidence would be destroyed. He had taken a pragmatic decision at the time, the only realistic choice in the circumstances, and he would now take action to ensure no harm had been done. A body would be chosen, the nation would get its burial, and he alone would know what had happened.

He settled back in his seat with a sense of relief at this resolution, happy with the conclusion that he had acted sensibly and in everyone's interests.

Back at the barracks his Commanding Officer was in the Officer's Mess and took him to one side when he reported back.

'Success?' said the CO.

'Yes, sir. One body delivered as instructed.'

'Good. No problems?'

'We had a problem on the way out but managed to make up time.'

'No cutting of corners?'

'No, sir. We had to dig up a few bodies before we found what we wanted but we got there in the end.'

The Colonel gave him a long look. 'Good. We need just wait and see how events unfold now.'

Peter took his leave and went back to his room where he sat for a few moments without moving. Then he took the metal container from his pocket, carefully removed the photograph and gazed at the face staring back at him. The woman had long curly hair and an expression that he found quite bewitching. The tilt of her boater, the curve of her lips, the smile that caused her mouth to part; he had seldom, if ever, been so struck by an appearance. There was a subtle humour in her expression, a hint of playfulness and, he imagined, the suggestion of a free spirit, a joie de vivre. A joie de vivre that he sometimes saw in others, that he would like to embrace, but which had been so absent from his life to date.

But the smile was not for him, it was for a man who was now dead, whose remains, at that very moment, were lying in a chapel in St Pol, and Peter knew that this woman would never know what had happened to her loved one. She may have received a statement informing her that he was 'Missing in Action', no more.

He looked into her eyes as if seeking a message but she looked straight back at him blankly and opaquely, giving nothing away, observing him from a different time and place in a haunting indifference to his feelings.

He turned the photograph over to see if he had missed anything but there was no writing, no name, nothing to tell him who she might be.

So he picked up his metal waste paper bin and placed it on the floor in front of him. Then he reached for the box of matches he used to light the pipe he occasionally smoked, placed the photograph to one side, looked at the face again, hesitated, then lit a match and set fire to the corner of the paper as he held it above the bin. He watched as the face slowly disappeared in the flames, only dropping the burning photograph into the bin at the last moment when his fingers could withstand the heat no longer.

For a few seconds he watched as the final corner of the photograph curled and blackened and when the flame was gone he sat back and shook his head slowly as he contemplated the finality of his action, wondering if he would ever live to regret it.

Midnight, 7 November 1920

Brigadier General L.J. Wyatt and Lieutenant Colonel E.A.S. Gell spoke briefly to the armed soldiers at St Pol chapel who had been standing guard outside the main door since the Reverend Kendall had left earlier that evening.

On entering the chapel they surveyed the scene. In the dim light they could make out four bodies laid out side by side on stretchers, each one covered by a union flag. Beyond them, in front of the altar, was a plain wooden coffin.

Flickering candles positioned around the walls cast shadows over the scene.

The men spoke sparingly before Brigadier Wyatt closed his eyes, moved from side to side to deliberately disorientate himself, stepped forwards with arms outstretched, groped in front of him and then rested his hands on the first body he came to.

'That one,' he said, 'that is our Unknown Warrior.'

Between them the two senior officers carefully lifted the the remains and laid them out in the coffin as neatly as they could before screwing the lid down. Then they stepped back and paused a moment.

'Thanks be to God,' said the Brigadier, 'what happens to the others?'

'They will be reburied locally by Reverend Kendall,' said the Colonel.

'Good. Our job is done here. Thank you Colonel.'

With that the Brigadier departed, leaving Colonel Gell to finalise arrangements.

THE TIMES NEWSPAPER

THE LAST JOURNEY. A PROUD SALUTE FROM FRANCE.
MARSHALL FOCH'S FAREWELL
(from our special correspondent) Boulogne Nov 10 Midday 1920.

'The body of the nameless Warrior chosen to remain through the centuries the symbol of the plain men of our islands is on its way across the sea, and rode home through the mist to its resting place at Westminster. The echoes of the Field Marshall's salute, fired as the British destroyer Verdun put out to sea bearing the body, have hardly died away, but the Verdun has already disappeared in the thick haze with the French destroyers which were waiting for her outside.

The Warrior has gone with the simplest and the most fitting of ceremonies. France sent her great Marshall Foch and men from some of her hardest tried regiments to salute the returning soldier as he passed from French soil. The townspeople crowded round the processions' route through Boulogne and paid sympathetic farewell to the representation of the hundreds of thousands who died, as one Frenchman put it 'for our country as much as his own.'

As the sun was sinking yesterday afternoon an army ambulance arrived at St Pol with the body, which had been bought 'from the Ypres front' and last night the Unknown lay in simple state, guarded by Poilus, in the library of the officers mess on the edge of town. The rough pine coffin, covered with a solid and torn Union Jack, was carried from the officer's chateau by eight non-commisioned officers, drawn from the various arms of the Service, and including an Australian and a Canadian.

A SWORD FROM THE KING

'French officers of the Boulogne area, with General Diebold at their head, and a number of British officers were there to salute the dead, and there were autumn flowers strewn on the floor of the library, which had been quickly converted into a Chapelle Ardente. The pine coffin was stripped of its flag and placed inside the oak coffin which had been sent to receive the body. It is a plain, iron bound coffin with a sword from the King's personal collection fastened to the lid and bearing the inscription

'A British Warrior who fell in the Great War 1914/1918.'

'Then men from the eighth regiment, a regiment with a fine record that has just won for it the Legion of honour, mounted guard, and by turns two of them watched all night. At about 10. O clock this morning the coffin, bound in the worn Union Jack, was placed on a French army wagon drawn by six horses and, with the eight British non-commissioned marching beside it, was taken to the neighbouring junction of three roads, the old toll bar known as the 'Dernier Sou'. The sky was grey and a thick mist laid over the sea.

'Soon Lieutenant General Sir G. MacDonogh, the King's representative, and a number of other British officers arrived, and then Marshall Foch drove up. Next, after a salute from the trumpets of the French cavalry, the procession moved off as the tender melancholy of Chopin's funeral march filled the air. Children and representatives of local associations were at the head, followed by seemingly endless ranks of cavalry with the marines and infantry next. Then came the coffin, followed by a number of wreaths – from the French Government, French army, French navy, and the Corps of interpreters – and immediately behind marched Marshal Foch and Lieutenant General MacDonogh. Then came officers, and after these more troops.

'Along streets bordered with be-flagged Venetian masts, past the silent watching crowd, the cortege passed through the town to the Quai Gambetta, where the Verdun, with her motto 'on ne passe pas', was moored, her crew mastered on deck.

MARSHALL FOCH'S PLEA

'There was a brief address from Marshall Foch who, with his usual grave eloquence, evoked the memories of British heroism that are conjured up by the names of Ypres, Somme, Messines, and all the other memorable battlefields, and pleaded that the sacrifices symbolised by the body of the unknown soldier there should serve to keep the two countries united in victory as they were in war.

'After Lieutenant General MacDonogh had replied, the troops astern and the marines aboard presented arms, and the 'Marsaillaise' and 'God Save the King' were played.

'Then the eight NCOs slowly hove the body of their comrade aboard the Verdun, while the ensign easing astern was slowly drawn down to half mast and the illustrious French Marshall, alone by the gangway, stood gazing at the coffin of the unknown British soldier. Then the poilus placed wreaths over the coffin, Lieutenant General MacDonogh went on board, and very soon – at about a quarter to twelve – once more to the strains of 'God Save the King', the Verdun cast off and steamed rapidly *away with an A.B. standing with bent head and reversed arms at each corner of the coffin. Then, as the destroyer slipped into the thick mist, the 19 rounds of the Field Marshall's salute boomed out. The Unknown Warrior was on his way home to the land whence he came.'*

CHAPTER 14

October 2011

'It seems very likely it was Daniel Dawkins who wrote the letters to Joyce,' said James Marchant. He was sitting in a café opposite Sarah Harding.

'How do you know?'

'It all fits. He joined up at the start of the war and served with the 6th Berkshire Light Infantry until he went missing in action near Ypres.'

'Which was when?'

'October 1917.'

Sarah looked at the photocopies Marchant had laid out across the table. 'And the other Daniel?'

'There's no record of him having even joined up.'

'So that's it then. We've found my true grandfather.'

'Almost certainly. He served with the 6th Berkshire Light Infantry between 1915 and 1917 so he would almost certainly have been at Messines Ridge which is what he wrote about in one of those letters. He referred to two soldiers, one called Timbo who I believe was a private Timmings, the other Fletch, a private Fletcher.'

'October,' said Sarah, 'and his last letter to Joyce was in late September – so that fits.' On one of the photocopies was an old black and white photograph of a group of soldiers.

She held it up and studied the grainy image. 'Is that them?'

'Yes. 5 Platoon. He mentions that at some point.'

'They look terribly stern.'

'All portraits do from then. Remember they had to sit still and face the camera for a number of seconds before the exposure took. No smiling – that's why everyone from that era looks so severe.'

'Of course.' Sarah was looking along the two rows of faces. 'I wonder which was him.'

'I can tell you.' Marchant handed her another piece of paper with two rows of names. 'Someone wrote their names on the back.'

Sarah looked at the names and then at the photograph. 'Third from the left at the rear,' she said to herself. Her finger pointed to a man who stared back at her without expression. 'So that's him.' She gazed at his face. 'My God.'

Marchant pointed to a date below the names. 'July 1917,' he said, 'a month after Messines Ridge. They're all there; Dawkins, Fletcher, Timmings, a young officer called Lieutenant Latham and a Sergeant Barnes.'

'Wow.' Sarah couldn't draw her attention away from Dawkins' face. 'So there's my grandfather.'

Marchant watched her. 'Do you need a moment?' he asked. She pulled out a tissue from her bag and blew her nose. 'No, I'm OK. It's just…'

'A bit overwhelming?'

'Yes.' She finally put down the photograph. 'Actually, I might just get some fresh air.'

'I'll stay here and guard the seats.'

Sarah stepped outside and Marchant watched her through the window as she lit up a cigarette in the street. She smiled at him and waved. He waved back and then studied his papers until she returned.

'Do we know anything more about him?' she asked as she sat down.

'Surprisingly little, I'm afraid,' said Marchant, 'just a sentence or two – which is rather strange – all my information has come from more general stuff.'

'Is that odd?'

'Possibly. I'll do some more ferreting around later but have you found out anything more from the school records?'

She shook her head slowly. 'No. Sorry, I've been rather busy at work.'

'No problem.'

'But there is one thing.'

Marchant looked up. 'What's that?'

'Dad was more lucid today. He was mumbling away but I heard one distinct word.' She paused.

'What word exactly?'

'Diary.'

'Diary? His?'

'I don't know. I was never aware of him keeping one.'

'Lord, that would be of interest.'

'I know. I've been searching through Dad's belongings but can't find anything. He's never referred to any diaries in the past and I've been through all his files but there's no mention of them.'

'Well, keep searching.'

'I've rather run out of places to look.'

Marchant finished off his coffee and tapped the table as he thought. 'Safety deposit box? Anything like that?'

'Not that I know of.'

'Attic? Cellar? The back of some wardrobe? If he's never mentioned them they may be well hidden.'

'Why?'

'Why? Why would someone hide their diaries? Because they contain some secret information, of course.'

'Ah.'

'And given everything we've found out so far that's potentially very significant.'

Sarah studied him. 'You've got that look again,' she said.

'What do you mean?'

'Animated. Full of energy. On the hunt.'

He laughed awkwardly. 'How odd. Are you implying my normal demeanour is one of abject lethargy?'

Sarah leant forward and patted his knee. 'Not every compliment needs to be back-handed.'

Marchant looked about him. They were in a Starbucks which wasn't his choice but was conveniently situated for both of them. There were eight other people in the room, two serving behind the counter, two men in suits by the window, two women on a leather sofa, a single woman reading a book and a man standing at a tall round table near the coffee machine fiddling with his mobile phone. Cars were moving slowly along the street beyond the large window. Grains of sugar, spilt earlier as Marchant had fumbled with a small white cylindrical package, formed a pattern on the wooden surface in front of him.

'I'm going to see a film later,' he said suddenly, 'would you be interested?'

'What film?'

'Once upon a time in Anatolia.'

'I'm not sure I want to see a spaghetti western.'

'It isn't. The titles' a play on the Sergio Leone film.'

'I know that really.'

Marchant looked at her directly for the first time in over a minute. 'You know that?'

'Once upon a time in Anatolia. A long, slow Turkish film about a man helping police find the body he buried.'

'So you've read the reviews.'

'You're not the only one who reads the reviews.'

'Of course not. I'm sorry, how patronising of me.'

Sarah touched his arm. 'I doubt many people would know about it,' she said, 'and it's not quite the chick flick to take a girl to on a first date. But I'm on.'

'First date.' He said it more as a question than a statement.

'It's a loose term.'

He was looking into his coffee cup again. 'Good. It's on at a cinema near Tottenham Court Road. What say we have something to eat afterwards?'

'Excellent.'

'We'll need to get going.' He stood up. 'That wasn't too difficult after all.'

'What wasn't?'

'Arranging a date. Cinema, meal ......,' he paused, conscious of where his words might be leading. 'That's how it goes isn't it?'

Sarah smiled. 'The pause after the word 'meal' sounds rather intriguing,' she said as they stepped out into the street. She put her arm through his. 'Thank heavens you're a gentleman.'

On the tube they returned to the subject of the diary.

'If your Dad has made some records that would be really useful,' said Marchant, 'so far we've just been speculating, we need more facts. We think Peter Harding was on one of the digging parties, we know he was at the service, we know he married a woman who was written to by a soldier called Daniel who went missing in 1917. Everything else is just joining a series of unrelated dots – which is the domain of conspiracy theorists.'

Sarah thought this through. 'So would he have known anything about Daniel?'

'Good question. We don't know if he ever saw those letters. In which case it's simply a matter of him marrying a woman who had previously been in love with a soldier who went missing in the war. There must be thousands of cases like that.'

'But it does all seem a bit too much of a coincidence,' said Sarah. 'My dad says 'Unknown Soldier' when I ask him who Daniel was and then, lo and behold, we discover the man who subsequently married Daniel's girlfriend was involved in the choosing of the Unknown Soldier. What's the likelihood of that happening?'

'Fair point.'

The train pulled into a station, the doors opened, people came and went, the train moved off again.

'But listen,' said Marchant, 'a man is walking past a phone box.' He leant forwards and emphasised his words with a movement of his hands. 'The phone goes off and he decides to answer it. It's his wife who says something important's cropped up. He says 'but this isn't my office, I've gone for a walk and I was just passing a phone box when it rang.' 'Well, whatever,' she replies, 'I must have got a digit wrong, but Uncle Harry has fallen ill – can you get to the hospital right away?" He looked sideways at Sarah. 'Fate? It was meant? Some strange mysterious force at work? Or coincidence?'

'It sounds highly improbable.'

'Yes, but sooner or later it will happen. Of the thousands of wrong numbers called every day sooner or later something bizarre like this will occur.'

'Every day?'

'OK. Every week, year, whatever. The point is that people will then say 'it's fate, it's mysterious, it's something spiritual. It's serendipity'. But it's not, it's coincidence. Extraordinary coincidences are bound to happen now and then.'

'Ever the rationalist.'

'What else is there to be?'

'So you're not a religious man then?'

'I'm just saying that it's all too easy to get swept away by anecdote when a bit more thought will reveal the real truth.'

'So you're not a religious man then?'

Marchant laughed. 'I close my mind to nothing but no, even though I come from a Catholic family I wouldn't describe myself as a religious man. How about you?'

'I also come from a Catholic family. I was educated in a convent.'

'Like Hattie.'

'Ah. Hattie.'

'Why 'Ah. Hattie?"

'Oh, nothing in particular.'

The train came to halt.

'This is us,' said Marchant, 'prepare yourself for a sore bottom.'

* * * *

The cinema was old fashioned with a small screen and uncomfortable seats. The people in the foyer were of a certain type, earnest, intellectual, speaking quietly with an air of erudition, as if they, the few, had the subtlety of mind to appreciate such an obscure film.

'I love places like this,' said Marchant, 'no popcorn for a start.'

They sat near the back and, after a busy day, both had brief periods of sleep during the first half of the film, waking to find that not much had changed in either the landscape or plot. They emerged past nine o'clock.

'What do you think?' asked Marchant.

'I think the description 'slow moving' didn't quite do it justice.'

He laughed. 'Yes, I did wonder at one point if we'd ever find that bloody body.'

Sarah followed him out into the street. 'I can't quite work out whether it was a work of genius or whether I've just been conned out of two hours of my life,' she said.

'The audience seemed moved. No one wanted to leave.'

'Perhaps they understood something at a deeper level than me. I'm probably not heavyweight enough for this sort of thing.'

'I wouldn't say that.'

They were standing in Shaftesbury Avenue. 'I don't know anywhere to eat round here,' said Marchant.

'There's a little place on the way to Covent Garden,' said Sarah, 'I went there with my husband once or twice.'

'Let's try that then.'

As they walked they analysed the film some more and Marchant talked about the layers of meaning. He mentioned existential enquiry, the characters shifting views of the truth, the ripple effect of crime and death on those who come into contact with it.

'God,' said Sarah, 'I just got a police procedural drama with rather a slow plot.'

Marchant smiled. 'I'm probably overanalysing. That's an unfortunate habit of mine. I must sound rather pretentious.'

'Oh no, it's nice having things explained. Anyway, it was rich in character and atmosphere and I thought the cinematography outstanding.'

He looked sideways at her to check if she was taking the mickey.

'Seriously,' she said with a grin, 'I enjoyed it and I think it's one of those films that will stay with one. Thanks for taking me, James.'

'I can never quite work out if you're being serious or not.'

'James, I liked it. But why the title 'Once upon a time' ...'

'I guess because it's about a series of disillusioned men who obsess about the past.'

'Ah. Of course. Now, this is the place.' They had stopped outside a small Italian restaurant with low lighting and red checked tablecloths. 'Oh, the past, what happy memories.'

They both looked through the extensive menu but settled for pizzas that were too large for normal plates and arrived on wooden boards. Marchant drank beer, Sarah white wine. A couple to their right scarcely said a word to each other throughout their entire meal, awkwardly examining their food, the other customers and the fish swimming in circles in a large tank by the entrance. In contrast, and slightly to their embarrassment in such close proximity to their silent neighbours, James and Sarah maintained an uninterrupted stream of dialogue as they ate. They talked about their pasts, finding they had played on the same beaches in Cornwall as children, possibly at the same time, that they both had domineering mothers and that they shared a passion for reading but had diametrically opposed tastes in music.

'And was your Dad fun?' asked Sarah.

'Oh yes. He was devoted to his profession but he had time for the family.' He pushed a slice of pizza around his plate. 'He was an exceptional man really.'

'And, as you said, hard to live up to.'

'Did I say that?'

'Yes.' Sarah waited for him to respond.

'Well, that's true of most people isn't it?'

'Some more than others I'd say.'

'I see.' Marchant took a swig of beer. 'There may be something in that.' He looked into his glass. 'It's a tough one, isn't it?'

'I wouldn't know, I'm not a man.'

'I had noticed.' Marchant took a handkerchief out of his pocket and blew his nose. 'But tell me more about your ex-husband.'

Sarah smiled at the change of subject. 'Oh, as I said, a complete shit.' She described her difficult marriage and then asked Marchant about his past relationships. He told her of the only real love of his life who ended up marrying another man because he had been too reticent in revealing his feelings for her.

'I guess I was a bit too shy,' he said, 'I only discovered some time later that she had been waiting for me to make a move. I'd rather imagined she was out of my league.'

'And what's happened to her?'

'Happy marriage, two children, pleaseant and successful husband. The bastard.' Marchant laughed but couldn't disguise the wistfulness in his voice.

'And what about Hattie?'

'How do you mean?'

'Are you in love with her?'

'Good God, no.'

'You talk about her a lot.'

'She's my cousin for God's sake.'

'Step cousin.'

'Even so.'

'And you said the marriage had gone stale.'

'It's still a marriage. And remember, we are a Catholic family – she'd never leave him.'

'Even if there's no marriage left?'

'Even if there's no marriage left. That's how it works – for better for worse – it's deeply ingrained in the psyche.'

'I left my husband.'

'Well you're not Hattie.'

'Evidently not.' Sarah was sitting quite still, her eyes fixed on his. He edged forwards and half reached out his hand before withdrawing it and fiddling with his napkin.

'I'm sorry,' she said, 'I didn't mean it to come out that way.'

Marchant waved away her apology. 'Perhaps we should pay the bill,' he replied.

It was their turn to sit in silence, just as the couple on the next table finally discovered something to talk about.

'Will you be OK getting home?' asked Marchant.

'I should be, yes. But I might need to hurry to catch the last train.'

Again, he marginally leant forwards and Sarah waited for him to speak but, after some more fiddling with his napkin he turned, caught the waiter's eye, and began looking in his wallet for his debit card.

Once the bill was paid they walked to the nearest underground station and at the point where they needed to head in opposite directions Marchant leant forward and kissed Sarah, slightly mis-timing his movement so that his lips brushed the side of her nose.

'Sorry,' he said.

She smiled. 'You take a girl out to the slowest moving film in history then don't even kiss her properly at the end of the evening, what on earth are we going to do with you?' She pulled him towards her and kissed him softly on the lips. 'Perhaps,' she said, when they were apart again, 'you need a little more practice at this dating thing.'

He chuckled at his own awkwardness. 'That,' he replied, 'sounds like a good idea.'

CHAPTER 15

June 1917

George Latham sat at his desk rifling through papers, unable to ignore the sound of his wife talking to her new friend Mrs Jackson in the drawing room. Since Mrs Jackson's visit some weeks back Elizabeth had seen her a number of times, on one occasion even travelling into Reading to meet up with her old cleaning lady at a public house. It seemed to George to be most inappropriate.

In front of him was a copy of the *Wiper Times*, a satirical paper written by a couple of young officers serving on the Western Front. He didn't know what to make of it. His first reaction had been one of outrage. Here were two officers responsible for maintaining morale in the trenches who were clearly making fun of their superiors, questioning the course of the war, complaining in as many words about their lot, spreading dissatisfaction and all to raise a few laughs. But when he had discussed it with his friend Ralph he had been forced to admit that perhaps it served a purpose. 'Humour is what keeps the men going,' said Ralph, 'black humour even more so. They're not suggesting mutiny or anything like that, they're just laughing at their circumstances. It's a good thing.'

George had been confronting his own opinions for some time now. He had read of Rudyard Kipling's torment at the death of his son, a boy Kipling himself had pulled strings to have enlisted. He saw in Kipling echoes of himself and when he'd read the words of the great poet *'if any question why we died, tell them because our fathers lied,'* he had been deeply moved. He had stared at the words, recalling his enthusiasm at Jeremy's signing up.

'Is it really a just and noble thing we're doing?' Jeremy had said to him one evening in the days before he went to France.

'Of course, it is, we're saving the civilised world,' he'd replied tetchily.

'Saving the civilised world. Creating a civilised world. Isn't that what people have been saying to justify slaughter since time began?'

George remembered the anger he had felt at the time. 'Your problem is that you think too much,' he'd said, 'you agonise over the whys and wherefores and overcomplicate the issues. We are being attacked by an aggressor. We are defending ourselves. You will be protecting the people of your country. There is nothing simpler or more noble than that.'

Jeremy hadn't responded and George had assumed his point had landed. But had it? Had his intellectual son just been humouring him, avoiding a full blown argument with his less cerebral father? Was there something in what the boy had said? Were things, as Ralph would say, more complex than good versus evil? George, a good sleeper all his life, even when the pressures of business had been intense, had taken to waking in the early hours in a cold sweat. Kipling's rhyme would revolve in his head and he would often slip quietly out of the house and go for a walk to clear his mind.

And then there was Elizabeth's relationship with this woman Jackson, the mother of a private soldier who, by the sounds of it, was a shirker and potential deserter. It would not go down well if the staff discovered a subaltern's mother was hobnobbing with the mother of one of his men – an unreliable one at that. But when he'd confronted her on it she had become untypically resentful, telling him that they were two mothers sharing their concerns in a way that men could not understand. The implication was that he was uncaring, glad to see his boy at war, unable to feel what she was feeling.

If only she knew. Yet he could not speak about it. Even with Ralph, his closest friend, there were boundaries that would not be crossed. He must deal with his worries alone, show fortitude, be the head of the family, a patriach others could look up to, someone from whom they might gain strength.

'....and if any question why we died, tell them because our fathers lied.'

He pushed the *Wipers Times* to one side and looked at some papers that needed signing but his brain felt out of focus and distracted.

The sound of Mrs Jackson leaving interrupted his contemplation. Elizabeth walked in to his study.

'So, she's gone,' he said, 'at last.'

'George, I don't understand your attitude to that poor woman,' said Elizabeth, 'she's extremely vulnerable and worried.'

'If only she'd stop snivelling all the time. Why can't she hold herself together like the rest of us?'

'Perhaps it's easier for some than others.'

'It's a matter of character.'

Elizabeth shook her head. 'No, George,' she said, 'it's a matter of a mother's love for her son.'

'You love your son and you don't go round weeping all the time.'

'Well that's different.'

'In what way?'

'I've been bought up to hide my feelings. As have you. Mrs Jackson hasn't benefited from the same upbringing as us – that doesn't make her a lesser person.'

George chose not to enter this argument. He had stated often enough his thoughts about class and upbringing having nothing to do with moral fibre and had no appetite for further discussion on the subject.

'Very well,' he said, 'but be careful, my dear. If her son turns out to be trouble we don't want to cause complications for Jeremy.'

'I will be.'

Having reached this stalemate the Lathams decided to go for an evening walk along the Thames and were soon making good progress in the direction of Henley with their two Labradors bounding along in front of them.

'Are you all right George?' asked Elizabeth when they stopped at a bench for a breather.

'Yes, why, don't I seem to be?'

'You seem to have been a little more taciturn than normal of late.'

George had a stick in his hands which he threw for one of the dogs. 'Well, it's a worry, isn't it?' he said.

Elizabeth watched the dog as it retrieved the stick and returned for another go.

'Those words of Kipling's ....' said George.

'I know dear,' said Elizabeth, interrupting her husband. 'I know. I've seen them on your desk.'

'They rather haunt me.'

'I know.'

They sat together on the bench, watching the dogs run back and forth, listening to the water of the river rippling past, letting the evening sun linger on their faces; small pleasures that in normal times would have provided a deep sense of peaceful satisfaction but which, on this occasion, failed to penetrate the layers of anxiety that had been their constant companions these past few months.

'Come on then dear,' said George wearily, 'let's get home. No point in dwelling on things beyond our control.'

CHAPTER 16

9 June 1917

Telegram from His Majesty the King to Field Marshal Sir Douglas Haig:

'I rejoice that, thanks to thorough preparation and splendid co-operation of all arms, the important Messines Ridge, which has been the scene of so many memorable struggles, is again in our hands. Tell General Plumer and the Second Army how proud we are of this achievement, by which in a few hours the enemy was driven out of strongly entrenched positions held by him for two and a half years.'

12 June 1917

Field Marshal Sir Douglas Haig to Sir William Robertson, Chief of the Imperial General Staff:

'If our resources are concentrated in France to the fullest possible extent the British armies are capable and can be relied on to effect great results this summer – results which will make final victory more assured and may even bring it within easy reach this year.'

For Field Marshal Haig the logic to press on after the success at Messines was overwhelming. After a pause for Plumer to bring forward his artillery and to see to the logistics of an army moving forwards the long planned offensive must continue. The armies needed to advance while the enemy was demoralised and on the back foot. The objective was to strike all the way to the coast where they would take Ostend and Zeebrugge and thereby prevent U-boats from disrupting the shipping lanes of the Channel. This would not only concentrate the German army in the north, taking the heat off the French who were near mutiny further south, it would also take pressure off the Russians in the east who, with their country in a state of revolution, were weak and close to collapse.

The War Cabinet thought differently. How could Haig proceed without full support from the French? How did he expect to advance the thirteen miles needed when previous campaigns had struggled to achieve half that distance? Why not wait until the French were recovered and the Americans, whose vanguard had already arrived in England, were ready to fight? Prime Minister Lloyd George was ever-mindful of the carnage of the Somme the previous year and that further heavy losses would have a disastrous effect on the morale of the nation. This was a nation that had now lived through three years of war, three years of formidable casualty lists in the papers, three years of shattered boys returning home and three years of hopes dashed, victories denied and repeated massacres with no ground gained.

The flag-waving patriotic enthusiasm of 1914 was long gone. Zeppelins were now dropping bombs on London, shipping was being decimated in the North Sea, people were wondering when the nightmare overwhelming their country would ever end.

And while the British politicians argued over whether to advance, and while thousands upon thousands of British troops made their way towards the Ypres salient, and while those who had fought to take the Messines Ridge recovered in reserve, playing football and holding field days and horse shows in the heat of a glorious summer, German engineers were sweating in the sunshine. Sweating as they built pillbox after pillbox and constructed stronghold after stronghold in the expectation of an imminent attack. And by the middle of July 1917 the German Army, rested, recovered and reinvigorated was fully prepared for whatever Haig might throw at them.

CHAPTER 17

July 1917

For over a month since the attack on Messines Ridge 5 Platoon had been rotating between the front and reserve in a confusing and debilitating contrast of circumstances. In reserve their routine was a strange combination of relaxing in the summer sunshine, endless parades to keep them busy, repeated polishing of buttons and bandoliers, extensive practices for the forthcoming assault and finally all forms of entertainment from attending amateur music reviews to playing football in a regimental league.

At the front the Germans mounted raid after raid on the British trenches in the search for information about when and where the next inevitable attack would come. They shelled the forward trenches repeatedly. In their turn the British sent out raids to capture prisoners and patrols to shore up defences.

June passed into July and still there was no word of attack.

One evening, after four days in the front line, Fletcher and Dawkins were preparing to go out on a night patrol when Timmings appeared in a hurry.

'Have you fucking heard?' said Timmings, 'we're getting that bastard Horrocks back as OC.'

'Fuck off.'

'We are. Sarn't Barnes just told me.'

Fletcher looked across at Dawkins. 'That's not good news for you, DD,' he said, 'he's got your number.'

'And I've got his.'

'The fucker's replacing Witheridge,' said Timmings, 'He's a Major now.'

'That's all we need,' said Dawkins, 'a bleeding cock horse of a bastard to order us about. I thought having Barnes was bad enough.'

Lieutenant Latham appeared. 'All ready?' he asked.

'Have you heard the news, sir?' said Timmings, 'Major Horrocks is taking over as OC.'

'It would be strange if I wasn't aware,' said Latham, 'as I've just been to a briefing with him.'

'We know him of old, sir,' said Dawkins.

'I believe so.'

'Talked of us, has he?'

'He mentioned that he was once commander of this platoon.'

'Tried to get DD into the glasshouse on some trumped up charge,' said Timmings but before he could go any further Fletcher interrupted him. 'Shut up, Timbo,' he said, 'you don't speak in front of Mr Latham about another officer like that.'

'Sorry sir,' said Timmings.

'Right,' said Latham, choosing to ignore Timmings' indiscretion, 'blacken up.'

The men applied burnt cork to their faces and hands before Latham checked their kit; each had, as well as their rifle, a sheath knife, a grenade and a cosh in case they had the opportunity to catch a prisoner.

The six man patrol, led by Lieutenant Latham, with Dawkins, Fletcher, Timmings, Peters and Johnston was to skirt round the edge of their forward trenches and, as before, make their way through No Man's Land to a small wood, little more than shattered tree stumps but one of the few not yet totally destroyed by shelling, where the Germans had been heard moving about on two previous nights. They were to watch for any German patrol, disrupt it if they found one, and leave behind a listening post.

'Keep close, only fire on my orders,' said Latham as they moved out of their trench and into the open.

'Fucking Hun will be watching for us,' whispered Timmings to Dawkins.

'Then keep your fucking eyes skinned,' whispered Dawkins.

It was a dark night with low cloud and the six men inched their way forwards on their stomachs until they came to a fold in the ground where they were able to walk almost upright to a point where they could see the outline of the wood up ahead. They stepped carefully, finding their way through a break in the barbed wire defences, passing shell holes where the sound of rats scavenging on dead bodies served as a reminder of the dangerous nature of their task.

The sound of a Verey light being fired had them freezing on the spot and when its glow lit up the empty battlefield, casting flickering shadows as it slowly fell to earth, they watched for any signs of life but the broken landscape was empty and desolate.

Latham shuddered as a chill passed through his body. He signalled for the others to move on and they set off behind him, their weapons pointing to either side, their eyes straining to detect any movement. Before long they arrived at the edge of the wood and they waited, listening, until they were sure there was nothing up ahead before following a small path that skirted round the trees in the direction of the German lines.

Dawkins tapped Latham on the shoulder.

'We'll be well within sight of the Hun once passed that corner,' he whispered.

Latham nodded and a few paces later he stopped and they worked their way into the wood. 'We'll stop and watch from here,' he said and the order was passed down to the end man.

Nothing significant happened for two hours. A few Vereys went off, a full moon appeared periodically from behind the clouds, the night grew colder. At one point the sound of raised voices coming from the enemy trenches just carried to them on the light breeze. More rats could be heard scurrying around in the grass and at times a smell of decaying bodies wafted in their direction.

'Looks like Fritz is having a night off,' whispered Fletcher.

'We'll be heading back shortly,' replied Dawkins.

Soon after this Latham appeared beside them. 'Nothing going on,' he whispered, 'we'll head back now. Fletcher, you and Peters stay here until just before dawn then come back the same way.'

'I've seen a good spot,' said Fletcher, 'just back there. Dip in the ground. We can cover ourselves in branches.'

A minute later the four men not on the listening post stood up silently and started walking back along the path.

'We'll just check round the other side on the way back,' whispered Latham.

The wood was the shape of an elongated diamond and they worked their way steadily to the southernmost tip where they'd arrived on the way out. They paused to listen then started heading north-west. Soon they came to the western tip where they stopped again. Here there was a wider track that they could see heading off along the side of the wood towards the northern point and then on to the German lines.

They worked their way round the corner, walked on a short distance and observed. Visibility was low but they could just make out the remains of a building in the fields. The air was very still. An owl hooted from somewhere in the wood.

'Nothing here, let's head back,' whispered Latham after five minutes and the four of them turned for home.

'Thank fuck for that,' whispered Timmings. They trod carefully, looking about them, stopping frequently to listen for sounds of enemy activity and soon were approaching the western tip again.

Suddenly Dawkins stopped and raised his hand.

'What is it?' asked Latham but at that very second, before Dawkins could reply, round the corner of the wood, directly in front of them appeared four German soldiers.

The two patrols, both returning to their lines, stopped and stood facing each other, weapons raised, no more than twenty feet apart. Nobody moved. The owl hooted again, a long and mournful noise that echoed through the trees. Another Verey went off in the distance but it's light didn't reach to where the eight men remained static, still as statues in the middle of the path.

Then one of the German soldiers very slowly and deliberately lowered his weapon. 'Kamerad,' he said, his voice calm and steady, 'Kamerad. Nicht fire.' He signalled to his men and they followed suit until all their weapons were by their side. The British soldiers remained with their rifles pointing at their enemy.

Than Latham slowly lowered his pistol. 'He's right,' he said, 'no point in us all dying.'

The German patrol leader moved gingerly forwards and held his arms open, his rifle in his right hand pointing to the ground, his left hand open and pointing to the sky.

'Nicht fire,' he said again and his men were also walking forwards.

Dawkins, who could hear Latham's shallow breathing beside him still had his rifle up. 'Steady, lads,' he said.

The Germans were now only a few paces away.

The other two soldiers had followed Latham's example and had lowered their weapons, leaving only Dawkins of the eight men with his rifle pointed at the enemy.

'Lower your weapon Dawkins,' said Latham. Dawkins half lowered his rifle. The German leader had stopped no more than ten feet away and was watching him intently.

'Nicht fire,' he said for the third time. 'Nicht killing.'

'Watch him,' said Dawkins, 'don't trust the bugger.'

For a few seconds there was no noise and no movement. The German patrol commander was smiling, his face just visible in the moonlight.

'We all want to live,' said Latham, 'they're humans just like us.'

The German commander started walking very slowly forwards and as he did so his right arm lifted a fraction. Instantly, instinctively, Dawkins raised his rifle and in one swift movement aimed and fired straight into the centre of the man's body. The German stared back at him, his face contorted in pain and surprise, before sinking to the ground. In an instant Dawkins had recocked his Lee Enfield and shot a second man at point blank range.

It was Timmings who was first to react and he shot a third man even as he was raising his rifle. The fourth took aim and fired but Dawkins had re-loaded again and his third shot hit him directly in the face.

No more than a few seconds had passed.

The smell of cordite lingered in the air and a small cloud of insects, disturbed by the arrival of the two patrols, now hovered again above the path as the darkness of the wood closed in around the English soldiers. A strangled groan came from the ground. 'I'm hit,' said Johnston through gritted teeth. The others turned to him and he was lying on the ground clutching his leg.

'Grab him, Timbo' said Dawkins, 'we need to move fast.'

Latham was staring at the four German bodies in front of him. Two were completely silent, two were moaning. 'My God,' he was saying, 'oh my God,' but Dawkins, who now had his rifle over his shoulder and was helping lift Johnston, took his arm. 'Leave 'em,' he said, 'come on sir, let's go.' Seconds later the four of them were running along the path as fast as they could, Johnston with his arms over Timmings' and Dawkins' shoulders, Latham leading the way. They continued on until they came to the southern tip of the wood where they paused briefly to check they weren't being followed before turning for home. Panting from their exertions they now walked in silence and when they reached the safety of their trench they climbed down and slumped to the ground, not making eye contact, breathing heavily.

A soldier who was on guard bent over them. 'Timmings,' said Latham, 'help this man get Johnston to the medics.' He watched as they shuffled off, leaving him alone with Dawkins.

The two men stood facing each other in the dark shadows of the trench.

'That was cold-blooded murder,' said Latham and his anger was almost tangible.

Dawkins didn't reply.

'They had their weapons by their side. They trusted us.'

Dawkins answered slowly, his voice betraying no tension, no remorse. 'No such thing as murder out here,' he said.

'It was wrong.'

'Wrong?' Dawkins spat out the word. 'Wrong? They were Huns. We're at war. He was reaching for his weapon.'

'That's not what I saw.'

'That's what I saw and it could be us dead and them back in their trench talking about the four tommies they'd just killed.'

Latham was shaking his head. 'They were looking us in the eye, they trusted us and we just shot them dead.' In contrast to Dawkins his voice was strained and high pitched, his whole being distorted by the raw horror of what had just happened.

'They were Germans, sir,' said Dawkins quietly. 'If we didn't kill 'em tonight they'd be dead before long anyway.'

Latham had his eyes closed and was bent over. 'Lord,' he said through his hands, 'how can you be so callous?'

'Callous?' There was a sudden edge to Dawkins voice. 'Callous?' He repeated the word as if it contained a terrible blasphemy. 'We're all dead out here, don't you see?' his voice was rising in volume. 'We're all dead, it's just some don't know it.'

Latham was rocking slowly backwards and forwards.

'You worry about killing,' continued Dawkins, 'and you're done for. Fucked. You'll end up like Pete Jackson.'

Latham opened his eyes and the two men faced each other, not speaking for a few seconds.

'When did you lose your soul?' asked Latham quietly.

'My soul?' Dawkins stepped back and lit a cigarette, his anger dissipating as he blew smoke out into the night. He offered one to Latham.

'I don't smoke.'

'Go on, sir, have one,' said Dawkins.

'No thanks.'

'My soul,' said Dawkins again. He was facing into the darkness, seemingly talking to himself, absorbed in his reflections. Then he turned to Latham and when he spoke he seemed strangely distant. 'Lost that a long way back.'

The next hour Dawkins spent alone in a small alcove someone had carved into the side of the trench, stretched out as best he could, allowing the cumulative exhaustion of the past years take hold, in a semi-conscious state, frequently drifting in and out of a light sleep. '*When did you lose your soul?*' The words kept returning to him. Images of mangled bodies appeared each time he closed his eyes and for once he couldn't prevent himself from recalling the men he had killed – not the ones at a distance, the ones close up, the ones he had faced and whose staring eyes had held his as he had thrust his bayonet repeatedly into their blood soaked bodies.

And then, suddenly, his uncle appeared in his imaginings.

Walking along the side of the canal, staggering from hours of drinking, shouting obscenities and bending to beat his cowering son. In a scene that returned to Dawkins in moments such as this, a scene that for years he had been forcing to the depths of his memory, the man's mean and ugly face appeared with a terrible clarity. His red pockmarked nose, his hand raised and then his shocked expression as the thirteen year old Dawkins lunged at him, sending him over the edge and into the shallows. It was as if Dawkins was back in that freezing cold water again, holding the bastard down as he struggled, pushing on his face, watching the bubbles rise, watching his eyes close and watching him sink to the bottom, being swallowed up by reeds, never to trouble his son or nephew again.

Dawkins writhed on his earthen bed, his body assaulted by the recollection of his first killing. '*When did you lose your soul?*' In truth, reflected Dawkins, perhaps he'd never had one.

Later, before they turned in, Dawkins came to visit Latham in his dugout.

'All right, sir?' he said.

'As much as circumstances permit.'

'I've bought a brew for you.'

Dawkins handed over a mug of tea.

'Thanks.'

The two men sat drinking their tea in the feeble light of the candle by which Latham had been writing his report and they chatted inconsequentially for a while about the coming offensive.

'What worries me,' said Dawkins, 'is that summer's passing. The ground is firm at the moment but I've been here before when it rains. Turns into a fucking quagmire, it does. And Flanders is the worst.'

'Well, from what I've heard I don't think we'll have too long to wait.'

'Good. Get it over with I say.'

'Anyway, there's a rumour going round that it'll be the 5th Army who'll be given the job.'

'Not us?'

'We might be on a flank.'

'That's General Gough's lot.'

'Yes.'

Dawkins considered saying something but held back.

'Go on,' said Latham, 'say what's on your mind.'

'Word has it that Gough's army ain't so smart.'

'Well,' said Latham, 'we'll find out soon enough.'

They sat opposite each other listening to the relentless sound of shelling.

'But you didn't just come in here to talk about the offensive,' said Latham.

'No, sir,' said Dawkins.

He looked at his Platoon Commander, still believing in the goodness of man, in the mercy of God, in the rights and wrongs of killing. 'Just wanted to say that Major Witheridge would have done the same thing,' he said.

'With that German patrol?'

'Yes.'

'You really think so?'

'I do. He knew the score.'

Latham, who was still shocked by the gruesome immediacy of the killings, studied Dawkins as he drank from his mug. 'It goes against everything I believe in,' he said.

'Then best not believe in anything.'

'Not believe in anything? What about goodness? Compassion? Care for your fellow man?'

Dawkins breathed out heavily. 'Those'll just get you killed.'

Latham looked at him incredulously. 'I don't believe you.'

'No?'

'I've watched you. I've watched you with Jackson and the others so don't tell me you don't believe in those things.'

Dawkins took his time to answer as he considered this contradiction. 'They're mates,' he said eventually, 'it's Fritz I killed.'

Latham finished his tea and threw away the dregs. 'Major Witheridge told me some men get by by hating the Germans. Is that true of you?'

Dawkins shook his head. 'Don't hate 'em,' he replied, 'flesh and bone, just like us.'

'Then how can you kill with such ease?'

Dawkins looked at Latham. There was only a couple of years difference in their age yet they were separated by a gulf of experience. 'Don't know the answer to that,' he said, 'often wondered though.'

A corporal came in to make a report and Dawkins remained silent as Latham discussed rotas for the following day. When the man had gone Latham shifted his position so that his eyes were level with Dawkins'.

'The men follow you, don't they?'

'Wouldn't know about that sir.'

'I've seen it. They see something in you.'

'They see some bugger that's survived longer than reason would have it. They see a bloke who says what he thinks. They see a bloke who ain't too windy. Other than that, they don't see much.'

'I've noticed that. You don't seem to fear death.'

Dawkins took time to answer. In the dim candlelight his eyes appeared opaque and sadly reflective. 'Fear it?' he said quietly, 'Oh no.' He leant towards Latham and his intensity was visceral. 'I don't fear it – I hope for it.'

CHAPTER 18

The Times November 12th 1920

PASSING OF THE UKNOWN
MEMORABLE SCENES
BRITAIN'S TRIBUTE TO THE DEAD

'*The first anniversary of the Armistice had a great meaning for the country. Armistice day this year had a still greater significance. It may be that never again will national sentiment in relation to the war have such an opportunity for expression as was given by the unforgettable ceremonies of yesterday.*

There were two outstanding events which cannot be repeated. The King unveiled the Cenotaph in its permanent form, and the Unknown Warrior was buried in Westminster Abbey whose grave for this and future generations will be a place of pilgrimage for the British race. The King, the Royal Princes, Lords, and all the people, all on a common footing, shared in a mighty tribute to the glorious dead.

It was a day of mellow sunshine. In the early morning mist lay lightly over London, but the vapours were dispersed as the hours were numbered, and at 9 O'clock the weather was the best that a November day can give. Long before dawn crowds had gathered in the hope of getting as near to the Cenotaph as possible when the barriers shutting off Whitehall should be opened but the ceremonies did not begin until 10. At that hour the coffin containing the body, which had been brought from France on Wednesday, was reverently lifted from the saloon at Victoria Station, where it had rested during the night, and placed on a gun carriage. The casket was covered in a Union Jack hallowed by many memories of the war, and on the flag soldiers placed side arms and a steel helmet. Field-Marshalls, Admirals and Air Marshall Sir Hugh Trenchard took up position as pall bearers, and to the roll of muffled drums, a procession, as representative of the service as could be made, moved out from the station into the crowded streets. A long route to the Cenotaph was traversed, and for nearly an hour silent but impressive homage to the dead was paid by hundreds of thousands through whose motionless ranks the cortege passed.

THE CENOTAPH UNVEILED

In Whitehall, when the procession approached, the Cenotaph, freed at last from scaffolding and tarpaulins, was draped with the National flag. The King, in the uniform of a Field-Marshall, stood near the Colonial Office waiting to step into his place as Chief Mourner. Near him were the Prince of Wales, the Duke of York, Prince Henry, the Duke of Connaught, the Archbishop of Canterbury, the Prime Minister, and many members of the government. The King's first act after the arrival of the procession was to step forward to the coffin and place upon it a wreath of laurel leaves and crimson flowers.

A brief service followed. Massed choirs from the city churches led the multitude gathered around in signing the hymn 'O God, our help in ages past,' and the Archbishop of Canterbury recited the sentences of The Lord's Prayer. Then, as Big Ben, in the clock tower of the Palace of Westminster, sonorously sounded the hour of eleven the King faced the Cenotaph and placed a finger on a button. Veiling flags fluttered down, and the memorial which authority caused to be created for a temporary occasion, but which the nation, with one voice, demanded should be made permanent on its original site, stood revealed in simple grandeur for all to see.

At this high and solemn moment all noise ceased. The silence had begun, men and women disciplined their bodies so that for full two minutes scarcely a finger moved. The stillness remained unbroken until buglers sounded the appealing notes of the 'Last Post'. There was little more to come before the journey to the grave of the Unknown Warrior was resumed. The King placed the first wreath at the base of the Cenotaph. The Prince of Wales gently laid his tribute of laurels by the side of that of the Sovereign, and the Prime Minister, the Adjutant-General, and the representatives of the dominions and colonies added homage for the United Kingdom and the Empire.

AT THE ABBEY

The last scene in the Abbey has no parallel in history. Simplicity dominated all that was done. The coffin, born by non-commissioned officers of the Guards, passed through a hundred wearers of the Victoria Cross. Famous men of the forces were the pall bearers. The King walked behind and was followed by Princes, Peers and statesmen. Choir and congregation sang the hymn 'Lead, Kindly light,' and as the Dean recited the committed sentences the King scattered over the coffin soil bought from the battlefield. Two more hymns were sung, one of them Kipling's 'Recessional,' and the service ended with the throbbing of drums and the clear call of bugles sounding the Reveille.

Tens of thousands of people who could have no place by the Cenotaph or in the Abbey during the morning walked past the memorial or the grave of the warrior during the afternoon and evening in columns which were never broken. Men and women waited long hours to pay their tribute, or even to take a place at the end of a long file of those who wished to have some part, no matter how humble, in the proceedings of the day.

Today the pilgrimage will be renewed. The Dean of Westminster announces that the grave in the Abbey will be left precisely in the same condition today as yesterday, and the Abbey will be open from 10.30 am for those who wish to pass by.

11 November 1920

Peter Harding, chosen for duty at Westminster Abbey as a recognition of his involvement in locating the Unknown Warrior, was tasked with showing guests of honour to their seats. There were one hundred of them, all women, chosen because they had lost their husbands and all their sons in the war. There was a solemn mood in the building and he found himself, like the others around him, speaking in hushed tones.

Most of the widows were seated when he spotted the Reverend George Kendall, the padre who had received the bodies in St Pol, standing to one side, observing the gathering of the congregation. He walked across to him.

'Hello Harding,' said the Reverend, 'made it back OK the other day?'

'Yes sir. I see everything went smoothly from then on.' Peter stepped back to let a soldier with two lines of medals on his chest go by.

'One of the VCs' said Kendall.

'I had no idea I was part of such a big thing.'

'I think it's taken us all by surprise.'

'They say there are hundreds of thousands lining the streets.'

Kendall spoke to another padre as he walked by. 'The country's never seen the like of it and I doubt it ever will again.'

At that moment the organ began a quiet and mournful hymn and the deep tones echoed through the Abbey, heightening the aura of expectation.

'That man who just passed me,' said Kendall quietly, 'he's the one who had the idea in the first place.'

Peter looked at the back of the officer who stopped, as if aware he was being watched, turned and smiled.

Peter smiled back. 'I see he has the MC.'

'Yes. David Railton's his name. A quite exceptional man.'

'I thought it was all the Dean's idea.'

'That's what a lot of people think but it was definitely Railton. He came up with it when serving as a padre with the soldiers at the front.'

Peter watched Railton as he shook hands with a soldier before continuing on his way towards the knave. ,

'His personal flag will be on the coffin,' said Kendall, 'I guess that will be some form of recognition.'

A widow appeared and Peter showed her to her seat.

When he returned to his position Kendall had moved on and Peter found himself standing next to a colonel. They chatted briefly and the colonel asked Peter how he came to be on duty. Peter, keeping an eye out for any remaining widows needing assistance, didn't stop to consider before answering.

'I was leading one of the digging parties,' he said.

The Colonel turned to face him. 'I think you are meant to keep that under your hat.'

Peter immediately regretted his indiscretion. 'Of course, I apologise, I was distracted.'

The Colonel smiled. 'Not to worry,' he said, 'but be careful what you say. Much store has been set on this business of total anonymity.'

'Of course.'

The service was about to begin and the Colonel looked at his watch. 'I must find my seat,' he said. He hesitated briefly. 'As a matter of interest, where was your body placed in the chapel?' he asked.

'I was the last to arrive. Furthest on the right.'

The Colonel nodded and Peter detected the slightest smile. 'In which case,' he said, 'I will make every effort to forget this meeting and to ensure I never meet you again or find out who you are. Good day to you.' And with that he set off towards his pew, leaving Peter open mouthed and confounded by what had just been said.

Kendall reappeared. 'I think all your widows must be in by now,' he said, 'you should go and find somewhere to sit.'

Peter pointed to the Colonel who was easing his way towards his seat. 'Who is that officer?' he asked.

'Him? That's Colonel Gell. He helped General Wyatt choose the body – although that's not something being made known to the general public at present.' He reached out to shake Peter's hand. 'Enjoy the service,' he said, 'I believe it will be something quite extraordinary.' And then he was gone.

Peter stood transfixed. His mind was racing. Gell's words circled in his brain until they converged into a staggering conclusion: the body he had recovered from an unmarked grave, the one he had delivered from the battlefield of Ypres, the one with a photograph of a girl in a side pocket; that was the body chosen in St Pol and that was shortly to be buried in the Abbey as the Unknown Warrior. It had to be – otherwise why had Gell made such an issue of insisting he should never know who Peter was?

At that moment the choir began singing a hymn and as the choristers stepped outside their voices just carried to the congregation. Peter felt unsteady at the realisation of what had just taken place, humbled by his part in this unfolding drama, and as he made his way towards a chair he wondered how significant this might be for him in the months and years ahead.

The hymn ended and the Abbey descended into silence. A solitary bell tolled. Then, after a minute of keen anticipation, the words 'I am the resurrection and the life' floated in through the building and as Peter looked about him he could see that everyone was transfixed by the gospel, many with their heads bowed, the widows to his front clutching handkerchiefs, the dignitaries staring resolutely ahead. Above him the towering arches of the Abbey seemed to capture the very mood of the occasion as they rose proudly, magnificently, towards the vaulted ceiling. A short while later the coffin appeared at the north door, borne by NCOs of the Coldstream Guards, and Peter listened to the sound of their footsteps as they made their way through the Quire. He watched as they emerged and progressed slowly up the length of the Nave, passing between one hundred holders of the Victoria Cross before reaching the graveside near the Great West Door. A deep hush was broken only by the sound of the pall bearers lowering their heavy load onto metal poles across the open grave. Then Dean Ryle's voice, clear and measured, carried through the Abbey as he read a prayer.

The service had begun and the enormity of the moment settled heavily on those present. As the organ sounded Beethoven's 'Equale for Trombones' not a soul moved, not a word was spoken, so that the singing of 'The Lord is my

Shepherd' which followed came as a great release, a chance to exhale and give voice to emotions so tightly constrained. A lesson from the Book of Revelation was listened to in complete silence. Then, as the choir gently sang 'Lead Kindly Light' the congregation strained as one to catch a glimpse of the coffin being lowered into the grave.

As the King sprinkled earth from a Flanders battlefield onto the wooden lid Dean Ryle's words 'Earth to earth, ashes to ashes, dust to dust ...' rang out through the Abbey and it seemed to Peter that their meaning had never before been felt so deeply as in that moment. After prayers were spoken the congregation sang 'Abide with Me,' and when they came to the final words of 'God of our Fathers' – 'Lest we forget, lest we forget,' it seemed a great wave of feeling surged through the building.

The Dean spoke the blessing then paused and a sound, very faint at first, like a train in the far distance, came from somewhere in the Abbey. It took a second for Peter to recognise it as a roll of drums before it grew in volume and swelled in a crescendo, filling the Abbey with a reverberating roar before it died away again, growing quieter and quieter until, with no discernible ending, it ceased.

Silence: punctuated only by the quiet sounds of weeping filtering through the abbey. Peter felt goose bumps over every part of his body.

Buglers sounded the Last Post and the Long Reveille and then, to the sound of the 'Grand Ceremonial March' played by the band of the Grenadier Guards, the King and all the dignitaries started making their way towards the Great West Door and out of the Abbey.

Peter watched as the holders of the Victoria Cross filed past the grave and he didn't move as the Cathedral slowly emptied until finally only those officiating remained.

He noticed that The Reverend Railton was beside him.

'Quite beautiful, don't you think?' said Railton.

Peter nodded. The two men stood side by side for a few seconds, not speaking, reflecting on the immensity of the occasion.

'Profoundly moving,' said Peter.

Railton held out his hands as if to include the departed congregation in their conversation. 'Too large to truly comprehend,' he said and his words made perfect sense. He turned and shook Peter's hand. 'David Railton.'

'Peter Harding.'

'George Kendall tells me you led one of the digging parties.'

'Yes, sir.'

Railton smiled warmly and patted Peter on the shoulder. 'In which case you can be proud to have been a part of this.'

'Thank you. And I understand you were the one who had the idea in the first place.'

Railton waved away the suggestion. 'One of many people,' he said, 'across the world. These ideas gather their own momentum.'

An officer approached Railton. 'We are about to place your flag over the coffin, sir,' he said.

'Of course. I'll be along immediately'. The officer walked off and Railton shook hands with Peter again. 'Lest we forget,' he said, 'I think that won't happen now,' and the kindness in his eyes spoke powerfully to Peter. Railton placed a hand on his shoulder. 'Thank you,' he said. 'Thank you for what you have done,' and he walked off towards the north aisle.

Peter made his way to a quiet corner where he sat down. He heard the great doors being closed. He watched as officials gathered in prayer books from the aisles, going about their business discreetly, unaware of being observed. The organ began playing again. Images of the body in the coffin and of the girl in the photograph intermingled in his mind as he reflected on the part he had played in the burial of the Unknown Warrior. He lowered his head into his hands and as he did so the question the Reverend Kendall had asked in St Pol came back to him.

'Can you confirm you have absolutely no knowledge of who it is whose remains are in that sack?'

It was a question that kept returning to him and was beginning to weigh heavily on his mind.

A short while later the doors were opened and two lines of people immediately entered through the North Door and moved slowly through the Abbey to file past the grave. Peter walked outside and he could see the queue snaking into the distance. A policeman asked him to stand back.

'These are all to see the coffin?' said Peter.

'Yes, sir. Thousands and thousands of them. It's caught us on the hop.'

Wooden barriers were being erected as they spoke.

'Well good luck,' said Peter and began walking away from the Abbey towards Whitehall. Thousands more people were milling around and when he came near to the Cenotaph he had to divert into a side street to pass the crowds. Traffic was just beginning to move around Trafalgar Square and he contemplated catching a bus to Picadilly but decided to carry on walking to the 'In and Out' where he was staying the night. When he finally made it to the club he went to his room, changed into civilian clothes and walked down to the bar.

Two officers he knew were chatting about the day and he joined them for a drink.

'The two minutes silence was the moment that will stay with me most,' said one officer, 'I swear the whole city came to a complete halt.'

'The whole country by all accounts,' said the other, 'factories, shops, offices – all silent.'

'All for someone unknown.'

'That makes it even more extraordinary.'

Each of them had been on duty and they compared notes on their collective experiences.

'I wonder how many out there imagine it's their son or husband in that coffin.'

'Thousands of them, I'd guess. Wouldn't you be out there if you'd lost a son?'

'Probably.'

Peter sat back as the two officers carried on talking, speculating as to who the Unknown Warrior might be.

'The story is that they dug up bodies from different battlefields and one was chosen out of four in some kind of secret ceremony.'

'I'd have my money on the Somme.'

'Why's that?'

'That's where there would have been most unaccounted deaths.'

'What do you think Harding?'

Transported back by the conversation to the cemetery near Ypres, Peter took a moment to come back into the present.

'Sorry,' he said, 'what did you say?'

'Who is the Unknown Warrior?'

'Surely the point is that nobody knows.'

'Someone must.'

'Why?'

'Someone always does.'

'Not on this occasion. They'll have gone to great lengths to ensure that.'

'Well I'd be surprised, it's very difficult to keep something this big entirely under wraps.'

Peter stood up. 'Another one?' he asked.

'Why not?

The three men had another drink before moving into the dining room for a late lunch and it was mid afternoon before Peter returned to his room. He lay on his bed to read a book but found himself unable to concentrate and decided to go for a walk. He crossed over into Green Park where large numbers of people were still hanging around, talking to strangers about their shared experiences, still soaking up the atmosphere, reluctant to go home. The water on the lake was perfectly still, the leafless trees static against the grey sky.

His steps led him, inevitably, to Parliament Square.

Here the crowds were thicker and he skirted round to the far corner where the queues leading up to the Abbey stretched off into Victoria street. Policemen were marshalling the mourners but the people stood quietly, shuffling forward every now and then, patiently waiting their turn to pay their respects to the Unknown Warrior. The majority were women, but there were men also and some children, their faces largely empty of expression, the drabness of their clothes contrasting with the vivid colours of the flowers and wreaths they held in their hands.

Peter walked slowly towards the Abbey, looking at the faces in the queue, and he stopped when he reached the steps up to the main entrance. The policeman he had spoken to earlier was still on duty and they talked about the day and speculated as to how many people would pass through the doors to view the coffin.

'How are the queues?' asked Peter.

'Growing by the minute. We're stretched here.'

'Anything I can do?'

'They might need some help inside.'

The officer let Peter in and he quickly appraised the situation. The two queues leading up to the coffin were orderly enough and soldiers were trying their best to move people towards the grave as discreetly as they could but everyone was wanting to lay their flowers and linger as long as possible. Two cathedral volunteers were dealing with the mounting piles of flowers but were being hampered by the bodies of the mourners.

Peter took up a position near where the volunteers were struggling and began ushering people on.

'Thank you. Thank you so much. Please move along now,' he found himself repeating, and to the more persistent lingerers 'I'm sorry, you have to keep moving, there are many thousands more waiting.'

Most followed his instructions politely, some hesitated, some he needed to take by the arm to usher them away. An army officer appeared and Peter asked him to find more help.

The mourners kept coming. Peter looked at his watch; he had been here for over an hour. Each mourner was wanting their moment with the dead soldier who, in each of their minds, was perhaps their son or lover or father. For them it was a moment of deep significance, one to extend as long as they could, for him it was a moment to keep as short as possible. He checked along the line of people stretching to the Great West Door and something caught his eye. Amongst the many dark hats a contrasting lighter one was visible. At that moment an old woman directly in front of him prostrated herself on the ground and he had to help her up and steer her gently to a pew where he sat her down. When he looked back at the queue the lighter hat was closer but the wearer still not visible. Another mourner needed encouraging to move, then another. A man in a corporal's uniform appeared and said he'd been told to report for duty and Peter told him to watch for a few minutes to see what needed to be done. He glanced up. The hat was closer, but the wearer's face was still obscured.

He stepped back, manoeuvring himself into a position whereby he could more clearly see the faces of the mourners as they approached the coffin. The hat was no more than twenty feet away now and he could see it was a straw boater with a blue ribbon tied around the rim. His hands were so tightly clasped that he could feel his pulse quickening. Then the owner of the hat was at the front of the queue and standing directly in front of him. It was a young woman and as she gazed at the coffin he stared at her face. She looked up briefly and as her eyes made contact with his she smiled.

He stood completely still, transfixed, unable to move. It felt to him as if someone had dimmed the lights in the cathedral and shone a spotlight on the girl smiling up at him. It was a smile he recognised. He seemed unable to breathe properly.

Then she bent down to place a small bunch of flowers at the edge of the grave before looking back at him. She smiled a second time.

'I think I've got it,' said the Corporal.

Peter didn't answer him.

'Sir, I can see what needs doing, you can leave me to ....'

They were interrupted by a woman who wanted to check that her flowers wouldn't be crushed.

'We'll do the best we can to ensure they won't,' Peter said to the woman, his words coming out unevenly.

'You see I lost my two boys,' she said.

'I'm so sorry.'

As the woman began telling him about her sons he looked over her shoulder and spotted the girl in the boater turning away and heading off towards the exit.

The woman reached forwards and gripped Peter's arm. 'Where was God when they were killed?' she asked, her voice filled with desperation.

He took her hand. 'He was with them, Madam, he was with them.' He turned to the Corporal. 'Help this lady on, please Corporal,' he said. Another mourner asked him a question about the coffin and as he answered he looked up but the straw boater was no longer visible. Finally he was able to leave his post but another surge of bodies blocked his way before he manged to push through to a vantage point by the pulpit. He jumped up the steps and scanned the mass of heads below him. At first he saw nothing but then, at the far end of the Abbey, he saw a flash of colour. He watched it for a second but by then the girl had already reached the Great North Door and before Peter could even re-enter the throng of bodies the young woman had stepped out into the dark of the London streets.

*The honour guard is drawn up outside the Chateau near Boulogne
where the coffin of the unidentified soldier was kept overnight.*

Procession passing through Boulogne, 10th November 1920.

Homecoming of the Unknown Warrior at the Cenotaph, London.

The funeral of the Unknown Warrior at Westminster Abbey.

CHAPTER 19

October 2011

After two days of repeated searching of her father's belongings, Sarah finally discovered an envelope tucked deep into a previously unnoticed pocket of one of his old briefcases. She pulled it out and opened it. Inside was an unusual looking key and some bank details on a piece of paper.

'Got it!' she said out loud and reached for the phone.

Marchant answered immediately.

'Safety deposit box,' she said, barely able to contain her excitement.

It took Marchant a second to realise what she was saying. 'Safety deposit box?' he replied, 'you've found one?'

'I think so.'

'I'll be around as soon as I can.'

Only four hours later they found themselves in the foyer of the Lower Regent Street branch of Lloyds Bank where an official led them out of the grandly marbled and pillared ground floor and down some winding concrete steps into a dimly lit basement. They waited as he unlocked a fortified gate before ushering them into a large room with rows of serried metal drawers. He walked down the row, checking numbers and stopping in front of one labelled 1920.

'Interesting number,' said Marchant.

'I believe it was at the family's request,' said the official, 'I'm not aware of it's significance.'

Sarah was staring at the drawer. 'I am,' she said.

He held up his key and Sarah took hers out of her pocket. Together they stepped forwards and unlocked safety deposit box 1920. The official carried the drawer to a green baize table and stepped back.

'I will leave you to examine the contents,' he said and melted into the background.

'Here goes,' said Sarah and opened the lid of the box.

Inside were two leather bound books. She took one out and placed it on the baize. On the cover it said: 'Diaries, Peter Harding 1918 – 1926.'

Marchant leant over to look. 'My God,' he said, 'So they're Peter's. That's a real bonus.'

'You open it,' said Sarah.

'No. It's yours.'

'No, please. I want you to be the first to make any discovery. You're the historian.'

Marchant gave her an enquiring glance but then nodded his head. Carefully he opened the book and turned to the second page.

'*14 March 1918. Arrived in Heuveland at 2pm and was shown to my billet. Interview with the CO. Inspected the guns at 5.30pm. Dinner in the officers mess. Bed at 10.30.*'

Marchant carried on reading the entries for the next few days, typed on blank sheets of paper that had been hole punched and filed. Each entry was as brief as the last.

'This is what we've been after,' he said, 'Amazing. This is where we fill in those gaps.'

Sarah gripped his hand. 'Let's go back to your place.'

Marchant placed the diaries in a backpack and zipped it up.

'Hold onto that for dear life,' said Sarah.

They caught a taxi to Redcliffe Square and walked up to Marchant's flat. He opened the bag and placed the books on his desk. Sarah pulled up a chair to sit beside him.

'Go on then,' she said.

He opened the second book and the first entry was from 1927. He turned to the back and the final entry was 1969.

'Looks like he kept things brief,' he said, 'either that or there'll be some big gaps.'

A slip of paper fell out that had been placed in the middle of the diary and he read the short paragraph.

'*Dad's Diaries.*

They sum up a life that witnessed two world wars.

I served with him in WW2, we experienced D Day together, we both survived when many around us were killed.

These diaries provide a clue as to the extraordinary times he lived through and what he was asked to do for his country.

They are a record of a unique period of history and will have a decided significance for many decades to come.

Stanley Harding.'

'Interesting,' said Marchant, let's go back to the first book.'

He put the second diary to one side and opened the first. The two of them sat side by side reading each entry with Marchant, the faster reader, waiting at the bottom of each page for Sarah to catch up.

'Rather as I remember him, a dry old stick,' said Sarah after a few minutes.

'It takes a certain skill to make something quite so unexciting,' said Marchant, 'and I should know, I conduct research for a living'.

Each day was described with great brevity and was simply a record of events. *'Inspected the guns. Visited 14 Regiment. Had lunch at the chateau with Major Andrews.'* There were no observations, reactions or descriptions of anything in detail. Even major events of the war were simply recorded in statistical terms: *'5th Army advanced and took 2,000 prisoners,'* being a typical entry.

'Let's skip a few pages,' said Sarah.

Marchant rifled through the book.

'There are some long gaps between dates,' he said, 'it seems he lost interest after a while and only wrote things down on significant days.'

He stopped at 11 November 1918 and the same day in 1919. On both occasions Peter Harding had allowed himself marginally more expression than normal but only just. *'November 11 1918. Armistice Day. The war is over. The nation celebrates. Toasts raised in the officers mess and much back slapping. Gone to bed feeling the worse for wear. Thank God it's over.'*

Then he skipped to 7 November 1920.

'Given a strange mission by the CO to visit graveyards and dig up a body. All very secret. Held up en route with a damaged wheel and needed to execute the mission in a hurry. Delivered the body to St Pol just in time. Part of a bigger thing. Significant moment and dramatic day.'

Marchant stopped reading. 'Yes! So that confirms he was on a digging party.'

'Read on.'

The 8th and 9th were of little interest but on the 10th Harding had travelled back to London.

'Informed I will be on duty in the Abbey to show guests of honour to their seats at the burial of the Unknown Warrior. Travelled back to England by train and boat, arriving London 5pm. Quick visit to the Abbey for a briefing then on to In and Out where I shall stay for three days.'

Marchant glanced at Sarah. 'Turn over?'

'Yes.'

He turned the page.

'*11 November 1920. The burial. Arrived at Abbey early for final rehearsal. Large crowds gathering throughout the city. Showed guests of honour (widows) to their seats. Immensely impressive service. Walked back to In and Out through thick crowds. Had late lunch with Cole and Smith. Walked back to Abbey, along Thames, back to Abbey again. Asked to help with queues of mourners passing the grave. Saw girl in photograph.*'

'What girl?' said Marchant.

'Wait.' Sarah finished reading. She looked at Marchant. Her hands were to her face, she was trembling. 'What girl?' she said, 'What photograph?'

'What photograph indeed.' Marchant was already turning to the next page. 'This could be what we've been looking for,' he said, his voice unusually animated, 'my God, we could be onto something after all.'

CHAPTER 20

July 1917

'We're going back to Pop,' said Timmings, his face shining at the thought, 'I'm going to get right fucking pissed tonight.'

It was the morning after the patrol and orders had come through that B Company was to be relieved and they were to return to the reserve for a week.

Poperinghe had become the town of choice for the British Army serving in Flanders, its cafes and estanimets filled to bursting point every night where vin blanc could be bought for one franc a bottle and eggs and chips were served in huge quantities.

By midday 5 Platoon was marching westwards in blazing sunshine along narrow roads, their tunics forming dark patches of sweat where their equipment pressed against their bodies, their feet swelling in their boots. To their astonishment, they had only been on the move a few hours when they came to a small train station and were ushered aboard a train that was to take them back to Poperinghe.

At Poperinghe station the company was pointed in the direction of a village not far from the town and after only twenty minutes they came to an archway beyond which a cobbled square was surrounded by a large farm and a series of outbuildings. It all seemed very ordered with soldiers dressed in smart clean uniforms directing men to their accommodation. 5 Platoon were shown to a large barn where camp beds were laid out in neat rows.

'Fuck me, it's the frigging Ritz,' said Timmings as they each chose somewhere to lay out their kit.

Before long an orderly led them to another building inside which three huge vats of water were joined by planks. The first was filled with hot, soapy water that was already turning a greyish-brown in colour, the second was slightly cleaner with no soap, the third was cleaner still, the water looking distinctly colder. The men stood in a row and stripped off, leaving their service dress in a bundle under their hats and handing in their underwear to go to the fumigator. Having shared the indignities of living for days in trenches together there was nothing new to them in the way of humiliation and they laughed and joked in their nakedness, eagerly anticipating the cleansing water, their bare white arses contrasting with their tanned arms and faces, their cocks dangling loose and swaying as they jostled for position.

The only exception to the jollity of the moment was Private Peter Jackson who covered his genitals with his hands and bowed his head.

'Got something to hide, Jacko?' said one of the soldiers.

Jackson didn't reply. The soldier was about to say something further but noticed Dawkins' expression and held back. They filed along the first plank, holding on to a rope slung across the whole area, and then they plunged into the water where they splashed about and washed themselves until encouraged to move on to the next vat.

Once they had been through the entire process and had dried themselves off there was another orderly issuing underwear.

'These bleeding long johns are even worse fitting than the last lot,' said Fletcher, pulling them up near to his nipples. The others laughed at the sight but Dawkins was observing him closely.

'What is it DD?' said Fletcher.

'What's that?' asked Dawkins, pointing at Fletcher's bare arm.

'Some kind of rash.'

'That's a blister.' Dawkins took Fletcher's arm and examined it. 'You're blistering up mate, you'd better get yourself to the MO.'

'It's nothing, just an itch.'

'Where's Peters?' asked Daniel.

'Over here,' came a voice.

Daniel walked over to where Peters was just receiving his clothing, took his arm and examined it. 'You've got it too,' he said.

'What're you saying, DD?'

'Fuck me. Mustard gas. There must have been some left in the soil where you did that OP.'

'Left there?'

'From when Fritz lobbed it over the other day. Some must have seeped into the ground. You need to get to the medics fast.'

When they recovered their uniforms Dawkins had Fletcher and Peters inspect theirs carefully and they found evidence of where the gas had soaked through.

'All on the front,' said Fletcher, 'where we lay on the ground.'

'How do the blisters feel?' asked Dawkins.

'Itching, ' said Fletcher, 'beginning to hurt.'

'Sarn't,' called Dawkins, 'Sergeant Barnes!'

'What is it Dawkins?' asked Barnes, coming over to where they were standing, 'not wanting to complain about our kit are we?'

'These men have got blisters, Sargeant, from that mustard gas.'

Fletcher and Peters showed Barnes their arms and he examined their faces which were also now beginning to blister up.

'Right, straight to the medics,' he said, 'back to the casualty stations. We don't want you infecting the others.'

'It's not contagious Sargeant.'

'I'm not risking that. Orderly!' Sergeant Barnes had turned to one of the men directing the bathing process, 'get these two men straight back to one of the casualty stations.'

'But I'm on duty here, Sargeant.'

Sergeant Barnes stood close to the man. 'Do as I say, soldier,' he said, his face, as it always did when he was angry, reddening, 'these men have mustard gas burns. If they don't get to the medics right now they'll be dead by morning. Do you understand me?'

The soldier, intimidated by the force of nature confronting him, stepped back. 'Yes, Sarn't, right away.'

'I'll go with them,' said Dawkins.

'No you won't Dawkins,' said Sergeant Barnes, 'you've got duties here.'

'I'll be back straight away Sergeant,' said Dawkins, 'and I can make sure they get the help they need.'

Sergeant Burns hesitated.

'I'll be back before dark,' said Dawkins, making it easier for his Sergeant, 'if I don't make it you can put me on a charge.'

Sergeant Barnes looked at the other men who were watching with interest to see where this might lead.

'Out of the mercy of my bleeding heart then, you can go,' said Barnes, 'and you've got four hours or I'll do just that.'

By the time they arrived at the reception tent of the clearing station the blisters had spread and both men were short of breath. Parker's eyes were inflamed and Fletcher was reporting abdominal pain. There was a queue of men waiting to be seen by a nurse and the orderly helped the two men onto stretchers to await their turn. Dawkins observed the scene and then strode up to a young nurse who was tending to another casualty.

'I'd like you see my mate next please love,' he said.

She didn't look up as she told him he'd have to wait his turn.

He stayed standing close beside her.

'I said he'll have to wait his turn,' she repeated.

Still Dawkins didn't move. Finally the nurse looked up.

'His name's Fletch,' said Dawkins, ' he's been out here a long time and his wife's pregnant.'

'I've heard that one before.'

'Yes, but Fletch's special.'

'That's what they all say.' The nurse turned to make her way to her next patient but Dawkins took her arm. 'What's your name, love?' he asked.

She stopped and looked up at him. 'Maggie.'

'Maggie, I'm Dan. I've been here since the start of the war. I've seen hundreds of men die, close friends many of them. I can't see another one go.'

The nurse wavered.

'You're a lovely looking girl,' said Dawkins, fixing her with his clear blue eyes, 'I know you'll want to help me. It would mean all the world.'

The nurse held his gaze and the subtle changes in her expression told him he would get his way. 'Please,' he said, 'do it for me.'

'Very well. Just this once.'

'You're a darling and I won't forget it.' Dawkins led her to where Fletcher was lying. 'And this is his mate, Peters, you might as well see to him as well.'

As the nurse bent over Fletcher, Dawkins took his hand. 'This is Maggie,' he said, 'best nurse in France. She'll see you all right.'

Fletcher grimaced but Dawkins detected the faintest smile as the nurse began applying ointments to his skin. With an effort Fletcher leant forwards and Dawkins lowered himself until his ear was close to his mouth.

'Same old Dan,' croaked Fletcher, 'See you back at the front.'

Dawkins was back in time to avoid a charge and discovered, as he had suspected, there were no duties to perform after all. The men were stood down and many had already drifted off into Poperinghe.

'You coming?' asked Timmings.

'Why not?

'How's Fletch?'

'He'll live but he's in for a rotten couple of days.'

'Poor bastard. Think he'll get a blighty?'

'No. Peters might though. Not as strong as Fletch.'

Dawkins noticed Jackson sitting on his own. 'Coming into Pop?' he said.

Jackson shook his head.

'Yes you are. You need a drink. No discussion.'

Unwillingly Jackson stood up and, through more of a reluctance to resist than any enthusiasm for a visit to an estanimet, joined Dawkins and Timmings as they set off.

'I'm on guard later,' said Timmings.

'Better not get too pissed then.'

They walked slowly to enable Jackson, whose leg was shaking as much as ever, to keep up and soon were in the outskirts of the town, passing an old factory with the words DELOUSING STATION painted prominently on the wall. In the main street a group of officers were standing chatting outside a hotel and Timmings noticed Mr Latham.

'Hello, sir,' he said.

'Hello, Timmings, what are you up to.'

'Same as you, sir.'

'What, a quiet evening of bridge and some civilised discussion?'

Timmings laughed. 'No, sir, going for a drink.'

'Well, have fun.'

'What's it like in there?'

'Very nice. Unfortunately it's only for officers.'

'We'll be heading for Café des Allies, bit more lively there.'

'We could meet up later if you want in Talbot House,' said Latham, turning to Dawkins.

'Maybe, sir. Let's see how it goes shall we?'

The three soldiers saluted and were heading off when Latham called Dawkins back.

'I gather Fletcher and Peters have been taken ill,' he said.

'Yes sir. Picked up some mustard gas at that listening post.'

'Not nice.'

'No. They'll survive though.'

'I'll visit them first thing.'

Latham looked towards Timmings and Jackson who were walking away. 'I'm sorry if I was unfair to you last night,' said Latham quietly.

'Unfair, sir? Not aware of it.'

'Suggesting you were callous. Suggesting you had no soul.'

'Water off a duck's back, sir.'

'Are you sure?'

'Of course. If I can take Fritz lobbing shells at me I can take a few words from you.'

'Well, that's good to hear.'

Dawkins smiled. 'Not much gets past my defences,' he said.

'Well, that's fine. Have a good time this evening.'

'And you, sir. They say the barmaids in Pop have a soft spot for posh young English officers.'

'Then I'll report back to you in the morning.'

In the Café des Allies a Belgian was playing familiar tunes on his squeeze box and everyone was joining in with the choruses. Dawkins, Timmings and Jackson sat drinking at a table singing along and after a couple of hours Dawkins had found his way to the front and was leading on one of the songs, a glass of wine in his right hand, his left resting on a waitress's waist.

'*The monk lamented his grief and shame,*
the monk lamented his grief and shame,
the monk lamented his grief and shame –
so he fucked her back to life again,' he sang and everyone cheered raucously.

Unsteadily he made his way back to the table. Timbo was swaying and knocked over a glass as Dawkins passed behind him.

'Steady,' said Daniel, 'didn't you say you were on guard tonight?'

'Fuck. I forgot.'

'No more drink for you, mate. You need to sober up. Get yourself some water.'

Timmings grinned foolishly. 'I'll get someone to stand in for me.'

'No you won't. They're all here.'

'Jacko. You do my guard?' said Timmings.

'He's as pissed as you are,' said Dawkins. He called over a waitress and asked for a jug of water. 'You'd better hope Sergeant Barnes won't be waiting up for you.'

Timmings seemed to take the advice and began drinking the water when it arrived before heading off to the latrines. Dawkins looked at Jackson. 'Cheer up Pete,' he said, 'this is meant to be fun.'

Jackson stared at the table, apparently oblivious to the noise all around him. His hands were shaking. His face was contorted in self pity.

'I've had enough, Dan,' he said, 'I can't do it again.'

'Do what?'

'The front. I can't do it again.' His voice was cracking as he spoke.

'You'll have to. There's no choice.'

'Dan, I can't.' Jackson looked up and there were tears in his eyes. 'I can't do it. I can't go back.'

'What do you mean you can't do it? What are you saying?'

'I'll do a runner.'

'Fuck off.' Dawkins leant forwards. 'Desert? They'll shoot you if they find you.'

Jackson had his head in his hands. 'That would do me fine,' he said quietly.

Dawkins pressed Jackson's hands on to the table top to stop them moving. 'Listen,' he said. Jackson's head remained lowered. 'Listen.' Dawkins grabbed Jackson's hair and lifted his face. 'You have a mum back home waiting for you. You stick this out for her. You don't go and get yourself fucking shot and let her live with the shame for the rest of her life. You don't bring that on your family. You've made it this far, the war's turning, you can make it to the end.'

Jackson shook his head slowly.

'And I haven't stuck by you all this time, fucking protected you, helped you at the front just to see you say 'fuck it'. That's not on, Pete.'

Dawkins let go of Jackson's hair and his head slumped down again. Then he looked up. 'You've been good to me, Dan, ' he said, 'you've been my friend. But I can't do it.' He was now crying openly.

'Fuck's sake,' said Dawkins and handed over a cloth, 'don't let them see you like this.'

Mademoiselle in the family way,' sang everyone around them. Jackson wiped his eyes. 'I'm sorry, Dan,' he said, 'I've let you down. I'm sorry.'

Timmings chose this moment to reappear. He didn't notice Jackson's distress and helped himself to a large glass of water. 'Ought to be getting back,' he said.

'I'll come with you.'

'I'll be fine. Just point me .... point me ... er ... in the fucking right direction, Dan.' His words were coming out slurred and disjointed. Dawkins stood up. 'I'm coming with you,' he said. 'Pete, give me a hand.'

Between them, Dawkins and Jackson manhandled Timmings out of the café and into the street, but they had only gone a few paces when they were stopped by the Military Police. They were questioned as to their unit and where they were heading. Dawkins held Timmings upright as best as he could and Timmings managed to answer the questions in a slow slur.

'Make sure you get him back without any bother,' said one of the MPs.

'I'll do that.'

Timmings grinned as the MPs walked away. 'And you can kiss my arse,' he said.

'Come on, let's get going.' Dawkins looked round. 'Where's Jackson?'

'Fuck knows. He buggered off while we were talking to the red hats.'

Dawkins stared at his friend. 'Which way did he go?'

'Didn't see. That way maybe.' Timmings pointed loosely down the street. 'But it could have been that way.'

'Shit!' Dawkins saw a low wall and helped Timmings onto it. 'Now,' he said, 'don't move from here. I'm going to look for him. Don't move.'

Timmings laughed. 'Don't move. Yes sir. To the right. Quick march. As you were.'

'Listen, do as I say. If you move from here I'll fucking brain you.'

Leaving Timmings lolling on the wall Dawkins ran down the street but there was no sign of Jackson. He ran back, checking Timmings hadn't moved, and searched the other way. Then he went back into the Café des Allies but he wasn't there.

When he returned to the wall Timmings was lying down and asleep. Dawkins shook him awake.

'Fucking idiot's done a runner,' he said.

'Runner?'

'Don't worry. Let's get you back.'

Dawkins helped Timmings up and they started walking in the direction of their billet. It would take them over half an hour and Timmings was on guard in forty minutes. The street was filled with soldiers in various states of drunkenness and a few local women walked amongst them plying their trade. They passed a shop that was open and selling tobacco and biscuits to any soldiers with money still to spare.

'This night's turning into a fucking nightmare,' said Dawkins but his young friend wasn't listening. Every now and then he fell over and Dawkins had to help him up so that by the time they reached the farm with one minute to spare Timmings was in a state of complete dishevellement.

They snuck in through a side entrance and made their way to the barn to collect Timmings' rifle.

'No sign of Barnesy, we might just get away with this,' said Dawkins as he steered Timmings towards the guard post but as they turned a corner Sergeant Barnes was standing, waiting.

'Late for duty,' said the Sergeant.

'Only just Sergeant,' said Dawkins.

'I'm not talking to you, Dawkins.' Sergeant Barnes walked forwards and put his face close to Timmings.

'You reek, you little bastard.'

Timmings tried his best to stand upright.

Sergeant Barnes smiled. It was a sly smile, a smile of self congratulation as he anticipated a moment of victory in his long-standing feud with the small group of soldiers he had come to detest. 'Drunk and disorderly,' he said. 'Corporal!' He shouted for the guard commander who appeared instantly. 'Lock this man up for drunk and disorderly and dereliction of duty.'

'Yes, Sargeant.'

Sergeant Barnes turned to Dawkins and he couldn't conceal his pleasure. 'First Field Punishment for this little shit,' he said, 'or I'll be very much mistaken.'

The next morning Timmings was up before the new Company Commander. Major Horrocks sat behind a trestle table with Sergeant Barnes and Sergeant Major Perkins standing on either side of him. Lieutenant Latham was in the background. Horrocks didn't look up as Timmings was marched in but made a point of slowly finishing what he was reading. When he finally raised his eyes he stared at Timmings for a long time before speaking.

'Read out the charge, Sergeant Barnes,' he said.

Barnes did as ordered, embellishing Timmings' state of drunkenness and adding in a number of derogatory statements apparently uttered by Timmings at the time he was marched off to the glasshouse. For good measure he implied that Private Dawkins had also behaved in an insubordinate manner.

At Dawkins name Major Horrocks bristled.

Once Barnes had finished Horrocks sat back in his chair. He was not a tall man but there was a quiet air of menace about him. His face was clean shaven, his hair short and neat, his uniform immaculately pressed. The way in which he held his head at a marginally backward angle gave the impression that he was permanently looking down his nose at people.

'What a despicable wretch you are,' he said to Timmings. 'As the Duke of Wellington might say, scum of the earth.' He spoke in a slightly nasal way that accentuated his refined accent, giving it an arrogant, supercilious tone. 'Drunk for duty is, in my view, one of the most serious crimes a soldier can commit.' He stood up and walked round the side of the table. 'It is putting your fellow soldiers in danger. It is an act of gross selfishness. What do you have to say for yourself?'

'I'm sorry, sir. We came back from the front and I were letting off steam. I got pissed and forgot about the duty.'

'Forgetting is no defence.'

'Sorry, sir, I fucked up, I know.'

'Don't you speak like that in front of me, man,' said Horrocks fiercely, his face distorting as he struck the desk with his hand, 'I will not have swearing in this court.'

'Sorry sir.'

Horrocks sat back down, suddenly calm again, and looked at the charge sheet.

'Lieutenant Latham?' he said without looking up at Latham.

'Yes?'

'Do you have anything to say?'

'Yes sir, I do.' Latham waited until Horrocks looked up. 'In mitigation, Private Timmings commited a considerable act of bravery at Messines Ridge, going forwards alone to take out an enemy pillbox. He saved many lives. Major Witheridge was planning to commend him for his bravery.'

'Sadly, Major Witheridge is no longer with us.'

'I am aware of that.'

Both men stared at each other across the table.

'So you think that excuses his behaviour last night, do you?' said Horrocks.

'No sir, I am just saying that it might be taken into consideration.'

'I see.' Horrocks wrote something on the charge sheet. 'Field Punishment Number one for one week,' he said, 'take him away Sergeant,' and he waved his hand to indicate the session was over.

Latham watched as Timmings was led out and was turning to leave himself when Major Horrocks called him back.

'Latham,' he said, 'a word.'

Latham faced him across the desk.

'I don't like it when officers try to defend reprobates like Timmings. It's bad for discipline.'

'I was simply making a statement about his good work at Messines.'

'I will repeat myself. It's bad for discipline.'

Latham stood in silence.

'I've been talking to Sergeant Barnes,' said Horrocks, 'he says you get too close to the men. You're too friendly with them.'

'I get on well with the men sir, yes, but I wouldn't say I'm too friendly.'

'Well that's the impression you give. And Sergeant Barnes is a sound man, I can tell.'

Horrocks stood up again and he walked over to Latham. 'So,' he said, 'a word of advice from one with considerably more experience than you.' His grey eyes held Latham's gaze with a complete absence of warmth. 'Some of the men in your platoon are trouble makers. They are not to be trusted. Timmings is one. Dawkins is another. In fact Dawkins is the ring leader. Do not befriend them or you will live to regret it. Keep your distance from them and certainly enter into no confidences with them. Your job is to send these men to their likely deaths and there is no room for friendship or sentiment between an officer and his soldiers. It only leads to trouble and misunderstanding.'

Latham noticed that as Horrocks spoke he very seldom, if ever, blinked.

'Do you understand me?' said Horrocks.

'Fully sir.'

'Good. I'll be watching you with interest. Dismissed.'

Latham stepped outside and made his way to his platoon's billet where there was a flurry of activity taking place. 'What's up?' he asked Sergeant Barnes.

'Jackson's gone missing, sir. Failed to make it to morning roll call.'

'When was he last seen?'

'Dawkins was the last to see him – in a pub in Poperinghe last night.'

'So what do you think's happened?'

'When I asked Dawkins he said Jackson was making out he couldn't take it any longer so I suspect he's deserted, sir. MPs have been alerted. They'll want to talk to Dawkins to find out why, if he suspected Jackson might go AWOL, he did nothing about it.'

'I was under the impression that Dawkins had his hands full trying to get Timmings back for his guard duty.'

'More important to stop a man from deserting sir. That should have been his main concern.'

'And I imagine you've already made this point to the MPs.'

Sergeant Barnes reddened slightly. 'Dawkins was at the centre of all the trouble last night, sir. He'll need to answer for his actions.'

Latham stood very still, his gaze fixed on his Sergeant, and Barnes stared back at him.

'Get him here.'

'Dawkins?'

'Yes. Get him here now.'

'I think he may be on guard sir.'

'Sergeant Barnes, I won't say this a third time. Get Dawkins here now.'

Sergeant Barnes managed to achieve an expression that was just short of insubordination. 'Very well, sir,' he said, 'if you think that's really necessary.'

He returned with Dawkins a few minutes later.

'Tell me the circumstances surrounding Jackson's disappearance,' said Latham.

Dawkins explained how Jackson had disappeared when Timmings had been answering the MP's questions.

'And what did you do?'

'I sat Timmings down on a wall, sir, and went to look for Jackson. I ran up and down the street and looked in the pub but he wasn't there. Then I went back to Timmings and helped him back here.'

'And what did you think might have happened to him?'

'He was in a low mood sir, so I was worried about what he might do. I thought he might top himself. So after I'd seen to Timmings I went back into the town and looked for Jackson again but couldn't find him.'

'Did you think of telling anyone?'

'No, sir. He might have just gone for a wander. He's done that before and been back for parade so I didn't want to cause him trouble.'

'You didn't think of speaking to the Military Police?'

'Not them, sir. That just complicates it. Better to deal with such things ourselves.'

'So what do you think has happened to him?'

'I think he might have done a runner. I was keeping an eye on him to get him back here with Timmings but, as I said, I lost him when we were with the red tops.'

'And have you told what you've just said to me to Sergeant Barnes here?'

'Haven't had a chance to, sir.' Dawkins looked directly at Sergeant Barnes. 'He just asked me if I was with Jackson last night and what state he was in.'

'I see. Thank you Dawkins.'

Dawkins saluted and left. Latham paced up and down for a few seconds before turning to Barnes.

'So, let me get this right, Sergeant Barnes,' he said, a slight tremble in his voice, his words coming out slowly, 'you spoke directly to the Military Police, suggesting they should question Dawkins about his role in Jackson's disappearance before you bothered to find out the full facts from the man himself?'

'When a soldier goes missing sir you need to act quickly.'

'Answer my question please Sergeant.'

'I did go to the MPs, yes.'

Latham observed Barnes, noticing fully for the first time the piggy shiftiness about his eyes. 'You don't think your first loyalty is to the men in this platoon? To me? To ascertain the facts with the men who have fought beside you before running off to the police and making false accusations?'

'False accusations...?'

'Sergeant Barnes, you've implicated private Dawkins in aiding a soldier to desert when it seems the exact opposite is the case. Dawkins, who has been on active service now for over two years. A man who has shown courage under fire on a number of occasions.' Latham's voice was now rising in volume. 'Frankly, I find that despicable.'

Barnes stared back at Latham but said nothing.

'And you talk to the new OC about me behind my back. You tell him I'm too close to my soldiers without ever mentioning this to me. What am I to make of that?'

Still Barnes said nothing.

'Tell me, what am I to make of a man who is disloyal to his soldiers and disloyal to his officer?'

Barnes, normally so ready with a cutting riposte when challenged, remained silent. His anger was evident from the expression on his face and in the way he held his body but he seemed unable to find the words to counter the accusations being levelled at him. Latham waited.

Finally Barnes spoke. 'I resent what you say deeply,' he said. 'I fought at Mons.

I was here at the start of this war. I have more experience than you, Dawkins and all the rest of this fucking lot put together. I am a professional bloody soldier.'

Latham stepped forwards until they were only a foot apart. 'Then behave like one,' he said, 'and we might just be able to fight the real enemy and not ourselves.'

CHAPTER 21

11 November 1920

Peter Harding stopped to catch his breath. He had first run up Whitehall, then Great George Street towards St James's Park and was now working his way along Victoria Street. Every now and then he stopped to search for the boater with the blue ribbon but it was nowhere to be seen. His only hope now was that the girl might live south of London and was walking towards Victoria station.

He felt a strong need to speak to her even though he had no idea what he would say when they met. He looked ahead and stepped into the road to pass the heavy mass of people making their way slowly along the pavement.

A taxi honked at him but he remained on the road and started running again. The street lights only dimly lit the way and he knew his chances of finding the girl were receding by the second. He bumped into a man who stepped out in front of him and he nearly lost his footing, apologising over his shoulder as he hastened on.

Victoria station was filled with people standing shoulder to shoulder in a dense fog of steam and smoke in front of the departures board. The excited hubbub of conversation mingled with the heavy sound of engines in the background. Peter made his way to the platform barriers and walked from numbers one to eight, looking into the faces of the men, women and children waiting for information, but amongst them there was no girl in a boater.

He walked to the other platforms but it was no different and as he stood by a newspaper stand traversing the station with his eyes a sickening feeling of realisation swept over him: the girl in the photograph who had filled his thoughts these past few days and who had briefly entered his life was gone. His opportunity to meet her had passed and he would never see her again. He took out his pipe, lit it and sought to lessen his disappointment in comforting puffs of tobacco while the people all about him carried on their business oblivious to his anguish.

Slowly, despondently, he started making his way to the exit near Grosvenor Gardens.

It was then, at the extent of his peripheral vision, that something caught his eye. A lighter colour again, surrounded by grey, moving steadily towards the underground entrance.

Peter started walking quickly in that direction but every few yards he had to force his way through the bodies in his path. At first he was polite, asking people to move aside as he nudged his way forwards, but when he saw the boater descend below street level he started pushing harder, elbowing away those reluctant to move without a word of apology.

He caught up with her in the queue for tickets, barging his way in front of a woman who gave him a long look, opened her mouth to say something but then thought better of it.

He stood behind the girl, catching his breath as she bought her ticket. She was wearing a dark blue coat and her hair was bundled up beneath the boater. He heard her say 'thank you,' and she turned. For a second she was studying her ticket and it seemed she might walk away without noticing him but then she looked up and their eyes met.

'Hello,' she said.

'Next.'

Peter stared at her.

'Come along, sir, we haven't all day.'

Peter turned to the booth and said 'a single please.'

'Where to?'

'Bayswater,' he replied, naming the first station that came to mind. The man issued him the ticket and he turned. She wasn't where she had been standing and he looked round anxiously.

'You're the man from the Abbey,' came a voice. He swivelled and there she was, standing slightly to one side, waiting for him.

'Hello. Yes. And you're the woman at the tomb.'

'I am.'

They were standing in the way of a stream of people wanting to pass and Peter ushered her to one side. They stood facing each other.

'Where are you heading?' he asked.

'Paddington.'

'Same direction as me. Let me accompany you.'

'If you want.'

He led the way down to the platform and they stood side by side waiting for the train.

'When I looked up at you in the Abbey you gave me such a long look,' she said.

'I'm sorry. You stood out from the others. Perhaps something struck me about you.'

'I see.'

The train arrived and they managed to find one seat. The girl sat down with Peter standing over her.

'My name's Peter Harding,' he said.

'I'm Joyce. Are you a soldier?'

'Yes.'

'Officer?'

'Yes.'

'I thought so. Why aren't you in uniform?'

The train set off with a lurch and Peter grabbed the leather strap above him.

'I was just helping out. If you don't mind me asking, who were you mourning?'

'My fiancée.'

'I'm sorry.'

'He went missing in 1917.'

'I see.'

'Were you out there?'

'Yes. I'm in the Royal Artillery. I saw the last year of the war. What about your fiancée?'

'He was in the infantry. He was in France from the start.'

Joyce was holding her boater in her hands in front of her. The train stopped and people got on and off.

'Three years ago,' said Peter once the train was moving again, 'where was he serving when he went missing? Ypres?'

'Yes. How did you guess that?'

'That's where most of them died that year.'

Joyce looked down. 'We never did find out what happened to him.'

A man in the seat next to Joyce stood up and Peter sat down beside her.

'That must have been very hard to cope with,' he said.

'It was.' She was gripping the straw of her hat firmly, curling the ribbon around her fingers. 'I was pregnant you see.'

'Oh.' He could think of nothing appropriate to say so fell silent. She appeared to slip into some kind of reflection so he left her to her thoughts until they arrived at Paddington.

She looked up. 'You've missed your station,' she said.

'Oh! My mind was elsewhere. But it's just a short walk back. Why don't I see you on to your train. Where are you going to?'

'Taplow.'

'Come on then.'

They walked into the main station and looked at the board. The next train was in forty minutes. 'Can I buy you a coffee or something?'

'Something would be nice. Something strong.'

They left the station and found a nearby pub where Joyce asked for a brandy.

'I feel I've earned it,' she said as they sat down in a small corner booth, 'what are you doing in Bayswater?'

'Oh, I'm meeting a friend. I'm staying a couple of nights in London before heading back to France.'

She took a large gulp of the brandy and shuddered.

'What a day,' she said.

'Yes.'

'I can't believe the numbers.'

'Thousands upon thousands.'

'And what was your job in the Abbey?'

Peter described how he had officiated at the service and he described the widows he had shown to their seats. Then he talked about the 'In and Out' and the friends he was catching up with while back for the three days. He asked her about her child and she said he was a boy whose name was Stanley and that he was now over two and a half years old. She told him about her home in Taplow and how her parents looked after Stanley while she worked.

Then he asked her about her fiancée.

'His name was Dan,' she said, 'Daniel Dawkins.' She paused as she thought of him. 'He was the love of my life.' Peter waited for her to continue. 'A real man's man, always surrounded by friends, always the leader.'

'He sounds a good sort.'

'Oh, he was that.' She circled her hands around her glass. 'He wasn't one for talking about his feelings and he didn't write much but I know he had a good heart. I met him at school – he'd run away from London and a local farmer near where I lived had looked after him until he signed up. He'd had a bad time of it up till then but you wouldn't have known it.'

'And he was at the front for over two years.'

'That's right. We began to think he was indestructible. He always said it was just luck but I used to think maybe there was something special about him, that he was being looked after ....'

Peter waited for her to continue.

'.... until the day the farmer appeared at the door to tell me he'd heard Dan had gone 'Missing in Action'.'

'I'm sorry.'

'I still kept believing he was alive somewhere. That he'd come home one day.' She looked up at Peter. 'But it never happened.'

Peter placed his hand gently on her shoulder. 'People say it's the not knowing that's the hardest bit.'

'They're right. Days, weeks, months. It was a terrible time.'

She described her struggle to feed her son and the long lonely evenings when she tried not to think of Daniel. Peter bought her two more brandys and two more pints of bitter for himself and her words kept on tumbling out, one after another in a long, vivid account and it was as if a dam had been breached and the weight of her recent memories, kept at bay these past years, finally broke their confines and rushed out in a wave of emotion.

Peter listened, entranced, until, exhausted by her monologue, Joyce slumped in her seat and he had to hold her to prevent her from falling to one side. There were tears in her eyes. 'He was such a fine man,' she whispered and Harding nodded as she leant against his shoulder.

By then she had missed her train but when they returned to the departures board they saw there was another leaving shortly. Peter took her to the platform and opened the door of a carriage.

'I would very much like to meet with you again,' he said.

She looked at him and her eyes were red. 'I don't get out much these days,' she replied.

'In which case I will come and visit you in Taplow when I am next in town.' He took a notebook and a fountain pen out of his pocket. 'Write your address here.'

She wrote down the details of her parents house as he watched. The guard blew his whistle.

'Time to go,' she said wistfully. He helped her up into the corridor.

'Two weeks,' he said, 'two weeks until my next leave. I will come and see you, I promise.'

'Thank you,' she said, thank you for listening.'

CHAPTER 22

1 August 1917

George Latham sat in his study and put down his newspaper.

'It's started again,' he said.

'What is it darling?' came his wife's voice from the next room.

'They're at it again. Another offensive,' he said.

Elizabeth hurried into the room. 'What are you saying?'

'It's all over the papers – the attack has finally begun.'

He held open the newspaper and showed her the headlines.

'How's it going?' she asked.

'Going well by the sound of things.' He picked up the paper and started reading extracts;

'Our armies broke the German line and effected an advance to a depth of between three and four thousand yards...'

'..... our forces were subjected to heavy counter attacks, which, however, were successfully warded off...'

'.....the enemy had strengthened their means of resistance, had bought up many additional guns, and had massed supports at all critical points. Their precautions were to no avail, for our special correspondent explicitly states that yesterday's advances reached the precise distance which was planned for the first day's operations....'

'....it is too soon yet to estimate in detail either the prospects of this formidable offensive or the present actual results. All that is clear is that a substantial slice of Belgium has already been wrested from the invader, that the Ypres salient is disappearing, and that many points where there was deadly fighting in 1914 and in the early days of 1915 are once more in British hands.'

'Well that sounds marvellous,' said Elizabeth.

'It does sound good, yes. But it also says *'yesterday's fighting may be no more than a beginning of operations.'* There's a long way to go yet.'

'How about Jeremy?'

'We don't know. I've heard that the 5th Army were going to be the main force, in which case he might not be involved.'

'He'd want to be part of a successful assault, surely.'

George shook his head slowly. 'I don't know. Listen to this; *'....the weather conditions were not very favourable during the 24 hours before the battle..'* That throws up some familiar images. I'm not sure anyone would want to be part of that.'

Elizabeth rested her hand on her husband's shoulder.

'You really have changed, haven't you? You would never have said something like that three years ago.'

'No.' His eyes were scanning the paper again. 'No I wouldn't. Perhaps I'm just that much wiser now.'

They spent the day pottering. They gardened after morning coffee, they walked the dogs along the Thames, they ate cold meats for lunch and went into Reading to buy some basic supplies in the afternoon.

'I have some news about Mrs Jackson's son,' said Elizabeth from the passenger seat as they drove home in the early evening.

'Oh, yes?' George kept his eyes on the road.

'He's deserted.'

George said nothing.

'It's terrible for the poor woman.'

'It was coming.'

'That doesn't make it any easier for her.'

'He'll be shot when they find him.'

'She's beside herself with worry.'

George started to say something but stopped himself. He turned the wheel as they came to the road for Sonning.

'Say it,' said Elizabeth.

George sighed. 'The man's a coward,' he said, 'he's been trying to avoid his duty since we first heard of him. He doesn't deserve our sympathy.'

Elizabeth pressed her feet into the floor. She sat upright, her jaw tensed, her eyes looking anywhere but at her husband. They arrived at the driveway to the house and George parked up. He stepped out of the car but Elizabeth stayed seated. He walked round to her side and opened the door.

'I don't mean to upset you my darling but that's how I see it.'

Slowly she climbed out of the passenger seat and now she looked at her husband directly. 'In which case,' she said icily, 'I take back what I said earlier. You haven't changed at all.'

The evening was spent with Elizabeth in a cold fury and no amount of concessions from George would mollify her.

'Listen,' he said as they sat drinking coffee after their dinner, 'you can't do this. I am a compassionate man at heart but my feelings are with those out there who are facing their fears as men. People like Jeremy. It's no good for them having to deal with someone who runs away at the first sound of gunfire.'

'The first sound of gunfire? What on earth do you mean?'

'Very well, perhaps not the first ....'

'That boy served in your beloved Somme. He has been out there for over a year. He has seen countless friends killed in the most horrific manner. Can you imagine what that must do to a young man?'

'So have many others and they fight on.'

'But many don't. I'm hearing more and more of soldiers whose minds have been ruined by their horrific experiences. There's even a hospital for officers who have cracked. It's perfectly ghastly. And you sit here in your armchair and judge this boy who has reached the end of his tether. You judge him. Shame on you George. Shame on you.'

Elizabeth spoke these last words with such fervour that George was rendered speechless for a moment. Then she burst into tears. He reached forward to pat her shoulder but she brushed him away.

'I'm sorry Liz' he said.

'How will you react if Jeremy comes home a broken man?' said Elizabeth through her tears. 'Will you say he deserves to be shot?'

'Of course not but that's not ...'

'It is the point. It is. Anyone can be broken. We have no idea what it's like, no idea.'

She dabbed at her eyes with a handkerchief.

They sat in silence.

'I'm sorry,' said Elizabeth, standing up to leave the room, 'I'm sorry to get so emotional. Silly little woman. But it's been three years, George, three years and now we welcome another offensive when young men slaughter each other in their thousands in a muddy field in Belgium. Men. Men sending men to their deaths and for what? A few thousand yards. Have we all gone completely mad?'

'Perhaps we have.' George had his eyes closed and rested his forehead on his hands. 'Perhaps we have.' She walked off without saying any more and he watched her head upstairs. Then he stood up and walked wearily to the French windows and stepped out into the garden. The dogs bounded up to him and they ran up and down oblivious to his torment as he made his way through the rose beds towards the summer house. The lawn had just been mown and the smell took him back, as always, to playing here on the wooden swing his father had built and which he had replaced when the children were young. He remembered pushing Jeremy back and forth, back and forth, every evening, day after day, and the boy's laughter as he rose higher and higher, to the edges of safety, and how pleased he was that his son showed no fear. Face adversity. Resolution and courage. That's what he had taught Jane and Jeremy. Resilience. No giving up. Had that been wrong? Surely not.

He looked back to the house and could see Elizabeth through the bedroom window looking out at him. He sat down on the seat of the swing.

Men who have cracked. Broken lives. He had been hearing more and more talk of these things recently. Shell-shock. It was a phrase being bandied around frequently.

But what was it? He had assumed a failure of nerve. A weakness of the mind. And yet. The previous year Ralph had talked to him about the Austrian doctor Sigmund Freud and his practice of psychoanalysis and though he had said at the time he thought it was complete nonsense it had caused him to reflect.

Reflect on the time when he was turning forty and his brother had been killed in a riding accident. His business had been failing, he had debts, his young wife Elizabeth, under strain with an illness whilst bringing up two small children had become remote, his workforce had become restless and infiltrated by militants. He had fallen into a pattern of waking in the middle of the night and not being able to get back to sleep, of lying in bed in a cold sweat, of thoughts racing away from him, of worrying about things that would normally have been of no consequence.

He had, of course, turned it around. The business survived and then flourished, the militants were ousted, Elizabeth strengthened, the children matured, his marriage survived and bloomed.

But he had been through dark days and nights and he had, at his lowest ebb, questioned the very state of his mind. Was this what was happening to these men?

He sat on the swing and thought back to those bad times. 'You judge him'. The phrase had stung. Judging others. He had been accused of this before but had always considered it to be a compliment, a recognition of his firmness of opinion, his commitment to high standards.

He pushed with his legs and started swinging in a low arc.

But what could he possibly know of what that man Jackson had been through? Of the horrors he might have witnessed? Elizabeth was right. Who was he to judge another man? How could a failing business, a difficult marriage or a cash flow problem compare with being shelled interminably, of being surrounded by death, of witnessing friends blown to pieces?

And yet he himself had nearly cracked.

George swung slowly back and forth, smelling the grass and the roses, looking back at his large red brick house, feeling the warmth of a summer evening and knowing, deep inside him, that, in spite of his wife's words, his world was indeed changing forever.

The following morning he was first in the shop to buy newspapers and he read the front pages as he walked home. Elizabeth, as always, had returned to her normal bright self and it was as if their row had never taken place.

'Liz, I want to say ..'

'No.' She held up her hand. 'No. I understand. I know what you're going through. It's done and said.'

'But ..'

'No, George, I mean it. I know you are working things out, I know it isn't easy. I respect you for it. Let's leave it at that.'

She poured them both out some coffee while he laid the papers out, first picking up *The Times*. He read slowly, absorbing each phrase, picturing the battle taking place across the channel.

'So, how's it going?' asked Elizabeth.

'Shall I read it out?'

She looked over from the stove. 'Yes please.'

George picked one report from a correspondent.

'There has been no material change or further advance today but we have been busy consolidating under the vilest weather conditions and making good the gains of yesterday,' he read. *'Captured German officers and men speak, according to their temperament, in lavish admiration or bitter hatred of our guns. Our infantry is loud in their praise.*

Not only was the timimg of our barrage almost everywhere perfect, so that our men could go behind it as behind a protecting wall, but the destruction of enemy trenches and gun positions and the like was extraordinary.

'We hear from German prisoners that one battery of their artillery was so smashed in the preliminary shellings of the days before the attack that it had to renew its crews nine times and restock with guns five times.'

'How terrible,' said Elizabeth.

George read a few more passages about the British successes. His eyes scanned the pages.

'But listen to this,' he said. *'I have said that the weather to-day has been of the vilest, and it is well we made our attack yesterday. Since last evening it has rained pitilessly, so that the ground is everywhere dissolving, and it is impossible to see even a hundred yards..... One result is that the battle has been fought practically without any aerial observation, a fact which should have been altogether in the enemy's favour ...'*

'My God, it must be grim out there.'

'But at least we're making ground,' said Elizabeth as she placed George's cooked breakfast in front of him and he couldn't be sure if she was being sarcastic or not.

'Hang on,' he said, 'there's a German report here, that's unusual.'

'German?'

'Yes, from one of their papers. The Times is repeating it in full.'

'That is unusual.'

George fell silent as he read the report, periodically taking mouthfuls of scrambled eggs and sipping at his coffee.

'Well?' said Elizabeth, 'what are they saying?'

'I'm not sure I should tell you.'

'What do you mean?'

'I mean it's probably just propaganda.'

'George, I'm a grown up, I can make my own mind up on things.'

'Very well.' George drank some more coffee and began reading.

'German Official report 1 August.

The great battle of Flanders has begun, one of the most tremendous of the third year of the war, coming to an end to-day with promises of success.

With masses such as have never before been used in any period of this war, not even in the east by Brusiloff, the English, and in their wake the French, attacked yesterday on a 15 mile front between Noordschoote and Warneton. Their aim was a lofty one. It was intended to deliver an annihilating blow to the 'U-boat pest' which, from the coast of Flanders, is undermining England's mastery at sea. Densely packed attacking waves of the closely placed divisions followed each other; numerous Tanks and cavalry units took part in the battle. After the fortnight's artillery preparation, which in the early morning of July 31 increased to drumfire, the enemy penetrated with tremendous pressure into our defensive zone. In some sectors he overran our lines situated in crater positions, and at some points temporarily gained considerable territory.

George paused and finished his coffee.

'In an impetuous counter attack,' he continued, *' our reserves threw themselves against the enemy, and in bitter hand to hand engagements, which lasted throughout the day, drove him either out of our fighting zone or back into the foremost crater field. To the north and north-east of Ypres the crater fields captured by the enemy remained deeper; in this section Bixschoote could not be held any longer.*

Fresh attacks advancing in the evening could bring no turn in the battle in favour of the enemy. They failed before our newly arranged battle lines. Our troops report heavy casualties on the part of the enemy, who fought regardless of sacrifices.

The brilliant bravery and dash of our infantry and pioneers, the heroic endurance and the excellent effect of the artillery, machine guns and mine-throwers, the intrepidity of our airmen, and the most faithful fulfilment of duty on the part of our scouts and other auxiliary arms, and especially the purposeful, quiet leadership, offered certain guarantees for the termination of the battle in our favour...'

He stopped and closed the paper. 'As I said, propaganda.'

Elizabeth had sat down opposite him as he was reading and she now held her hand to her mouth.

'Bolstering their morale,' said George.

'But what's the truth?' said Elizabeth. 'Who should we believe?'

'Our correspondents of course.'

'But remember last year. They hardly told the truth then.'

George looked at the German report. He sighed heavily. 'Who knows, Liz,' he said, 'who knows? Nothing is what it seems these days.'

After breakfast he decided to visit his friend Ralph and after a phone call set off in the Lanchester towards Henley. The road was empty of traffic and he arrived in time for morning coffee.

'You were lucky to catch me in,' said Ralph, 'there's a lot happening at the moment. I'm heading into town shortly.'

They sat down in Ralph's study and George told him about the conflicting reports in *The Times*. 'You have contacts, Ralph,' he said, 'what's really going on out there?'

'It's not pretty,' said Ralph.

'I read about the rain.'

'But you may not have read that the bombardment of the past two weeks has destroyed the drainage system. Remember, this is a very low lying area, only rendered habitable by an extensive network of managed canals. The whole place has become one giant quagmire.'

'Isn't there a plateau there?'

'The Gheluvelt. It's a key objective of this assault and held by the Germans these past years.'

'And?'

'Still held by the Germans. The reports of shattered pillboxes are true – but there are many more of them, solidly built, able to hold up to thirty men. They would be a formidable obstacle in dry conditions – in a giant bog I shudder to think how our men will fare.'

George had known Ralph since they were young men and he knew he wasn't given to exaggeration.

'How many casualties on the first day?'

'You won't like it.'

'How many?'

'Twenty thousand. Maybe more.'

'Oh my God.'

'When that German report talks of 'heavy casualties' it isn't a lie – although they don't mention they've lost similar numbers in the past weeks.'

'Forty thousand men dead.'

'Probably more. It's all beginning to sound sickeningly familiar.'

The telephone in the hall rang and George could hear Ralph speaking somberly to someone at the other end.

'George, I have to go. The one thing I suppose that's a slight comfort to you is that it's the 5th Army taking the brunt. I don't think Jeremy will have been involved to date.'

'But he might be soon.'

Ralph was putting on his hat and coat. 'I fear he might,' he said, 'we can but pray from here on in.'

17 August 1917

General Sir Hubert Gough studied the last in a long line of situation reports from the sectors.

After sixteen days of intense fighting the 5th Army had been reduced to an exhausted, depleted force that had all but lost its heart. Since 31 July they had suffered more than fifty thousand casualties as advance, counter attack, advance and counter attack had played out across the Flemish landscape.

The heavy rain that had started on the very afternoon of that first day of the offensive had continued without let up for another four days. After a short period of intermittent sunshine the remorseless downpour returned again to deepen the misery of the troops, many of whom by then had spent over a week soaked to the skin, catching what little sleep they could in water filled trenches and shell holes, protected only by leaking ponchos from the unrelenting elements.

It had been the wettest August in living memory and the advance had ground to a halt in impossible conditions.

After more than two weeks of fearsome battle the Gheluvelt Plateau was still in German hands. The Passchendaele Ridge remained a distant objective. Many of those who had escaped death in assault were being blown to pieces by the shells that fell constantly on their defensive positions.

It had been a particularly bad day and General Gough sat alone for a while, his face drawn, fighting the numbing demoralisation that had been growing inside him these past weeks. He considered the options facing him. Then he called for his driver and was soon on his way to Field Marshal Haig's headquarters, rehearsing his arguments to himself in the back seat of the staff car.

At HQ he spoke to the Commander-in-Chief of the impossibility of their task. He clarified the alarming loss of men, the exhaustion, the difficulties of resupply, the appalling conditions, the guns sinking into the mud. He described the painfully slow movement of the infantry across water logged shell holes that was so fatiguing that only the shortest advances were possible. He informed the Commander-in-Chief that tactical success was not possible, or would be too costly under such conditions, and advised that the attack should be abandoned.

But Haig was committed to his strategy and confident it would work in the end. The war of attrition would continue.

'Send two divisions of the 2nd Army to bolster the 5th' he said later to his staff officers, and the instruction was relayed to General Plumer who, for the past two weeks, had been watching events unfold, witnessing the disaster befalling the 5th Army and awaiting the inevitable order to send his troops into battle.

CHAPTER 23

August 1917

'Jesus fucking Christ,' said Timmings, 'have you ever seen anything like that?'

The men of 5 Platoon had just disembarked from a train and, after no more than a five minute walk, had rounded a corner to be confronted by a scene of extraordinary devastation.

In front of them, stretching as far as the eye could see through the morning mist, was a brown, slithering, ocean of mud. In the foreground two tanks, three quarters buried, their barrels pointing crazily to the sky, were seemingly being swallowed up by the land. Beyond them a network of duck boards criss crossed this vast swamp, on the horizon shattered trees poked up from low ridges.

They watched as a team of engineers encouraged their reluctant mules to negotiate the temporary footpaths that snaked around water filled shellholes.

'Blimey. Welcome to hell,' said Dawkins.

A platoon of men being relieved approached them. They were caked in mud, their heads were down, they appeared haggard and at the limits of their endurance.

'All right, Corporal,' said Dawkins to one of the soldiers as he passed.

The man looked up, his eyes sunken and unrecognising, his shoulders bent under the weight of his kit.

'Aye,' he replied in a Scottish accent, 'cushy enough.'

Dawkins looked along the pathetic line of men. 'Not that many of you,' he said.

'Aye, that there are,' said the man. His voice carried with it a weariness that made each word appear an effort of will. 'Only ten left.' He looked back over his shoulder and gestured towards the mud. 'You'll be meeting the rest shortly.'

Dawkins offered the man a bar of chocolate which he slipped into his pocket.

'Best of luck, then,' said the corporal and carried on his way, plodding slowly, placing one foot carefully in front of another. His straggle of soldiers followed and not one sad, pitiless face looked up as they passed, not a single word was exchanged as they left the battlefield with an exhausted disregard for the new arrivals.

'Poor bastards. They're all in,' said Fletcher.

'Beyond that,' said Dawkins.

The platoon fell silent at the prospect of what lay ahead. They stood on the duckboards in deep contemplation, imagining themselves returning one day as these men had, their numbers decimated, their bodies and minds reduced to the most basic forms of life focused only on survival.

'Keep moving up there.'

Dawkins looked up to see Sergeant Barnes urging them on.

'And keep away from the edges.'

They needed no reminding of this order. They had heard the stories of the past weeks of soldiers, mules and horses of the 5th Army that had lost their footing, slipped over the edge and sunk within seconds into the thick, glutinous mud that surrounded the paths. Some had been pulled out by straining comrades, many had disappeared below the surface with terrible cries of anguish.

'Someone give that man a nudge,' said Dawkins.

Fletcher, the blisters on his body still healing and his generosity of spirit tested by the pain he had been suffering, laughed. 'First opportunity, DD,' he said, 'Plop. In he goes. Then let's see who wants to rescue him.'

Sergeant Barnes appeared beside them.

'Something funny, Fletcher?' he said.

'Everything, Sergeant.' Fletcher stood up and rested on his rifle. 'The whole bloody set up. Makes me want to weep with laughter.' He surveyed the desolate landscape.

'I'll have you weeping if you don't get a move on.'

'Yes, sergeant.'

They were led to a pillbox that had been captured from the Germans on the first day of the offensive.

'As the man said, cushy enough,' commented Fletcher as he surveyed the large room, 'at least it's dry.' They were lucky. Instead of being stuck in rat-infested holes, 5 Platoon were to have a roof over their heads for the next twenty-four hours. And the weather was improving. Between them and the German lines the ground was firmer although there wasn't a blade of grass to be seen in any direction.

'Never know, we might have missed the worst,' said Timmings as he unloaded his shovel, his bombs, his ammunition and his pack into a corner.

'That's good coming from you, Timbo,' said Dawkins.

Timmings had spent the previous week being marched back and forth at the double in full kit by merciless regimental police determined to make his first field punishment an experience to remember. Each morning and evening, to heighten his disgrace, for an hour he was tied to a wagon wheel in full view of the Regiment. Twice he had been cut down by Australian soldiers, bemused by the British Armies' fanatical adherence to discipline and eager to make a mockery of this contempt for human decency. Both times he had been strung up again by the RPs.

'True,' he replied, 'me shoulders are still fucking aching.' He sat down and Murphy nuzzled up beside him. 'All a fucking great adventure for you mate,' he said, stroking the dog under the chin.

'Did you see Major Horrocks at the station?' said Dawkins, 'strutting around as if he owned the fucking place, arrogant bastard.'

'He'll be the second to get a shove,' said Timmings.

'Careful with your words, Timbo,' said Fletcher, 'we might all think it, best not say it.'

The men set about making themselves comfortable, pleased that Barnes was establishing himself in another pillbox fifty yards away. Lieutenant Latham appeared.

'Hello sir,' said Dawkins, 'fancy a brew.'

'Good idea.'

Latham sat down on a bench left by the Germans and as Dawkins began boiling some water they started chatting about the stalled offensive. Fletcher had seen wave after wave of soldiers being bought into the casualty stations on stretchers, all needing to be washed down before the surgeons could get anywhere near their wounds. He had spoken to a corporal from the Lancashire Fusiliers who said some pieces of ground had been won and lost more then ten times. Dawkins had heard that the pillboxes on the plateau were as good as impregnable. 'So what next, sir?' he asked Latham.

'I know very little more than you do,' said Latham, 'other than the fact that General Plumer has been given the job of revitalising the attack over the next few weeks.'

'So we'll be seeing some action before long,' said Dawkins.

'Sooner rather than later, I'd imagine. Staff seem keen for us to keep hammering away at their lines and make gains wherever possible.'

A shell whistled overhead and some men instinctively ducked.

'Take it easy,' said Dawkins who had carried on cleaning his rifle without flinching, 'If it has your name on it, you'll get it. If it hasn't you won't.'

'Thanks for that DD,' said Fletcher.

'It's a fact,' said Dawkins. 'If you're alive there's no need to worry. If you're dead you can't worry. Simple.'

'If only it were.'

'It is.'

Fletcher laughed. 'Dan, if I was as certain about anything as you are about everything I'd consider myself opinionated.'

'Don't give me all that stuff, Fletch. There's life and death, that's all there is to it.'

'And good and bad, and right and wrong?'

'You said it mate.'

Fletcher smiled at the familiar path the conversation was taking. 'Well I guess, as you say, it keeps things simple.'

'That's the best way, Fletch. No point in troubling yourself about what might or might not happen. Just get on with it. Accept it or you'll go mad.'

'Like Jackson,' said Timmings.

'Ah. I do have some information there,' said Latham. 'He's been found.'

Dawkins was pouring out a mug of tea and he stopped, kettle poised in mid air. 'Where?'

'Some village. He was hiding in an outhouse where he was found by a farmer who reported him. He's back at HQ.'

'Court martial then.'

'Of course.'

'Will they shoot him?' asked Timmings.

'I doubt it. They might sentence him to death but my guess is they'll commute it and send him back here. That's what tends to happen now.'

'I was on a firing squad,' said Dawkins.

The others looked at him. 'I didn't know that DD,' said Timmings.

'Not something to be proud of, Timbo.'

Dawkins stirred his tea.

'Go on, then,' said Timmings, 'tell us about it.'

'Not much to tell.'

'Come on Dan, when was it?'

Dawkins looked reluctant to speak.

'Come on, Dawkins,' said Mr Latham, 'I think we'd all be interested to hear.'

Dawkins sighed. 'Very well,' he said, 'First year.' He looked at his audience.

'Late 1915. It was a bloke called Fraser – he went mad as a bull. Ran around screaming and refused to fight. One of the corporals knocked him out and when he came to he scarpered when no one was watching. They caught him soon enough and he was court martialled the next day.'

'And you shot him?' said Timmings.

'Me and a few others. They issued one of us with a blank to steady our nerves but I could tell when I fired it wasn't me. Odd thing was, this bloke who'd been howling around the place putting the wind up everyone went all quiet when the time came. They lined him up against a wall just at sunrise and offered him a blindfold but he said he didn't need one. He just stared at us, calm as fuck, daring us to do it.'

'So it was all a show?'

'Often wondered about that Timbo, but I think it was the guns – he couldn't take the noise. I think it was actually hurting his head in some ways.'

'Where did you aim?' asked Fletcher.

'The heart. We weren't many paces away so it wasn't hard although some of the lads hands were shaking so much they had trouble with it.'

'But not you.'

Dawkins looked into his tea. 'It was a job to be done,' he said, his voice flat and emotionless. 'He was a deserter.'

The men fell silent at this until Dawkins, refilling his mug, continued.

'The thing I remember was the padre,' he said, 'his voice. There was something to it as he read a prayer and if ever I was to believe in him up there that was the moment. It was ethereal.'

'Ethereal? What the fuck's that?' said Timmings.

'Out of this world,' said Fletcher.

'That's right, Fletch. One of the officers used the word and I asked him later. Out of this world. That's what it was like. We stood there, this body slumped in front of us, dawn breaking and the words, all about forgiveness and being loved and all that, just sounded out in this vicar's voice.' Dawkins' stopped talking and the others waited. 'All tender like and compassionate,' he said and there was a catch in his voice. 'I'll never forget it, that's for sure.'

Fletcher put a hand on his shoulder. Dawkins' eyes were closed as he recalled the scene. 'After this the padre walked along the line and placed his hand on our shoulders, one after another. He said nothing but it was comforting enough.' Dawkins was speaking slowly and it seemed to the others he was struggling with each word. 'He had kind eyes, I remember. Made us all feel much better somehow.'

'Who was he?' asked Latham.

'Never met him before or since but someone said his name was Railton. David Railton. I won't forget him, that's for sure.'

Latham was set to ask another question but Dawkins stood up. 'Need a piss,' he said but the others noticed his eyes were wet as he left them.

'Fuck me,' said Timmings, 'never seen Dan like that before.'

'Leave him be for a moment,' said Fletcher but just then a soldier appeared at the entrance to the pillbox. 'Mr Latham, sir, the OC wants all officers to report to HQ.'

'Here we go,' said Latham.

'Attack, sir?' said Fletcher.

'Who knows. We'll find out soon enough.' He picked up his weapon and left the building.

A short while later Dawkins reappeared, fully composed as if the previous conversation hadn't taken place. 'What's up?' he asked.

'Mr Latham's been called to HQ.'

'We'll be attacking soon, then,' he said. 'Have you noticed he's fallen out with Barnes?'

'I have,' said Fletcher, 'my guess is it's about Timbo's field punishment.'

'Might be,' said Dawkins, 'might be about me.'

'How's that?'

'When you were having it cushy having all those nurses back in the field hospital Barnes as good as told the fucking red tops that I'd helped Jackson escape.'

'That would make sense.'

'What, that I'd help Jackson escape?'

'No, of course not. I mean it makes sense that Barnes would try to heap the blame on you. It takes the heat off him if there's a scapegoat and who better to take the rap than that troublesome bugger Dawkins.'

'That's true.'

'So what happened?'

'I overheard Mr Latham give Barnes a roasting. Accused him of being disloyal to the platoon.'

'Bloody hell.'

'Barnes was well pissed off.'

'That's not good, the Platoon Commander and platoon Sergeant falling out.'

'I've seen it before. One usually wins out in the end.'

'My money would be on Barnes,' said Fletcher, 'the nice guys tend to get stuffed by the bastards out here.'

'We'll keep an eye out for Mr Latham,' said Timmings.

'Keep an eye out for yourself, mate,' said Dawkins, 'that's all you can do out here.'

They were bombarded throughout the day but the pillbox was solidly built and even near misses failed to shake the foundations. They took it in turn keeping watch but the enemy, like them, was hunkered down, resting before the inevitable next push.

At midday some bread, cheese and stew arrived and, in a respite from the shelling, they risked taking the bench outside and sat in the sun behind the concrete bunker, hidden from view from the enemy, eating their lunch.

When he'd finished eating Dawkins reached into his pocket, pulled out the metal container he carried with him, opened it and looked at the picture of his fiancée.

Timmings looked over his shoulder. 'Ain't seen that for some time,' he said.

'Get it out now and again, Timbo. Nice thing to do.'

'I'd give her one,' said Timmings.

Dawkins laughed. 'Don't think that's going to happen, Timbo.'

'When'll you get married?'

'Next year perhaps.'

'And you love her?'

'I'm marrying her, you daft bastard.'

'How often do you write?'

'Not much of a writer, Timbo,' said Dawkins, 'anyways, send a letter every week and they worry when they don't get one. Every month or so, that does me. I sent her one after the last assault, I'll send her another one shortly.'

'Wish I had a girl.'

'Time for that Timbo. You'll have all the girls you could want when this is over.'

A while later Mr Latham approached them with his orderly beside him.

'Right,' he said, 'I have some orders, let's go inside.'

In the pillbox he told the men about an attack they were to make on some farm buildings that evening. 'Us, 6 and 7 Platoons,' he said, 'it's a strong point that's changed hands a few times and the staff want it back.' He described the land between them and the farm. 'It'll be heavy going,' he said, 'thick mud still, but not as bad as we've seen and at least it's not raining.'

'That makes it all hunky dorey then,' said Dawkins.

Latham ignored him. 'We'll spread out at 1750hrs and advance at 1755hrs behind a bombardment. Now here's the plan.' He outlined how the three platoons of B Company would approach the barns and the first to arrive would throw in mills bombs before entering the buildings which were mostly rubble and fallen timbers but still provided protection for riflemen and machine gunners. Once they had taken the objective A Company would follow up to reinforce the position. 'Everyone clear?' asked Latham. The men nodded. 'Good. I'll go and brief the others.'

After that there was a buzz of conversation as the soldiers discussed the plan until a corporal said 'Right. Enough chat, get to work.'

The talking stopped and the men started going about their business quietly and methodically, not looking at each other as each of them managed the tension in his own way. Some packed and repacked their kit as if orderliness would give them strength. Some read old magazines to take their minds elsewhere. A few wrote letters. Dawkins and Fletcher chatted, Timmings fell into a disturbed sleep.

'It's the anticipation that's the killer,' said Fletcher.

'Bullets, Fletch, they're the killer.'

At 1730hrs Sergeant Barnes appeared. 'Move out in twenty minutes,' he said, but all the men had been ready for some time.

'I think I'll have a last shit,' said Timmings.

'Good idea,' said Fletcher, 'it'll help you run faster.'

At 1748hrs they stood poised at the doorway and the bombardment began, shells landing just to the east of their position. Dawkins shook hands with Fletcher and Timmings.

'Move out,' said the corporal, and they stepped outside. The rest of the platoon was emerging from other bunkers and within a minute all thirty of them had made their way into the line of trenches that linked the pillboxes. Over to their left the men of 6 Platoon were forming up in a similar way, to the right, 7 Platoon.

They stood against the walls of the trench, not moving for over a minute, watching as the exploding shells in front of them started a gradual creep across the fields towards the enemy. They gripped their rifles, rearranged the packs on their backs. A few mouthed words of prayer.

'We need to be right behind that,' said Dawkins and it was as if Mr Latham had heard him because at that moment he blew his whistle, four minutes early, and 5 Platoon started advancing. 6 and 7 Platoons hesitated, their officers unsure whether to stick to agreed timings or use their initiative but Latham was waving them on and they too began to advance.

Ninety men set off at a walk, trusting that the barrage in front of them would hide their movements and keep the enemies' heads down. They advanced slowly, their feet sinking into the mud so that within only a few paces their boots were heavy and their legs aching. Beyond the explosions the barns, a few hundred yards away, could be seen intermittently. Timmings stumbled and with the weight of mills bombs to carry he had to be helped up by Dawkins and Fletcher who were on either side of him. Just behind them, in the centre of the platoon, Mr Latham was keeping an eye on the formation to make sure they advanced as one, now and then shouting for somone to keep up.

For a few minutes they made decent progress without any fire being returned but then a soldier shouted 'There!' and they all spotted the Germans running out of their bunkers and taking up positions in their trenches. Seconds later a hail of fire swept across the field and 5 Platoon was directly in its path.

Dawkins, in spite of the weight of his equipment, began running. He could hear his own breathing, coming in loud pants as each step he took through the mud required a supreme effort. He looked to his right and Fletcher was keeping pace with him. He looked to his left and there was no sign of Timmings. He kept on running but the bullets were whistling through the air and men were falling all around him.

'Dan,' Fletcher was shouting, 'Dan, get down.' He looked back and saw that only three or four men from the platoon were with him and at the same time he heard a machine gun open up and Fletcher was over to his right in a shell hole so he ran towards it and jumped in. The water was above waist height but he didn't notice the cold. Together they peered over the rim of the crater and not a single man of 5 Platoon was standing.

'Are they all gone?' shouted Dawkins.

'About half. Rest have gone to ground.'

'Fuck me.' Dawkins looked over to the left and he could see that 6 Platoon, less exposed to the enemy trenches than 5 Platoon, was making better progress and was nearing the farm buildings.

'We'd best wait here a minute,' he said.

'Timbo took one,' said Fletcher.

'We'll get him on the way back.'

The barrage had now reached the enemy trenches and there was a lull in the firing. When Dawkins next looked up 6 Platoon were at the barns and throwing in bombs at a tremendous rate.

'Let's go,' he said and scrambled out of the shell hole. Off to his right he could see Lietenant Latham and a few others doing the same and they all started advancing again as fast as they could and this time, what with the barrage and with the Germans distracted by the assault on their barn, the fire coming at them was less intense. Then it stopped altogether and they half ran, half walked the last hundred yards until they reached the enemy line where they jumped down with bayonets fixed. Not a single living soul was in sight, only a few dead bodies strewn across the bottom of the trench, victims of the barrage, barely visible above the stagnant water that now sloshed up to the British soldiers' knees.

'Where the fuck is Fritz?' said Fletcher.

'They'll have retreated.'

Dawkins walked along the trench until he found Lieutenant Latham who was looking dazed. Sergeant Barnes was beside him, gasping for breath, his hands on his knees, oblivious to the dead German soldier leaning against his left thigh.

'Looks like 6 Platoon have taken the farm,' said Dawkins.

Latham nodded.

'How many of us made it?' Dawkins asked Barnes.

'Give me a fucking minute,' wheezed Barnes. He sat down on a ledge, bent forwards and removed his helmet. Sweat was trickling down the side of his face, his hair was plastered across his skull.

Dawkins turned to Latham. 'I'll go and check,' he said. He made his way as fast as he could along the trench until he came to members of 7 Platoon then worked his way back, passing Sergeant Barnes whose eyes were closed, and Mr Latham who was trying to write a note to be taken back to Company HQ on a piece of paper that was rapidly disintegrating in his hands. When he had reached the last man in 5 Platoon he returned again to where Latham was now standing, looking about him.

'There's eleven of us made it, sir,' he said.

'Eleven?'

'Yes, sir.'

Latham was trying to make sense of what was happening.

'A Company should be with us shortly. We need to hold on until then.'

'Eleven?' said Latham again, 'out of twenty eight? Is that all that's left?'

'Yes.'

'My God.'

Dawkins peered over the top of the trench towards the enemy lines. 'Fritz will counter attack soon,' he said, 'we need to be ready.'

'Of course.' Latham shook his head. 'Sorry, I'm a little disoriented...'

'Happens to everyone sir. Now, we need to get the men facing forwards.'

'Yes.'

'I'll take the ones that way,' said Dawkins, pointing towards where Fletcher was already standing and aiming his weapon to the east, 'if you take the ones down there.'

Sergeant Barnes, totally exhausted, tried to raise his body. 'Catch your breath Sarn't' said Dawkins, 'we'll be here some time.'

Latham, recovering his equilibrium, headed off and Dawkins worked his way back towards Fletcher, speaking to each man in turn and telling them to take up position.

'We've lost more than half our men, Fletch,' he said.

'We must look for Timbo.'

'I'm off to do that now.'

Fletcher knew Dawkins too well to point out the dangers. 'Good man,' he said.

Dawkins left his kit and rifle with Fletcher, climbed out of the trench and started running back towards where he'd last seen Timmings. He passed the shell hole where he and Fletcher had sheltered and then scanned the ground ahead of him. At the point where they'd come under fire he came to a body every few yards and he checked each one. Finally he found Timmings who was lying on his back, held up above the ground by the kit underneath him.

'Timbo,' said Dawkins, 'it's me, Dan.'

Timmings groaned.

Dawkins checked his body but there was no obvious wound.

'Where were you hit, Timbo?'

Timmings just managed to point to his middle and then Dawkins saw the red of his blood mingled in with the mud that covered his entire uniform.

'I'm going to get help,' he said, 'you wait here.'

He started running towards the bunker they had set out from less than half an hour earlier, oblivious to the fact that in contrast to the recent ear-shattering sounds of the assault there was now only a disorientating quiet.

A company was forming up and preparing to move when he arrived and he found the CSM issuing orders. 'Sarn't Major,' he shouted, 'Sarn't Major Swift. We need stretcher bearers out there. There's men dying in that field.'

CSM Swift quickly appraised the situation. 'I'll send them right on behind us,' he said, 'we're just moving now.' He spoke to a soldier who ran off and then a whistle blew and the whole company of men started moving out of the trench. Dawkins walked with them, covering the same patch of ground for the second time that day. He spotted two men following behind with a stretcher so he joined them and led them to where Timmings was lying exactly as he had been left.

'We're back,' he said, but Timmings didn't reply.

'Timbo, we're back. You've got a blighty there mate.'

Timmings didn't move.

'Timbo, son,' said Dawkins and he dropped to his knees beside his young friend, taking his cold hands in his. 'Timbo, think of all those birds waiting for you back home.'

The two soldiers with the stretcher who were crouching beside him glanced at each other.

'Timbo. Timbo.' Dawkins was shaking Timmings.

'He's dead, mate,' said one of the stretcher bearers. 'Nowt we can do for him now.' He leant down and closed Timmings's eyes. Then the two men stood up and went off in search of other wounded soldiers.

Dawkins stared at Timmings' still face for a few seconds then he lay down beside him in the mud and looked up into the sky. He watched the sun pass behind a cloud and emerge again the other side. He watched a bird, one of the few remaining in the area, swoop up and down. He watched a biplane in the distance move along the horizon. An image of his mother came to him. He seldom thought about her these days but he could see her quite clearly, lying on her bed, defeated by illness, looking up at him one last time before letting out a final wheeze. He took Timmings' hand the way he had taken hers and held it tightly. 'I'm sorry, Timbo,' he whispered, 'I failed you lad.'

He closed his eyes and felt the mud seep through his clothes. The renewed sound of battle seemed distant and of another world. It would be good to lie here peacefully, he thought, to escape with Timmings to somewhere where there were no guns, no hails of bullets, no orders to attack – and it would be right. Right that he, of all the men at the front, should be the one to die.

His mind drifted for what seemed to him a long time but must have been only a few seconds before a burst of fire from off to his right bought him back to the present. The others would need him. And so, knowing once again that he must ward off the dark thoughts that had threatened his resolve for so many years he turned, craned his neck to see what was happening up ahead and, with a powerful effort of will, forced himself to stand up. He was alone in this stretch of land with only the dead around him. He took a deep breath, stepped forward, gritted his teeth and then, with leaden feet, taking no mind of any fire that might come his way, he started walking back towards what remained of 5 Platoon.

CHAPTER 24

November 1920

Peter Harding grew up in an austere upper middle class family where meals were taken in a large and draughty dining room in almost complete silence. Dinner would be announced by a gong and the Harding family, dressed in black tie, would sit formally round the long mahogany table night after night, barely communicating, enduring a painful evening ritual that had changed little in generations.

His father was a remote man who had inherited an estate that he could barely afford to run and who had little energy left to engage with his wife and child.

His mother was a cold and uncaring woman, married for her money, disappointed by life, never loved by her parents nor her husband and so unable to pass on love to her son. She seldom touched Peter from the day he was born, leaving any demonstration of maternal affection to the Irish nanny.

So it came as something of a relief to Peter when, at the age of seven, he was sent away to boarding school. Here his ability on the sports field gained him acceptance amongst his peers and, though he was never considered to be an amusing type, he was generally admired for his reliability, steadiness and sense of purpose. Having no apparent need for friendship gave him a certain confidence and he was respected for being his own person, doing his own thing, possessing what was referred to by his Masters as 'strength of character.'

In direct contrast to many of the other boys, he enjoyed term times and dreaded the holidays. For weeks on end in the summer he would be stuck in the family home in the country with only his parents, the servants and a collection of animals for company. There was little to do other than go for long walks, read books or attend dreary music evenings listening to local women singing sentimental arias with exaggerated passion.

Not having a sister and attending an all boys school meant he grew up knowing little about the opposite sex. The few girls he did meet at social occasions he found impossible to talk to as they had nothing in common with a boy whose interests extended little further than rugger, cricket and the adventure stories of G.A Henty.

On leaving school he went straight into the Army, another all-male environment, and so it was that by the age of twenty-two Peter Harding was a man who was awkward with women, did not enjoy holidays and knew virtually nothing about life outside formal, masculine establishments.

Yet in November 1920 as he served with his regiment in France he could think of little other than the day his leave would begin and he could return to England to see the young woman he had met in London two weeks earlier.

He didn't fully understand his feelings other than knowing that she had captivated him and he couldn't get her out of his mind. From the moment he had seen Joyce's photograph at the cemetery in Ypres something about the way she looked had taken hold of his senses as nothing had done before. Meeting her and listening to her talk about Daniel and Stanley and her life as a mother alone with her small child had only added to his enthralment.

He knew that her love was for a man who had been dead for three years but that seemed not to matter. She was alone and in need of someone to support her and he realised with a compelling certainty that he was the man to provide that support. He knew nothing of love but imagined he already loved her and that she might in turn come to love him.

The second half of November passed slowly but the 28th finally came and Peter boarded the train home with a keen sense of anticipation. He seldom travelled to his family house these days, preferring to stay in London at the club or in a flat loaned to him by a friend from the Regiment. On arrival in the capital he caught a bus to the flat in Pimlico and settled himself in for the evening. He had written to Joyce the previous week and arranged to meet her at Taplow station at eleven o'clock on the 29th. He would take her out for lunch and suggest she come with him to see a play in London the following day.

In the morning he woke early and arrived at Paddington in good time. On the train he tried to read a newspaper but, unusually for him, his mind kept wandering so he watched the stations go by; Iver, Langley, Slough, Burnham. He stood up and waited at the door for Taplow to appear in the distance and then the train was slowing and he took hold of the handle.

The train stopped in a cloud of smoke and he stepped down onto the platform. There were only four others alighting and he followed them to the exit and stepped out into the station concourse.

'Hello, Peter.'

Joyce was wearing a long coat but instead of her familiar boater she had on a woollen hat.

'Joyce,' he said, shaking her hand, 'It's very good to see you.'

He called a taxi and they drove to her house where her parents, Jack and Mary, greeted him warmly. Mary was holding a small boy in her arms who she handed to Joyce. Jack asked Peter about France and they talked about his journey back via Paris, Calais and Dover.

'This is very cosy,' he said, looking round him at the small living room. Heat was blasting out of a wood burning stove and a kettle started whistling as he was offered a biscuit and asked to sit down in one of the deep armchairs. The smiling parents, the warmth, the comfortable furniture –so very far removed from his memories of home.

'Joyce tells us you met her at the Abbey,' said her father.

'Yes, I was helping out. I was on duty at the service.'

'We didn't make it to town but the village stood in silence on the green.'

'It was an extraordinary day.'

'That it was.'

'Joyce lost her fiancée,' said Mary, 'he was 'Missing in Action'. So it meant a lot to her.'

'I know.'

'Here,' Mary went to the mantelpiece and took down a photograph.

'Mother, please,' said Joyce.

'Peter will be interested,' said Mary, 'won't you Peter.'

'Of course.'

She handed him the photograph. It was of a man in his early twenties, in uniform and staring determinedly at the camera.

'It was taken on his last leave,' said Mary, 'over three years ago now. We never knew he wouldn't be coming back. We thought he was invincible, you see. '

'Mother.'

Mary's eyes were filling with tears but Peter hardly noticed as he looked at the photograph. So this was Daniel Dawkins. As he examined the resolute features of the soldier he couldn't prevent the image of a graveyard near Ypres coming into his mind. Of pulling a decomposed body out of the earth, laying it on the ground, examining it for any means of identification, placing it in a bag and driving it to St Pol.

'Are you all right, son?' asked Jack.

Peter tore his gaze away from the photograph. 'Yes,' he said softly. 'Yes, fine, thank you. He was a good-looking man.'

Joyce placed her boy on the rug and took the photograph from Peter. 'Peter won't be wanting to go through all that again,' she said to her parents, 'he lost friends in the war also.' She put the photograph back on the mantelpiece. 'Let's have some coffee, Mum.'

After they had drunk their coffee Peter walked with Joyce down the hill to the Taplow House hotel, leaving the boy with her parents.

'It's very posh,' she said, 'I've lived round here all my life and never been inside.'

'Well let's see what the food's like.'

Joyce gasped at the prices but Peter insisted she eat what she wanted and she chose clam broth followed by duck. He ordered a bottle of Chablis and to go with their cheese he asked for two glasses of port. It was growing dark outside when they finally began the walk home.

'Are you very rich?' asked Joyce.

'Not at all.'

'I've never had a meal like that before.'

'I thought we might have another tomorrow in London.'

'In London? Heavens. I'll need to ask my parents if they'll look after Stanley.'

'There's a play on at the New Theatre with a young chap called Noel Coward. I thought you might like to see it.'

'A play?'

'Yes. A comedy.'

'You are rich!'

Peter laughed. 'Seriously, I'm not. It's just that I've got a bit of cash built up for leave.'

'Well, I'm glad. I wouldn't want you to be rich.'

'Don't worry, I never will be.'

'Tell me about your family.'

'That's not a very interesting topic.'

'Go on, I'd like to hear.'

'Well,' said Peter, 'they're not at all like yours.' He told her about the cold house in the country, of the long silences, of the time he was late for dinner because he had stopped to help someone who had fallen from their horse and how his father had been so furious he had not spoken to him for twenty-four hours. He told her of the day he came home at the end of the war to find his father was away on a business trip and his mother, after ten minutes of polite conversation, had withdrawn to her room, leaving him to eat alone the cold remnants of an earlier meal left out for him by the housekeeper.

He described growing up without brothers or sisters, boarding school and his passion for reading and sport. As he talked Joyce made sympathetic noises. 'What a heartless childhood,' she said, 'I can hardly imagine it.'

'One gets by,' he replied.

They passed her parents house and walked along the river all the way to Bray before turning back. As they passed the large houses that looked out over the Thames Joyce asked Peter if he lived in anything similar and, although his family home was larger than any of them, he laughed and said, 'nothing nearly so grand.'

Back at the house Jack and Mary welcomed the couple back in as if they had been away for weeks and Mary produced tea and cake which they ate cramped on the chairs in front of the stove. The boy, Stanley, was playing with a toy plane which he offered up to Peter who took it and formed swooping movements in the sky much to Stanley's amusement.

'Oh, he favours you,' said Mary, 'he's normally wary of strangers.'

'He's a lovely little fellow,' said Peter.

'He's got the looks of his father already,' said Mary, ' but he needs a man to play with.'

When Peter left that evening Mary kissed him on both cheeks and put her arms around him in a way his mother never had. Jack shook his hand firmly.

'And will we be seeing you again soon?' asked Mary.

'Mother,' said Joyce, 'Peter's a very busy man. He's an army officer. He can't be travelling out to Taplow all the time.'

'Actually, I was rather hoping Joyce might come with me to see a play in London tomorrow,' said Peter.

'Of course,' said Mary, 'that would be a grand idea. We can look after Stanley can't we Jack?'

'Of course we can,' said Jack, 'delighted to. It's not often Joyce gets to see a play in London. You don't want to miss that.'

'Are you sure?' said Joyce.

'Absolutely. I'd love to have the company.'

They agreed the details and Joyce offered to walk with Peter to the station. As they left through the front door Peter looked back and noticed Mary smiling at Jack.

'They're a delightful couple, your parents,' he said as they made their way down the hill.

'They took a shine to you.'

He didn't reply.

'I'm sorry Mum's so forward, she doesn't get to meet many men like you.'

'She was charming.'

They walked beside each other and when they approached the station Peter reached into his wallet. 'Here's some money for the train journey tomorrow,' he said.

'No, Peter, I don't need that. We can afford it.'

'I know you can, but I want tomorrow to be my treat. I want to give you a special day. Please, take it.'

'Very well.' Joyce took the money and placed it in her pocket. 'You're very kind. It's been lovely getting to know you better.'

'Tomorrow, then.' Peter reached out his hand and shook hers. 'I'll look forward to it greatly.'

The next day went well. The play was only mildly amusing but the experience of sitting in the stalls of a London theatre, drinking champagne in the interval and dining at the Criterion afterwards was a novel one for Joyce who spent most of the evening grinning at her good fortune. When she finally arrived home at past midnight her parents were up waiting for her. Mary insisted she run through every detail, wanting to know what all the women in the audience were wearing and what was on the menu at the restaurant, and when Joyce went upstairs to her bedroom at one in the morning Mary followed her up. Stanley was asleep in a large cot and Mary sat down on the bed.

'I'm so happy for you,' she whispered.

'Mother,' said Joyce, 'it was just one night out.'

'Has he asked to see you again?'

'Yes, but he's only back here for another week.'

'I could see the way he looked at you.'

'Mum! I hardly know him.'

'Do you love him?'

'Mum, I've only met him a few times.'

'Well I think he's special.'

Joyce was laying her clothes out on a chair. She shook her head. 'He's very nice. Very attentive. He seems to know a lot about everything.' She put on her nightdress. 'But he's not Dan.'

Mary frowned. 'You can't go on comparing any man you meet to Daniel. You did that with poor Patrick and also with that young farmer. You have to look forwards now. And also...'

'Also what?'

'Also he's a wealthy man, Joyce. A gentleman. He can look after you and Stanley.'

'That's enough, mum. Stop trying to marry me off.'

'I'm just saying.'

'I know what you're saying and I can look after myself thank you. Now, I need to get some sleep.'

Mary leant forwards and kissed her daughter.

'I'm just saying a nice officer like Peter won't come by that often and he's obviously in love with you.'

'Mum. Stop it. Off you go. I'll make my own decisions in my own time.'

'Very well, dear.' Mary stood up and looked down at Stanley, asleep on his back, a curl of hair falling over his face. 'Let's see what tomorrow brings, then.'

Peter met up with Joyce twice more over the next two weeks, on the second occasion taking her and Stanley along the river to Windsor in a boat he had borrowed for the morning. Later in the day, after an early supper with her parents, he walked with her to a pub in Maidenhead before catching his train back to London.

'So,' he said, 'I return to France tomorrow.'

'Yes.'

Peter reached forwards and took Joyce's hands. 'I've grown very fond of you, Joyce,' he said.

'And I of you. And thank you so much for all the treats.'

'I find I can't stop thinking about you.'

Joyce sensed what was coming and looked away.

'Joyce,' said Peter, 'I love you and want you to marry me.'

She closed her eyes. 'But we hardly know each other.'

'Yes we do. Yes we do. I feel I've known you all my life.'

'But Peter,' Joyce searched for something to say, 'there's Stanley.'

'I will love Stanley also. He will become my son and I'll give him the love I never received as a boy. I'll look after both of you.'

Joyce shook her head. 'It's all so fast ....' she said, 'I don't know what to say.'

'You don't have to say anything. Just think about it.'

Joyce took a deep breath and then looked Peter firmly in the eyes. 'But what if I don't love you?' she said.

Peter gripped her hands. 'You may learn to,' he replied.

'But what if I love someone else?' whispered Joyce, 'someone who is no longer with us?'

Peter kept holding on to her hands tightly. 'I know,' he said quietly, 'I know.' He slowly let go of her. 'And I will have to accept that and live with it.' He ran his hands over his face. 'And I will ask no more than that you trust me and like me for who I am and one day,' he stroked a tear from the side of her face, 'one day, with the passing of time, I hope you may find you come to love me as much as you love Daniel.'

Over the next few months whenever Peter had the opportunity he would return to England to visit Joyce. They would go for walks along the Thames, enjoy lunches in pubs, make trips up to London. One day he took her to the 'In and Out' where he introduced her to his friends and though she said later that she was awed by the surroundings and all the smart accents, she amused the assembled company with stories of mixing up orders when working in a shop and misplacing important documents as a secretary.

'You've found a live wire there,' said one of Peter's friends and his fellow officers laughed at how solid old Peter had somehow conspired to land such a cracker.

During this period the mention of marriage cropped up periodically and each time Joyce said she was 'thinking about it'. While Peter confided in no one as to his hopes and plans Joyce spoke frequently with her mother, verbalising her feelings about a man she was growing ever fonder of but admitting that that deep, unfathomable consciousness, that profound awareness that this was the man she was destined to live with for the rest of her life, still eluded her.

'I knew it from the very first day I met Dan,' she said.

'Dan is dead, dead for over three years now,' said her mother abruptly, increasingly frustrated by her daughter's reluctance to make a decision that would radically alter her life for the better.

After that Joyce avoided the topic with Mary but one day, late in the evening, it was Jack who finally helped her make up her mind. Mary was out and Joyce, for the first time, spoke to her father about her doubts and confusion.

'I don't know about what you felt for Dan but I'm thinking it was a rare thing,' he said. 'When we were courting I wasn't so sure about your mother. She was the one who wanted to marry. I didn't feel that spark you talk of, I just knew I wanted to be with her. That was enough in the end. Love, if that's what you want to call it, came over time. I'd be lost without her now.'

Joyce sat in silence, her father's words resonating in her mind. 'Thanks, Dad,' she said finally, resting her head on his shoulder, 'that's what I needed to hear.'

CHAPTER 25

August 1917

When Dawkins reached the German trench where he had last seen what was left of his platoon men from A Company were swarming in and Fletcher, Lieutenant Latham, Sergeant Barnes and the others appeared to have moved on. Nobody seemed to know what exactly was happening. Finally he found Sgt Major Swift who told him that the men of 7 Platoon were heading back down the line and 6 Platoon, who had taken the farm, were to be relieved shortly. CSM Swift then went off and Dawkins began checking to see if any of his men were still around.

'You, man, where's your rifle,' came a voice that he recognised.

He turned and Major Horrocks was standing a few yards away, apparently without a trace of mud on his uniform. 'Oh, it's you Dawkins,' he said. He signalled for Dawkins to come closer to him.

Daniel didn't move.

'Come here when I tell you to, Private Dawkins,' said Horrocks.

Dawkins walked up to him until his face was close to the Major's.

'I will say again, where is your rifle? Where is your equipment? It's forbidden for men to abandon their weapons.'

Dawkins, who was passed any sense of caution, took his time to reply.

'And where's yours, sir?'

'I beg your pardon?'

'Where's your weapon? Where's the mud on your uniform? Where were you when your company advanced?

'How dare you ....'

'I've just taken this trench while you watched from a cosy bunker. I 've seen over half my platoon wiped out. I've run half a fucking mile to try to rescue one of my best mates who died as I tried to help him. And you ask me where's my fucking rifle?'

Horrocks, unsettled by the closeness of Dawkins, stepped back.

'Now listen here, I will not have you speak to me in this manner...' he said but Dawkins had stepped forwards again and was even closer.

'No, sir. You won't. Because now I'm going to leave you and I'm going to find my rifle and my kit, and I'm going to find what's left of my platoon, and you're going to watch me go and you're not going to say anything because you and I both know what's really happened here.'

Major Horrocks, his face ashen, started to say something but at that moment CSM Swift appeared and, seeing the look in Dawkins' eyes as he spoke to his Company Commander, and knowing him of old, called out.

'Dawkins,' he shouted, 'Fletcher is along the trench waiting for you. Go along now.' He turned to Major Horrocks. 'Sir, We're consolidating here, Major Templeman is in that dugout over there wanting to speak to you about the withdrawal of your company. The CO is with him.'

Horrocks, looking shocked and temporarily lost for words, stared at Dawkins. 'We need to move fast, sir,' said the Sergeant Major.

'Very well,' Major Horrocks replied. He moved closer to Dawkins. 'I'll deal with you shortly,' he said.

'Fine by me, sir.'

The CSM stepped between the two men. 'Dawkins,' he said, 'do as I say. Go now.' Dawkins gave Major Horrocks one last look, said 'right away Sarn't Major,' and walked away.

He met up with Fletcher who had remained behind while the remnants of 5 Platoon had set off back to their original start point.

'Good of them to wait,' said Dawkins.

'Mr Latham wanted to but Horrocks insisted he set off immediately.'

'Did he now.'

'What about Timbo.'

Dawkins just shook his head in a way that any soldier of experience recognised immediately.

'Poor little bastard.'

Both men leant against the walls of the trench as if the strength in their legs were finally failing them. Fletcher offered Dawkins a cigarette which they smoked slowly, not talking.

'So that shit didn't do him any good,' said Fletcher finally but neither of them laughed.

'Maybe he's the lucky one,' said Dawkins.

Fletcher, who was familiar with Dawkins' nihilism, shook his head. 'Come on, let's go,' he said wearily.

As Dawkins put on his kit Murphy appeared at their sides.

'Hello, my furry friend,' said Dawkins, 'I'd forgotten about you.' He picked up the dog and cradled him in his arms. 'You've got more lives than a bloody cat, you have.'

When they were ready they set off, facing into the low evening sun, walking slowly with Murphy trotting along beside them, his belly grazing the mud. Every so often the dog stopped to sniff the rich mixture of smells of the battlefield and they had to encourage him on. When they reached the small incline where Timmings had fallen Dawkins stopped. The body was gone already, taken away by stretcher bearers to a mass grave along with all the others who had died that afternoon. Fletcher spotted a twig and jammed it into the mud to mark the spot. Murphy sat beside it and looked up at them with an expression that suggested he knew what had happened. The two men took off their helmets and they stood in silence for a few seconds.

'Best be getting back now,' said Fletcher.

Dawkins nodded and they turned west again, towards the bunker, towards the paths made of duckboards, towards the reserve trenches, Poperinghe, Paris and England. And at that moment it seemed to the two men, lone figures in a ruined landscape, that though their country could be reached in less than a day, their homeland was a lifetime away.

Back at the bunker Lt Latham was waiting for them and he helped them with their kit.

'Timmings?' he said.

'Didn't make it, sir.'

'Oh.' Latham, not yet a seasoned fighter, not yet numbed from sentiment like the older men under his command, closed his eyes and his body seemed to falter as he considered the news of yet another death.

'I'm sorry,' he said.

'We all are, sir.' Dawkins sat down on the ground. 'But it's done. He's gone.' He lit up another cigarette and watched the smoke curl up to the concrete roof. 'I could do with a brew, mind.'

'Let me do that.' Latham boiled some water while the men, a small enough number now to all fit in the one bunker, lay on the ground, a few of them falling asleep, others just staring into space. Sergeant Barnes seemed to be having trouble moving about.

'Take it easy Sergeant Barnes,' said Dawkins who, along with Fletcher and Mr Latham, was the only one who didn't seem shattered by the exertions of the afternoon. 'Reckon you're too old for this game.'

Barnes nodded. 'My knees are fucked,' he said. He was having trouble keeping his eyes open.

Fletcher and Dawkins exchanged glances. Latham handed out tea to those awake. An hour passed with little movement or conversation. Then, just as it seemed the whole front had settled down into an uneasy quiet, a lull after the day's exertions, there was a loud explosion. Dawkins stood up, opened the door and peered out into the dusk towards the distant German lines where A Company were consolidating the gains of the afternoon. There was another explosion, followed by another, then a whole series, a bombardment as heavy as their own had been earlier, and all the shells were falling on the captured trenches.

'Counter attack,' said Dawkins.

The others followed him outside and they watched as bomb after bomb fell on the farm that 4 Platoon had earlier captured and the trench where A Company were holed up. Then their own guns opened up behind them, targeting the German artillery, and more explosions could be heard in the distance but the barrage didn't lessen in intensity.

Latham had acquired a set of binoculars on their last spell in reserve and the men took it in turns to watch events unfold.

'Infantry are attacking,' said one of the soldiers. He handed the glasses to Latham. 'It's growing dark,' he said, 'I can't see much but you're right, I can see flashes of rifle fire.' The others stared across the fields, straining their eyes in an attempt to see the battle unfold. The bombardment had stopped. 'There's bombs being thrown,' said Latham. Pinpricks of light were just visible to the naked eye and in the occasional larger flash the shadows of running men could be seen.

Then it went quiet. The eleven soldiers of 5 Platoon, no longer able to see anything as night settled in, unsure of what was happening to the east, stood outside their bunker and waited.

'I've seen this before,' said Fletcher.

'What?' said Latham.

'Time and time again. We take a trench, they counter attack and take it back. They take a trench, we counter attack and take it back.'

'And they're taking it back now.'

'I believe so, sir.' Fletcher's face was just visible. 'I'll wager we'll see what's left of A Company returning shortly.'

He was right. Twenty minutes later the first of them arrived, staggering up to the bunker and collapsing to the ground. More drifted in over the following half hour, making it back under cover of darkness in ones and twos, any military formation long forgotten as they struggled back over the unforgiving terrain. Most appeared traumatised, many were wounded, some were crying out in pain.

Last in was CSM Swift. He looked about him at his men, some of whom were crowded in to the bunker with 5 Platoon, the remainder now in the trenches around them.

'Carnage,' he said.

Latham handed him his flask and the Sergeant Major took a swig.

'Finish it,' said Latham.

The CSM gulped heavily and handed the flask back. 'Corporal Jenkins,' he said to a soldier who was standing nearby, 'take two men and check on how many made it back.'

'Yes, Sarn't Major.' The Corporal left and the CSM began describing how shell after shell fell on them followed by waves of Germans who had swarmed into the trenches they'd left only hours earlier. 'By the time the bombing stopped we were already heavily depleted,' he said. 'It was impossible. The Major ordered the retreat just before he took one in the head.'

'Major Horrocks?' said Latham.

'No. Templeman. Horrocks left earlier.' He cast a glance in Dawkins direction. 'He said he needed to get back to his men.'

'So we're back where we started,' said Latham.

The CSM gave him a long look. 'In terms of ground gained, yes sir.'

Shortly after that the Corporal returned. 'Somewhere's around twenty-five got back, Sarn't Major.'

'Twenty-five.' The CSM seemed hardly able to say the number. 'Out of over a hundred.' He looked at Latham. 'Not back where we started at all, sir.'

'So where's Major Horrocks now?' asked Dawkins.

CSM Swift shrugged. 'Somewhere in these lines,' he said, 'I imagine you'll be hearing from him soon.'

* * * *

At 2100hrs orders came through for what remained of A Company to withdraw. More troops were coming up to relieve them shortly.

'That'll leave us alone to defend the area,' said Fletcher,

'You'll be all right, Fritz won't do anything more tonight,' said CSM Swift, 'he'll be as buggered as we are.' Wearily he picked up his equipment and prepared to move off. He saluted Latham. 'Good work earlier, sir, I'm sorry we weren't able to finish the job.'

Latham saluted back. 'We all did our best,' he replied.

The CSM, a grizzled veteran who had been observing young subalterns come and go these past few years, who had watched them arrive as little more than boys, full of enthusiasm and keen to make a mark, and had seen them die as men, cynical and resentful after facing the realities of warfare, paused before answering. He studied Latham's face.

'That's all we can do, sir,' he said, 'good luck to you.'

He left and his soldiers followed him out until only the men of 5 Platoon remained. Dawkins organised a guard rota and they settled down for the night. It was unusually quiet. After talking in low tones the few men still awake lay down on the ground and one by one they fell asleep.

Then, quite unexpectedly, at midnight the door opened and Major Horrocks appeared with three soldiers behind him. Latham was jerked awake from a dream by Horrocks shaking him on the shoulder.

'Latham,' he said, 'wake up.'

Latham came to and the others began to rise.

'I'll speak to you outside,' said Horrocks to Latham.

Once they were alone Major Horrocks ran through the situation. The farm had been taken back by the Germans after some intense fighting. Thirty men from B Company had been killed, more than that wounded. They were to be relieved in the morning by a battalion of the North Staffordshire Regiment.

'It has been a bad day,' said Horrocks, 'a very bad day. But we were so near. We were so close to a glorious success this afternoon.' He paused for effect. 'It would have been a feather in the Regiment's cap. We can't let that go to waste.'

Latham's face was motionless as he listened.

'So, Latham, I want you to take six men and have another go at those barns before dawn.'

Latham stood in stunned silence.

'Did you hear me?' said Horrocks, 'I want them taken back.'

'With six men?' said Latham, 'when a whole company failed to do it?'

'Yes, with six men. You will have the advantage of darkness. The Germans will be complacent after their victory and I imagine those barns will be lightly defended. They will be ripe for the plucking. With a small force you can sneak up and surprise them and kill them with bayonets. I'll be with the rest of what remains of the company coming up behind you.'

'Even under darkness it will be impossible.'

'I'll choose not to have heard that, Latham. This is a direct order.'

Latham questioned the tactics of what Horrocks was asking him to do but the Major, becoming agitated by the clarity of his subaltern's objections, became increasingly belligerent. 'You will attack,' he said finally, 'as I have ordered you to, and we will cease this conversation now.'

'I see,' said Latham.

Horrocks called for his men. '0200hrs it is then,' he said to Latham as they appeared from inside. He handed Latham a piece of paper with the instructions for the attack typed neatly on its front. 'I expect nothing but the best from 5 Platoon.'

Latham watched them go and marshalled his thoughts before going back inside and relaying the orders. When he had finished the men looked at each other incredulously.

'Suicide, sir,' said Fletcher, 'that's what that is.'

'Yes, but it's an order from my Company Commander,' said Latham.

'If you ask me,' said one soldier, 'I think we should forget it.'

'That's not an option,' said Latham.

The small band of men began discussing how they might best execute that order in a way that would ensure as many returned alive as possible. Dawkins barely contributed to the conversation, biding his time and listening to the plan unfold until they reached the moment when it came to choosing the six.

'You'll need me,' said Sergeant Barnes.

'No, Sergeant,' said Latham, 'not this time. We'll need to be quick on our feet.'

'I'll go,' said Dawkins, 'after all, it's me he wants out of the way.'

'What's that?' said Latham.

'He'd like to see the back of me.'

Latham stared at Dawkins in amazement. 'That's a shocking thing to say.'

'It's a fact, sir. He knows it, I know it. So be it.'

Latham was so taken aback he was temporarily rendered speechless and so

Barnes spoke up.

'Very well,' he said, 'Dawkins it is. Fletcher, you'll want to go, I imagine. Smith, Clarke, Summerfield, Wilson, you're the fittest, you can join them.'

The men left off the list objected but Barnes overruled them. He suggested the patrol take minimum kit so that they could move swiftly and then he started organising ammunition.

'Dawkins,' said Latham, 'a word.'

The two men stepped outside.

'That was a very serious accusation you just made,' said Latham.

'I'm sorry sir, I was out of order.'

'What made you say it?'

Dawkins relayed the conversation he had had with Horrocks in the German trench.

'Shit,' said Latham.

'It goes back a long way,' said Dawkins, 'When he was Platoon Commander. He couldn't take it that I knew more than he did and that I didn't mind telling him so.'

'Was there any specific incident?'

'One or two. One time he got stuck behind a wall when we needed to cross some ground. Couldn't move. I had to drag him out and force him into the open or we'd have have been stuck there when Fritz advanced.'

'Did anyone see that?'

'No. And I've kept it to myself. But you can see why he's got it in for me.'

Latham considered the implications of what had just been said.

'So are you saying he's prepared to see us all killed out of some sort of feud with you?'

Dawkins looked up to the stars. 'Wouldn't go that far, sir, but he's got grudges and there's times he doesn't think straight, that's for sure.'

'And we're on the receiving end of it all.'

'That's about it – and, as you said, it's an order. We both know that if you disobey you'll be the one that gets it. There's no choice.'

Latham looked out into the night, in the direction of the barns. 'We'll talk about this later,' he said.

'I rather doubt that sir.'

* * * *

The men fell into an uneasy sleep, those chosen for the patrol waking repeatedly to lie in the dark, alone with their imaginings, listening to the troubled breathing of their fellow soldiers. Some shouted out from where they lay, their bodies writhing as the awfulness of what they had witnessed came back to them in vivid nightmares that continued as they slipped in and out of consciousness.

At 0400hrs Latham and Fletcher were wide awake.

'Can't sleep sir?' said Fletcher.

'No, and you?'

'No.'

They started chatting quietly about Fletcher's family. He had been married four years and had two sons. They then talked about Timmings and Fletcher told Latham how Timbo had been in and out of trouble ever since he was a young lad and how he was set up for a life on the margins of society until the Army had given him some stability and purpose.

Dawkins was snoring beside them.

The door opened.

'Who's that?' said Latham.

The sentry appeared. 'It's Colonel Parker, sir,' he said, 'with another officer'.

Latham jumped up and saluted as the Commanding Officer stepped into the bunker. Behind him was a tall man who walked with a slight limp and whose right arm seemed to hang unnaturally by his side.

'At ease, Latham,' said Colonel Parker, 'this is General Deveraux.'

'I'm sorry to intrude,' said the General, 'we won't take much of your time.'

Dawkins had woken and was also standing. 'Hello Dawkins,' said the CO. 'How are things?'

'Cushy as ever sir.'

The Colonel smiled. 'We've just been with Major Horrocks,' he said, turning to Latham, 'I believe you have orders to attack Borry Farm shortly.'

'Yes, sir,' said Latham, 'in about an hour.'

'I see. May I see the instruction.'

Latham reached into his pocket, pulled out the piece of paper and handed it to the CO. Colonel Parker read it carefully and then placed it in his pocket. The General observed without speaking.

'Well, Latham,' he said, 'the situation has changed. There will be no attack.'

'No attack, sir?'

'No. We need to consolidate. Bring up our guns. General Deveraux has made it clear he wants no more advances until we are fully prepared.'

'I see, sir.'

The Colonel looked about him at the soldiers listening intently to his every word. 'I suggest you now take a well earned rest. The Staffordshires will be here in a few hours. I'm sorry if you've had a sleepless night unnecessarily.'

He looked at Dawkins. 'And are you behaving yourself, Dawkins?' he said.

'As best I know how, sir.'

'That's all we can ask for.'

The General stepped forwards and saluted with his left hand. 'Thank you, men,' he said, 'I wish you well.' He smiled, saluted again and left the bunker.

Latham, Dawkins and Fletcher stared at the door. Fletcher let out a long sigh.

'Well there's a fucking turn up,' said Dawkins.

All the others had woken up now and Latham explained what had just happened.

'I'm not dreaming this am I, sir?' said one of the soldiers.

Latham laughed. 'No. It's a fact. We're not to attack – the General has withdrawn the order.'

'Thank God there's some sense up there after all,' said Dawkins.

'We live to fight another day,' said Latham. Instinctively he went round and shook hands with each man in turn. The last he came to was Dawkins.

'We do, indeed, sir,' said Dawkins, 'and before we do that I'm off back home on some leave and when I return we'll visit Pop and this time, Mr Latham, sir, you'll get pissed with your men and that's an order from the troops.'

Latham sat down on the bench, the nervous energy that had been keeping him going for the past twelve hours finally evaporating.

'That I will look forward to,' he said. He leant back and closed his eyes and as his soldiers laughed and slapped each other on the back and talked about their extraordinary reprieve he fell, almost instantly, into a deep and dreamless sleep.

CHAPTER 26

October 2011

In James Marchant's flat Sarah Harding stood in the doorway to his study and watched as he examined her Grandfather's diaries. Marchant was bent forwards and every now and then he would hurriedly write something in his notebook.

'How are you getting on?' she asked as she entered the room and placed two coffees on his desk.

'Making progress' he replied. He pointed to an entry in Peter Harding's diaries.

30th November 1920. '*On leave. Went with Joyce to a play in the West end and dinner at the Criterion. Joyce returned to Berkshire. Stayed at In and Out again.*'

'First mention of her name?' said Sarah.

'Yes.'

They read on. Stanley was first mentioned on 8th December; '*Took Joyce and her small son Stanley for a trip along the river, ending up with lunch at the Thames Riviera. A most pleasant day.*'

'Lord, an expression of feeling,' said Marchant.

Sarah flicked on a few pages. 'Look at this,' she said and pointed to an entry. '*Introduced Joyce to friends at the In and Out. On good form.*'

'Does he mean he was on good form?'

'No. He'd have been referring to her. She was quite a raconteur. I can just imagine it, Joyce holding forth and Peter listening in the background.'

'Would he have been OK with that?'

'Oh, yes. Although ...' Sarah looked up from the diary, '... he must have been a little jealous of the attention she got. I remember Mum once saying that most of their friends were because of her.'

'Maybe he enjoyed it. Perhaps she bought things to the marriage he'd otherwise have missed.'

Sarah smiled. 'That's a fairly shrewd observation, James.'

He smiled back. 'Thank you. I'd like to think I have some psychological insight from time to time.'

They came to the end of the first book and started working their way through the second, reading about Hardings's various promotions and postings and the arrival of the Second World War where Peter and Stanley had both been involved in D-Day.

Marchant stretched and stood up.

'Right,' he said, 'so where does that leave us?'

'You tell me.'

He started pacing the room as he often did when thinking aloud. 'Well,' he said, 'it confirms he was on a digging party and it confirms he was at the service. He refers to seeing 'the girl in the photograph' and he talks about Joyce a while later.' He stopped at the window.

'Brilliant. What would we do without your great investigative mind at work.'

'Wait.' Marchant was pacing again. 'So do we assume the girl he saw in the Abbey, the girl in the photograph, was Joyce?'

'Of course. They appear within a week of each other.'

'Exactly. So here's the question. Where did he first see that photo?'

Sarah was standing beside him. 'Well, we know Joyce was Daniel Dawkins' fiancée.'

'Yes.'

'So we can hazard a guess it was his.'

'Yes. But they would never have met.'

'I know that, different Regiments, different times.'

'So how did Harding get to see it?' Marchant stopped his pacing. He put his hand on Sarah's forearm. 'Unless..,' he said, ' it was on the body he dug up on the seventh of November.'

Sarah put her hands to her mouth. 'Oh my God.' She ran one hand through her hair, waving the other in front of her. 'So it's Daniel's body Peter digs up and it has Joyce's photo on it.'

They stood facing each other. 'In which case,' said Marchant, 'it's just possible we have a direct connection. That's quite a thought.' He stared down at the diaries. 'And that photo is of real significance – if we can find it, it will link Peter Harding directly with Daniel Dawkins via Joyce.'

'Oh my Lord.' Sarah grasped Marchant's hands. 'Oh my Lord. I need a drink.'

She made her way into Marchant's small kitchen and found a bottle of Burgundy in the fridge. She poured out two glasses and returned to his study to find him writing more notes. 'It must have been a shock to him when he saw her in the Abbey,' she said.

'Of course. But my guess is he wouldn't have mentioned the photo to her. He'd been given very specific instructions that the body he had to dig up must be unrecognisable. I can't see him admitting to anyone that he'd pocketed a photo that might give away that body's identity.'

'And of all people not to her.'

'Why do you say that?'

'Well think about it from her angle. How would a girl feel if a stranger she's just met tells her the reason he's interested in her is because he's found her photo on the body of her dead lover that he's just dug up?'

'So he'd have kept it a secret from her.'

'I'd have thought so.'

'You think he could do that?'

Sarah held up one of the diaries. 'You've read these,' she said, 'he wasn't exactly a demonstrative, open type. I can imagine him keeping his cards very close to his chest.'

'OK. But whether he tells her or not, he holds onto the photo, meets her, falls in love with her and subsequently marries her. In which case, he's bound to find out at some stage that her previous lover was Daniel Dawkins and that that was the man he dug up. So he knows the identity of the Unknown Soldier and at some stage he tells his son Stanley who, as his life is ebbing away ninety odd years later, whispers 'Unknown Soldier' to his daughter. That's you by the way.'

'Bloody hell.'

Marchant was at the window again. 'But let's slow down a bit,' he said, 'I'm heaping one speculation upon another here.'

Sarah watched him as he moved each hand in turn as if physically balancing evidence.

'Let's sit down,' she said.

They sat down beside each other on his sofa.

Marchant started writing again. 'Right,' he said, 'firstly, we know he dug up more than one corpse because he contacted Charlie Matthews' mother. In fact, records suggest each party had to disinter a number before they found one that was unidentifiable.'

'Go on.'

In which case who's to say the photo came from the body that was delivered to St Pol?' Sarah waited for him to continue. 'Maybe he dug up Dawkins's corpse, found the photo and so put the body back in the ground before looking for another.'

'Why would he have kept the photo?'

'I don't know but it's just as likely, in fact more likely than that he kept something off the body that he then took away.'

Sarah sighed. 'You have a point there.'

'In fact,' continued Marchant, 'who is to say that the photo even came from one of the bodies he dug up? It might have come into his possession some other way, completely separate from the diggings.'

'But we know he could never have met Daniel.'

'True, but all I'm saying is there's no specific evidence that that photo was on the body he dug up and delivered to St Pol.'

'Although it's likely.'

'Yes. Likely.'

Sarah shook her head in frustration. 'You said firstly, what else?'

'Well, we're assuming it was Joyce in the photo. As we don't have that photo we don't have a direct link between it and her. It might just be a coincidence.'

'Oh, come off it. We know that within days of spotting 'the girl in the photo' Peter was writing about Joyce and her small son Stanley who just happened to be exactly the right age to have been fathered by Daniel. We know Daniel was Joyce's lover because we have the letter. Are you telling me this is just another one of your famous coincidences?

'I know, I know. It seems unlikely. But it's not proof. Not solid evidence.'

'OK. Anything else?'

'Well, even if the photo did come from the body he handed in at St Pol we know it was only one of four that were laid out in a row from which one was chosen by a man with his eyes closed long after the parties had gone. There's no way he could have known his was the one picked.'

'Perhaps he met that guy later and was told.'

'That would never have happened. It was a Brigadier sworn to secrecy and, as I said, even he didn't know which one he chose.' He pointed to the diaries. 'So, what I'm saying is that though these are of great interest they certainly aren't enough to make a watertight case. I couldn't go public with them yet, I'd be torn to shreds.'

'Oh, so you're thinking of going public? That's news.'

Marchant stopped moving and stared at the diaries as if willing them to reveal more secrets. 'Just a figure of speech,' he said.

Sarah patted him on the shoulder. 'Really? I said it would be hard to resist.'

Marchant pursed his lips and Sarah noticed the intensity of his expression as he studied the closely typed pages. She picked up the first diary again and started flicking through it. 'He could have been a bit more expressive,' she said, 'a bit of emotion, a bit of description, even a bit of humour. Who was he writing this stuff for?'

'Himself.' Marchant didn't look at her as he spoke and it almost seemed as if he were talking to himself. 'An ordered mind like his likes to record things in chronological order so that he can check on facts at a later date if necessary. It's a logical process, nothing to do with emotion.'

'Takes one to recognise one.'

He didn't reply.

Sarah went back into his kitchen and returned with the bottle of wine.

'James,' she said. 'James.' He looked up reluctantly. 'Time's moving on and I have something planned for this evening. We can always come back to this later.'

'What?'

'I thought I'd take you out dancing. A bit of exercise might do us both some good.'

Marchant sucked in his breath. 'I was worried you might have remembered that.'

'Come on, it was a deal. I watched the slowest film in history, it's your turn to practice a few spins.'

'But we're on to something here.'

'It's not going to go away.'

He closed the diaries as if it pained him to do so. 'Very well. I guess I can use the excuse of two left feet no longer. But us rational types aren't very good at that sort of thing.'

'That's not strictly true. It takes a logical mind to master the steps. People like me might be good at all the twirls and movement but it takes a certain type of analytical brain to remember all the sequences.'

'Then perhaps I'll be a natural. When do we need to be there?'

'8pm.'

He looked at is watch. 'Then we'd better stop drinking this wine and I'll make you a sandwich before you set off. Take the diaries with you. I'll pick you up at 7.45pm.'

* * * *

Marchant couldn't stop thinking about the diaries as he finished off his work that afternoon. There must be something else he hadn't yet discovered, something that would make his case watertight. He finished work at 5.25pm in order to give himself half an hour to get ready, twenty minutes to walk to his car and an hour and a half to drive to Sarah's house to be there for 7.45pm. Roadworks at a busy junction delayed him for ten minutes and, being a man who was never late for anything, he had to talk to himself sternly to remain calm.

He made up five minutes by speeding on a dual carriageway and arrived at 7.50pm.

Sarah opened the door in a dressing gown with her hair turbaned in a pink towel.

'Oh,' said Marchant, 'I was worried I was late.'

'No, it's me, sorry, I got engrossed in some work and didn't spot the time.'

She let him in and he paced her living room while she dried her hair. He looked at his watch repeatedly.

'Help yourself to a drink,' she shouted down, 'I won't be long.'

He didn't answer but sat down and distractedly read an article in a magazine about the refurbished interior of a country home, all straight lines, white walls, flat uncluttered surfaces which seemed to him a misjudged anachronism in an eighteenth-century house.

'How's it going?' he shouted up at 8.15pm.

'A couple of minutes.'

He walked up and down examining the paintings on Sarah's walls, reading the titles of the books on her shelves.

She appeared at 8.25pm in a bright red blouse, a tight pair of jeans and high heels.

'Right, let's go,' said Marchant.

'And?'

'And what?'

'How do I look?'

He admired her outfit. 'Very sexy if I might say so.'

'Good.' She in turn looked him up and down. 'And I think the suede brogues and thick corduroy trousers will wow them on the floor this evening.'

They arrived at 8.35pm and a lesson was already in full swing. Sarah stood opposite Marchant in a long line of women facing an equally long line of men.

'And finally to the fourth move,' said a smiling man with a broad Scottish accent into a microphone. He then explained a series of manoeuvres that they practiced a number of times, first unaccompanied, then with music. Marchant had no trouble understanding what to do and as Sarah moved around him, swaying her hips as she interlinked her arms with his, she cast him an admiring glance. 'You're a natural,' she said over her shoulder.

There was a pause while everyone caught their breath then the Scotsman was cracking a joke to a flurry of laughter. 'Right,' he said, 'let's be doing the whole thing then. Ladies, move four men to your left.'

Sarah smiled. 'See you shortly,' she said.

'What, you're leaving me?'

'Yes. But I'll be back soon.'

Marchant noticed a grim-faced women edging towards him. She had dyed blond hair, a very short dress, a pronounced cleaveage and a roll of fat that protruded from beneath her tight, frilly blouse. He estimated her to be in her mid-sixties.

She stopped directly in front of him and stood, unsmiling, waiting for the music to begin. 'We were late, I missed the first three moves,' he said hurriedly by way of an advance apology, but then the music started up and the voice in the speakers said 'from the top....'

The woman held out her sweaty hand which Marchant grasped and, glancing to his left and right to see what those on either side of him were up to he attempted a swivel but she remained steadfastly on the spot.

'Wrong way,' she hissed.

'Sorry.'

He stepped forward and backwards, his partner reluctantly doing the same. The music was running at a high tempo and there was no room for thought but Marchant, continually looking around him, did his best to follow the moves of those on either side and he progressed across the floor with his joyless partner in a series of jerky, uncoordinated steps. On the second move he stepped on her toe and she let out a loud yelp. On the third element, in his utter confusion, he turned too sharply, slipped, and fell over. He righted himself rapidly as she stood, hands on hips, glaring down at him. At last they reached the fourth move and he was managing to regain a modicum of respectability but then turned left instead of right at a crucial moment and his arm struck the woman across the side of her face. She stopped in her tracks, rubbed her cheek bone, then put her hands on her hips again. At that moment the music stopped and Marchant looked back at his disgruntled partner. Her face was a picture of resentment as she leant towards him and said, with venom, 'that was humiliating.'

'Well I'm very sorry.' Marchant replied.

'It's a bit late for that,' she said as she turned away from him.

'Yes, and fuck you too,' he said under his breath. He stood panting at his exertions and noticed he was sweating profusely. A sickly smell reached his nostrils and he remembered that the shirt he was wearing was one that had lain damp in the washing machine for too long; the sour stink of damp clothing was beginning to be reactivated. He stepped back a little.

'Ladies, four more men, find another addonis to woo you and glide you to paradise.'

Marchant groaned and contemplated running for it but already a tall woman, immaculately dressed and with an imperious manner was opposite him.

'How do you do, my name is Lavinia,' she said, offering a hand.

'James. I have to tell you I'm a complete novice.'

'Very well James, then we'll hold each other close,' said Lavinia, stepping towards him. She smelt of lavender and he wondered if her perfume was chosen to go with her name.

'Oh.' On approaching him she instinctively withdrew. Then, out of politeness, she closed in again but not before Marchant noticed a barely detectable wrinkling of her nose. The music began.

'Just follow me, James,' said Lavinia and she began the first element with a swivel that he had come to recognise. Then she stepped forwards and backwards which he also recognised.

'I think I might be getting it,' he said as he gradually took the lead, and they moved smoothly together through all four elements even though she seemed throughout to be arching her neck further back than was entirely necessary.

'You're better than you said, James,' said Lavinia once the music had finished and they were standing facing one another, 'perhaps we can meet up later.'

'Meet up? What, for a drink?'

Lavinia smiled. 'I meant for a dance but a drink might be nice also.' She shook his hand again. 'Perhaps after a shower. Goodbye for now.'

Two more compulsory swops of partners later he slunk off to the bar where Sarah found him, already half way through a pint of lager.

'How was that?' she asked.

'Possibly the most torrid fifteen minutes of my life.'

'Oh.' Sarah looked surprised, 'didn't you enjoy it?'

Marchant glared at her. 'What, dancing with four separate women to moves that I don't know, striking one across the cheek, stepping on her toes, and actually falling over at one point,' he shook his head in awe at what he had just experienced, 'and you think perhaps I might not have enjoyed it?'

'I'm sorry about that.'

'So am I.'

Sarah looked sheepish and put her arm over his shoulder. 'I am very sorry,' she said, 'me and my timings. I'll make it up to you later.' She flinched. 'What's that smell?'

Marchant looked around the hall at the couples who were now dancing again. 'That, Sarah,' he said, 'is the smell of naked fear.'

They stopped to buy fish and chips on the way home and by the time they were back at Sarah's house Marchant had calmed down and was trying to see the funny side of things. As they sat on tall stools at a bar in her kitchen, eating off chip paper and drinking coca cola he described his embarrassing few minutes with the alarming first woman and Sarah began giggling.

'Oh, I know her,' she said, 'mutton dressed as lamb. She's desperate to look good on the floor – that was bad luck getting her.' Marchant shook his head at the recollection. 'I really am terribly sorry,' Sarah said, leaning forwards to put her hand on his arm but she was struggling to contain her laughter. 'I get so absorbed in this stuff I can't imagine anyone not enjoying it.' She looked at her watch. 'Listen, it's past ten thirty, I think you'd better spend the night.'

'I've got things to do in the morning.'

'You can get up early.'

He looked at her. 'Well, it's a thought.'

Sarah smiled. 'Don't worry, I have a spare room,' she said.

'Well,' Marchant dipped a chip in some mayonnaise. 'Why not then.'

'I'll find you a spare tooth brush.'

Sarah left him finishing his food while she made up a bed.

'I think I might have arranged a date earlier,' he said when she returned.

'What?'

'Don't sound so astonished. My second dance, a woman called Lavinia – she said she might be up for a drink later.'

'You asked her for a drink?'

'I didn't mean to but that's how she took it.'

'Well, you are a dark horse.' Sarah put her hand on his arm. 'Although Lavinia is a notorious nymphomaniac.'

Marchant raised his eyebrows. 'Really?'

'Of course not, I've never met her before.'

'Well, that's disappointing.'

'Perhaps you should come next week, find Lavinia again, ask her out.'

Marchant sipped from his can. 'Sarah, I hate to disappoint you, but I will never set foot in that hall again.'

'Shame. You're such a natural mover.'

'Don't be ridiculous.' He stood up. 'Let's have another look at those diaries before we turn in.'

'Do you really want to do that now? At this time of night?'

'Yes. Why not?'

Sarah smiled enigmatically. 'Very well.'

They took their glasses into her living room, sat on her sofa and started re-examining the two books.

'There's something odd here that I can't quite pin down,' said Marchant, 'something we're missing.'

Sarah flicked through the pages. 'It's the lack of emotion that intrigues me.'

'I know. And to think men like Sassoon and Owen were writing such powerful stuff around the same time.'

Marchant looked again at the entry for the 7th November.

'Given a strange mission by the C.O to visit graveyards and dig up a body. All very secret. Held up en route with a damaged wheel and needed to execute the mission in a hurry. Delivered the body to St Pol just in time. Part of a bigger thing Significant moment and dramatic day.'

He stopped reading and paused. 'Hang on, repeat what you just said to me.'

'What, about the lack of emotion?'

'That's it.' He ran his finger over the page. 'Look at it again.'

Sarah read the lines out loud.

'What strikes you about that?'

'Part of a bigger thing?'

'No. The last sentence.'

'Significant moment and dramatic day.'

'That's it!'

'That's what?'

'Emotion. It's out of place. He hasn't used a phrase like that before. He's simply recorded events without any comment or reaction.'

'I see what you mean, an expression of feeling.'

'Well, almost. At least an observation which is something I don't think we've seen before.'

'Maybe that's because it was so unusual.'

'Maybe.' Merchant had his eyes close to the page. 'Hang on a sec. What's this?' He was forming a small aperture with his fingers to peer through. 'Have you got a magnifying glass?'

'Probably, yes.'

'Can you get it.'

Sarah left the room and came back a few moments later with a magnifying glass. Marchant leant forwards and examined the writing.

'Good Lord,' he said.

'What is it?'

'Look.'

He passed over the diary and the glass. 'Look at that last sentence,' he said.

Sarah studied the page. 'It's slightly different.'

'That's right. The typewriter ink is ever so slightly darker.'

'As if it's been added later ..... and look,' Sarah angled the book so that Marchant could see better, 'is that a full stop he's covered up with the bottom of the S?'

Marchant peered hard at the capital letter. 'Well spotted. Yes. He's very carefully placed the S to do that.' He sat back. 'Let's think this through. He writes the diary entry on the 7th in his normal factual style then, some time later, adds the words 'Significant moment and dramatic day. Why would he do that?'

'To add emphasis?'

'Possibly. Or maybe something more than that, maybe he's very subtly drawing attention to the entry.'

'What do you mean, some kind of signal?'

'I don't know. But it's certainly odd and, as he says, significant.'

'So he's marking this day in some way?'

'Possibly. And 'dramatic'. That's a strange word to use; he's never, in a year of fighting, used an adjective in that way.'

'Strange.'

'I wonder if there are any more entries like this.' Marchant started flicking through the pages and examining each one. Sarah looked over his shoulder.

'Here,' he said, 'look at this.' He pointed at an entry on 14th April 1926. '*Joyce amused by these new friends*.' 'Same thing, slightly different ink.'

'Intriguing.'

They came to the end of the first diary and Marchant reached for the second. Sarah looked at her watch. 'It's getting late, James,' she said, 'why don't you take these back with you in the morning and have another look. In the mean time it's time for bed.'

'Just give me a few more minutes.'

Sarah sat back and watched Marchant as he minutely examined each page. She yawned. He was entirely absorbed in his task.

'Well, I think I'll leave you to it,' she said eventually.

She stood up but he wasn't listening. She tapped him on the shoulder. 'The spare bedroom's at the top of the stairs on the right. Next to mine. I'll leave a towel on the bed.'

'Thanks.' Marchant looked up briefly. 'I think we might be on to something here.'

Sarah smiled, leant down and kissed him on the cheek.

'Great.' She stood behind him and rubbed his shoulders. 'I'll make things up to you another day then.' She let her hand rest on his arm but his attention was already back on the next page of the diary so she quietly slipped out of the room and up to her empty bedroom.

CHAPTER 27

September 1917

Three years before Peter Harding was introduced to Joyce's parents, Jack and Mary, Daniel Dawkins, back on leave again, had sat in their kitchen drinking tea and trying to keep conversation away from the front. To their many questions he answered briefly, giving few details, playing down the horror and giving the impression that the men were well looked after and the war would be won shortly.

'I think that's enough questions, Dad,' Joyce said, interrupting Jack's thirst for knowledge of the war.

'But I'm interested, love.'

'I know, but Dan's tired and he'll want to forget about all that for the moment.'

'Why don't you take Dan for a walk to the pub,' said Mary, 'I bet he hasn't been to one of those in a while.'

'We do now and then,' said Daniel, 'when in reserve. They call them estanimets over there.'

'But Mum's right,' said Joyce, 'some fresh air's what we need. We'll be back for dinner.'

It was a glorious autumnal evening and the low sun was in their eyes as they walked down the hill and crossed over the bridge into Maidenhead. Joyce linked her arm in Daniel's and they spoke little as they enjoyed the warmth on their faces. An old man passed them and he raised his hat to Daniel who nodded stiffly in return.

'Have you still got that dog with you?' asked Joyce.

'Murph? Oh yes, he'll be with us to the end I'd imagine.'

'That's so sweet.'

'He took it bad when Timbo died.'

'Timbo's dead?' Joyce stopped and stared at Daniel. 'You never said.'

'You never asked.'

'How, when?'

'Last month. We were trying to take some barns and he was hit right at the start.'

'Oh, my Lord.' Joyce seemed rooted to the spot. She had her hands to her face. 'Oh, I'm so sorry, Dan, he was one of your best mates.'

'That he was.'

Joyce moved closer to Dan and put her arm around him. 'I'm so sorry,' she said again but he removed her arm.

'Don't make a fuss of it,' he said, 'it's done, no use raking it up.'

'But he was so young, just a boy, it's so sad...'

'No,' said Daniel, 'Joyce, please don't.'

'Don't what?'

'Don't say it's sad, don't go over it. He's dead, I live. Let's get to the pub.'

Joyce stared at him, not able to think of anything to say until he took her arm again and started walking.

'Can't think about it,' he suddenly said, 'can't think about it or you'll fall apart.'

Joyce looked across at him and his face was set, his chin jutting forwards in what she imagined was a determined attempt to control himself, to remain strong, to keep unwanted emotions at bay. She had seen this look often before. As they walked together she thought back to when they had first met and she remembered when he had talked about his childhood and the father who had deserted his poverty stricken wife and son, the mother who died of tuberculosis, the uncle who beat him and who died in an accident, and his words made perfect sense to her. *'Can't think about it or you'll fall apart.'* He'd been doing that all his life.

They came to The Bear, an old coaching inn on the Bath Road and Daniel bought Joyce a cider and himself a pint of bitter.

'I need to tell you something, Dan,' said Joyce when they were sitting at a corner table, sipping at their drinks.

He put down his glass and looked across at her.

'I'm going to have a baby.'

Daniel didn't move. His eyes remained firmly on Joyce's, his hands on the table. He didn't speak.

'Say something Dan,' said Joyce, 'you're making me nervous.'

His face suddenly broke into a grin. 'That's grand,' he said. 'That's grand. How many months?'

'Four you idiot, that's when you were last back. It was Brighton I'll bet.'

'Let me feel.'

Joyce pulled open the long cardigan she was wearing and Dan noticed her small bump for the first time. He reached forward and placed both hands on it. 'Our child,' he said softly, 'now that's something.' He kept feeling the bump, moving his hands gently side to side.

'That's enough for now, Dan,' said Joyce, 'you can feel him later.'

'Him? It might be a her.'

'It might be but I have a feeling it'll be a boy. A little Dan.'

'A boy to remember me by.'

The words slipped out before he could stop them and Joyce sat back in alarm.

'Don't say that, Dan, you'll be the best of fathers, you'll be there for him, I know you will.'

'Of course, love.'

Daniel also sat back, picked up his glass and downed the rest of his pint in one large gulp. 'This is cause for a celebration,' he said, 'I'll have another of these.'

'Not for me, I think I should take it easy for his sake.'

'You do that.'

Daniel walked to the bar and the barmaid smiled at him.

'Another pint, please,' he said, 'I'm to be a father.'

'That's marvellous,' said the barmaid as she pulled the pint. She looked over at Joyce. 'You'll make a lovely family.'

Daniel turned and looked over at Joyce who was sitting smiling back at him and it was then that the enormity of the barmaid's words hit him. He steadied himself against the bar. He saw Joyce as if at a great distance, still smiling but through layers of sadness. He saw her alone with the child, pushing it in a pram, waking at night to deal with its crying, reading it to sleep in the absence of its father.

'Are you OK, love?' said the barmaid.

He didn't reply but without looking to either side of him he headed for the door and walked out into the street. He turned left towards the river but had no sense of where he was heading. Thoughts began to engulf him and he staggered as if drunk until he came to a bench where he lay down and stared into the sky. For a moment he was back beside Timbo, then at his mother's bedside, then he was in that canal pushing with all his might, watching his uncle's eyes wide with fear, hearing the thrashing of his feet, feeling the splashes of water as they rose repeatedly and crashed against his face until the body went still, the face disappeared to the bottom and Daniel, dripping wet, shaking from his effort, struggled up to the bank to comfort his cringing cousin and warn him to never speak of this to no one, ever.

He looked up to see Joyce staring down at him.

'Dan,' she said, 'my poor boy. What's all this?' She sat on the bench and cradled his head in her arms and for the first time in his life he cried unashamedly, his body wracked with convulsions as wave after wave of memories flooded his mind until he subsided into a deep sleep and Joyce held him like that until he finally awoke, looked about him and asked where they were.

Later, after Jack and Mary had gone to bed, Daniel stepped outside and lit up a cigarette. He looked over the tops of the trees and watched them swaying gently in the breeze. He listened to the quiet of the evening and enjoyed for a while the absence of shellfire. After two years of living in close proximity to others it was good to be alone, to be free to wander, to have time and space to think.

On a whim he headed up the hill and came to an imposing building set back some distance from the road. Taplow Court. As a teenager he had been bought up here one day with two other farm labourers to help move some hay for the landowner, a Mr William Grenfell. Afterwards they were given tea by Mrs Grenfell and had been joined by her younger son Julian. For some reason, although Julian was ten years older than Daniel and from a vastly different background they immediately felt easy together, seeming to recognise in each other something that separated them from the rest. Daniel had come to the house a few times after that to help in the gardens at busy periods and each time Julian had sought him out. One day, Julian suggested Daniel join him at dawn to shoot pigeons in the woods towards Cliveden and this had become a regular activity. They would creep through the undergrowth before separating to drive birds towards each other, working together with an instinctive understanding.

'You know what makes us so alike?' said Julian one day as they counted their birds, 'in spite of our many differences?'

'Tell me,' said Daniel.

'We're hunters. We're both natural hunters.'

Daniel had looked down at the dead birds lined up on the ground at their feet.

'More than that,' he said and he started stuffing the still warm bodies into his backpack. 'We're killers.' He laughed uneasily at the thought. 'Natural killers.'

Another pigeon suddenly appeared ahead of them, only briefly visible between the trees, and with one easy movement Daniel picked up his shotgun, aimed and fired, bringing the bird down fifty yards away. Julian watched his young friend and smiled.

'Perhaps you even more so than me,' he said.

Now Daniel strolled along the driveway towards the Tudor styled front of the house and when he reached the great front door he stopped and waited. A dog barked inside and a short while later a man with an imposing moustache and an aristocratic bearing appeared.

'What do you want?' asked the man.

Daniel stood facing him. 'Mr Grenfell, sir?'

'Yes.'

'It's Dan. Daniel Dawkins.'

The man came out and inspected him.

'Daniel?' he said, 'what on earth brings you up here at this time of night?'

'I'm back for a short leave,' he said, 'and I was wondering about Julian. I know he joined the Royal Dragoons but I've heard nothing since. I thought if he was home we might go to the Oak and Saw for a nightcap.'

'William, who is out there?' came a woman's voice from inside.

'It's Daniel,' said Mr Grenfell, 'do you remember? the lad from the village.'

Mrs Grenfell appeared in a dressing gown and nightcap. 'Daniel?' she said, 'of course I remember him. Who wouldn't remember Daniel.'

'He's asking about Julian.'

'Oh.'

William Henry Grenfell, Baron Desborough, put his arm around the shoulder of his wife Ettie and together they faced Daniel and he sensed from the way they stood what was coming.

'You'd better come inside, Daniel,' said Mr Grenfell. He led the way into a large room with high backed chairs. 'Can I offer you a whisky?'

'That would be good, sir.'

As William poured out two whiskies Ettie asked Daniel about where he was serving.

'Near Ypres,' he said, 'with the Berkshire Light Infantry.'

'Oh,' she turned to her husband, 'isn't that who Reginald's son is with?'

'Yes, dear.'

Ettie turned back to Daniel. 'Perhaps you'll know him, Daniel, his name is Michael Horrocks.'

'Major Horrocks. Yes, he's my Company Commander.'

'Oh, what a coincidence.'

'Well, I know most of the officers in the Regiment.'

'I suppose so. He was a troubled boy, I'm pleased to hear he's made it to Major.'

'Troubled?'

Mr Grenfell joined them and gave his wife a warning look not to be indiscreet but she took no notice. 'He was a sickly child,' she said, 'always in and out of bed, never able to join the others. I'm afraid Julian may have been a bit rough with him.'

'Bullied him?'

'I wouldn't go so far as to say he bullied him but I always thought Julian and the other boys were rather mean to him.'

'I see.'

'I hope he's turned out all right.'

'I'm sure he has dear,' said William, 'but we shouldn't be talking like this.' He handed Daniel his glass. 'Now Daniel.' He looked up at a portrait of his son on the wall. 'I'm afraid to say Julian's no longer with us. I'm surprised you hadn't heard.'

'I'm sorry to hear that, sir.'

'It's over two years ago now,' said William, 'he was standing talking to a bunch of officers when a shell landed nearby. A splinter hit his head.'

'I see.'

'And Billy died two months later,' said Ettie, 'both gone, just like that.'

Daniel watched her and noticed how she spoke matter of factly, as if describing the death of her pets and not her two sons, and he wondered what anguish was concealed behind her upper class manners.

'Julian was a good man,' said Daniel, 'he would have been a strong officer.'

'Oh, he was that,' said William and he went to a desk and returned holding a letter. 'Read that.'

A phrase had been underlined and Daniel read it out loud. 'I adore war. It is like a big picnic but without the objectivelessness of a picnic. I have never been more well or more happy.' He nodded. 'Sounds like Julian,' he said.

'Is that how it is?' asked Ettie.

Daniel considered her question before answering. 'I can see what he means,' he replied, 'he's talking about the comradeship, the excitement, living at extremes, but ...' he paused and Ettie leant forwards, 'but no, it's not a picnic. It's a living hell.'

He noticed Ettie flinch marginally at his words but he knew he was right to speak the truth. 'Perhaps he was lucky to die in that first year,' said Daniel, 'before the real horror began.'

'I don't think he was lucky at all.'

William was standing behind Ettie and he placed his hands on her shoulders. 'There's not been much luck around these parts recently,' he said.

'No sir, that's true.' Daniel swirled the ice in his whisky. 'Wrong place, wrong time I guess.' He took a long sip and felt the coolness in his throat.

'It's fate,' said Ettie, 'that's what I believe.'

Daniel looked her in the eyes and saw the desperate need she had to make sense of the tragedy that had so devastated her family. 'Perhaps it is Ma'am,' he said, 'perhaps there's some reason to it we don't understand.' He finished his whisky and stood up. 'But I must be off, my fiancée will be waiting up.'

William and Ettie stood also and as William led Daniel to the front door Ettie went off to another room. When she joined them again she had what looked like a small pamphlet in her hands.

'I'd like you to have this, Daniel,' she said as she handed the pamphlet to him. He looked down at it.

'What is it Mrs Grenfell?'

'Julian wrote poetry and some of it was published. It was a side of him not many people saw – I'd like you to have a copy.'

Daniel flicked through the slim volume. 'Thank you,' he said, 'that will mean a lot to me.'

Suddenly Ettie reached forwards and she embraced Daniel and pressed her face into his chest. 'Be safe, my boy,' she said as she clung to him.

He patted her back and looked at William who, in spite of his aristocratic demeanour and commanding presence, at that moment had the haunted look of a defeated man. Ettie still held Daniel with an unnatural strength. Slowly he prised himself away from her and William took her in his arms.

'I'll come and visit again when I'm next back,' said Daniel but, as he turned and walked down the driveway, he knew his words sounded hollow and empty.

Back at Joyce's house Daniel let himself in quietly. Joyce was waiting for him.

'Where did you get to?' she asked.

'Took a walk up to Taplow Court.'

Joyce had known for some time about the deaths of the two sons and the gloom that had since settled over the place. 'Did you see anyone?'

'Yes, the baron and his wife.'

'I see.' She noticed the pamphlet in his hands. 'What's that?'

'Some poems.'

'Julian's?'

'Yes.'

'He was quite famous for those.'

'Didn't know that.'

'Do you want to read them?'

'Later maybe.'

'Very well. I'll make us some coffee.'

Joyce went into the kitchen to boil some water, leaving Daniel to himself. When she returned he was sitting on the sofa with the poems unopened in front of him.

'What do you want to do tomorrow?' she said.

'Let's go for a bike ride.'

'That's a good idea.'

They sat in silence. 'You're not saying much, Dan,' said Joyce after a while.

'Not that much to say,' he replied, 'I think I'll turn in.'

The next day they rode their bikes to Windsor and on through the great park but Daniel seemed more distracted then ever and Joyce became wary of interrupting his thoughts. When they stopped at a pub Daniel perked up a little and they explored names for the baby but on the way home he rode ahead until they came to a grassy bank before Brunel's railway bridge where he stopped and waited for Joyce to catch up.

She sat down beside him and together they watched a barge head up river towards Boulter's lock.

'I was wondering if I should look up Pete Jackson's mum,' said Daniel.

'That's a nice idea. You're a good man, Daniel Dawkins.'

Daniel lay back and rested his head on his hands, staring into the sky as he had done the previous day. 'No I'm not.'

'Of course you are.' She also lay back so that they were side by side, watching clouds move slowly to the east above them. 'You always do good for people. I've never known you do anyone any harm.'

It was a while before Daniel replied. 'Then it's my turn to tell you something,' he said.

Joyce looked across at him, alarmed by the the tone of his voice.

'You know my uncle died when I was a lad?'

'Yes, you told me some time back.'

'I killed him.'

Joyce closed her eyes.

'I pushed him in the water and jumped in after him then I held him down until he stopped breathing.'

Joyce had her hands to her mouth. Daniel sat up and looked across the water, talking as if to himself. 'I killed the bugger and all these years I've lived with it, never telling anyone, not even you.' He was sitting very still. 'And the thing is, I didn't feel bad about it. No remorse, none of that sort of thing. I just killed and that was it.' He turned to her. 'That's not right is it?'

'But you were just a boy.' Joyce's voice was trembling. 'Just a boy, you were defending your cousin. You were doing a good thing. You're a good man, Dan, everyone knows that.'

'But now it's been happening again. I've been killing these last two years. Lord knows how many. Too many to count. I shot a man on a firing squad and I didn't blink. I killed four men last month when I needn't and I felt nothing. Nothing. It's as Julian Grenfell once said to me. I'm a killer and that's it.'

'No, Dan, no.' Joyce took his hands in hers.

He looked away again. 'You see I'm not a good man, Joyce. I'm bad. I've known that all along. I killed when I was thirteen, I've been killing these last two years. I've no right to be a Dad. I'll be killed myself and I'll rot in hell and it'll be a good thing.'

'No.' The word came out of Joyce's mouth with an edge that surprised him. 'No, Dan, that's not true. You're a good man. A strong man – everyone knows that. You've saved lives.' She was gripping him fiercely. 'You protect the weak, don't you see that? Look inside yourself, Dan. Your mum, your cousin, Timbo, Pete. You've been protecting others all your life. You've only killed because you've had to. It's war, Dan, it's war. That's what's bad.'

Daniel shook his head. 'No, love,' he said, his body heaving from the power of the revelations coming out of him. 'It's the end of the line. I've been waiting for it. It's been long overdue.'

Joyce took his face in her hands and forced him to look at her.

'No Daniel. No. I'll not have you talk like this.' Her voice had a steely edge to it he had never before heard. 'I'll not have you go soft on me, you of all men.

You're to be a father and a husband and it doesn't matter what you think, you have responsibilities. You'll see out this war and you'll come home and you'll come to see you're the best of men. You killed your uncle because he was a bad man and you were protecting his boy. You've killed Germans because they're the enemy. Anyone whose been through what you have would shut down their soft side, you're no different, so you stop feeling sorry for yourself. Be a man Daniel.' She was shaking with the power of her intent. 'If you think you've done bad things then you do good things to turn that round, you don't just give up.'

Then, as if the force of her resolve had run its course, she leant forwards and hugged him. 'There's always hope,' she said softly, 'and you'll be the best of dad's. Don't you ever forget that.'

Daniel faced her and sucked in air. He didn't reply but stood up and walked down to the water's edge. Joyce watched as he walked up and down, looking across to the houses on the other side of the Thames, his hands in his pockets, his collar up. Finally he returned to where she was standing, waiting for him.

'I'll tell you what, Joyce,' he said, 'you know me better than I know myself.' He smiled at the thought. 'But you're wrong about one thing and I've only just realised it.' He leant forward and kissed her. 'I'm not your rock, you're mine.' Then he picked up his bike and set off back towards the house leaving her watching his back, holding her belly, her mind a whirl of emotions as she wondered what the next few months would have in store for her and her unborn child.

When she returned a short while later he had one of the poems open in front of him. She picked it up and he watched her, not speaking.

'Can I have a look?' she said.

He nodded.

'*Into Battle*,' she read out loud.

He said nothing as she read each verse slowly to herself, then, when she had finished, he took the pamphlet from her.

'*The blackbird sings to him...*' he read to her,
'*Brother, brother, if this be the*
Last song you shall sing, sing
well, for you will not sing another, brother sing.'

Joyce made him repeat it. 'And what does that mean?' she asked when he had finished.

'I don't know love,' he replied as he took her in his arms, 'never really understood poems.'

'*If this be the last song you shall sing, sing well*,' she read again. 'Maybe it's as I said. Maybe there is time to turn things round.'

'Perhaps that's what it means,' said Daniel, 'perhaps you're right.' He put his arm around her shoulder. 'And I guess we'll find out before long.'

CHAPTER 28

October 2011

James Marchant rubbed his eyes and looked at his watch. 11.35pm. Two days had passed since he and Sarah had discovered Peter Harding's diaries and he had been examining them for four hours without a break. Pages of notes written in his precise handwriting were scattered across the floor of his study.

The phone rang. 'It's me.'

'I was going to phone you myself, I might be making some progress...'

'Dad's on his way out.'

Marchant, so absorbed in his work, took a second to register. 'On his way out?'

'Dying, James. They don't think he'll make it until morning.'

'Oh, I'm sorry.' He couldn't think of what else to say.

'He's had a stroke and he's in a coma.'

'Do you want me to come round?'

'No, no need. My brother's on his way.'

'Well,' Marchant struggled for words, 'my thoughts will be with you.'

After a brief conversation he put down the phone and then poured himself a glass of water.

He gathered up the pieces of paper and laid them out on his desk. All the phrases he had found from both diaries that showed evidence of having been added later he had written down. Peter Harding had done a good job of disguising his additions but the slight change in colour of the ink was just detectable.

Using a magnifying glass Marchant had spotted ninety-four changes in total and had written each of them down.

He looked at his sheets of paper. Mostly, the additions consisted of one short sentence added to the end of an entry for the day. On 17th July 1958 Peter and Joyce had gone sailing and after a typically brief summary of their trip the phrase *'delayed in the Doldrums for three hours'* had been added. On 5th May 1965, four years before his death and clearly not well Peter had visited his old club, the In and Out, to meet up with friends and had later added *'Food better than normal.'* On 4th September after the description of a function Peter and Joyce had attended the words '*A dreadful affair,*' had been inserted.

Marchant looked up and down each sheet to see if anything leaped out at him but he was tiring and decided to leave it to the next day. He had two meetings to attend in the morning both of which required some preparation so he would work on the diaries in the afternoon. He wondered if he should call Sarah back but decided against it.

The next day he hurried home after his meetings and on the way received a text. 'Dad died soon after 9 this morning.'

'I'm coming down,' he replied.

In his flat he picked up the diaries and his notes and stuffed them into a briefcase before setting off. On the train he took out the papers and looked through them. The sentences that had been added seemed random and made no sense in themselves; they provided extra detail to the events of the day and included some arch observations but there seemed no pattern to them. So why had they been added?

On a visit to London in 1926 Peter had inserted '*the city is busier then I have ever seen it.*'

After a trip to the theatre he wrote '*left with divided opinions.*'

Following a brief holiday in France in 1955 he had written '*quiet and beautiful but still brings back memories.*'

Marchant scanned up and down looking for any links or similarities but even though he felt certain there was a code or pattern of some sorts, it eluded him.

At Stanley's house he found Sarah and her brother Michael having a cup of tea.

'I'm so sorry,' he said.

'He was very old,' replied Michael, 'it must have been a thankful release at the end.'

They talked rather formally about arrangements before Michael said he had to go.

'Sarah tells me you've identified the writer of the letters to our grandmother,' he said to Marchant as he put on his jacket.

'Yes. A fellow called Daniel Dawkins.'

'So, he's our true grandfather.'

'It would seem so.'

Michael let out a long sigh as if expelling years of doubt and uncertainty. 'It's somehow rather comforting to have a name,' he said wistfully, 'what sort of man was he?'

'We're trying to find out. At the moment we don't know much more than that he was a soldier who died in 1917.'

'It's funny that Joyce never talked about him.'

'Perhaps she thought it was for the best.'

'Yes.' He reached out to shake hands with Marchant. 'That would make sense – she always wanted to do the best for everyone. And of course Dad only knew Peter.'

'Yes.'

Michael kissed Sarah on the cheek. 'Well, let us know anything you find out,' he said, 'and thanks so much for being here for Sarah.'

When he was gone Sarah came up to Marchant. 'I need a good hug,' she said.

He held her against him, her face in his shoulder.

'That's nice,' she said, 'Michael's not very tactile.'

'Have you eaten anything?'

'No.'

'You need to. Let's go out.'

They found a pub and talked about Stanley over their food, Sarah reminiscing about her father's hobbies, and holidays in Cornwall, and his wife, her mother, who had died at the age of seventy-five leaving him a widower for the last ten years of his life.

'He was a lovely man,' she said, 'very kind. Like Joyce, always wanting to help others – I think it got in the way of his career over the years.'

Marchant listened, asking the occasional question, letting Sarah go back through time until she was reminiscing about her grandfather, Peter.

'Tell me,' he said, 'was Peter someone who liked puzzles?'

'In what way?'

'Word games, playing with words and phrases, that sort of thing?'

'Possibly. I remember him playing scrabble if that's what you mean but, as we've discussed, he wasn't very imaginative – it was Granny who had the creative mind. But why do you ask?'

'Maybe for another time.'

'No. I'm fine. What is it?'

'Well, those added entries we found in the diaries, I think there might be some kind of riddle in there.'

'Riddle?' Sarah was fully back in the present. 'Tell me.'

'Are you sure ….?'

'Yes. What sort of riddle?'

Marchant leant forwards. 'Well,' he said, 'I've looked through both diaries and searched for alterations like the one we found on the 7th November 1920.' He told her how he had stayed up the previous evening copying down all the additions and how there were ninety-four in all and they seemed to make little sense but there was something, he was sure, that linked them together.

'Where are your notes now?'

'In the house, I bought them with me.'

'Let's have a look.'

'Are you sure you want to at this time?'

'Absolutely. I need something to focus on.'

Marchant paid up and they walked back to Stanley's house, her arm through his. 'Thanks for coming,' said Sarah as they approached the front door, 'it was sweet of you.'

'It wouldn't have said much for our relationship if I hadn't.'

'Our relationship.' Sarah savoured the word. 'I like that. Our relationship.' She took out her key and opened the door. 'And I still owe you something for that painful night of ceroc.'

'What sort of something?'

'Let's wait and see.'

In the living room he laid his papers out on the floor and they kneeled in front of them examining the phrases.

'They were fond of riddles in those days,' said Marchant, 'playing with letters and words, devising simple codes, that sort of thing.'

'Ssshh.'

Five minutes later Sarah let out a gasp.

'Got it,' she said.

'What?'

'Well, it's obvious.'

'Not to me.'

'You're not very clever really, are you?'

'It's something I've learned to live with.'

She smiled. 'Look for similarities.'

'That's what I've been doing.'

Sarah leant forwards and put a mark against three of the sentences. 'Right, look at these. What do you see?'

'*It was extremely dilapidated*,' Marchant read aloud, '*everyone agreed it was a dud.*' '*It was kept going by dependants.*'

'And?'

He stared at the words.

'Dependants. Dilapidated, Dud?' said Sarah.

'Oh my God.'

'Two D's in each word.'

'I can't believe I didn't spot it.'

'It's easy to miss. Sometimes it's the thing right in front of your nose that you don't see.'

'Right.' Marchant stood up and started pacing. 'Two Ds. Of course. Daniel Dawkins.'

He went to the back of the first diary and pulled out the note Stanley had written. He read out loud.

'Dad's Diaries.

They sum up a life that witnessed two world wars.

I served with him in WW2, we experienced D Day together, we both survived when many around us were killed.

These diaries provide a clue as to the extraordinary times he lived through and what he was asked to do for his country.

They are a record of a unique period of history and will have a decided significance for many years to come.

Stanley Harding.'

'Dad's diaries. D Day. Decided. It couldn't be clearer.'

He had his fingertips steepled as he spoke. 'Perhaps it was Stanley who made the additions, using his father's old typewriter.'

'That's a thought.' Sarah was flicking through the diaries again. 'And look,' she was pointing to the 7th November 1920. '..... *Delivered the body to St Pol just in time. Part of a bigger thing. Significant moment and dramatic day.*'

'Dramatic Day. Heavens, staring us in the face.' Marchant gathered the papers together. 'OK. We need to pull out every sentence with a word with two Ds in it. Have you got some scissors?'

Sarah found two pairs of scissors and they began cutting out strips. They ended up with thirty-two which they laid out on the carpet.

'I've had an idea,' said Marchant and he picked out '*Delayed in the doldrums*,' and put it at the top. Below it he placed '*A dreadful affair*.' Below that he put '*Needed to dredge the river*.'

'I see what you're up to,' said Sarah and she started handing him strips until the first letter of each line read out a name: 'Daniel Dawkins'.

They knelt over the bits of paper.

'I'm shaking,' said Sarah.

'So am I.'

For a few seconds they didn't move nor speak. 'Go on, ' whispered Sarah and her voice was trembling. Underneath the line that read '*Simply too dowdy for words*,' Marchant placed '*Under the dado rail was what appeared to be a painting by Turner*,' followed by '*Not a dependable type*.'

Marchant was moving his hands swiftly now and in less than a minute he had the words 'Unknown Soldier' laid out in front of him.

Sarah grasped the arm of a chair to support herself. There were five strips of paper left. 'My turn,' she said. She moved the last two words so that there was a gap between them and the first two. Then she placed '*I suspect interest will dwindle rapidly*,' followed by '*she discarded the rest*.'

They sat back temporarily. 'I can hardly do it,' said Sarah, 'over to you.'

Marchant picked up the last three strips and placed them in order. '*There was discord afterwards*.' '*He was a bit of a dandy*.' '*Everyone agreed it was a dud*.'

'Oh, my Lord,' she said

All the pieces were in place.

'Daniel Dawkins is the Unknown Soldier,' said Sarah. She looked at Marchant who was kneeling with his hands on the ground, staring at their handywork, shaking his head in disbelief. She put an arm over his shoulder.

'Extraordinary,' he said, 'truly extraordinary.' He couldn't take his eyes off the words laid out on the carpet. 'If it was Stanley who did this he went to great efforts. I'm guessing Peter must have told him the whole story at some stage and warned him never to reveal the secret – but he couldn't resist recording it somewhere for someone to find one day.'

'And that's what he was hinting to me when he said 'Unknown Soldier'.

'Yes.' Marchant looked at her and his eyes were as intense as she'd ever seen them. 'As a code it's pretty crude but it's served its purpose. And here we are now, nearly a hundred years on, staring at the truth.'

Sarah gave him a hug. 'This is quite something.'

Marchant stayed in her embrace for a few seconds then stepped back and started pacing the room again. 'This could be it. This could be the final piece we need – it links everything we've discovered together.' He was imagining the intense interest amongst his peer group this discovery would cause. 'Then again,' he said, stopping to face her, 'that's what they thought about Hitler's diaries.'

'And?'

'They were fake.'

'Oh.'

'It ruined more than one man's reputation.'

'Heavens.'

'So, as I've said before, if your evidence isn't rock solid, if there's the slightest doubt, if there's something you've missed or interpreted incorrectly than they'll be down on you like a pack of hyenas.'

'Who is they?'

'Historians. Journalists. You can be torn apart.' His face betrayed the conflict raging inside him.

'But these aren't fake.'

'No. That's right.' Marchant's eyes were glistening, his whole body tense. 'So maybe it's time for bravery. Time to stand up and take the biggest risk of my life.'

Sarah stared at the picture above her father's mantlepice. It was of a galleon in a storm, the sea breaking over it's bows and the helmsman struggling to steer a course. She looked at Marchant who seemed transformed from the stiff, reserved man she had first met into a force of nature straining at the leash. 'My God,' she said, 'to think this all began with me innocently finding some letters in a file.' She reached out to take his hand. 'What in God's name have I set in motion here?'

CHAPTER 29

September 1921

The marriage of Peter Harding and Joyce Sheppard was a small affair held in the Taplow village church with a reception at the Taplow House Hotel paid for by Peter. His parents sat stiffly in their pew, his mother in a dark maroon dress and peacock feather hat, his father in morning suit and polished brogues, while Joyce's parents laughed and joked with their friends on the other side of the aisle, all dressed in ill fitting suits and plain dresses.

At the reception Joyce worked her way round the room, introducing cousins to cousins, adults to adults, children to children. She ensured Peter's mother was comfortable on an upright armchair and bought members of her family to meet her, cajoling them to approach the stern, unsmiling woman who was casting disapproving looks at the noisy children chasing each other through the legs of the expensive furniture.

Peter was less comfortable mingling, preferring to keep an eye on his father and playing with the young Stanley, helping him to build a tower out of napkins and paper cups and holding him proudly when he tired.

'Peter, this is my friend Barbara,' said Joyce at one point, 'we met by the Thames three years ago.'

'Yes, you've mentioned her,' said Peter, 'I was so sorry to hear about your husband.'

'Thank you. Joyce was terribly kind at the time.'

'I gather you never did discover how he died.'

'No, one of the 'Unknowns'. Like so many others.'

'A very sad business all round.'

'Barbara and I often walk along the river when you're away,' said Joyce, changing the subject, 'she's got a dog called Monty who loves to chase rabbits.'

'Remember when we first met,' said Barbara, who was on her third glass of champagne, 'and D ..' she suddenly stopped herself.

'Yes, Dan talked about his dog Murphy,' said Joyce. 'I remember. It's OK, Barbara, Peter and I have no secrets.'

'No, of course not.'

Peter smiled benignly at Joyce. 'I know about Daniel,' he said, 'though not his dog.'

Joyce explained how Murphy lived with the soldiers of 5 Platoon and at that moment Peter's friend Stephen Cole appeared with another bottle of champagne in his hand and was soon in deep conversation with Barbara.

Stanley grabbed his mother's leg and Peter looked at his father who appeared to be falling asleep.

'I'm right, aren't I?' said Joyce, 'we have no secrets?'

'You should know me well enough by now,' said Peter, 'I'm a pretty straight-forward sort of fellow.'

'Yes I do.' Joyce put her arm around him and they kissed. 'I'm a very lucky woman,' she said, 'to have found such a dependable type.'

Peter made a short but sincere speech and his family left soon after, missing the impromptu singing and dancing which, Peter noted later, was probably a good thing.

With the party still going, Peter and Joyce slipped away quietly and made their way up to their bedroom. Peter undressed carefully, hanging up his suit in a wardrobe, placing his cufflinks in a small leather box and folding his shirt, socks and underwear over the back of a chair. He then lay in bed and waited for Joyce. Out of deference to his awkwardness she undressed behind a screen before slipping in beside him.

'You may now kiss the bride,' she said and giggled.

Peter leant over her and kissed her on the forehead.

'I think we can do better than that,' she said as she pulled him down towards her.

When, not long afterwards, she lay beside Peter as he snored gently Joyce forbade herself any comparisons between the exhilarating nights she had spent with Daniel and the awkward, rather formal performance she had just experienced with her husband. When Peter told her later that he had never before been to bed with a woman she reasoned to herself that with patience and encouragement he would learn over time to relax and become more imaginative.

They honeymooned in Venice and as they approached St Mark's Square over the water Joyce sighed at the beauty of the city. She didn't mention that Dan had often promised they would go there one day for a holiday. They stayed in a hotel overlooking the Grand Canal, visited the Doges palace, ate in small restaurants in magnificent squares and when they sat side by side in a gondola gliding silently through the narrow canals she watched other couples pass and dared hope that romance with Peter would grow in time.

Over the following years he proved to be the most thoughtful of husbands. He was devoted to Joyce and ensured she never went without. They moved into a house in Wimbledon where he cared for Stanley in a way he himself had never been cared for, teaching him how to play rugby and cricket, taking him on expeditions, relishing a family life that had eluded him in his youth.

And, in a way, Joyce's father had been right. She grew to realise how happy she was with Peter, how hard it was to imagine being without him, how he had become an integral part of her life.

And yet not a day passed when she didn't think of Daniel. Each time she looked into Stanley's eyes she would see his real father looking back at her. Sometimes, after making love with Peter, an act that always followed a predictable pattern, she would break her private rule and think back to the times when she would lie in Daniel's arms, slipping into a dreamlike state of brimming satisfaction. With Peter she silently welcomed the fact that the intervals between their love making grew greater as each year passed.

There was plenty of money for holidays but Peter seemed happy to return each year to the same hotel in Wales where they would go for long walks in the mountains and sit quietly in the evenings reading books and listening to the radio. Joyce, who liked meeting people and exploring foreign cities soon became restless with the boring predictability of her husband's routines and pushed for him to become a little more adventurous.

In 1933 he reluctantly agreed to go with her to Athens for a few days where they stayed in a hotel with rooftop views to the Parthenon and visited the National Archaological Museum in the afternoon before dining in a narrow street close to Monastraki. On the next table was an English couple of similar age to themselves and it wasn't long before Joyce was chatting to them about their itinerary.

As a third bottle of local wine was delivered in a metal flask, conversation moved on to the past and the woman turned to Peter and asked him how he'd met Joyce.

'I was marshalling a long line of people queuing to see the tomb of the Unknown Warrior and spotted her,' he said.

'At the Abbey?'

'Yes.'

'On the day itself?'

'Yes.'

'And what, she caught your attention somehow?'

'Yes, you could say that. And then I bumped into her shortly after at Victoria station and we recognised each other.'

The woman turned to Joyce. 'Why were you in the Abbey?' she asked, 'did you lose someone in the war?'

'Yes,' said Joyce, 'my fiancée. He went missing in 1917.'

'Oh.' The woman was temporarily lost for words.

'You were in the Army then?' said her husband to Peter.

'Yes, I was a gunner.'

The couple seemed unsure how to proceed from here and for once in such a situation Joyce didn't intervene to keep the conversation moving on. She watched Peter to see what he would say next.

Realising all eyes were on him he fiddled awkwardly with his napkin. 'You see I was on duty that day at the service,' he continued, 'and I only went back later to help out when I saw the crowds.' He was speaking even more slowly than normal. 'Then it was a great stroke of luck bumping into Joyce on the station like that.' He looked at the woman who was smiling at him. 'If I believed in fate I'd say that's what it was.'

'And here you are, almost twenty years on,' she said reassuringly, 'so fate played a good hand that day.'

'It certainly did for me,' said Peter. He looked across at Joyce who was fixing him with her gaze. 'And hopefully for Joyce too.'

The couple waited for her to speak. 'Of course,' she said, 'but I sometimes think it was more than just fate.' Her eyes remained focused on Peter.

'In what way?' asked the woman.

'It was almost as if Peter recognised me that day.'

The sound of a bazooki playing drifted down the street. A stray cat hopped onto an empty seat and was shooed away.

'It almost felt as if I did,' replied Peter, 'in some odd way.'

In the silence that followed a waiter arrived to remove their plates and ask if they wanted coffee. 'I sometimes have that feeling with people,' said the woman, speaking swiftly as if to hurry them on from the strange mood that had settled over the table, 'maybe you met in a previous life, or in a dream. There's lots of interesting things being said about such matters these days.'

'I'm not convinced by any of that,' said her husband and started to explain his doubts about the subconscious and its impact on behaviour.

As he talked Peter appeared distracted, avoiding eye contact with Joyce, watching the people jostling along the street, studying the menu. She sat still, saying nothing, looking at him now and then as if to challenge him to return her gaze.

And then the moment was passed as the couple entered into a heated discussion about Freud and Jung, the waiter bought the coffee, Peter and Joyce joined in the conversation, the bill was delivered, the two couples shook hands, they said what a pleasure it had been and went their separate ways.

On their way back to the hotel Joyce linked arms with Peter but though they walked through the streets of Athens together they spoke little. They barely noticed the ancient ruins, the restaurants closing down for the night, the musicians packing up to go home. Their minds were elsewhere, reflecting on the words that had been said and not said, on the looks that had been cast and the looks avoided, on the secrets and suspicions that had finally been hinted at but now hung in the air unspoken.

Back in their bedroom they undressed and Peter read in bed as Joyce lay on her side, looking out of a gap in the curtains at the night sky. She felt a sense of liberation that what had been preying on her mind all these years had finally emerged and though she'd said nothing specific Peter's discomfort had been telling. She had seen his uncertainty, his weakness, and in those moments in the restaurant she had felt a subtle shift in their marriage. She turned and looked at her husband and he smiled at her but carried on reading.

'Thank you for a lovely day Darling,' she said but even as she spoke she was thinking of the day when she had sat with Daniel by the Thames and told him to fight his demons. '*You are my rock*,' he had said to her that night and she now fully understood, for the first time, what he meant. She lay on her bed watching the stars above the Acropolis, listening to the traffic in the street below and re-evaluating her life. Daniel had been right. In spite of appearances, even without realising it, it was she who had been been the solid foundation of their union. It was her strength that had held them together. And now, once again, beneath the conventions and unwritten understandings of her times, underpinning the habits that had formed over years, it was she who held the balance of power in her marriage.

* * * *

When he was sure Joyce was asleep Peter closed his book and turned out the light. He lay on his back and thought through the evening. Ever since he had met Joyce he had said nothing to anyone about the real reason behind their meeting and month after month, year after year, the secret he had carried with him since that day in Ypres smouldered deep inside him. It flared up once in a while, burning ceaselessly, never dying out, never allowing him to be fully at peace.

'It was almost as if Peter recognised me that day.' The words had been spoken quite casually but their significance had struck deep into him. What did it mean? He recalled the day they'd married and she'd checked with him that they had no secrets from each other. Had she had suspicions all along? He dreaded the day when she might confront him fully about it.

He was still preoccupied with such worries when they returned to England but a few days later an idea came to him. He would go to visit David Railton. Since the time they had met briefly after the burial of the Unknown Soldier he had often thought of the padre, recalling his kind eyes and calm voice, and he began to imagine that if he were to talk to him and tell him about the photograph, of meeting Joyce and marrying her, of his conversation with the Reverend Kendall, of his certainty that it was Private Daniel Dawkins in that coffin, then this would be a great release. He had a burning need to talk to someone and by admitting to what had happened to the very instigator of the burial he might clear his conscience and unload a terrible weight off his mind.

Over time the idea grew until one day he decided he must act. He discovered that Railton was now vicar of a small village called Shalford in Surrey. Telling Joyce he had business in town he travelled to Guildford by train and then on to the village. On arrival he enquired where he could find St Mary the Virgin parish church and decided to follow a route that would take him via the river. As he walked he rehearsed once more what he would say to the vicar.

A wind had picked up so he turned up the collar of his coat and pulled his hat more firmly on to his head. For a few moments he watched the point where two bodies of water met then started walking in the direction of the church – but he had gone no more than a few paces when he saw, further along the river bank, a figure in a coat and hat similar to his just standing in the open. He approached and realised it was the very man he had come to speak to.

When he was a few paces away the man turned and looked at him.

'Good morning,' said David Railton.

'Good morning, sir.'

Railton stepped towards him. 'I know you, don't I?' he said.

'Yes, sir. Peter Harding. I met you very briefly in Westminster Abbey in 1920.'

'I remember.' Railton reached out and they shook hands. 'What brings you to Shalford, Peter?'

All of a sudden, faced with this defining moment, Peter doubted the wisdom of his visit. 'Oh, just visiting a friend. Only here for a short while,' he said, 'I'm just catching some air before returning to town.'

'Can I buy you a drink?'

Peter hesitated.

'Come on,' said Railton, 'there's a good place just up the road.'

'Very well. Thank you sir, I think I just have time.'

'Do call me David, please. I'm just an ordinary old vicar these days.'

Railton's car was parked nearby and he drove Peter to a nearby pub.

'They serve a very good pint here,' he said, 'now, tell me what you've been up to these past years.'

Peter described how he was still in the Army and ran through the various jobs he had done that had led up to his current posting as a staff officer at the War Office.

'So, you're what, a Major now?'

'Yes.'

'And married?'

'Yes. With one son. Although his real father died in the war.'

Railton drank his beer slowly. 'I don't believe any family wasn't affected in some way. How did he die?'

'No one knows. He was one of the 'Unknowns.''

'I see.'

'In fact ....'

Railton looked up at Peter. 'Yes?'

'In fact it could be him we buried in the Abbey.'

Railton leant forwards and touched Peter on his forearm. 'It could be indeed,' he said, 'that is surely the beauty of what we achieved.'

Peter was sitting very still and didn't reply. Railton observed him closely. A girl came up and asked if they wanted more to drink and both declined. 'You were on one of the digging parties if I recall,' said Railton. Peter fiddled with a beer mat, passing it between his fingers. He looked into Railton's brown eyes.

'That's right.'

Railton's voice dropped. 'Why are you really here, Peter?' he asked, 'why have you sought me out?'

Peter didn't reply.

'Is there something you want to tell me?' said Railton quietly. 'Is that why you've come here?'

At that moment it seemed to Peter that the room was very warm, the walls close, yet the other customers distant. 'I'm not sure,' he said, 'I did come here to tell you something but I'm not so sure now.'

Railton thought for a few seconds, watching Peter's face. 'Something to do with that digging party?' he said.

'Yes.'

Railton closed his eyes briefly and breathed out. 'You know, I've been half expecting this conversation ever since that day. It all went so smoothly....'

Peter was leaning forwards. 'I've been wanting to talk to someone ...' he began but Railton's hands were up.

'Perhaps I'm not the man to tell.'

Peter stared at him.

'If, as I suspect, you are about to say something – specific,' said Railton, 'about the body you dug up, then that may best be told to someone in authority.'

Peter felt sweat trickle down his neck. 'I do have something specific to say.'

'I see.'

An old couple who had been sitting at the table beside them made to leave and Peter stood up to let them pass. When he sat down again Railton grasped his hand.

'I can only imagine what secret it is you have been harbouring, Peter,' he said. His voice was quiet but resolute. 'But I can make an educated guess.' His eyes were unwavering. 'If it is what I think it may be this must be a heavy burden for you and I would like to help but I fear I have too much invested emotionally in this. There is too much history for me, too many hurdles faced, too many obstacles overcome for me now to be sanguine about anything you might tell me.' He released Peter's hand. 'So, though this may be selfish of me, for which I apologise, I think I would prefer to remain ignorant of anything you may have to say.'

Peter nodded slowly. 'I just want to do the right thing,' he said.

'The right thing?'

'Yes. To make the right decision.'

Railton smiled. 'Then that should be something for you to determine, and you alone.'

Peter looked surprised. 'But isn't that what you do? Tell people what is right and what is wrong?'

'Me? A humble vicar?'

'Yes, surely that's your job.'

'Oh no, you misunderstand my role.' Railton opened out his hands as he might when delivering a sermon. 'I advise, certainly, I inform others of my beliefs in the hope that they may benefit from forming similar beliefs, I tell them of the joy that comes from a relationship with God – but I hope I never tell them what they must do. I hope I never say 'this is right, this is wrong' or 'I am right, you are wrong'. After all isn't that the very thing that causes wars in the first place?' He took Peter's hand again. 'It must be up to each individual to make their own decisions – we can only hope to behave in a way that others may admire and choose to follow suit.'

Peter could feel the warmth of Railton's hand on his and it felt strangely as if some message was being conveyed through the tips of his fingers as they sat, unnoticed in their corner of the pub, communicating at a level unfamiliar to Peter.

'I will talk to someone in the War Office,' he said suddenly.

'You think that would help?'

'It might.'

'It might well.' Railton released his grip again. 'I usually find that for anyone living with some sort of lie, as I assume you have been for some time now, then admitting the truth proves a powerful relief.'

Peter bent his head and considered the vicar's words for some time before replying.

'Yes,' he said, 'yes, I believe I see that now.' He stood up with a renewed sense of purpose. 'Thank you, David,' he finally said, 'that has helped me considerably. It has helped clear my mind.'

The following week, after much consideration, Peter arranged to meet his old Commanding Officer, Tim Ballard, who was now a senior civil servant working in a different department to himself in the War Office. They met in an oak panelled office with thick carpeting and paintings from the Napoleonic wars on the walls. After some initial conversation to catch up on events since they had last met Peter came directly to the point.

'You remember that day, November the seventh when you gave me an instruction to travel to Ypres to dig up a body?' he said.

'Yes,' replied Ballard cautiously.

'Well there was one thing I didn't tell you on my return.'

Ballard's shrewd gaze held Peter's as he evaluated these words. His eyes turned downwards to examine the dark green leather that covered the surface of his desk.

'I'm not sure I'm going to like what I'm about to hear,' he said, looking again at Peter.

'No. I fear you won't. You see there was something on the body I delivered that I kept to myself.'

Ballard pursed his lips. 'And what exactly was that?'

'A photograph.'

'A photograph.'

'Yes.'

'A photograph of a girl.'

'Of a girl.'

'Yes.'

Ballard stood up and walked to the window.

'And?' he said, his back to Peter.

'And I found out who she was.'

'You found out who she was.'

'Yes.'

Ballard's habit of echoing Peter's words had an unnerving effect but Peter had rehearsed what he had to say carefully.

'In fact, I am now married to that girl and I know the identity of the man who was her fiancée in 1917.'

'Married.'

'Yes.'

Ballard turned and stood directly over Peter who was still sitting. He bent down so that their faces were close. 'The identity of the man you dug up and delivered to St Pol, you mean.'

'Yes.'

Ballard remained bent over, his face betraying a strange mixture of anger and shock. 'So let me be absolutely clear here,' he said, 'the body you dug up and which you stated to me and others had absolutely no means of identification, in fact had a photograph of a girl on it and you have found this girl, married her and found out from her who the man was.'

'Not exactly like that. I bumped into her, I didn't seek her out. And she volunteered the details of the man, I didn't ask her for them.'

'My God.' Ballard went back to his desk and sat down so that he was facing Peter again. He began writing on a sheet of paper with a fountain pen with Peter sitting in silence opposite him.

'And what was his name?'

'Daniel Dawkins.'

'Regiment?'

'6th Battalion the Berkshire Light Infantry.'

'Rank?'

'Private.'

'Anything else I should know?'

'I haven't told my wife about this. I have kept it entirely to myself – I am the only one to know this thing up until now.'

Ballard looked up but it was some time before he spoke. 'What on earth possessed you to be such an utter fool?' he asked.

Peter leant forwards. 'Believe me, sir, it was not something I did lightly.' He then described the journey out to Ypres, the moment the ambulance went into the ditch causing a long delay, the digging up of Charlie Matthews and the other bodies and finally his discovery of the photograph on Dawkins' body just as they were about to leave for St Pol with no time left.

'And that photograph, where is it now?'

'I burned it almost immediately.'

Ballard wrote this all down. 'And you say you bumped into the girl, where was that?'

'She was one of the mourners who visited the grave when I was on duty. It was an extraordinary coincidence.'

'Indeed. And a most unfortunate one.'

Peter half smiled. 'You might say that, I suppose.'

Ballard looked up. He was not smiling. 'Your mistake, of course, came at that moment.'

'You mean I shouldn't have said anything. Should have ignored her.'

'That's exactly what I mean.'

Peter nodded slowly. 'Don't think I haven't agonised over that,' he said, 'but hindsight is a fine thing.'

'Yes.' Ballard folded up the piece of paper he had been writing on and placed it carefully in an envelope. 'It is, but we must now deal with the reality of what has happened.'

'What will you do?'

'That's a good question.' Ballard stood and Peter did the same. 'I will give this some careful thought and will be in touch.' He started walking towards the door of his office. 'I will contact you shortly. In the mean time it goes without saying talk to absolutely no one of this.'

Two weeks later Peter was summoned up to the sixth floor of the War Office. He was shown into a large ornate room where three men were sitting around a table. He recognised them all; The Secretary of State for war and the colonies, the head of the Army and Tim Ballard.

Peter swallowed.

'Come in Major Harding,' said the Secretary of State. Peter walked across the wide expanse of Persian carpet. 'Please sit down.' Peter sat opposite the men and waited for one of them to speak. There was a musty smell to the room. Three white coffee cups, upturned on saucers, as yet unused, sat beside a jug on a silver tray. A painting of the Duke of Wellington hung above an ornate marble fireplace.

'Would you please repeat to us,' the Secretary of state said at last, 'what you told Colonel Ballard the other week about the events of November 1920.'

'Yes sir.' Peter cleared his throat and took a sip of water from the glass in front of him. 'It began when Mr Ballard, my Commanding Officer at the time, called me into his office ...'

Peter ran through the events of the 7 November with little interruption until he came to the point when he was asked by the Reverend Kendall to place the body he had delivered in the chapel.

'Were the other bodies already in place?' asked the head of the army.

'Yes, sir.'

'And do you recall the arrangement?'

'Do you mean how they were laid out?'

'Yes.'

'In a row sir.'

'And where was yours placed?'

'On the right as one looked towards the altar, sir.'

The Field Marshal cast a glance towards the Secretary of State. 'Carry on,' he said.

Peter described burning the photograph, meeting Joyce and listening to her in Paddington station as she talked about Daniel. He was asked a series of questions to confirm that he had never mentioned to Joyce or anyone else his finding of the photograph. He confirmed he had kept his secret to himself.

Then the Secretary of State, who had remained silent throughout the ten minutes Peter had been talking, spoke up.

'Major Harding,' he said, 'it goes without saying this is a situation of the utmost gravity.'

'I understand that, sir.'

'We have spoken to the Reverend Kendall and it would seem that when he opened the chapel in the early morning of the 8th November the empty space in the row of bodies was indeed the one on the right.'

'I see.'

'Which means that, almost certainly, your body was the one placed in the coffin.'

'I understand.'

'Which means, Major Harding, that in all probability the body that lies now in the Abbey and that is revered as the Unknown Warrior is, in fact, that of Private Daniel Dawkins of the 6th Berkshire Light Infantry.'

'Yes sir.'

A heavy hush fell on the room.

'Now,' continued the Secretary of State, 'there is something you may not know, Major Harding.'

It seemed to Peter that the room darkened marginally as the politician paused before carrying on. 'At the time he went missing in action Private Dawkins was up for court martial for retreating when ordered to advance.'

The words seemed to reverberate around the room. Peter closed his eyes and gripped the table. His mouth was suddenly dry.

'So what I'm saying, Major Harding, is that the Unknown Warrior, the body of the man lying in Westminster Abbey, the body representing those thousands of fine soldiers who sacrificed their lives for their country, the greatest symbol of heroism this country has ever had – belongs, according to the evidence you have just given us, to a man who was a coward.'

Peter sat unable to speak. He felt a dizziness overcome him and the three men opposite appeared to move out of focus. He shook his head in disbelief.

'Imagine,' said the Secretary of State, 'if that were ever to get out.'

CHAPTER 30

November 2011

Since working out the code in Peter Harding's diaries James Marchant had slept little. He was sitting on something of major significance and the excitement was hard to contain. On the one hand he was only too aware that all he had was one diary with a crudely fashioned code, a few links and the words of a dying man whose memory had been fading at the time. Any scrap of doubtful evidence, any tiny omission of detail would be pounced upon by experts and used to tarnish his reputation. Conjecture counted for nothing, facts, research and first hand accounts were everything.

So, a part of him was urging caution. And yet.... on the other hand the diary had been found. It was undeniably genuine. The code was unmistakeable. Peter Harding's involvement was clear. The link to Dawkins was beyond doubt and the dates all fitted. It was a compelling story and who was he to sit on it, to conceal a dramatic part of the nation's history for fear of being ridiculed? The thought of the recognition that would come his way for such a major find was hard to resist and he had begun to imagine receiving awards, being asked to speak at conferences and being paid large advances for books. His career which had been unspectacular to date would receive a major boost. Here, at last, was a chance to really make his name.

Three days after the find of the diaries Sarah invited him to her house to watch a documentary about a man called Fabian Ware. Ware had been the driving force in the creation of the Commonwealth War Graves Commission and it had been his determination that had led to the construction of the giant cemeteries in France and Belgium. Mention was made of the unknown warrior with a re-enactment of the choosing of the body at St Pol. Marchant and Sarah sat on her sofa as old film clips were shown of the King placing his wreath at the foot of the Cenotaph. The programme finished with a slow panning shot of Tyne Cot cemetery.

'That was interesting,' said Sarah, 'what did you make of that clip of the King?'

'It was odd. He seemed casual, almost disinterested.'

'Perhaps he was nervous of letting his emotions show.' She sat back and leant her head against his shoulder. 'So, where are we?'

'With Dawkins? With the Unknown Warrior?'

'Yes.'

Marchant switched off the television with the remote. 'With all this interest building about the centenary I think it's time I went public.'

Sarah took her time to reply. 'Are you sure?'

'Yes. I've been giving it a lot of thought, it's time to publish. I've written a paper and I'm going to send it off.'

'I see.'

He sat up and looked at her. 'You don't sound convinced.'

'I've been thinking about the pack of hyenas.'

'Don't imagine I haven't but, as I said, it's time to be brave.'

'What about the grain of history. You talked about the Unknown Soldier being an iconic symbol and ....'

'Did I say that?'

'Something along those lines. And you said the Establishment would never allow it ....'

'Fuck the Establishment.'

Sarah also sat up, surprised to hear him swear like this, disconcerted by the strident tone of his voice. 'But you've talked about it being part of the fabric of the nation, how it means so much to ....'

'But it was nearly a hundred years ago, most of them are dead.' Marchant stood up and started pacing again as he always did when thinking hard, as if his brain needed movement to work at its best.

'I thought it was a symbol for soldiers through all ages.'

'Yes, yes.' He appeared irritated at Sarah's misgivings. 'But don't you see, it's about the truth, about revealing what needs to be revealed.'

Sarah sat still and watched him. In recent emails and phone conversations she had noticed Marchant's increasing forcefulness. From being a man of extreme courtesy and deference he had suddenly begun talking over her, not listening, finishing her sentences. It was as if he was being driven forwards by a force that was at odds with his character and it worried her that he seemed to be ignoring his own advice. 'Oh is it?' she said as she gave him a long, challenging look. 'And there I was beginning to think it might be about your ego.'

'My ego?' Marchant stared at her. 'Don't be ridiculous.'

Sarah stood up and joined him by the window. 'This wouldn't have anything to do with your father would it?' she asked.

'What on earth do you mean? He's been dead nearly twenty years.'

'I know that, James,' she said, 'I'm just saying that you're a man I've come to admire deeply. A man of principle and intelligence. But even the best men can get carried away when trying to prove themselves.'

'It's not like that at all.'

'Isn't it? Don't forget this is my family we're talking about here.'

They stood glaring at each other, Marchant tense, Sarah composed.

'Just give it some thought,' she said.

'I have. I've been thinking of little else these last few days.'

'Then think hard about why you're doing this. Think about what it will really achieve.'

He didn't reply. She put her arm round him. 'All I'm asking is that you give it a few days more. Be absolutely sure you're doing the right thing before you do something irreversible.' She kissed him on the cheek. 'Do that for me, if for no other reason.'

Troubled by Sarah's words Marchant decided to visit Westminster Abbey the next day. Ignoring his own determined belief in rationality he imagined that, perhaps, coming face to face with the tomb of the Unknown Warrior might reveal a certain clarity to him, a wisdom of ages, an insight from a different dimension.

He caught the tube to Westminster and walked the short distance to the Great North Door of the Abbey where he was surprised to find he needed to pay to enter.

'We are entirely self-funding,' said a verger when Marchant questioned him, 'we receive no financial support from the State, the Crown or the Church of England.'

'I didn't realise that.'

'So, your gift is welcomed.'

'My pleasure.'

Marchant looked at the leaflet he had been given and noted the recommended route around the Abbey.

'Anything in particular you wish to see?' asked the verger.

'I'm actually most interested in the tomb of the Unknown Warrior.'

'Turn right here and it's at the end of the nave.'

'Thanks.'

Marchant started walking and as soon as he turned the corner he could see a small group of people up ahead, gathered in front of the Great West Door. He hesitated. The people were standing round an oblong of red poppies. He thought he felt a slight breeze pass through the Abbey. He stood still and breathed deeply, sensing that his work over the past weeks was culminating in this one moment. He looked up at the soaring vaults above him, rising skywards to proclaim the greatness of God, and he began walking slowly but his feet felt heavy and he could think only of Daniel Dawkins wading through mud as he advanced towards the Passchendaele ridge.

He reached the tomb and the polished black marble glistened under the lights of the Abbey. He began reading the words on the gravestone.

'Beneath this stone rests the body of a British Warrior unknown by name or rank brought from France to lie among the most illustrious of the land and buried here on armistice day 11 Nov: 1920....'

The people who had been surrounding the tomb moved on and Marchant found himself alone. An organ practice that had been filling the Abbey with the sounds of a Bach concerto came to an abrupt end. The Great West Door opened briefly, cast a shaft of light over where Marchant stood in front of the grave, then closed again. The air was still now, time moved slowly, the weight of history had never felt so powerful to him.

'You know, it's the only floor tomb in the Abbey which is never walked on,' came a voice.

Marchant looked up to see the verger he had spoken to earlier standing beside him.

'Even at a coronation, the procession goes round it.'

'That's extraordinary.'

'It's as strong a symbol now as ever it was.'

The two men looked down at the words inscribed on the marble.

'I wonder who is under there,' said Marchant.

'Many thousands have.' The verger noticed the intensity of Marchant's gaze. 'Might he be someone from your past?'

'In a funny way, he might.' Marchant briefly closed his eyes and an image of Dawkins came to him in vivid detail. 'But not a relation of mine.'

'It has a strange effect on people,' said the verger, 'a pull like no other. I see it time and again.'

Marchant found himself leaning forwards, his head lowered. 'Yes. I think I know what you mean.'

The verger stepped back to leave Marchant alone for a few seconds but he was hovering nearby.

'Where is David Railton's flag?' asked Marchant.

'Just here.' The verger pointed to a neighbouring chapel. 'We tend to call it the Warrior's chapel.'

Marchant studied Railton's Union Jack, the very same flag that had covered the coffin on its final journey to the Abbey. He read the inscription on the wall describing how that had come about and then he looked at the nearby pillar where the ship's bell from HMS *Verdun* had been hanging since 1990 when the ship was broken up.

'All very moving,' he said.

'Indeed.'

The verger's attention was caught by a foreign tourist and he left in the direction of the quire. Marchant made his way slowly round the Abbey, following the guided route via Henry VII's Lady Chapel, Poet's corner, the cloisters and back, once more past the tomb of the Unknown Warrior where he stood in silent study before making his way out into the street via the Abbey shop.

He felt unsettled, his senses disrupted, his reason affected by what he had just experienced, and he walked along the street taking no notice of those passing him by, as if enveloped in a strange fog that separated him from his immediate surroundings. He thought of Peter Harding walking the same streets nearly a hundred years earlier, then, as his steps led him towards Green Park, he began to see through Daniel Dawkins's eyes, to see this world of civilians going about their daily business unaware of his presence amongst them, to feel the unbridgeable gap between their world and his.

Disoriented he sat down on a bench to recover his equilibrium. 'Something to do with your father,' Sarah had said. Was that really what this was all about? Was he really seeking to prove himself to a man who was no longer alive? It was an unsettling thought. A pigeon approached and pecked at his shoe, a bicyclist raced past, a jogger stopped to do some stretching exercises. He closed his eyes and tried to marshal his racing thoughts.

'Excuse me, can I sit here?' asked a woman, pointing to the space beside him.

'Of course. I was just off anyway.'

On the move again he decided, for the first time in a long while, to take the afternoon off. He might go and see a film but first he would just walk. He would meander, in no rush, and look at buildings, perhaps visit a gallery or an exhibition, eat something by the river, enjoy being alone with no agenda or deadline.

He began walking and soon he reached the Thames, leaving behind the Houses of Parliament, looking over towards the London Eye. On a whim he decided to catch a boat towards the docks and minutes later he was travelling across water, feeling a breeze on his face, not listening to the commentary, taking in the sights, noting all the new buildings, passing the Festival hall, the Tate Modern, the Globe.

He couldn't stop thinking about the tomb. There was a solidity to it, a sense of wonder, even something majestic about its position at the very entrance to the Abbey. Generations had come to see it, widows had knelt and wept beside it, soldiers had bowed their heads and thought of dead comrades as they guarded it.

But if he had been hoping for some kind of sign from his visit as to how he should now proceed it had not come to him. What part he was now playing in the tide of history still remained unclear. 'Be absolutely sure you're doing the right thing,' Sarah had said. But what was the right thing?

The next day, in a search for more clarity, he went to the Imperial War Museum to see if he could find out anything more about Daniel Dawkins.

He made his way to a room lined with shelves of military records and sat himself down behind a computer. After typing in his personal details he began his research, as before, by looking up the Berkshire LI and then narrowing it down to 5 Platoon of the 6th Battalion. He typed in August 1917 and the familiar names appeared: Lieutenant Latham, Sergeant Barnes, Dawkins, Fletcher, Timmings, Jackson.

He typed in 'Daniel Dawkins. Private. 6 BLI.'

As on his previous searches all that came up was 'Volunteered 1914. Served with 6 BLI 1915 – 1917. Missing in action October 1917'.

He looked at the screen and pondered. Then he typed in 'Jeremy Latham. 2nd Lieutenant 6 BLI.' Three paragraphs of information appeared. He did the same for Sergeant Barnes and there was a whole page describing his time in Mons in the first engagement of the war, his time in a training depot and then his role as Platoon Sergeant in 1917. Each member of the platoon had at least one paragraph to their name, including Jackson who had been court martialled – all except Dawkins.

For over fifteen minutes Marchant tried a series of approaches to get at what he was after but he kept coming up against dead ends; it appeared that, apart from this minimal description, there was nothing further to be said about Private Dawkins. It was almost as if someone, at some stage, had deleted the details.

Suddenly, Marchant became aware of a presence behind him. He turned and a woman in a dark suit was standing and peering over his shoulder.

'Can I help you?' he asked.

'Mr Marchant?'

'Yes.'

'I wonder if you might come to meet the Head of Curation.'

'How do you know my name?'

'You logged in.'

'You make a note of everyone who logs in?'

'Not normally.'

Marchant frowned. 'So what's this about then?'

'I don't know. All I can say is that Mr Phillips has asked me to bring you to speak to him.'

'Well I'm actually rather busy here.'

'He said it was very important.'

The man who had been working beside Marchant looked up enquiringly.

'It seems I've set something off,' said Marchant.

'How intriguing.'

'Please Mr Marchant, I think you should come with me now,' said the woman. He looked up at her impassive face.

'Very well,' he said, 'if it's entirely necessary.'

'I believe it is, sir.'

After walking down a series of corridors Marchant was shown into an office where a man in a tweed suit stood up to shake his hand.

'Mr Marchant,' he said, 'thank you so much for coming to see me.'

'I understand there was little choice.'

'Well,' the man looked slightly embarrassed, 'we couldn't, of course, force you but I'm most grateful you came anyway. Please, do sit down. I'm John Phillips, Head of Curation.'

'What's this about?'

'I'm afraid I'm not sure.'

'So you ask to see me about something that's very important and then you tell me you don't know why?'

'Yes, it must seem odd but you've obviously triggered something.'

'Triggered what?'

Phillips looked at the woman. 'Thank you Miss Charlton,' he said, 'I can take it from here.' Miss Charlton left the room and closed the door.

'I'll be frank with you Mr Marchant, I don't know exactly but there are one or two files which, when opened by the same person on a number of separate occasions, raise some kind of alarm.'

'Alarm?'

'They set off a number of procedures.'

'Which file are we talking about here?'

'I'm not at liberty to disclose that at the moment.'

'What can you disclose then?'

'Very little.'

'So what am I doing here then?'

'Waiting.'

'For what?'

'For someone from the Ministry of Defence to come and speak to you.'

'The MOD? And what if I don't want to wait?'

'I think, Mr Marchant, given the level of security messages I have received, that that would be a mistake.'

The army officer who arrived sixty-five minutes later wore an expensive grey suit. His striped tie, pocketless shirt and regimental cufflinks marked him out instantly to Marchant as of a certain type who judged others by how they dressed and who viewed themselves as being members of an upper elite. However, he spoke with such a pronounced drawl that Marchant suspected he had risen up from humbler origins.

'Mr Marchant,' he said, not smiling, proffering his hand, 'Major Hall.'

Marchant reached out and noted the unnaturally firm handshake.

'Hello, Major Hall,' he said, 'have I set claxons off in the MOD?'

The Major sat down opposite him. 'As a matter of fact you have, yes.'

'Well, I've been hanging around here for over an hour for you to come and interview me. What on earth is going on?'

The Major chose not to answer him immediately, instead placing a folder on the table between them.

'I'll get straight to the point, Mr Marchant,' he then said, 'you have accessed information on a soldier called Daniel Dawkins on a number of occasions in the past month and six times this morning.'

'I know that.'

'Why?'

'Just general research.'

'But you looked him up six times.'

'I've looked up a number of soldiers from his platoon a number of times.'

'But why the interest in the first place?'

'I'm a historian. I've been looking into the Berkshire Light Infantry. I had honed my investigation down to 5 Platoon of the 6th battalion as they suffered heavily at Passchendaele. Nothing more than that.'

'Have you been commissioned to do this research?'

'Yes.'

'Who commissioned you?'

'Someone wanting to trace her grandfather.'

'Dawkins?'

'As a matter of interest, yes.'

'So it is Dawkins you're interested in.'

'Well, yes.'

'So why didn't you say so?'

'Because, frankly, it's none of your business.'

The Major had clear blue eyes that fixed Marchant with an unwavering gaze. 'In fact it is my business.'

'Why?'

'We can come to that later. What have you found out?'

'Look, is this some sort of interrogation?'

'Not yet. I'm simply trying to establish some facts.'

'This is all very strange.'

'Please, just answer my questions and we can clear things up quite swiftly.'

Marchant took a breath. 'As I've said, the platoon suffered heavily.'

'And Dawkins?'

'It would seem he was one of the ones who died, probably on the 9th October.'

'And nothing else?'

'No.'

'I see.' The Major looked across at Marchant. 'Well, I'm here to tell you to cease your enquiries as of now.'

'I beg your pardon.'

'You are to stop your research into this soldier.'

'Stop my research? What are you on about?'

'Information on Dawkins is classified.'

'Classified? He died nearly a hundred years ago!'

'Nevertheless.'

Marchant held Major Hall's gaze. 'Is that why there's so little about him?'

The Major shrugged.

'I thought there was something odd going on.'

'Odd as may be, you are to stop investigating him.'

'And what if I don't?'

'Don't stop your research?'

'Yes.'

'Then you will be held accountable for your actions.'

'What does that mean?'

The Major leant forwards. 'We're not playing games here, Marchant. This is a very serious matter.'

'I've no doubt about that but if I'm in some way being threatened I'd like to know why.'

'Let's not use the word threatened, I'm simply telling you, in the national interest, to stop.'

'In the national interest?'

'Yes.'

'So something that happened in 1917 is still to be supressed for the national interest. It must have been pretty momentous. You've got me intrigued now.'

The Major sighed. 'The easiest way forward from here is for you to simply accept my advice.'

'Oh, advice is it now? I thought it was an order.'

'Very well, my order.'

'And who are you to give me orders? I'm a civilian remember, not a serving soldier.'

Major Hall sighed again. 'Listen, Marchant, I am asking you, advising you – ordering you if that's how you like it, to leave Dawkins alone. That is the wisest thing for you to do. I strongly recommend you heed my words.'

Marchant shook his head as he gathered his thoughts. 'I'm sorry, I need more than this. We live in a free country. You can't just walk in here and tell me to stop looking things up.'

'I can actually.'

'On whose authority?'

The Major considered this turn in the conversation. 'All right,' he said after a while, and opened the folder on the table and pointed to a document.

'You see this?'

'Yes.'

'It's a memorandum dated 1933,' he said, 'and marked top secret. It is signed at the bottom by the then Secretary of State for war and the colonies.' He turned it to show Marchant the signature.

Marchant examined the heading. 'Christ!'

'Yes, Christ. It has been updated by the staff officer in my role over the years. Only he and the Minister for Defence at the time gets to read it. It is covered by the Official Secrets Act. It has the highest level of security. And ...'

Marchant was trying to appear as calm as possible but his heart was racing. The Major was watching closely for his reaction.

'And it states quite clearly that anyone who shows an undue interest in Corporal Dawkins must be dissuaded from doing so.'

Marchant said nothing, his hands clasped tightly together under the table.

'In the thirties that meant anyone requesting to look at his file. Today we have an alarm that goes off when someone tries to access information repeatedly.'

'And what information there was about him has been mostly removed.'

'Yes.'

The small room was warm and Marchant was sweating.

The Major leant towards him. 'Mr Marchant, I believe you know more than you are letting on,' he said.

'I've told you all I know.'

'We both know that's untrue.'

'So what is it I'm supposed to know? What is the great secret about this man Dawkins?'

'That's what I'm trying to find out from you.'

'But I'm asking you.'

'What I know is not the issue here, it's what you know that matters.'

Marchant, the nervous tension in his body rising, stood up. 'With all due respect, Major Hall, we're going round in circles here.'

The Major also stood. 'Look, let me be absolutely clear about what is going on,' he said. He came round the table to stand close to Marchant. 'You are a sophisticated man, a researcher, your job is to find clues in what you read. It is my belief that you have stumbled upon something significant about this man Dawkins – hence your particular interest in him. I, on the other hand, have a file that has been passed on over the years that states in no uncertain terms, and is signed by no less than a cabinet minister, that anyone trying to find out about Dawkins is to be dissuaded from doing so. It is really very simple. I don't know exactly what you've found out so far but you must stop.'

'Yes, I've got that message.'

Marchant remained standing, uncertain, trying to work out his best strategy.

'Perhaps I can tell you one thing to help convince you,' said the Major.

'Go on.'

'This must go no further than these walls.'

'Very well.'

'Will you promise me that?'

'Yes.'

The Major placed his hands on the table and leant forwards. 'The final entry in Dawkins' file is that he was to be court martialled for refusing to advance when ordered to.'

'What?'

'He was up for cowardice.'

'My God.'

'Daniel Dawkins was a coward, Mr Marchant.'

The word hung in the air. Marchant sat down heavily and Major Hall sat down beside him. The room was stuffy, the computer whirred, the spotlight shining down on the table seemed unusually intense.

'That's hard to believe.'

'It's clearly documented.'

'So, the U.....' Marchant stopped himself but too late.

Major Hall stared at him. 'Indeed.' He nodded at their mutual understanding. 'I think we both know what we're talking about here.' He closed the file. 'So, let's be frank about this, Marchant. You're researching Dawkins because you believe there's a link with the Unknown Soldier. Am I right?'

Marchant didn't reply.

'I'll take that to mean 'I am.'' Major Hall leant forwards, his fingers intertwined. 'Well, I don't know how you have made that link, I don't know the details of what you may have unearthed in your research, but I'm now going to make an intuitive leap and surmise that you have come to believe that the body in the Abbey belongs to this man Dawkins.'

Marchant, faced with the Major's logic, stared back at him before nodding slowly.

'In which case,' said Major Hall, 'if you are right – and I'm not saying you are – but if you are right, then the man they buried, the body that has acquired a mythical status around the world – is that of a coward.'

Marchant sat, temporarily unable to speak. He looked down at the file. 'That's a lot to take in,' he said at last.

'Of course. And you'll now understand why it's my job to dissuade you from doing anything that would be against the national interest.'

'And if you don't manage to dissuade me?'

The Major opened his hands outwards. 'That would be a big mistake on your behalf.' He shook his head. 'Think about it. There will be considerable interest in the First World War over the next few years with all sorts of ceremonies and events held to commemorate the centenary. I should imagine there will be a particularly high profile service held in Westminster Abbey in November 2020 with dignitaries from around the world attending. Just imagine .....' he searched for the right words, 'just imagine the reaction if anything were to damage the credibility of that.'

'I am.'

'Good. Keep on doing so. It can't happen.'

'They won't let me?'

The Major allowed himself a slight smile. 'To be precise, we won't let you.' He removed a form from the folder. 'So, I have a piece of paper here for you to sign,' he said, 'stating that you will cease your investigations forthwith and that any information you have pertaining to Corporal Dawkins you will keep strictly to yourself.' He placed it in front of Marchant. 'I can not advise you strongly enough to sign it now.'

Marchant felt the room closing in on him. He took three deep breaths. 'I need to think about this,' he said.

'Just sign.'

'I can't. I have to clear my head.'

'Well, I've warned you.'

Marchant stood up. His mind was spinning. 'Give me a couple of days to think about it,' he said.

CHAPTER 31

October 1917

'What's up with Sergeant Barnes?' asked Fletcher, 'he's gone dead quiet of late.'

'Something's got to him,' said Dawkins, back with the Regiment, his last leave already seeming far away.

'It was that attack on Borry Farm.' Fletcher took a sup of beer, 'he's not been the same since.'

The two men were back in Poperinghe and were to return to the front shortly.

'I think he's finally found out that he ain't invincible,' said Dawkins.

'It was that moment,' said Fletcher, 'when we reached the trench and he was all in. He saw you take over. It affected him someways.'

'Well he's off my back so whatever it is I'll have some more of it.'

'Mr Latham did OK after his wobble.'

'They all wobble at some stage. Kids at school one day, leading men over the top the next – what can you expect?'

There was singing going on all around them but Dawkins and Fletcher had little appetite for jollity. Since Timmings' death and the loss of over half the platoon they had retreated into their own tight circle of two, scarcely speaking to the new soldiers who had arrived from England, quietly going about their business, drained to their limits by the remorseless disorientation of a rotation system that saw them move repeatedly from the relative comforts of reserve, up the line to the waterlogged trenches, and back again. It had become a strange and debilitating existence, with new recruits entering their lives constantly, living in close proximity to them for a while, and then disappearing in an instant, either to be evacuated back to a field hospital or to die, like Timbo, alone in a boggy field far from home.

As with other men who had survived more than one advance, Dawkins and Fletcher, without truly acknowledging it even to each other, had resolved to make as few friends as possible, to keep their distance, to survive solely for themselves.

They had agreed to meet Mr Latham at Talbot House, one of the few establishments where officers and soldiers could mingle and have a drink together.

They finished their beers and started walking up the street but hadn't progressed far before they saw Major Horrocks with a staff officer coming towards them. Without exchanging even a glance they crossed over onto the opposite pavement but Horrocks, with presumably the same thing in mind, did likewise at exactly the same moment. Once set on their new course neither party could double back and they met a short distance down the road. Dawkins and Fletcher saluted.

'Good evening, Dawkins,' said Major Horrocks.

'Evening, sir.'

The four men stood awkwardly facing each other.

'Out for a drink?' said Horrocks.

'Yes sir. Just the one or two. Wouldn't want to risk getting drunk before returning for duty.'

Horrocks laughed awkwardly. 'Very wise.'

'Fletcher here has promised to keep an eye on me, sir. Make sure I don't do anything silly.'

'Good.'

'I'm sorry to say Private Timmings' punishment was rather wasted sir. He may have learnt his lesson but he took one the very next day so he never had the opportunity to put his learning into practice.'

Horrocks pursed his lips and his eyes flickered between Dawkins and the officer beside him. He turned to Fletcher. 'Well, keep an eye on your fellow soldier, Fletcher,' he said, 'we wouldn't want Dawkins to go the way of his young friend now,' he looked straight at Dawkins, 'would we?'

Fletcher stepped forwards in front of Dawkins. 'No sir. Thank you, sir. And have a pleasant evening.'

Horrocks hesitated, saluted back, gave Dawkins a long look, and then continued on his way.

'Don't bait the sod,' said Fletcher, 'no good will come of it.'

'I've got his measure,' said Dawkins, 'don't you worry.'

Fletcher made no comment.

'When I was back home I spoke to some people who knew him when he was a boy,' said Dawkins.

'You did?'

'Yes. The Grenfells. They live in a mansion above Taplow and I used to do work for them. I got to know their son a bit. Anyway, she said Horrocks was a weedy lad, put upon by the other boys.'

'That would make sense.'

'You think so?'

'Think about it Dan. Why does he hate you so much?'

'Because I don't put up with his high and mighty bollocks.'

'Yes, but why else?'

'Because I stand up to him.'

Fletcher stopped walking. 'You're everything he's not, Dan.'

'How do you mean?'

'You're a good-looking lad, popular, strong. He's a cowardly little runt. All he's got over you is his rank and that's why he uses it so much.'

'Fuck me.'

'Compare him to Major Witheridge or Colonel Parker, Dan.'

'Both good officers.'

'Yes, because they're strong like you. They don't need rank to make them what they are.'

'And Mr Latham?'

'Not yet but he'll get there.'

They began walking again. 'So you reckon Horrocks's not just an evil little bastard?' said Dawkins.

'It's never that simple, Dan.'

Dawkins nodded as he considered his friend's words. 'Might just be getting to realise that, Fletch,' he said, 'perhaps I should have listened to you once in a while.'

'What, I'm not all piss and wind?'

Both men laughed but they had arrived at Talbot House. They walked in and found Mr Latham in the bar.

'What can I buy you men?' asked Latham.

They both chose beer and soon the three were sitting at a corner table, sheltered from the general noise by a wooden partition. They talked of anything but the war. Fletcher polished his glasses as he described his plans to start a small building business one day, Latham told them about his hopes to go to university.

'What've you got in the way of family, sir?' asked Fletcher.

'Father, mother, one sister.'

'How are they doing?'

Latham told them about his family and they questioned him about his privileged upbringing. He went on to speak about his sister's work as a nurse and then explained how the tone of his father's letters had changed over the past months, from being full of enthusiasm for 'kicking the Hun' to a more sobre, sometimes even wistful take on events.

'What about you, Dawkins?' he asked, 'we've never heard much about your family.'

Dawkins shrugged. 'That's because there ain't much to say.' He lit up a cigarette. 'My Dad buggered off when I was three, my Mum died when I was twelve. I was bought up by my auntie and uncle for a while..... until he fell in a ditch and died.' He paused and the others waited for him to continue. 'Did a runner then and was taken in by a farmer.'

'That sounds hard.'

'Life's hard, sir.' He grinned. 'Unless your dad's a rich fucking buinessman and you live in a bleeding mansion in the village of Sonning with a Lanchester in the drive and servants to cook your meals.'

Latham looked back at him unsure how to take this but Dawkins punched him playfully on the arm. 'Only taking the piss, sir. Only odd fucking thing about it is how you've come out a decent enough bloke.'

Latham laughed and the three men sipped at their beer.

'But I'm to be a dad,' said Dawkins.

'A father?' said Latham. He looked at Fletcher. 'Well that's great news. Do you know this?'

'I do. Dan tells me most things although I'm glad to say he left out details of the conception.'

Latham turned back to Dawkins. 'And I guess the mother is the girl in your photograph.'

'Might be. Might be one of the other six girls I met on leave.'

'You ...'

'Of course it's her. What do you think, sir, I shagged my way round Berkshire?'

'Of course not. I'm sorry.'

Dawkins laughed. 'Only ribbing you again.'

They talked for a while about Berkshire and Dawkins mentioned The Grenfells and their son Julian.

'I've heard of him,'said Latham, 'he wrote some poems that were published, you know.'

'I didn't but his mum gave me a copy of them.'

'They were different from the other poets writing from the front.'

'How come?'

'He wrote positively about war. About the friendships and such like.'

'Well, as I said to Mrs Grenfell, he didn't get to live through the Somme, did he?'

At that moment Sergeant Barnes walked past them. He was on his own.

'Sergeant Barnes,' said Latham, 'join us for a drink?'

Barnes stood looking at them uncertainly but then nodded and said 'just a quick one.'

Fletcher went to buy Barnes a beer.

'We were talking about what we'll do when we get back home,' said Latham.

'If, you mean,' said Barnes, 'if you get back home.'

'That goes without saying.'

'I'll put my fucking feet up,' said Barnes, 'that's what I'll do.'

'Knackered, Sergeant?' said Dawkins.

'Knackered?' Barnes settled himself into his seat and his shoulders were hunched. 'You could say that, Dawkins, yes.' His chin lowered towards his chest, 'aren't we all?'

Latham and Dawkins observed Barnes, both noting how the harsh physical environment of the trenches was wearing the man down, making him old before his time and blunting the edge of his bitter anger.

'Your wife'll look after you,' said Latham.

'My wife?' Barnes laughed with a weary resignation, 'she hates me. As do the kids. They see me as a complete bastard.'

'You surprise me, Sarn't,' said Dawkins.

The two men glared at each other and Latham fiddled with his beer mat. 'We all have our human side, Dawkins,' he said.

Dawkins nodded, his eyes still on Barnes. 'Beginning to understand that, sir,' he smiled, 'but some hide it better than others.'

At that moment Fletcher reappeared with more beers and saved Barnes from having to reply. The men settled back in their seats and listened to the young singer who was working her way round the room, sitting on knees and flirting with each soldier in turn.

'You did all right at that farm,' said Barnes to Dawkins after a while, 'I'll give you that.'

Dawkins was watching the singer who was approaching their table. 'Steady on Sergeant Barnes,' he said as she ruffled his hair, 'I'm a live cunt if I remember it correctly. You don't want to go all soft on me now.'

The following day Private Jackson appeared amongst them again. Court martialled, his sentence to death had been commuted and he had been sent back to the front to be part of the forthcoming assault. He appeared unannounced, accompanied by a red hat who handed him over to the the CSM who in turn handed him over to Sergeant Barnes. As Sergeant Barnes marched him into the lines the men averted their eyes, not wanting to be associated with his shame, nor to be tainted by his cowardice.

Dawkins watched as Jackson unpacked his kit and told him to step outside where he offered him a cigarette.

'So, you've had a fine run of it since we last saw you,' said Dawkins.

Jackson didn't reply.

Dawkins described what had been happening since Jackson had been away and told him about the forthcoming assault. 'In the meantimes,' he said, 'you keep yourself to yourself. The lads'll give you stick but you ignore all that.'

Jackson nodded.

'I saw your mum when I was back on leave,' said Dawkins.

Jackson stared at him blankly.

'She's holding up. Seems to be seeing a bit of Mr Latham's mum which is bloody strange if you ask me.'

'I'm alive,' said Jackson suddenly.

Dawkins looked at him. 'I can see that.'

'I should be dead, you see, but I'm alive.' As he spoke he looked at Dawkins with a new and disconcerting intensity. 'I'm being looked after.'

'Well that's all nice and dandy then.'

Jackson smiled as if at Dawkins' naivety. 'You'll see,' he said.

'I will, will I? That's good then.'

'And I'll look after you, Dan.'

Dawkins noted the emptiness of Jackson's gaze. 'Well that's good of you, Pete.' He put his hand on Jackson's shoulder. 'And there'll be opportunity enough for you to do that shortly.'

In the afternoon the company was called to the square where Major Horrocks addressed them. With the sound of a bombardment that had been pounding at the enemy for over two weeks as a backdrop, he told the men that the next phase of the assault would take place in two days. They were to move forwards that evening.

'We fight for our King and Country,' he said, his voice rising at each significant word, 'it is a noble thing we do, it is our destiny, it is our duty.'

The men stood in silence, their faces impassive, and when he had finished speaking a hush descended on the gathering, each man looking straight ahead, the new arrivals straining to appear calm, the old hands, what there were of them, showing no emotion.

Horrocks, impressed by his own rhetoric, gazed out at his troops in the certainty that his words had inspired them, taking their expressions for a quiet determination bought about by the wisdom and passion of what he had said.

The Sergeant Major dismissed the parade and the men filtered off to their billets. Dawkins and Fletcher went off to the cookhouse for a brew and stood smoking apart from the rest of the men who were gathered in small huddles, some talking rapidly, some already escaping into solitude.

Since the conversation in Poperinghe the previous evening both men had been unusually quiet.

'Nobility of warfare,' said Dawkins, 'killing for King and Country. What a load of arse.'

'We'll be testing it again shortly,' said Fletcher.

'Aye.'

'At least we've got Plumer in charge again.'

'That's true.' Dawkins stubbed out his cigarette. 'But they'll be well defended and in depth. Not looking forward to it if I'm honest, Fletch.'

Fletcher looked at his closest friend, the man he had so often seen fearless in assault. 'That's unlike you, Dan,' he said.

Dawkins kicked at a stone and watched it roll away. 'Suddenly all seems a bit different, Fletch. Less clear.'

'Knowing you're to be a dad?'

'That's about it.'

Fletcher put his hand on Dawkins shoulder. 'So you're like the rest of us after all,' he said.

Dawkins smiled. 'Perhaps I am.' He looked Fletcher in the eye. 'Tell me.' He paused. 'Do you think I'm a good man Fletch?'

Fletcher kept his hand where it was. 'You're one of the best, Dan.'

'You think so?'

Fletcher took his time to reply. He came closer to Dawkins. 'What's this about then?' he asked.

'How do you mean?'

'I've not known you talk like this before.'

'Like what?'

'Like talking about yourself. Questioning things. You've never let that guard down, Dan, you've always been this rock in the middle of us all.'

'Rock?' Dawkins smiled at the thought. 'That's what Joyce once called me.' He lit up another cigarette and Fletcher waited for him to continue. 'But I've never really felt like that, Fletch.'

'I know.'

Dawkins looked into his friend's eyes. 'You're a wise old bugger, aren't you.'

Fletcher now pulled Dawkins towards him and the two men held each other for the first time since they had met over a year earlier.

'We all have our secrets, Dan,' Fletcher said over his friend's shoulder, 'we all have our fears and doubts.' He patted Dawkins's back. 'And I don't know what yours are but one thing I do know is you're a good man and you deserve to see out this war.'

Dawkins in turn patted Fletcher on the back. 'Pete Jackson says he'll be looking after me,' he said, smiling at the thought.

The men separated and grinned at each other.

'Then there you are, Dan,' said Fletcher, 'nothing can go wrong.'

'Maybe not, Fletch,' Dawkins replied. 'Maybe I'll make it after all.'

CHAPTER 32

June 1976

To an outside observer the marriage of Peter and Joyce Harding appeared a happy one and in many ways it was. They seldom argued, they enjoyed walks together, they shared a passion for their dogs and they lived a comfortable existence in their Wimbledon home. But ever since that day in Athens when the nature of their first meeting in the Abbey was so obliquely aired it remained a distancing presence, always lurking in the shadows of their relationship, never revisited but never forgotten.

Peter remained devoted to Joyce and as the years passed he was happy enough to take the back seat and defer to her on the majority of decisions. He never talked to her about his visit to David Railton nor his interview in the War Office when Major Ballard had told him of Dawkins's cowardice charge. For her part Joyce appreciated the secure life he provided for her, his decency, his care for her child, but the passion she had felt for Daniel and that she hoped might blossom with Peter never truly did.

When he returned from the Second World War in 1945 she had been enjoying her independence and it was strange having him back in the house slipping into his familiar patterns of behaviour. He grumbled about the Labour Party, pottered in his workshop, listened to sport on the radio.

She often met up with her friend Barbara who still lived in Berkshire and they continued their pattern of having lunch at a pub before taking their dogs for a walk. One day they found themselves looking across to Windsor.

'That day we met seems a lifetime ago,' said Barbara.

'It is.'

They sat down on the grass and let their dogs wander.

'It's odd to think how things might have turned out of if they'd both lived,' said Barbara.

'I try not to.'

Barbara, who had never remarried, looked across at Joyce. 'But Peter is a marvellous husband.'

'Oh, that's true. I've nothing to complain about.'

One of the dogs came up to them with a stick in its mouth and Barbara threw it into the water. 'He's a good man, Joyce,' she said, 'you've been very lucky.'

Joyce was remembering that day when Daniel had told her Dave would be dead and had then pedalled off on his bike at speed as if trying to outrun the terrible truth. She could picture him quite clearly sitting on a wall, his bike on its side, his face set in that determined way of his when holding himself together. 'I know. Of course I have,' she said, 'it's so churlish of me to make comparisons.' She let out a long sigh. 'But I just can't help it once in a while.'

In their fifties Peter and Joyce began holidaying apart. It was never fully discussed but one year when he was fishing in Scotland she decided to go on an organised tour of southern Spain and soon she had developed a taste for foreign travel where she could meet new people while visiting sites of historical interest.

She remained an attractive woman and received plenty of attention when away on her own but if Peter was worried at the close friendships she formed with the various men she met on these trips he never said so. When she was just turning fifty-five a wealthy Italian man she met in Rome pursued her for three days, taking her out for meals and buying her flowers. He urged her to leave the boring Englishman who had not even telephoned to see how she was, and when he kissed her at the door of her hotel bedroom she almost gave in to the need for one last night of excitement, one last reminder of what it was like to be transformed into a different place beyond the routine of her life.

But she resisted his flattery and though she met up with him a few times afterwards she made it clear that while she always looked forward to his company and enjoyed the romance of their meetings she would never be his lover. She knew that if she did have an affair she would struggle to keep it secret and she would never want to hurt good old Peter who had remained a loyal, supportive husband for so long.

And so their life continued, living together but moving further apart as their interests, never close, diverged over time.

Then one day in the early summer of 1976 Joyce was sitting having breakfast in a small hotel on the edge of Lake Trasimeno when the tour guide approached her to say there was a telephone call she needed to answer.

It was Stanley at the other end of the line, informing Joyce that Peter, who had been ill for a while, had had a stroke and was not expected to live more than a week.

'I'll catch the first flight home,' said Joyce.

On the way back she had mixed emotions. Sadness that the man she had lived with for nearly sixty years and who had been a good friend and companion over that time was coming to the end of his life, excitement that this might represent a new opening for her, a chance to really start exploring the world.

She found Peter propped up in bed with Stanley at his side. Peter was frail and appeared to have shrunk in the week Joyce had been away; his cheeks were hollow, he had problems moving his limbs, his eyes were glazed. Yet he was still lucid and he asked the nurse who had been employed to look after him to leave the room.

'I don't have long,' he said in a throaty whisper, 'and I have something to say that's very important.' He looked at Stanley. 'Would you leave us alone for a minute?'

Stanley looked at Joyce. 'Of course,' he said.

When they were alone Peter reached up weakly and Joyce took his hand. 'I have a secret I need to tell you that I have been keeping for most of my life,' he said, 'and I hope you won't feel badly about me for what I'm about to say.'

Joyce looked down at him and blinked. She had somehow always known that this moment would come. Ever since their eyes had first met in the Abbey and the intensity of his look seemed more than just a stranger's gaze she had guessed there was more to their meeting than just chance. Her suspicion that he was concealing something from her, confirmed on that night in Athens, had always been with them wherever they were and she knew that one day, in its own time, the truth would emerge. So this was that moment.

'Go ahead, my darling,' she said, scarcely able to formulate her words. 'I won't feel badly about you.'

Peter paused to gather himself. 'It begins on the seventh of November 1920 when I am called in to see my Commanding Officer...' He asked for some water and Joyce helped him sip from a glass. 'That's the day my life changed completely.'

It was early evening and as Peter talked the light in the room started to fade. Joyce sat listening silently as he described the orders he was given by his CO in France. He explained the drive to the cemetery in Ypres, the puncture, their late arrival and how they had begun digging up bodies. He stopped for another drink of water. 'At one point it seemed we would fail in our mission which bore down on me heavily,' he said. 'I was feeling quite desperate but finally,' he paused, 'finally we dug up the body we needed.' His voice was weak but steady. 'It was an enormous relief. We bundled it up into a sack and put it into the ambulance.' He closed his eyes briefly. 'But there was one thing that happened then that is what I need to tell you now.' He paused again as if gathering his energy then he looked straight at Joyce. 'At the last minute I found something on the body that we had missed. It was a small container. I looked inside it and there was a photograph. It was a photo of ....'

'Oh my Lord,' said Joyce. 'Oh my Lord.' Peter fell silent. 'It was me, wasn't it? It was a photograph of me.'

'Yes, my darling, it was of you.'

Joyce's hands were at her mouth. They were shaking. Peter lay still, his voice mouthing words but making no sound. The room was dark now, the only sound that of the heart monitor whirring in the background.

'So you recognised me in the Abbey.'

'Yes.'

'And it was Daniel. The body you delivered was Daniel's,' said Joyce, her voice trembling.

Peter took a long time in answering. 'Yes, my dear. I believe it was.'

Joyce began sobbing. 'You've kept it from me all this time,' she whispered.

'My darling, I had no option.'

There was a long moment when neither of them spoke.

'Go on,' said Joyce after a while, 'carry on.'

'I burnt the photo that evening,' said Peter, 'so there would be no evidence.' He pointed to the jug on his bedside table and Joyce gave him some more water. Then Peter told her about the service at the Abbey, speaking to the officer who had helped choose the body in St Pol, volunteering to help later with the queues of mourners, seeing her as she approached the coffin and recognising her immediately from the photo.

'And you followed me to Victoria station.'

'Yes.'

'Of course.'

Joyce switched on a sidelight and Peter looked up at her, his eyes damp, his face drawn. 'From the moment I saw that photo I have loved you more than I can describe,' he said, 'and that has never changed.'

Joyce started to say something but Peter squeezed her hand faintly.

'No, let me finish,' he said. He described his meeting with Railton and his visit to the War Office. He told her of the confirmation that his body had been the one chosen – but he didn't mention being told that Daniel was up for court martial. 'I know it is a terrible secret I have held,' he finally said, 'and many times I have thought of telling you, but it has been bigger than the two of us. Too big to tell.' His voice faltered and when, after a long pause, he spoke again he could hardly be heard and Joyce had to lean forwards. 'And I couldn't face the thought of losing you,' he said. He closed his eyes. 'And now you know.'

Joyce looked down at him and as he slipped into unconsciousness she bent forwards and kissed him on the forehead. Then she left the room quietly and walked down to the kitchen. She made herself a cup of tea and sat thinking. So, the two of them had met within feet of Daniel's corpse. When she had first looked up into Peter's eyes she was within touching distance of Daniel's coffin. In those few seconds the man she so loved and the man she would come to marry had been beside her there, briefly locked together in time and space, joined for a moment in an eternal triangle of grief, hope and death. No wonder he had never mentioned it – as he said, it would have been too much to bear and he would have lost her. She wondered if that was why she'd never really pressed him for an answer in spite of all her doubts. Perhaps, she thought, after all this time she had known the truth all along but had feared to face it.

Stanley came into the room. 'Are you OK?' he asked. Tears were streaming down the side of her face.

'Mum?' He reached out his arms and she pressed her face into his chest as he patted her gently on the back. 'Is he gone?' Joyce shook her head. He held her and she was limp in his arms. 'What is it then?' he said once her sobbing had subsided. She leant back and looked at him. 'One day,' she said, 'I'll tell you, but not now. I can't tell you now.'

Peter died at 8.43 that evening but not before pointing Joyce in the direction of his bureau where his diaries were neatly laid out. She took them to him and he managed to murmur '7th November'. She read the entry for 1920.

'But you don't mention the photo,' she said.

He strained himself to speak. 'Two d's,' he whispered and she read it again.

Joyce studied the diary. 'Dramatic day,' she said, 'Ah. I see. Two Ds for Daniel

Dawkins. You old bugger, that's opaque even for you,' and, for the last time in his life, Peter smiled.

Later that evening, with Peter's body awaiting the arrival of the undertaker, she went to a file she had kept secret all these years and took out Daniel's last three letters to her. She re-read them all. Earlier ones she had burnt, feeling in some way that they were a betrayal of Peter's love for her – but she had never been able to destroy these last three, the only link up until now with her dead fiancée. After reading them she went to Peter's bureau and pulled out a folder marked 'Joyce' that contained all their letters to each other when she had been away travelling. Very carefully she placed Dan's letters at the bottom of the pile and determined never to read them again.

The day after the funeral she caught the train into town and visited Westminster Abbey for the first time since that day in 1920. When she came to the tomb of the Unknown Warrior she stood motionless for a long while and when her knees buckled she was helped off the floor and taken to a pew by a verger and some American tourists who fussed over her until she had recovered her composure.

'It's a hallowed place,' said a kindly face, 'I'm not surprised you were overcome. I sure felt something myself.'

Over the next few weeks Joyce read the diaries a number of times but could find no further coded reference to Daniel. She began to agonise over what to do: her husband was dead and she was left alone with the secret of her first love's burial. It would be a betrayal of Peter to share that secret with others, yet a betrayal of Daniel to let that secret wither and die.

She thought of telling Stanley but decided that must only happen when she, like Peter, was at the end of her life. She considered telling Barbara but talked herself out of it. hen, a few months later an idea came to her. On a tour of the Great War cemeteries that she finally felt up to attending, she found herself with half an hour to spare before the coach arrived. Sitting in the foyer of the hotel she was completing a crossword when she came across a clue; 'Keeping a secret. For your eyes only'. The answer was easy; 'code'.

'Yes,' she said out loud. She had her solution.

Throughout the day as she visited the graveyards around Ypres her plan developed. As she stood in silent reflection amongst row upon row of gravestones at Tyne Cot she listened intently to historians describing the events of 1914 to 1918. She walked the very ground Daniel might have covered, looked east towards Germany the way he must have done, and stepped past craters in the earth where shell holes had once provided cover for men trapped in No Man's Land. And then she knew, with an absolute certainty, exactly what she would do.

In the hotel that night, when the rest of the party had gone to bed, she began constructing sentences and she smiled to herself as she imagined digging out Peter's old typewriter and carefully adding these into his diaries.

One day she would tell Stanley about the photograph and tell him what to look for in the diaries and then he could do with it as he wished. In the meantime the secret of the Unknown Warrior was safe with her. It would be hidden away in a safety deposit box that she would organise on her return and the clues she would hide amongst Peter's solid prose would wait for the day an inquisitive mind unearthed the truth about Daniel Dawkins's final resting place.

CHAPTER 33

6 October 1917

George Latham picked up the pile of letters that had landed on his doormat and looked through them.

'Elizabeth,' he shouted into the drawing room, 'a letter from Jeremy.'

Elizabeth joined him immediately. 'Come on, then ' she said, 'open it.'

They sat at the dining table and read together.

'*My Dear Mother and Father,*' it began, '*I am writing to you from the relative comfort of a pillbox we captured from the Germans yesterday. It has been a great stroke of luck – it seems to have been some sort of HQ and the men have been smoking cigars and drinking Rheinwine in a sort of reckless abandon. I fear if the OC were to turn up now he might find us all quite drunk – but, frankly, we are past caring.*

It has been a bloody few weeks.

Since the 20th September there have been non stop advances, attacks and counter attacks as we fight our way towards the Passchendaele Ridge. Luckily for us the weather has been better so the ground has been firmer under foot but the place still resembles a kind of lunar landscape, full of craters brimming with fetid water, pathways weaving through what can only be described as lakes of mud and villages reduced to rubble after the repeated bombardments from both sides.

The talk here is of victory and we have indeed made advances. Our new tactics, practiced repeatedly before we moved up, seem to be working. I can't say too much but we are nullifying the Hun's counter attacks quite effectively.

But at a terrible cost. Once again I have lost eighteen men in the past two weeks out of a platoon of less than thirty. From when I first arrived in France there is only myself, Sergeant Barnes, Corporal Gregson, Dawkins, Fletcher, Jackson (tell his mother he is surviving) and Haniford left. I have to admit one gets quite inured to it all after a while.

New men arrive every day and it is a terrible shock to them.

Two days ago we waited in a trench for an early morning advance and one young soldier kept calling out 'Mum. Oh Mum.' The Germans must have heard him and *it was disturbing the others. I tried to reason with him but he just kept on wailing 'I can't do it, I want my Mum,' and the men were shouting 'send him 'f***ing back to his Mum,' so I told him he was being a coward and I'd have him court-martialled but he still kept on wailing until Dawkins appeared and slapped him fiercely on both cheeks. That silenced him and a moment later he fell into a deep sleep.*

But he was killed the next day so he never will get to see his mum.

Dawkins seems to have changed since his last leave. Maybe it's discovering he is to be a father but he suddenly seems less certain about everything. He was attached to one of the skirmishing parties the other day and I'm sure I saw him looking nervous and having to steel himself before setting out which is most unlike him. Before he went out he asked me to keep hold of a photograph he keeps in a metal container. It was of his fiancé, a beautiful girl, the one who is bearing his child. I said I would look her up when I got back if he didn't make it.

But he did and I was gladly able to return it to him. I wouldn't have enjoyed that conversation.

And so it continues. We will be relieved shortly and then the whole routine of back to reserve before returning to fight another day will recommence. We are all very weary. I still pray to God for strength and mercy but I'm rather beginning to wonder if he's listening.

I am due leave in a couple of weeks so will pass on details as soon as I have them. I can't wait to see you all again.

My love to Jane,
And my love to you,
Jeremy.'

Elizabeth closed her eyes. 'That poor boy,' she said, 'calling out for his mother then being killed. It's inhuman.'

Even though it was still mid-morning George poured himself a brandy.

'Ralph tells me there's debate at the highest level as to whether to call it all off,' he said, 'Haig feels victory is within his grasp but Plumer and Gough, even with the successes of the past few weeks, are shocked by the number of casualties, and Lloyd George is questioning whether we'll ever free those damned ports.'

'I wish they'd call it off tomorrow.'

'So do, I, Elizabeth, so do I. Wish. That's all we can do.'

CHAPTER 34

November 2011

The thought that he should have contacted Major Hall by now was preying on James Marchant's mind as he left an appointment in Jermyn Street. The meeting in the Imperial War Museum had changed everything. The fact that he had triggered an immediate visit from a staff officer at the MOD just by clicking on the name Daniel Dawkins a few times had come as a shock in itself. To then be told that Dawkins, a man he had imagined all along to be heroic, was in fact a coward up for court martial was seriously disconcerting. Twice the previous day he had received texts from the Major requiring a response and he knew the only sensible thing to do was to comply with the man's demands – but the thought of signing that form, even though he now realised that going public could lead him into all sorts of trouble, seemed so final that he found himself procrastinating.

Sarah was up in London for the day and as he walked towards towards the bar where he was due to meet her he wondered how much he should reveal of what had been said.

She was sitting at a corner table with a glass of wine and after he'd bought himself a beer they chatted inconsequentially for a few minutes.

'You've gone rather quiet these past couple of days,' she said.

'I've been thinking.'

'About going public?'

'Yes.'

They sat in silence for a few seconds and he could tell from the set expression on her face that her attitude had been hardening.

'Well you know my thoughts on that.'

He didn't reply.

She circled the rim of her glass with a finger.

'Here's how I see it, James,' she said, leaning forwards now and looking him straight in the eye. 'My grandfather Peter Harding decided to keep his secret. He kept it all his life, knowing it was too big a thing to reveal, too devastating to release, telling, we assume, only Joyce who then, again we assume, told my father, both of whom also kept silent for year after year.'

Marchant nodded slowly. 'Go on.'

'And so is it really up to us now to reveal that secret? Do I want to be the first in my family to publicise something that my father and grandparents guarded so keenly for all that time?'

'Believe me, these thoughts have been going through my mind.'

'Good. They need to.' 'And anyway,' she continued, 'even if we had solid, incontrovertible evidence, DNA, tooth analysis, all that, even if we could say one hundred percent we knew it was Daniel buried in the Abbey – which we can't – it would be wrong to reveal it. Simply wrong.'

'Because ...'

'Because? Because? For God's sake, because, as you've said to me a number of times, the idea of the Unknown Warrior, the importance of it to millions of people around the world, the history, the symbolism – we simply can't destroy that out of ....'

'Vanity. I think that's what you said the other day.'

'Yes. Vanity.' Sarah took his hand in hers. 'You see, James, it seems to me this is a case of your career versus my family's integrity – and our friendship.'

He stared back at her.

'It's that binary, is it?'

She sat back. 'No. No, that came out wrong. But James, I heard something on the radio yesterday – in one of your strange coincidences the subject of the Unknown Soldier came up in a discussion on the First World War and someone described how up to a thousand women actually dreamt that it was their own son who was being buried. The Reverend Kendall was besieged by people convinced it was their loved one who was chosen in that French village. It's that big. That important. You just can't do this.'

Marchant sat in silence. 'I think I'll pop out for some fresh air,' he said, 'I won't be long.'

Outside he walked slowly around the block. 'My family's integrity. Your career. Our friendship. ...' These were tough words. He passed shop windows with no awareness of what was beyond the glass, he crossed a street without looking, he bumped into a man who had stopped to hail a taxi.

Then his phone rang.

'Mr Marchant.' The voice was immediately recognisable.

'Yes. Hello, Major Hall.'

'We're becoming impatient, Mr Marchant.'

'I would imagine so.'

'So, you must sign today or ..'

'Or?'

There was a pause. 'Or there will be consequences, Mr Marchant.'

For a second an image of being held in a small cell and tortured until he signed came to Marchant. He even managed to smile at the thought.

'Well, you'll be pleased to know I've decided,' he said.

'And?'

'And I'll sign your damned piece of paper.'

Back in the bar Sarah was in conciliatory mood.

'James, I'm sorry. You're the least vain man I've ever met, I shouldn't have accused you of that.'

'That's OK.' It was his turn to take her hands. 'You were right. I got carried away by the thought of making a name for myself – and you pulled me back in the nick of time.' He paused. 'And you were also right about wanting to make my father proud of me. It clouded my judgement.' He said it calmly but the pressure of his grip revealed the depth of his feeling.

'Oh, James.' Sarah closed her eyes briefly. The sound of a police car could be heard in the distance.

'So,' he said, 'as you've said, the best thing, the right thing morally, is for us to become the latest custodians of the secret.' He was speaking quickly again, regaining control of his emotions. 'We've picked up the mantle and we'll pass it on to the next generation. We'll keep the diaries hidden and leave the clues for someone else to find one day.'

Sarah squeezed his hands. 'It's the right decision. I think your father would approve.'

'I've come to see that.'

'I can't stop thinking about Daniel,' she said, 'I just keep picturing him out in France in those terrible conditions and being killed with no one there to see what happened to him.' She sighed at the thought. 'I wish we could have found out more about him.'

'Yes, I'm sorry we haven't been able to. But we can try looking in other areas.'

'You said it was odd there was so little about him from the military angle.'

'Yes.'

Sarah looked at Marchant quizzically but said nothing. She gazed out into the street. 'I bet he was a brave man,' she said.

Marchant didn't reply and when she looked back at him he averted his gaze.

'What is it?'

'Nothing.'

'Something's up. You're being evasive, I can tell.'

'No, just tired.'

'James, look at me.'

He turned his face towards hers.

'I've come to know when you're holding something back and I can tell you are now. What is it?'

'I don't think I can tell you.'

She leant forwards. 'James, if you value our friendship and you have something important you're not revealing then you must tell me. I need to know, I need so much to know the truth about my grandfather.'

'You won't like it.'

'Tell me.'

Marchant swallowed but held her eye. 'He was up for court martial for cowardice when he went missing.'

'What?'

'It seems Daniel refused to advance when ordered.'

'Refused to advance? No, that can't be right.' Sarah looked aghast. 'Tell me how you know this.'

'I've been visited by a man from the MOD.'

'You've what?'

Marchant took a deep breath. 'When trying to find out more about Daniel I was paid a visit.'

Sarah was motionless. 'Tell me.'

He hesitated before speaking but then, choosing his words carefully, he ran through his visit to the Imperial War Museum, the Head of Curation's intervention and the arrival of Major Hall. Sarah listened, her face registering shock, sadness and finally anger in quick succession.

'I simply can't believe it,' she said when Marchant had finished.

'Well, I'm not making it up.'

'No, I can't believe Daniel was a coward.'

'The men from the Ministry do.'

'Then they must be wrong. There must be more to this.'

Marchant put his hand on hers but she brushed it away. 'Wait a minute.' She stared at him as she thought things through. 'This is why you're not going public, isn't it? I see now. It's because you've accepted their word for it. You've let them bully you into brushing the whole thing under the carpet.'

'That's not true.'

'Isn't it?' In her fury and disappointment Sarah's voice was suddenly harsh and accusing. 'Are you sure, James? Are you sure that when you told me a few minutes ago that by being the new custodians of the secret would be the right thing to do morally, what you really meant was that you were buckling under pressure from some bloody military bully?

'That's completely unjustified. You're the one who has persuaded me to keep silent, not the sodding major. You need to calm down.'

'Calm down? Calm down? You've just told me my grandfather, a man I had come to believe was a great man, a brave and sensitive man, was a coward – and you ask me to calm down?'

'Well you insisted I tell you the truth and that's what I've done.'

'Then fuck you!' Sarah's eyes were brimming with tears. 'Fuck you with your calm, rational bloody analysis, this is my flesh and blood we're talking about here.'

'Don't you accuse me of having no feelings.' Marchant's resentment was clear from the tone of his voice. 'This has emotional impact for me too you know.'

They sat facing each other, their frustration and bitterness hanging in the air.

'Then do something about this.' Sarah downed the last of her wine, stood up and picked up her coat. 'Do something positive and find out what really happened out there.' She threw some change on the table and started walking but stopped and turned. 'I'm beginning to wish I'd never found those fucking letters,' she said, then she turned her back, nodded at a waiter, and stepped out into the street.

CHAPTER 35

8 October 1917

To those soldiers in the 2nd Army who had survived the two weeks since the 20th September, the Ypres Salient held a particular horror.

Crossing the Ypres – Yser canal over a temporary bridge one entered a wasteland of shattered swamp that rose gradually towards the Passchendaele Ridge. German soldiers on the higher ground trained their machine guns on wooden pathways that zig-zagged between brimming shell holes. Giant rats, gorged on the bodies of fallen soldiers, ran hither and thither amongst the heaps of rubble that had once been villages. Bubbling streams linked lakes of liquid mud. Blackened tree stumps littered the landscape. Bodies of fallen soldiers lay everyhere, many half buried, many below the surface, sucked in by the saturated sponge that was the salient; gurgling, spitting mud, emitting a stench of death like no other place on earth.

'Abandon hope all ye who enter here,' said Dawkins.

The men of 5 Platoon surveyed the scene.

'End of the world,' said Fletcher, 'That's where we are. The end of the bleeding world.'

'Might just be,' said Dawkins.

It had taken them five hours to reach this point and the new men were all in. It was dusk and they were to attack at 0500hrs. Everyone was shivering and many had streaming noses and sore throats as an epidemic of fever swept through the battalion. The rain had returned in a furious horizontal movement that soaked already sodden clothing, finding gaps and chilling flesh that was clammy and turning blue with the cold. They followed one another in single file, slithering on the duckboards, often grabbing the man in front to avoid falling off the track and into the mire that would drag any living thing under in seconds.

A guide led them to a series of trenches that were filled above knee height with putrid water where every few paces foul smelling bubbles rose to the surface as the soldier's boots squashed air out of the lungs of unseen corpses.

On arrival at their destination the men slumped into an exhausted torpor. Twenty minutes later Lieutenant Latham gathered together his Sergeant and Corporals. Dawkins, promoted yet again, was amongst them.

'Reveille at four, attack at five, normal drill,' was the extent of Latham's orders, 'get what sleep you can. Good luck.'

The men heated a sorry brew of lukewarm tea and ate cold rations in silence before huddling together for warmth. Private Peter Jackson sat alone with only Murphy the dog for company. Since his return to the front Jackson had been behaving strangely. He had ceased all communication with the other men and now only spoke to Murphy who spent much of the time curled in the top of his backpack.

Dawkins sat down beside him. 'So, back over in the morning,' he said.

Jackson smiled benignly, as if keeping a secret to himself.

'I won't be beside you this time,' said Dawkins, 'I have to lead the section. But you'll be all right. Just keep level with the others.'

Jackson stroked Murphy. 'No need to be scared, Dan,' he said.

'What's that?'

Jackson smiled again. 'I can see it in your eyes Dan but there's nothing to be scared of,' he said, 'It'll all work out, don't you worry.'

'What do you mean Pete? What'll work out?'

Jackson was staring into the distance. 'Everything,' he said and Dawkins, while assuming that Jackson had finally lost all touch with reality, still felt unsettled by his unnatural calm.

The night passed slowly. With their energy fully sapped by the walk out from Ypres, the men remained in a kind of semi-conscious lethargy, any thoughts of the morning's assault outweighed by the more immediate need to protect themselves from the biting wind that whistled through the trenches.

The following morning they rose in darkness, cajoling their creaking limbs into action, eating the remainder of their rations and then waiting for the order to advance.

'Not much of a fucking bombardment,' said Dawkins.

He was right. The sappers who had been working day and night to build gun platforms had been defeated by the conditions and 5 Platoon were to advance behind a creeping barrage that was the most feeble of the campaign.

At 0455hrs a shell above them glowed white through the clouds and the battalion of men scrambled out into the open. As the soldiers took their first steps they entered a strange, disconnected place. Shells were exploding ahead of them, the guns were sounding from behind, but in those brief moments before the Germans reacted to their presence it was as if a calm had descended on their small part of the battlefield. They walked side by side, not talking, passing slowly through a temporary fissure in the fabric of the Western Front, crossing a narrow strip of land that for those precious seconds was peaceful and detached from the chaos surrounding them.

Then the enemy opened fire.

The younger soldiers ducked and shouted in terror but the older men rallied them and urged them on. Dawkins, for the first time he could remember, could feel the cold hand of fear grip his very essence so that the bullets whizzing past him seemed louder than normal, the explosions closer, the cries of men around him more terrible than before. He shouted encouragement to the younsters around him but his voice was thick and lacking its usual authority.

They had been going for no more than a minute when Fletcher fell.

Without a sound he simply sank to the ground. Dawkins stopped and dropped down to his knees beside him. Fletcher's right leg below the knee was hit and though he attempted to get up he fell over immediately.

'Stay down you stupid bastard,' said Dawkins, inspecting his wound. A shell landed nearby and he instinctively ducked. 'That's it for you, mate,' he said, 'no visiting Fritz today. Pain?'

Fletcher smiled at him. 'Nothing, Dan.'

'Good.'

'So this is what a blighty feels like.'

Dawkins was hastily wrapping a field dressing round Fletcher's leg. He looked up and the rest of the platoon were moving away.

'Yes, you bastard,' he said, 'fucking blighty at last.'

'See you then, Dan.'

Dawkins tied off the ends of the dressing and sat in the mud.

'Think you can crawl?'

'I'll give it a go but I've lost my glasses. I can't see too far ahead.'

Dawkins took a quick look round in the mud. 'Can't see them but there's a dip over there.' He pointed Fletcher in the right direction. 'It's not far. You'll make it.'

'Thanks Dan.'

'Right, see you, Fletch,' he said, and then he leant forwards and embraced his closest friend. The dripping stubble on their cheeks touched and Fletcher patted Dawkins on his back.

'Best of luck, mate,' said Fletcher, 'I'll be OK. You keep yourself safe now.'

Dawkins stood up. 'I'll do that, Fletch,' he said, 'bye for now, you've been the best of mates,' then he turned and began running to catch up with the others.

By the time he had caught up there was a lull in the bombardment and the enemy fire had intensified. A machine gun directly ahead of them was scything down anything that moved and men were falling with every few yards of ground gained. On their left flank 7 Platoon seemed to be faring better but away to their right there was no sign of anyone from 6 Platoon. Neither Lieutenant Latham nor Sergeant Barnes were anywhere to be seen.

'It's no good,' shouted Dawkins, 'we'll not make it.' Another man crumpled into the cloying mud even as he spoke. He looked swiftly to his left and right and estimated that only seven soldiers from the platoon were still with him. There was still some distance to the enemy front line and the slight mist that had given them cover earlier had completely cleared.

'Back,' he shouted, 'turn back.'

The men needed no encouragement and immediately took Dawkins lead as he ran back towards his own lines. On seeing his enemy retreating the German machine gunner, as if having no appetite for shooting men in the back, ceased firing and the British soldiers were able to shuffle across the ground in an exhausted trot. With no more than thirty paces to go Dawkins stumbled across Sergeant Barnes who was lying on his side.

'What's up, Sarn't?' said Dawkins, crouching down.

'Took one in the side,' said Barnes, struggling to get his words out.

Dawkins eased him over onto his back and could see where the sergeant had been hit.

'You'll live,' he said, 'let's get you back.'

With Barnes letting out agonised groans Dawkins helped him up and put his arm round his waist. Barnes then hopped on one leg until they made it back to the trench where they slithered over the top and down its steep side before landing in a heap on a duckboard that projected out of the scummy water at the bottom.

Dawkins propped Barnes up and looked about him. The seven others had all made it back but apart from them there was no one to be seen.

'Thought the next wave would be here by now,' said one of the soldiers.

'Must be a cock up, but they'll be here soon,' said Dawkins.

'What do we do now?' asked another soldier.

'Keep our fucking heads down, that's what.'

The soldier, one of the recent new recruits, could have been no more than eighteen and his teeth were chattering. 'Are we all that's left?' he asked.

'That we are.'

The boy stared at Dawkins in a state of utter bewilderment, unable to comprehend the scale of the horror that had befallen him. He shook his head from side to side but could find no more words to express his shock at the massacre he had just witnessed.

'We'll wait here until relief comes,' said Dawkins, 'get what rest you can.' He then lifted Barnes up and carried him to a bolt hole where at least they could be out of the rain.

It was here that Major Horrocks, alone apart from his orderly, Ennis, found them a few minutes later.

'What's happening here?' he asked.

'Sergeant Barnes is wounded, sir,' said Dawkins.

'I can see that. Where's Mr Latham?'

'Somewhere out there,' said Dawkins, pointing towards the German lines.

'So what are you doing here with these men?'

'We came back.'

'Came back?'

'Yes sir, we were down to eight men and were coming under sustained machine gun fire. It was hopeless, so I ordered the withdrawal.'

Major Horrocks looked around him with an expression of disbelief.

'Let me get this right, Corporal Dawkins,' he said, 'you told the men to retreat?'

'Yes.'

'You chose to ignore the orders – orders I might say that have come directly from General Plumer – to continue advancing until the enemy lines have been taken?'

'As I said, sir, it was hopeless, we'd all be dead by now if we'd continued.'

'Just answer my question, Dawkins.'

'Very well, sir, yes, I did.'

Major Horrocks pursed his lips. 'That is an admission of extreme cowardice, Corporal Dawkins.'

Daniel looked him up and down. 'And what would you call someone who doesn't even make it out of the trench in the first place?' he asked.

'I beg your pardon?'

'What would you call an officer who chooses not to advance with his men? A fucking coward of an officer who skulks in the safety of his lines while most of his company is wiped out in front of his very eyes.'

Major Horrocks stared up at Dawkins, his fists clenched as if he was about to strike the taller man. Dawkins looked down at him coolly.

'You'll pay for this,' said Horrocks, his voice distorted by anger.

Dawkins shrugged. 'And how will that be?'

'Ennis,' said Horrocks, his eyes still fixed on Dawkins, 'write this down.' The soldier took out a pencil and a sheet of paper.

'At...' he looked at his pocket watch, 'at 0535hrs on the 9th of October 1917, Corporal Dawkins of 5 Platoon, the 6th Berkshire Light Infantry admitted that, when confronted by light enemy fire, he ordered a withdrawal in direct contravention of orders to advance.' He was speaking slowly and deliberately to give Ennis time to write. 'He left his Platoon Commander and fellow soldiers to continue on the battlefield without him and returned to the safety of his front line. On his return, when challenged, he insulted his company commander in front of witnesses, using foul language.' He paused. 'Got that?'

'But sir,' said Ennis uncertainly.

'I said have you got that, Ennis?'

'Yes, sir.'

'I therefore recommend,' continued Horrocks, his voice dropping almost to a whisper, 'that Corporal Dawkins be court martialled for cowardice.'

Dawkins had listened silently as Horrocks spoke. 'I was wrong,' he said, 'you really are an evil little bastard, aren't you.'

Horrocks reached for his pistol and pointed it at Dawkins. 'One more word from you, Corporal, and I will shoot you here and now for your insubordination.'

Dawkins grinned. 'Oh, I doubt that.' He looked towards Ennis and Sergeant Barnes. 'This is the British Army. Even you aren't mad enough to summarily kill a serving soldier in front of witnesses.'

Major Horrocks continued to point his pistol at Dawkins. His hands were shaking. 'Witnesses indeed,' said Horrocks. He lowered the pistol, took the pencil and piece of paper from Ennis's hands and turned to Sergeant Barnes. 'Sergeant Barnes,' he said, 'Your signature as a witness, please.'

Sergeant Barnes, through half-closed eyes and with enormous effort, took hold of the pencil but held it in mid air, not writing.

'Sergeant Barnes,' said Horrocks, 'if you know what's good for you, you will sign this document this very moment.'

Barnes looked directly at Dawkins and still his hand hovered over the paper.

'You're on your way home, Sergeant,' said Dawkins, 'I'll be back out there shortly.' He pointed towards the enemy lines. 'Do the sensible thing.'

Barnes gazed at the piece of paper and then, very slowly, he signed his name. Horrocks immediately retrieved the paper and handed it back to Ennis.

'Ennis,' he said, 'sign this as second witness and then you will take it immediately to HQ and hand it in to the adjutant.'

Ennis hesitated. He looked at Dawkins.

'Do as the little cunt says,' said Dawkins, 'don't get yourself into trouble on my behalf, Enno.'

Ennis still hesitated but then he too signed, put the paper in his documents wallet and, with a nod towards Dawkins left them.

'And you, Dawkins,' said Major Horrocks, 'you will be arrested as soon as we have completed the next wave of this attack.'

'We? So you'll be joining me this time?'

Horrocks raised his pistol again. 'Don't push me, Dawkins.'

Dawkins stepped forwards so that his chest was up against the barrel of the pistol. 'I think, Major Horrocks, that I might just do that.'

He turned to Sergeant Barnes whose eyes were closed again. 'Sergeant Barnes,' he said, 'Sergeant Barnes.' Barnes stirred and opened his eyes. 'It looks like the mist is coming down again so we'll leave you now. The next lot will be coming up shortly.'

'Got it,' muttered Barnes.

'We'll be off to get Mr Latham back,' said Dawkins, 'me and the Major here.' A look of terror flitted across Horrocks's face as Barnes, mustering his last reserves of strength, reached out a hand. 'Then Good luck to you,' said the Sergeant and it seemed to Dawkins, as they spoke their last words to each other, that Barnes just managed to raise a conspiratorial smile.

Dawkins pushed past Horrocks into the open trench and he was right – the mist had descended again. Suddenly, with no warning, he grasped the pistol out of Horrocks' grip before he had time to react. He pointed it so that the muzzle was inches from Horrocks's face. 'So, let's be away.'

'What are you saying, Dawkins?'

'I'm saying I may need some help in getting Mr Latham back if he's out there wounded and that you're the one who'll help me.'

'Don't be ridiculous.'

'Me? I'm the ridiculous one?'

'Get one of these other men to help you, I'm the OC for God's sake.' Horrocks looked about him at the remaining soldiers of 5 Platoon. 'You, private, go with Corporal Dawkins here to find your Platoon Commander,' he said but before the words were out of his mouth Dawkins struck him across the side of his face with the pistol.

'Stay where you are lads,' he shouted, 'this is between me and the Major. You wait for the next company to arrive.' The men remained where they were, watching in disbelief.

Horrocks made to say something but Dawkins struck him again. 'Either you start climbing that ladder now or I shoot you and go on my own,' he said.

'Dawkins, listen to me..'

'Climb. You have three seconds.'

'Dawkins, I've done my share of fighting, you should know, it's just I can't do this, I can't go over again...' Horrocks voice, normally so self-assured, was now higher, his words coming out breathless and distorted.

Dawkins struck him a third time so that blood began to seep out of a weal in his cheek.

'Climb.'

With great reluctance Horrocks took hold of the ladder. 'I beg you, Dawkins,' he said as his boots found the first rung, 'I beg you, I've done this too often, it's too much ...'

'Climb.'

Slowly Horrocks climbed, his feet pausing on each step.

Dawkins followed directly behind him and when he was half way up he turned to the soldiers who were still standing where they had been, scarcely able to comprehend what they were witnessing.

'Whatever happens next,' said Dawkins, 'you saw none of this, do you understand?'

'Yes, DD,' said one of the men.

'It'll do no good for anyone for this to be talked about so I need you to swear on that.'

'Yes, I swear,' said the soldier.

'And the rest of you.'

The other men swore not to say anything.

'That's important lads,' said Dawkins, 'you remember that, it's between me and the Major now.'

Horrocks had stopped while this was happening and Dawkins now shoved him from behind.

'Climb.'

'Dawkins, I'll retract the court martial ....'

'Fucking climb or I shoot.'

Horrocks began climbing again with Dawkins pushing him as he laboured his way to the top. As they cleared the rim of the trench Horrocks knelt on all fours and gasped for breath. 'I don't think I can do this,' he said.

Dawkins knelt down beside him and grabbed his collar. 'Listen, Major Horrocks,' he said, 'you may have had it bad as a boy. There may be a reason you have to bully everyone around you, but that cuts no ice here. I don't give a fuck about why you've become the little shit you have because now it's time to do something good. It's time for you to be a real man and save someone else's skin. It's your last chance.'

Horrocks began wheezing and gasping for breath. 'I'm not well,' he managed to whisper.

'Do you think you're the only one?' Dawkins face was only inches away. 'Do you think the others don't all shit themselves at the thought of going over?' He pulled the Major up to his feet. 'I could hardly climb that ladder earlier, I can hardly put one foot in front of another today but I'm forcing myself. I'm forcing myself and that's what you're going to do now.' He took hold of Horrocks belt and started dragging him forwards. 'Now, we need to move fast while the mist still holds.'

The lull in the battle cast an eerie mood over the landscape. As Dawkins and Horrocks walked alone towards the enemy position they stumbled frequently across bodies of men who, earlier that morning, they had been conversing with in the trench. They passed the spot where Fletcher had fallen but he was no longer there. Many of the soldiers were moaning as they lay dying from their wounds, alone with their final thoughts, eeking out their last moments in excrutiating pain.

Dawkins recognised Wilson, one of the men who had been in the bunker the night they were ordered to attack Borry Wood. He was face down and choking on the liquid mud beneath him. Dawkins carefully turned him over and he stared up out of one eye, the left hand side of his face entirely missing.

'Take it easy, John,' said Dawkins but even as he spoke Wilson spluttered one last time and died.

The mist ebbed and flowed. Whenever it lifted they sank to the ground and acted dead, when it thickened they continued towards the point where Dawkins had last seen Mr Latham. They picked their way carefully through the rutted fields and Dawkins found himself imagining how this place would have once been; green, covered in grass or crops, the farmers tending to their cattle or sheep, farm buildings, fences, woods, sunshine. All gone now, only deep mud, shattered tree stumps, rain, disfigured limbs, dark clouds, pools of blood.

'Mr Latham,' he shouted out but there was no answer.

'He'll be dead,' said Horrocks, 'we might as well turn back.'

Dawkins continued walking. 'Mr Latham,' he shouted again.

'For God's sake, Dawkins, you'll attract every Hun machine gunner in the area.'

'Mr Latham.'

'Here.' The voice was very faint, coming from over to their left. Dawkins walked towards the sound, followed by Horrocks. 'Again,' he shouted. 'Here.' In a slight break in the mist they could see a shell hole, about twelve feet across, no more than thirty paces away.

'That's him,' said Dawkins, 'run.'

They began running but were only half way to the shell hole when quite suddenly the breeze picked up and the mist cleared. A volley of shots rang out and Major Horrocks let out a loud shout. Dawkins briefly looked across and Horrocks was being hit repeatedly, his body jerking one way and another as the rounds found their target. Dawkins mustered the energy to sprint the last few yards and as he jumped over the lip of the shell hole a series of bullets whistled past his ears, missing him by inches. The hole was deep with water only feet from the rim and it was a few seconds before he surfaced, spitting slime out of his mouth and grabbing at tree roots. He managed to gain some purchase on a narrow ledge and ended up crouching, water up to his waist, gripping the roots, his head just below ground level. Mr Latham was a couple of feet away, balancing on the same ledge.

'Close thing,' said Latham.

'Nice place you've found.'

'Bit wet and cold.'

'True.'

A single shot rang out and Dawkins looked up. 'Sniper. Someone else must be out there.'

'You came alone?'

'Major Horrocks was with me.'

'Major Horrocks?'

'It's a bit of a story. He was hit just then.'

Latham raised an eyebrow. 'The others?'

'Not many left. We turned back.'

'Slaughter.' Latham seemed to be having trouble getting his words out. 'Sergeant Barnes?' he said.

'Took one. So did Fletcher – but they'll be all right. I don't think Jackson made it out of the trench.'

Latham didn't reply.

'Major Horrocks told us to come straight back out again and attack.'

'And?'

'I told him to fuck off.'

What might have passed as a smile crossed Latham's face. 'Trouble then,' he said but though the two men were facing each other Dawkins struggled to hear him.

'I made him come back with me to find you,' said Dawkins, 'not sure he was too happy about that.'

Latham smiled again but said nothing. Dawkins reached out with his left hand and just managed to touch his officer's shoulder without losing balance. 'You all right sir?' he said.

Latham looked up. 'Might have been hit,' he said.

'Where?'

'Not sure. Below somewhere.' He spoke with an effort, each word accompanied by a grunt of pain.

Dawkins eyed the gap between them to see if he might reach out to check Latham's wound but to do so would mean losing his footing.

'Not much I can do until we get you back,' he said.

'I'll be OK.'

'Best not to talk then, conserve your energy.'

'Right.'

'But unless the mist comes down again we'll be stuck here till dark,' said Dawkins.

'Right.'

They waited. After a while the mist began to thicken again, enveloping the land in an unusual purplish light, its opaqueness lit up periodically by flashes of gunfire that came and went in waves of ghostly fluorescence. In a few more minutes they would be able to make a dash for it.

'Could have done with this half an hour ago,' said Dawkins but he was wondering at Latham's ability to move.

A breeze floated across the ruined fields, whispering through the debris of No Man's Land so that a strange sound came to them, as of a train in the distance, its engine beating in echos through mountains, its steel wheels screeching on tracks.

Latham's eyes were closed, his knuckles white as he gripped his tree root. 'Tell me about your girl again,' he said. His voice was little more than a whisper.

Dawkins changed his position by shuffling his feet along the ledge.

'My girl?' he said, 'what can I say?' He was watching the muscles round Latham's mouth as they tensed with each pulse of pain. 'Long curly hair, nice smile, kind face.'

'I saw that.'

'Don't speak.' Dawkins was picturing the photograph in his pocket. 'I met her at school. She stood out. Spoke up for herself, teased me, had a confidence the others never had. Wouldn't let me kiss her at first. She's funny. Makes me laugh. Always has something to say.'

'She loves you.'

'Yes. Yes, I believe she does. Fuck knows why. She was always cleverer then me, always reading something, she'll make a good mother.'

'And you a good father.'

'I plan to.'

They fell silent and listened to the battle going on to the south. The rain was forming small valleys in the mud as it flowed over the rim of the crater. The sky was dark now, as if night was falling prematurely. Visibility was down to no more than fifty feet.

Latham opened his eyes briefly and looked into the sky. 'Mist,' he whispered, 'Go.'

'I'll stay a while.'

'Go.'

'We will. Wait till it thickens a bit more. Choose our moment.'

'You. Leave me.'

'Won't be doing that, sir.'

'Brother, brother, if this be the
Last song you shall sing, sing
well, for you will not sing another, brother sing."

Dawkins listened to the words in his head and it was as if Joyce was with him, reading out loud. 'Understand it now,' he said.

'Understand what?'

'A poem.'

'What poem?'

'Just a poem.'

'Tell me.'

Dawkins recited the verse.

'Again.'

He repeated the lines.

'You're the brother,' said Latham.

'Guess I am.'

Dawkins could see Latham's hands were slipping on the roots so he took hold of his sleeve to prevent him from sliding under. 'Hold on, lad,' he said.

Latham's head was over to one side. 'You're a good man, Dawkins,' he said.

Dawkins thought back to his recent conversations with Joyce and Fletcher. 'Might just be after all,' he said. He was holding on with all his strength. Latham's eyelids were flickering and it was all Dawkins could do to keep him from going under. 'Hold fucking on,' he shouted but Latham's head was dropping.

Then the young officer suddenly opened his eyes one last time and stared directly at Dawkins. 'I did my best, Dad,' he said. Dawkins freezing fingers were losing their grip. 'Yes, you did, son,' he replied softly, 'I'm proud of you.' Latham looked at him through glazed eyes and smiled. Then his body slipped from Dawkins' grasp and Daniel watched helplessly as the young officer started slowly sliding down the muddy bank, his body limp, his lips apart, his eyes closed again until first his mouth, then his nose and finally his entire head disappeared beneath the stinking waters of Flanders fields.

Dawkins held on to the roots and watched the bubbles rise where his Platoon Commander had been squatting opposite him seconds earlier. He felt numb all over, his body and mind now distancing him from the horrors that surrounded him, protecting him, reducing him to a being that knew no pain, felt nothing, could withstand what no sane man could tolerate. A burst of fire raked above his head. The mist suddenly lifted again and the lines of fire from the German machine gun posts, hidden for the past few minutes, were visible once more. Then everything fell silent apart from the terrible groaning coming from the wounded soldiers strewn across the ruined land, exposed, unable to move, dying alone with nothing to relieve their suffering. The rain was driving down heavier than ever and Dawkins saw that the water level in the shell hole was rising rapidly. The salient was saturated and in a short while his crater would be filled and he would have to make a dash for it back to the trenches, his kit on his back, his feet sinking up to the ankles with each step, a lone figure making a bid for safety with no cover, no supporting fire and in full view of the German gunners.

Private Peter Jackson had been asleep when his platoon went over the top. On his own in a small dugout he had been missed by the sergeants and corporals as they gathered the men to advance and when nobody called for him he simply remained where he was.

Inured to the sound of gunfire it was voices that finally woke him. He peered out of his hide and saw Daniel shouting at the Company Commander. He watched as they ascended a ladder and disappeared out of view.

'Where the fuck have you come from?' asked one of the soldiers as he walked calmly past them towards the ladder. Jackson didn't answer but slowly assembled his kit.

'What's Dan up to?' he finally asked.

'He's gone out to find Mr Latham.'

Jackson looked down at Murphy who was standing beside him, his ears up, water dripping off his coat. 'Let's go find Dan,' he said and Murphy wagged his tail at the prospect of a walk.

In the past few days Peter's leg had stopped shaking. After more than a year of uncontrollable movement it had at last settled down as a strange serenity had come over him. The sound of shells no longer made him flinch. The cold, the rain, the hunger, the misery of life at the front seemed no longer to matter. A benign fatalism had taken hold of him and he was existing in a trance, once removed from reality, divorced from his surroundings.

He checked to ensure the pouch round Murphy's neck still had a small flask of whisky in it then he picked up the dog and climbed out of the trench. Once in the open Murphy jumped down and began trotting alongside him.

Peter walked in a straight line, heading in the direction of the German pillboxes, head held high.

'Dan,' he shouted, 'Dan. Where are you?'

At that moment a breeze blew the mist away and the whole battlefield was open in front of him. Bodies were strewn everywhere.

A series of shots rang out and Jackson could see, some distance away, two men running. One fell to the ground, the other seemed to dive for cover.

'Dan. I've got some grog for you,' he shouted.

There was no reply but he knew Dan would have made it to cover. Pete had come to realise in the last few days that Dan was indestructible. Bullets missed him, he was being watched by some benign spirit, he would survive while all those around him perished.

'I'm coming,' he shouted and he smiled at the thought that he too, Dan's friend, was unassailable and would survive this war. He bent down to pat Murphy on the back of his head and it was when he stood upright again that a single shot rang out across the salient and a sniper's bullet hit Private Jackson directly in the chest, exploding inside his ribcage and tearing his heart apart so that he was dead before his body even hit the ground.

*Soldiers viewing the smashed remains of a German
bunker and trenches at Oostaverne Wood.*

Dressing station at Messines Ridge, 1917.

Holding the line at Passchendaele during the Third Battle of Ypres.

Ypres-Zonnebeke Road

CHAPTER 36

November 2011

The anger James Marchant felt, both at himself for having inadvisedly told Sarah about Dawkins court martial, and at her for her accusation that he had simply buckled under pressure, propelled him into two days of frantic action. Leaving aside the work that was piling up on his desk he set about researching the men of 5 Platoon to see if he could gain any clues as to those last days that Dawkins was alive – and why he was up for court martial. He followed a number of leads but one by one they ended up in dead ends until finally he was left with only a single possible source of information: Lieutenant Jeremy Latham.

Marchant established that Latham had gone missing in the same assault as Dawkins and his body was assumed to be buried alongside the many 'Unknowns' in France. He had a sister called Jane who worked as a nurse during the war, had married soon after and had had two sons and a daughter. The eldest of her grandsons, now in his early sixties, had inherited from his father the family home in a village called Sonning and lived there still.

Marchant tracked down the number and called. A man answered and politely listened as Marchant explained his quest on behalf of a client to track down details of a soldier in his Grandfather's platoon in the First World War.

'I do have a file,' the man said, 'that my grandmother kept and passed down. I can't say I've looked through it in years but I've often wondered if it might be of historical interest – it has various letters and a few documents – so I'd be delighted to show it to you.'

'Thank you,' said Marchant, 'thank you so much. It could be very significant. Would you mind if I came over this evening?'

The man agreed and Marchant drove out to Sonning, arriving in darkness at a large house near the river.

'James Marchant? I'm Tony Sanderson,' said the man as he opened the door. He led Marchant into a study with leather chairs and a tall bureau where he gave him a beer and they talked about Jane Latham who had died in 1987 aged ninety-two.

'How much do you know about her brother?' asked Marchant.

'Jeremy? Very little, I'm afraid, other than that he went missing at Passchendaele when serving as a Lieutenant in the Berkshire Light Infantry.'

'But you say you have a file of his.'

'Well, not his exactly. I believe it was George Latham's – his father's.' He walked to his desk and picked up a file similar in appearance to the one containing Peter and Joyce Hardings' letters, 'this is it.' He handed it to Marchant who opened it carefully and started reading the first letter he came to.

'Why don't I leave you to it,' said Tony.

'Thank you.'

Marchant worked his way through Jeremy's letters, skimming over the early ones from his time at boarding school but then carefully reading those sent from the Western Front. It seemed Latham had been struggling to reconcile his religious faith with the Godless slaughter he was caught up in. There were a number of references to Dawkins and it appeared that the two of them had struck up a strange friendship.

Then Marchant came to Latham's last letter, dated 1 October 1917 and when he read the words '*Dawkins seems to have changed since his last leave. Maybe it's discovering he is to be a father but he suddenly seems less certain about everything,*' he felt a terrible sense of foreboding. '*He was attached to one of the skirmishing parties the other day and I'm sure I saw him looking nervous and having to steel himself before setting out which is most unlike him.*'

A cold shudder ran through Marchant's body. Had the Dawkins referred to in earlier letters as a brave and skilled soldier finally lost his nerve? Had he cracked and refused to go over the top? It was painful to contemplate.

He finished the letter and slumped back in his seat. So that was it. It seemed the Ministry of Defence version of events was accurate. He dreaded having to tell Sarah.

Tony Sanderson came back into the room. 'Interesting?' he said.

'Very. Very significant.'

'You think you might be able to do something with the letters?'

'Quite possibly. I'd need to look at them more closely.'

'I thought the one from the sergeant was quite poignant.'

Marchant looked up. 'What?'

'The letter from the sergeant to George Latham, didn't you see it?'

Marchant stared at the file in front of him. 'No.'

'Here.' Tony went to the back of the file and inserted in the flap was a letter written in poor handwriting, dated December 1917 with a High Wycombe address. Marchant turned it over and looked at the signature at the bottom. 'Sergeant Barnes,' he said, 'he was badly wounded at Passchendaele and never returned to the front. I wonder why he was writing to George Latham.'

'Read it,' said Tony, 'it mentions your man Dawkins.'

Marchant turned the letter back over and started reading.

'*Mr Latham, sir, I was platoon sergeant of 5 platoon, B company 6th Battalion The Berkshire Light Infantry between March of this year and early October when I was wounded and returned to England.*

Your son was 5 platoon commander during this time. I wanted to write to say a few words as Mr Latham spoke often of you and I thought you would want to know he was a brave lad.

We didn't always get on and I feel bad about that. But he made good decisions and the men respected him. He was leading the assault when we lost him. We came under heavy fire and were forced back and I was wounded. I'm sorry to say your son didn't make it back.

I need to tell you something, Mr Latham. In the assault almost the whole platoon was wiped out. It was a corporal called Dawkins who told the lads to retreat and it was the right thing to do but Dawkins fell out with the company commander, Major Horrocks over it. I've not told this to no one as it would be my word against an officer's but Horrocks had it in for Dawkins and he made a few of us sign to say Dawkins had refused to advance and should be court martialled. The others who signed were all killed in the next assault so it's just me left and I've been bothered by that signing and regret what I did.

Dawkins then went back out into no man's land to find your son and bring him back and he forced Major Horrocks to go with him but that was the last I saw of them.

I wanted to tell you this so you would know the men did their best for your boy. I'd ask you to not talk of this as I would be in trouble for criticising an officer but I needed to tell someone and I thought, as Mr Latham's father, you would be a good person to tell.

I am sorry for your loss but I wanted to get this off my chest and also let you know your boy did well,

Respectfully,

Bob Barnes.

Marchant sat reading and re-reading the letter. His body felt heavy in the chair, his feet stuck to the floor as if hypnotised. He was conscious of his heart pounding in his chest.

'What do you make of it?'

With an effort of will he looked up to see Tony Sanderson looking over his shoulder.

'Extraordinary,' he replied. 'Truly extraordinary.'

'I thought it might be.'

'It's of the utmost importance.'

'What, the bit about Dawkins?'

'Exactly. It completely changes our understanding of his final actions – I can't tell you what a relief that is.'

Sanderson smiled. 'Well, I'm pleased to be of help. Your client will be pleased.'

'Oh yes. You can't imagine how much. Would you mind if I took a photocopy of some of these letters?'

Sanderson patted his shoulder. 'Listen, take the folder. I can see you're a man who can be trusted and if there's some good to come out of this then it's the originals you'll need.'

'That's very kind of you.'

'Just make sure you bring them back in one piece.'

Ten minutes later Marchant was sitting in his car in Tony Sanderson's drive with the engine running. He dialled Sarah's number on his phone.

'Hello James.'

'You know you said 'do something positive' the other night?'

'Yes.'

'I have.' He was grinning as he spoke. 'I've got something to show you.'

'That sounds intriguing.'

'I'm coming round.'

'This evening?'

'Yes. I'm in Sonning at the moment and I'm setting off now.'

'Where's Sonning?'

'It's about fifteen minutes drive from Taplow. It's where Daniel's Platoon Commander lived. I've been reading his letters.'

'My God.'

'I think you'll be pleased with what I've found.'
'I'm at Dad's house preparing for the funeral.'
'I'll see you soon then.'

There was a hold up on the M4 and so it was past 10.30pm that Marchant finally arrived at the house. Sarah let him in and her excitement was hard to contain.

'Come on,' she said, 'let's see what you've got.'

They sat at the dining table with Marchant handing over one letter at a time, pointing out references to Dawkins while Sarah devoured every word. When they came to Latham's last letter she put her head in her hands. 'That's so sad,' she said, '*looking forward to seeing you all again.* He never did.'

'No.'

'But what do you make of that?' She pointed at the letter. 'He said Daniel was nervous all of a sudden.'

'I know. That really worried me.'

'So might they be right after all? Is that what you came to tell me? I thought you said I'd be pleased.'

'Well, there is one more thing.'

Marchant handed over the letter from Sergeant Barnes. He watched as Sarah read it. 'Oh my Lord,' she whispered, 'Oh my Lord.'

Marchant took her hand. 'It's been sitting in this file all these years,' he said. 'Just think of it. The very evidence that proves Daniel was brave to the end, undiscovered until now.'

There were tears running down Sarah's cheeks and she tried to speak but no words came out of her mouth. Marchant came round the table, sat beside her and gave her a hug. She looked at him.

'You're crying too, James,' she said, 'you're a bloody softy after all.'

11 November 2011

James Marchant stood with Sarah Harding in Trafalgar Square as the Last Post was played. The square was packed but when silence fell at the stroke of eleven the stillness was so complete that the chimes from Big Ben at the far end of Whitehall sounded clearly through the chill morning air.

Earlier they had listened to readings from television stars. After the silence they joined in with others throwing poppies in the fountain.

A recording from the Prime Minister rang out through loud speakers.

'We stand together,' said Mr Cameron, 'to honour the incredible courage and sacrifice of generations of British servicemen and women who have given their lives to protect the freedoms that we enjoy today. From the trenches of the First World War to the desert of Afghanistan, our Armed Forces have proved time and again that they are the bravest of the brave and the very best of what it means to be British. We can never fully repay the debt we owe them.'

When the ceremony was over they caught a tube to Paddington and then a train to Reading where Sarah's father was to be buried later in the afternoon.

There were few people in their carriage and they sat opposite each other looking out as the suburbs of London passed slowly by.

'I'm sorry I got so angry the other day,' said Sarah, 'it was unfair of me. I got things out of proportion.'

'That's OK, I shouldn't have told you about the MOD like that.'

'I'm glad you did – look what it led to.'

The train stopped at Ealing Broadway and the driver warned there would be a slight delay due to a red signal.

'I've contacted Major Hall in the MOD,' said Marchant, 'he's extremely interested to see Barnes's letter.'

'So what does that mean?'

'It won't change their determination to keep the identity of the Unknown Soldier hidden but it will mean the stain on Daniel's character will be removed.'

'That's great news.'

The train started again and travelled almost at walking pace before finally picking up speed after West Ealing.

'It's funny isn't it?,' said Marchant, 'how I got so carried away. It shows how easy it is to lose sight of what's right and wrong when the emotions take hold.'

'And that's in a measured, rational, well-educated type like you from a steady background.'

The train stopped at every station on the way to Reading and one by one what few people there were in the carriage got off until the two of them were alone. Buildings gave way to fields. The sun shone intermittently through the window. As they neared Taplow station Marchant, sitting opposite Sarah, leant forwards.

'How the wheel turns,' he said, 'here we are, a century on, in the place where Daniel grew up, where Joyce lived, where they walked to the river, where Peter took her and Stanley out for meals.'

'That's quite a thought.'

They looked up the hill towards the village and Marchant pointed out the towers of Taplow Court where one of the lesser known war poets had lived.

'I'm so pleased Daniel turned out to be a good man,' said Sarah, 'it 's hard to explain but it means a lot to me.'

'I think I understand.'

As the train crossed Maidenhead bridge Marchant came and sat beside her.

'It's an auspicious day,' she said, looking out at the woods between Maidenhead and Twyford, 'the day my grandfather was buried, the day my father will be buried.'

'You arranged it that way?'

'It seemed right.' She leant against him. 'So you said the other day that we would pass our secret on to the next generation.' She rested her hand gently on his leg. 'What exactly did you mean by that?'

He looked out of the window as the train slowed for Twyford.

'I suppose I meant pass it on to our children,' he said. His words lingered in the air. 'I was speaking figuratively, of course.'

Sarah nudged him in the side. 'Say that again,' she said.

'I was speaking figuratively.'

'No, the first bit.'

'Pass it on to our children.'

'That's the one.' She squeezed his leg. 'You old romantic, you, you're such a fast mover.'

CHAPTER 37

11 November 1920

George and Elizabeth Latham rose early on the day the Unknown Warrior was to be buried and there was little conversation as they took their breakfast in the conservatory. At 7am the driver arrived at the front door and they climbed into the back of the Lanchester.

'Reading first,' said George.

Soon they were on the Bath Road and fifteen minutes later the car turned into a narrow street of terraced red brick houses.

'Number forty-two,' said Elizabeth.

Mrs Jackson was standing in the doorway waiting for them. George opened the rear door of the car for her and she climbed in beside Elizabeth. George settled himself in the front passenger seat.

As the women talked behind him he sat in silence, watching the road and reflecting. It had been just over three years since his son had been reported missing, believed dead. For a time he had hoped beyond reason that Jeremy might turn up, perhaps concussed and suffering memory loss, perhaps wounded and being looked after in a French hospital, but as the weeks had passed so George had finally come to terms with the certainty that his son was dead. The letter he received from Sergeant Barnes had, in a way, been a comfort.

A month after receiving that letter a man called Fletcher, walking with crutches, arrived one evening at George's front door and introduced himself as having been in 5 Platoon. George welcomed Fletcher into the house and took him into the study.

'I thought you might like to hear about your son Jeremy, ' said Fletcher, 'he talked about you often, he told us about this house and the blue Lanchester. It wasn't that difficult to find the place.' George smiled. 'He admired you a lot, sir, we could tell that.'

Fletcher told George that he had been in hospital for the past months recovering from his wounds. He described the final disastrous assault in the Ypres Salient, the advance into driving rain, of how he had been wounded early on and how a friend called Daniel Dawkins had patched him up. He said that he'd crawled back to his lines but then fallen unconscious and woken up in a field hospital. He told George that Jeremy had been a good officer and well liked by the men.

'I wasn't with him at the end,' he said, 'but ...'

'I've had a letter from a Sergeant Barnes,' interrupted George, 'he saw Dawkins go out to try and recover Jeremy.'

'He sent it, did he? That's good.'

'You know about the letter?'

'I was in the same hospital as Sergeant Barnes and he told me what happened. I persuaded him to write to you.'

'I have you to thank then.'

'He was reluctant because he thought it might get him into trouble.'

'The business with Horrocks?'

'Yes.'

'I thought of taking it to a friend of mine who has contacts but decided in the end to respect Sergeant Barnes's request not to do so.'

'I think you did the right thing, sir. Dawkins died, Major Horrocks died. Joyce – that's Dawkins fiancée – won't have been informed of the cowardice charge. So, best left as it is.' Fletcher re-adjusted his legs. 'And Major Horrocks will have had a family – they wouldn't want to hear what happened at the end.'

'That's very reasonable of you, given that Dawkins was a friend.'

'The best of friends.'

'He must have been a very brave man.'

'He was at the end when he wanted to live.'

George didn't fully understand what this meant so made no comment. He offered Fletcher a drink and he accepted a brandy.

'I can't imagine what it must have been like for you all out there,' said George.

Fletcher looked about the room, at the rich fabrics, the book-lined shelves and the antique furniture and he thought of the time Dawkins had teased Mr Latham about his comfortable background. 'We lived with it at the time. We fought to survive, that's all we could do.'

'And you did. Survive, I mean.'

'Yes, and that's been very tough.'

'Surviving?'

'When all the others died. It's hard to live with.'

'I think I understand.' George noticed for the first time that the lines etched on Fletcher's face were those of a much older man. He walked over to the fire and stoked the embers. 'Guilt,' he said, 'it eats away at you doesn't it.'

'It does for those of us who made it back.' Fletcher stared into the flames. 'The guilt that comes from not being killed. Of seeing good men around you die and yet you live and you don't know why. The never ending sense that your continued existence is wrong in some way. It makes no sense but it sucks the joy out of life.'

George gave Fletcher an appraising look. 'You're very eloquent for a private soldier.'

Fletcher smiled. 'There was talk of a commission when I joined up,' he replied, 'but my eyesight wasn't up to it and I was happy to be one of the men after all. I never did tell the others.'

George stabbed at a log with a metal poker. 'Guilt,' he said again, 'I can see how troubling that must be.' He was shaking his head. 'But mine is a little different.' He faced Fletcher across the room. 'If any question why we died, tell them because our fathers lied,' he said quietly. 'You see, I pushed for my son to go and fight and now he's dead.'

Fletcher struggled to his feet and came to stand beside him. 'You did what you thought was the best thing at the time,' he said. 'You didn't kill him, the war did. We all had our reasons for joining up. No one knew how it would turn out. We were all victims of the circumstances we found ourselves in.'

George didn't answer. 'We all do what we think is right,' continued Fletcher, 'even Major Horrocks must have thought he was doing what was the best thing. We can't blame him for who he was.'

George considered Fletcher's philosophy. 'That attitude could excuse a lot of very bad behaviour,' he said, 'you have to draw a line somewhere.'

'Perhaps. Perhaps I'm too tolerant. But I prefer that to being too judgemental.'

George nodded slowly. 'I think my wife Elizabeth would go along with that sentiment. But it's a slippery path.'

'I know that. And, of course, certainty is what's needed at times.' Fletcher paused as he reflected. 'I noticed that in the trenches. That's why Dawkins was such a natural leader. But all those deaths – all that slaughter – what was the cause of all that if not certainty?'

'You mean I'm right and you're wrong so I must kill you.'

'That's exactly what I mean.'

George sighed. 'Perhaps none of us really know the answers,' he said.

The two men stood in silence.

'And what are you up to now?' asked George eventually.

'It's not easy,' replied Fletcher, 'I wanted to set up a building business but that's not going to happen now because of this,' he pointed to his right leg, 'and there's not much work around for able bodied men these days, let alone those with disabilities.'

George stood thinking for a few seconds then stepped closer to Fletcher. 'Then you will come and work for me. I need a man of your intelligence in the business.'

Fletcher stood as upright as he was able. 'I hope you don't think that's why I came here, sir,' he said.

George patted him on the shoulder. 'I wouldn't have made the offer if I did.'

The two men faced each other, unaware in that moment that their shared loss would unite them for many years of friendship to come.

'Then I would welcome the opportunity, sir,' said Fletcher.

The driver slowed down as he eased the Lanchester around Hyde Park Corner, avoiding the many people who were making their way towards Westminster Abbey on foot. Since the burial of the Unknown Soldier had been announced in the papers the whole country had been gripped with anticipation and the Lathams had decided they must be part of the event. George soon established that all the seats inside Westminster Abbey were taken by dignitaries and special guests so he and Elizabeth decided they would go to Whitehall and observe from there. Ralph had said he could sort out a good vantage point for them but they would need to set off in good time. Elizabeth had insisted they take Mrs Jackson with them.

The driver dropped them off on the Embankment and they began walking along the river. The crowds were already filling the road but by speaking to policemen and showing them a letter written by Ralph that bore a House of Commons stamp they were able to slip past barriers and work their way to a spot where they could see the Cenotaph.

Soon after they arrived the crowd quietened as the King, dressed in the uniform of a Field Marshal, appeared and took his place near the Colonial Office. With him was the Prince of Wales, Lloyd George and all manner of Royalty and government ministers.

George looked about him at the rows of faces lining the street and picked out the older men, wondering how many of them would, like him, be anxiously awaiting the arrival of a coffin that they dared hope might contain their son's remains. The early mist had cleared and it was a crisp November morning. There was a low hum of expectation echoing through the buildings of Whitehall. Flags fluttered loosely from the tops of buildings.

Then, in the distance, came the sound of drums beating out a funeral march. The crowd fell silent. George took deep breaths as the sound grew louder and it felt to him as if the insistent, mournful rhythm was striking deep into the very fabric of his soul. Then the procession was in sight, the drummers, the black horses, Field Marshal Haig, the gun carriage and the coffin, draped in a Union flag.

The procession stopped and the King stepped forward and laid a wreath of laurel leaves and crimson flowers on the coffin. He did this swiftly, almost casually, as if lingering would be more than he could contemplate.

George's hands were shaking.

Massed choirs led the singing 'O God, our help in ages past,' and George joined in, relieved to have a moment when he could open his lungs, breathe in fresh air and move about to ease the tension that was gripping him so fiercely.

Then they came to the fifth verse.

'Time, like an ever rolling stream,
bears all who breathe away,
they fly forgotten as a dream,
dies at the opening day.'

George faltered at the second line. His lower lip started trembling and his shoulders were heaving. He clenched his fists and dug his fingernails into the palms of his hands but he was struggling to control his emotions. Elizabeth, on one side of him, was staring straight ahead, unaware of her husband's distress and it was Mrs Jackson, finally calm and composed after her years of weeping, who noticed the tears coursing down George's cheeks. She reached out and took his hand.

When The Archbishop of Canterbury read the Lord's Prayer she put her arm round George's waist. At the end of the prayer she looked across at him and smiled and throughout the two minutes silence that followed she held him, their bodies pressed together, their minds finally convergent, two parents united in a deep bond of sorrow for their missing children.

They stayed like this as the buglers sounded the Last Post, their sombre notes the only noise echoing in the streets of London, and it was only when the last sound died down to be replaced by an extraordinary hush that Margaret Jackson finally let go of George Latham and he was able to stand tall, take a deep breath and once more adopt the demeanour he would expect of a gentleman such as himself.

CHAPTER 38

9 October 1917

Daniel Dawkins looked up into the sky, waiting for the mist that had earlier drifted across the salient to return. The rain had all but stopped but the shell hole continued to fill. He had expected another wave of soldiers to come by but as time passed he guessed that sense had finally prevailed and the attack had been postponed.

The water was up to his neck.

The bombardment had ceased, the machine guns had stopped firing, there was only the sound of wind and rain sweeping down unimpeded from the Passchendaele Ridge. Even the groaning from wounded men stranded out in the open had finally died down, leaving a hush that was more disturbing than any cries for help.

He thought of Fletcher and Sergeant Barnes and wondered if they had made it to the casualty station by now. He thought of Joyce and imagined what she might be doing at that moment. His fingers gripped the roots protruding from the muddy sides of the shell hole but the ledge on which he was perched was breaking up and he knew that soon he would lose his purchase. If he wasn't to drown and join Mr Latham beneath the surface of this rancid pond he would shortly have to draw on his last reserves of strength and drag himself out over the lip.

Something touched his helmet.

'Fuck off,' he shouted and shook his head to scare off the rat that would be scavenging the corpses, waiting for him to die. He felt a wet, shaggy mass of hair brush against his neck. Then a familiar shape came into view.

'Murphy?'

There was a small patch of levelled earth beside the roots and with one leap Murphy jumped down and ended up with his nose inches from Dawkins' face. He started licking Daniel's cheek.

'Murph, my old mate? How the hell did you find me out here?'

Keeping hold of the roots with his right hand Dawkins managed to manoeuvre his left so that he could stroke Murphy on the back of his head. Murphy nuzzled up to him and Dawkins felt the dog's cold nose rubbing up against his ear. For a while they stayed like that, touching each other for company, trapped in No Man's Land, man and dog alone together in their watery isolation.

Then Dawkins felt something dangling under Murphy's neck. 'Let's see what you've got here,' he said.

It was a pouch and with his one free hand he managed to open it and extract a small flask. He unscrewed the metal lid with his thumb and put the neck to his mouth.

'Oh, Murph,' he said, 'you little champ.'

The whisky burned his throat and he took another swig.

'Who sent you out here? Was it Pete?'

Murphy looked at Dawkins, his head tilted to one side.

'It was Pete, wasn't it. He sent you out here for me.'

The shelf under his feet loosened further and he was now balancing on one foot.

Then a thought occurred to Dawkins. He reached into his pocket and pulled out the small metal container he had been carrying these past months. 'Here,' he said, 'take this back to Pete, Murph. He'll know what it is.'

He slipped the container containing the photograph of Joyce into Murphy's pouch. 'He'll find her and tell her what happened.'

Murphy looked at him enquiringly.

'Go on, boy, go back to Pete.' Dawkins prodded the dog to jump out of the hole but Murphy wouldn't move.

The water was touching Dan's chin. His helmet was level with the ground.

'No fucking mist when you need it, Murph,' he said, 'Fritz'll be waiting.'

A few more minutes passed and he was needing to angle his head to keep his mouth from filling. The water was half up Murphy's small body but still he remained where he was. A rare ray of sunshine flickered across the shell hole and it seemed like a signal to Dan.

'Right, this is it then, Murph,' he said, 'can't wait any longer,' and, mustering all the remaining energy in his body, his feet scrabbling on the side of the shell hole, his right arm pulling on the roots, his left holding Murphy by the scruff of the neck, Dan hauled himself out into the open.

Above ground he knelt, panting from his efforts, his back exposed to the ridge, liquid mud dripping from every part of him, and faced west, towards home, towards Joyce, towards his unborn child, towards a life he had finally begun to believe might be possible. Murphy stood beside him. 'Go on then son,' said Dawkins, 'go and find Pete. I'll be right behind you.'

But Murphy wouldn't move so Daniel stood up and began walking. He stopped briefly to check Major Horrocks's body but then carried on in a straight line, his eyes on the horizon and his back straight. He could almost sense the German gunners lining up their sights but with each step he wondered if, as earlier, they would hold their fire out of a sense of fair play, a reluctance to shoot a man who was not threatening their position. He started whistling and felt a little light-headed as he watched Murphy scampering around his feet, sniffing at every object and body he came to. Could it be that Mr Latham was right? Could it be that there was some higher being watching over him, had been these past years, saw a good in him worth preserving? He smiled at the thought and for a few seconds was filled with a feeling of elation he had never before experienced but then a burst of machine gun fire sounded across the salient. An aimed and accurate volley it lasted only a few seconds and by the time it was over and quiet had descended once more Dan was lying face down, his blood seeping into the soil.

'Go on then, lad,' he whispered to Murphy, 'leave me now.'

Murphy licked Dan's face.

'They got me at last,' said Dan and his fingers stroked Murphy's back before falling to the ground. He tried to roll onto his side but was unable to move. He needed to lift his head but had no strength. His mouth was filling with rainwater and there was nothing he could do.

'Go,' he managed to say one last time, bubbles forming at the corners of his mouth. Then he closed his eyes and gave one last, long sigh.

Murphy sat beside him. Shells flew above his head as a new bombardment began. The mist came and went, morning turned to afternoon, nothing moved in the salient. Every now and then the small dog would nuzzle Dan's face but it was cold and unresponsive. Periodically the German gunners would fire aimlessly into No Man's Land to remind their enemy of their presence but the next wave of attack failed to materialise.

It wasn't until mid afternoon that Murphy, growing hungry, finally gave Daniel one last lick on his face and then started walking slowly back towards the trenches, his tail hanging low, the hairs of his belly dragging on the ground, stopping frequently to check if Dan was following. He came to Peter Jackson's body, sniffed it, paused a moment then carried on. He passed the scattered corpses of the men of 5 Platoon, all sinking from view as the mud slowly gathered them in, and he wove his way back towards where the next wave of men, fresh troops from across the Channel, had finally arrived and were nervously awaiting orders to advance.

He found his way down into a forward trench and scampered along the duckboards, weaving past putteed legs, hearing voices talking quietly. He ran and ran, heading in no particular direction until he came to a spot that was drier than elsewhere. He sat and curled himself up.

'Here, boy.'

Murphy looked up and a kindly face was bending down towards him. A pair of hands grabbed him and lifted him up.

He licked the soldier's face. Fingers stroked him under the chin.

'What are you doing here all alone?' asked the soldier.

Voices were shouting along the trench.

'Off shortly.' The soldier stood holding Murphy as men fixed their bayonets. 'Have to put you down now,' he said, then, 'Hello, what's this then?'

His hand was touching the pouch under Murphy's neck. He opened it and found inside a small metal container.

'Don't know what this is,' he said, 'a lucky charm is it?' He tried to open the clasp but it was jammed.

A whistle blew nearby and the soldier, one of hundreds who had been waiting for the order to advance, looked at the dog which in turn was looking up at him. Hastily, he stuffed the metal container into his trouser pocket. 'Wish me luck, then,' he said and Murphy watched as his feet disappeared up a ladder, over the top of the trench and towards the German army where gunners were preparing themselves once more for the next British assault.

EPILOGUE

On 11 November 1921 the stone in Westminster Abbey marking the grave of the Unknown Warrior was replaced by a new gravestone of black marble from Belgium, chosen by the Dean, the Right Reverend Herbert Ryle.

At the end of the service the Reverend David Railton carried his Union flag to the altar where it was dedicated before being raised in St George's chapel.

The Times had stated earlier that the flag (known as the padre's flag) *'should never leave those doubly venerable walls. It flew at Vimy Ridge and in the Ypres salient, on the Somme, at Messines Ridge ..... it served as the last covering for numbers of our dead; and it bears the glorious stain of their blood. It has covered the grave of the Unknown Warrior and now it is to hang near his resting place.'*

It seemed to those who knew him well that Railton was finally receiving the acknowledgement that was his due.

He often reflected on that day in Armentieres when he had come across a grave marked *'an unknown soldier (of the Black Watch).'* It was a day that had ultimately triggered scenes of mass emotional grief across the world: on the same day as the Unknown Warrior had been laid to rest in London, in France the *poilu inconnu* had been carried along the Champs Elysees in front of packed crowds before being buried beneath an arch of the Arc de Triomphe. Over the next few years unknown soldiers were buried in Belgium, Italy, Greece, Portugal and, on November 11th 1921, at Arlington National Cemetery in the United States of America.

After the war Railton served the Church of England in various roles until his retirement in 1945. In 1955, returning home to Inverness-shire from Battle, Sussex where he had been helping the Rural Dean, he accidentally fell from a moving train at Fort William railway station and died from his injuries.

By this time the Tomb of the Unknown Warrior in Westminster Abbey, the Tomb of the Unknowns in Arlington cemetery in Virginia, the Neue Wache in Berlin, the eternal flame burning beneath the Arc de Triomphe in Paris, the dozens of other sites in cities as far apart as Baghdad and Canberra, Ottawa and Warsaw, Athens and Kiev, Wellington and Moscow, Rome and Bandung had become sites of pilgrimage.

* * * *

David Railton, a modest man to the end, died knowing that he had played his part in this. He gained a quiet satisfaction from knowing that the grave beneath that marble slab in Westminster Abbey would continue to be a reverent place. It would, for generations to come, be a symbolic place, a beloved place, somewhere for thousands each year to come and quietly mourn their loved ones. And it would hold this spell over the nation because, as he had first envisaged, the body they had dug up from the killing fields of the Western Front, that they had solemnly carried across the Channel, paraded through London and buried in the Abbey was, and would always remain, that of an Unknown Warrior.

AUTHOR'S NOTE

This is a work of fiction based on fact.

In 1916 The Reverend David Railton did indeed come up with the idea of choosing a body from the battlefields of the First World War and subsequently burying the Unknown Warrior in Westminster Abbey.

The Reverend George Kendall, Brigadier-General Wyatt and Lieutenant Colonel Gell were involved as stated. The service on November 11th 1920 took place as described.

The battles of Messines Ridge and Passchendaele were significant events in the war and key figures such as Field Marshall Haigh and General Plummer were in command.

But Sarah Harding, James Marchant, Daniel Dawkins, Peter Harding and Joyce Harding are fictional characters and so their conversations with real characters are imagined. There were a number of fine Light Infantry regiments but no Berkshire Light Infantry. Lt Latham, Sgt Barnes, Fletcher, Timmings and Major Horrocks are also fictional characters.

Any resemblance of fictional characters to any real life characters is unintentional.

ACKNOWLEDGEMENTS

I am not a historian but have read a number of exceptional books in my research to give 'The Name Beneath The Stone' authenticity.

For the background and context of the First World War I found particularly helpful 'The Western Front' by Richard Holmes and 'Forgotten Victory' by Gary Sheffield. 'Forgotten voices of the Great War' and 'Last Post', both by Max Arthur, gave me a great insight into conditions for soldiers in the trenches. 'They called it Passchendaele' by Lynn MacDonald proved exceptionally useful in understanding the events and horrors of 1917.

'Her privates we,' by Frederic Manning, written by a soldier who survived the Somme and, after the war, wrote a novel based on his experiences proved to be truly inspirational for me and set the tone for my book.

For the choosing of the body and burial of the Unknown Warrior I read many articles and pamphlets but 'The Unknown Soldier' by Neil Hanson was the detailed account of events that fired my imagination and to which I referred throughout.

Finally, I'd like to thank The Times newspaper for allowing me to include excerpts from correspondents in 1917 and 1920.

In terms of editorial input I'd like to thank in particular Lucie Skilton and Liz Garner for their always valuable professional advice. Alexander Paterson helped me greatly with military procedures. I should also like to thank my friends Jeremy Fletcher and Julian Spooner for their honest feedback even when I didn't want it. And, of course, Zita, my wife, who has become my 'first reader' over the years and always the voice I listen to when needing reassurance that I've written something that will appeal to people other than just myself.